Vision World

By Marcello Antonius Versace Tino

Thompson and Prince

ISBN - 13: 978-0615929019
ISBN – 10: 061592901x

Library of Congress Code Number: 2013956418

Key Words: American Literature __ Science Fiction __ Dystopian Novels __ Quantum Physics and the Human Mind __ Revolution __ Political Novel __ Mass Media.

Book cover and logo designed by William Benson

The Second Coming

Turning and turning in the widening gyre
The falcon cannot hear the falconer;
Things fall apart; the center cannot hold;
Mere anarchy is loosed upon the world,
The blood-dimmed tide is loosened, and everywhere
The ceremony of innocence is drowned;
The best lack all conviction, while the worst
Are full of passionate intensity.
Surely some revelation is at hand;
Surely the Second Coming is at hand.
The Second Coming! Hardly are those words out
When a vast image out of Spiritus Mundi
Troubles my sight: somewhere in sands of the desert
A shape with lion body and the head of a man,
A gaze blank and pitiless as the sun,
Is moving its slow thighs, while all about it
Reel shadows of the indignant desert birds,
The darkness drops again; but now I know
That twenty centuries of stony sleep
Were vexed to nightmare by a rocking cradle,
And what rough beast, its hour come round at last,
Slouches toward Bethlehem to be born?

By William Butler Yeats

Chapter One

Merling sees himself as the sorcerer, the eye in the magic of imagination that can take a dot and turn it into a globe, a universe, a period at the end of a sentence that casts a spell. He is the magic at the core of reality, a part of the mystery that we call God. Today he is in the conference room of a control center deep below the ground looking at a 3D virtual reality image of a fawn chewing on a spike of wheat, munching the grain, savoring the kernels, the green fertile juices of the leaves. Merling tries to get beyond the image to the life within the dot itself, to feel the earth soft beneath its feet, the sun radiating through its fragile form like a warm bath of light while the wind blows through the sea of golden waves caressing its soft brown fur like the hand of God, my child, our home.

The fawn's mother is a few yards away, and his father with antlers like the Eternal Tree of Life sniffs the air, alert for danger, the snake in the garden, man, the hunters. The air smells of the sweet growth that the veins of life sprout from, the perfume of nature in the breeze, the earth, a few worms, a snail, the lady bug that has escaped the insecticide, and the foul odor of the chemicals, the black alchemy of the earth created by man to transform the bowels of the earth into phantom blood.

The stag whiffs the breeze, the wet mist like blue, and he sees emerald splashes from the corner of his eye, no scent of man, nothing moving but the hypnotic sway of the shoots of grain. His eyes, grown weary from scanning the field, dwell upon the fawn when a bolt of light rents the picture, strikes the child and drops the fawn dead upon the earth. The stag's mate jerks around, startled, shocked as another bolt of light frames her face in horror. He leaps helplessly, his horns pierce the air, and he is dead in the sky.

The ocean of blue turns red as he falls on a bed of gold green olive russet black with no mourning just petroleum soil and the sound of a sea of gold that is protected from the sky by bolts of lightning from a satellite named Zeus Two that looms in space. The three carcasses of meat lie in the field, dead, and they show up on the grid at the control center as three red blotches, three dots losing heat.

Brad Merling laughs, "Ladies and gentlemen, we'll have venison tonight."

Brad, who is the Chairman of the Alpha Commission and the head of Vision World, relishes the applause from the men and women from the Chinese Economic Planning Board who are attending the meeting. Brad notes the pleasure, and they should be pleased. Venison meat is going for a thousand dollars a pound on the world market, and fawn meat... My God, how these mandarins of the New China love their fawn at five thousand dollars a pound. He wants to burst out laughing at the hypocrisy of it all, but he only smiles and says, "And as you can see, our satellite surveillance system provides perfect protection for our fields. Penetration is impossible."

In the moment's pause he savors the three red blotches, the scene, and the pictures of death in the fields that are being projected as high definition holographic images into a conference room buried deep beneath the control center. Because of the highly advanced three-dimensional imaging technology, the projections seem real from any perspective, and the conference room, which is in reality a large safe encased in reinforced concrete, seems to be floating on air.

A white rectangular plane with lines that extend into infinity forms the conference table, and it is the axis of a panoramic view of the fields and blue sky, a vast sea of riches extended over two states. The men in the control tower seem like ghostly presences lurking around the conference room as they monitor screens that are vivid portals into the inner workings of Vision World.

Merling watches the electronic monitors controlling the automated machinery that tends to the fields. The screens reveal the data and infrared chemical analysis of the soil that is coming from a satellite. On one of the screens, he can see that the computer, based on the data, is directing yellow bug-like-tank-trucks with tubular sprays to feed the soil and monitor the water content.

He hears Ms. Yuong, the head of the Chinese delegation, say, "The satellite security system is very impressive, but it seems effective only against intruders who try to infiltrate the system in small numbers." She smiles slightly, "What if we were attacked by hungry mobs of people angered by the fact that we own and control all the best farm land in Montana?"

Merling laughs, "Unlikely, but let's pretend."

Merling turns to his security chief, John Hathaway, "John, do you think you can conjure up the starving masses for me?"

On one screen magnified for the easy viewing of the delegates, a graphic of the sector where the deer were slain appears as a grid. On the grid, new red dots begin to appear, thousands upon thousands of them.

Merling smiles, "Thank you, John. I'll take over from here."

He presses a button and a control panel appears as a pattern upon the surface of the table. He begins to touch the keys on the screen with fingers long and tapered like those of a concert pianist. Red warning lights flash through the room as data appears across the topmost borders of the panel, and a computer generated automated zombie voice pervades the room, "Priority One Intrusion!"

Merling looks at the red button flashing on the control panel, and he touches it gently as if he were touching the nipple of a woman's breast, and the game begins.

He touches a few more buttons, and on the screen appear three armored-troop-carriers loaded with armed personnel and heading for the field where they are joined by two remote control attack vehicles.

Merling marvels at how the nature of war has changed. It has been reduced to eye and hand coordination and the touching of buttons. He loves it. It's like the video games he played as a child where cartoon characters appeared and disappeared on the screen. In this game, death progresses across the screen in the form of two toy tanks that form the axis of a firing zone designated by a red square on the grid. As the vehicles penetrate the target zone, the red square begins to transpose itself on the target area.

Merling's face is blood red, glowing from the reflection of the screen. He looks at Hathaway and the monitors who are waiting for his next move. They are all appendages of him, the conduit to the conductor, human nerve ends in the system waiting to be triggered.

Brad smiles and fingers the red button once again, the ground opens up, and two heavily armed supersonic hover planes appear on launching platforms rising from an underground hanger. To heighten the drama, Merling raises the volume of the sound and fills the room with the roar of the engines as the warships soar off to battle. He then presses another button and a hologram of one of the remote control attack vehicles in the field appears, larger than life. It extends its firing arms, and the metal arms lock into place to the hum of electromagnetic force. Hundreds of firing ports, packed with photon charges and bundled together like the barrels of an old fashion Gatling gun begin to spin faster and faster until they are a blur of fire pulsating death, but on the grid, the attack vehicles look like lawn sprinklers gone wild as toy helicopters rocket the area with little splashes of red.

Merling's eye travels from the abstract to the real, the blood red reality of pure power, and he thinks to himself, fire is what makes us who we are. We Americans are the final bearers of the flame. This love of fire must have come with us as far back as our Aryan forefathers who wandered in the cold, worshipping fire, gold, the flame being passed on by tribal story tellers who looked into the campfire at night and saw the stars, the children peering from behind into the beyond at flaming chariots and warriors who were given the mysteries of the sun for the price of their immortal soul.

Fire is our power, and we have turned it into all its forms, and now after a history of war and conquest, molten steel, electrons turned into dynamos, now we can, like Zeus, rain death with a lightning bold and split an atom and create destruction far beyond what Zeus could ever imagine from his throne on Mount Olympus.

Merling looks at the aerial view of the field being projected into the room. He looks at the devastation. There is nothing left of the fields except that in the center of obliteration and the charred soil devoid of any life form, is a small intact plot of wheat with the remains of the deer lying there as if sleeping in a bed of gold, a medieval tapestry of tranquility fringed with terror, a dinner for the Gods.

Ms. Yuong studies Merling for a moment. He is tall and slim with silver white hair folded back like wings. His features are Trans-European. He is the spirit of the West marching through time into the American frontier, a magnificent predator whose character has been blurred by a world of numbers that has depreciated the poetry and the romance in the history of his genes. Ms. Yuong feels a shiver of cold run through her, but she is compelled to ask, "You're not bothered by this?"

Merling smiles and looks at her through steel blue eyes that seldom blink and says, "Feel reassured, Comrade. We take property rights very seriously in America."

Chapter Two

Colonel Dennis Martino, a military investigative officer for this sector of the United States, has been watching this exercise from the entranceway to the fields. He hears the whirling sound of the electromagnetic fields that generated the photon cannons wind down, and he watches the helicopters return to base through a sky that was once blue but is now gray with swirling snakes of smoke.

"Some barbecue, Sergeant. Do you know what's going on?" Denny asks.

The Sergeant shrugs. "I don't know, sir. I just work here."

Denny gets back into the army staff car, and his orderly drives off down the road into the charred remains of what was Paradise. Because so much of Denny's work these days is civilian and investigative, he isn't required to wear a uniform that is so symbolic of the sameness of his life. Even a suit and a tie he finds restrictive and uncomfortable. He opens his brief case, and he looks through his papers, the crisp white sheets, the clear black print, the illusion of order. Security is not normally his job, but General Shea was short a man today, so here he is.

Denny reaches into his coat pocket and pulls out a pack of Camel straights and lights up a cigarette.

He inhales deeply.

He's quite satisfied with the gesture, the inhalation of death. Yes, he smokes when nobody else smokes because a slow death of his own choosing is one of the few romantic gestures left to a man who can't find it in his heart to kill anymore. Denny remembers the first time that he had a cigarette. It was after his first battle. God, it tasted so good, the smoke that smothered the smell of death as he continued to breathe fire. At that moment he realized that all his life he tried to be good, to belong, to be like everyone else, yet the only time he was free was in the fire zone where his senses intensified. He saw for the first time the vivid color in the flowers, blood red, dancing in the sunlight, the jewel in a drop of water, the air vibrating with life in contrast to the oblivion of death, the darkness that swallowed up life like a black hole in space.

He became a junkie to the feeling and a lieutenant colonel at twenty-eight years old, a veteran of three wars. But he had a problem. Not only did his senses wake up, but his mind came to life as well. He began to think about things, and the more he thought, the more confused he became. What confused him most was that as he went from one war to another the enemy he fought became poorer and poorer. Finally, one day when he was on patrol in Columbia, the truth came into focus when someone took a shoot at him from behind a tree. In a rage, he pulled the trigger on his 60mm machine gun loaded with explosion shells. He literally sawed the tree in half and in the end he was looking at a burned out stump of a tree and a twelve-year-old boy with no shoes tangled in the fallen branches, dead. The boy was so thin that if Denny hadn't killed him he probably would have died of starvation. Denny had no stomach for it anymore. Even the dead deer made him nauseous now.

The irony is that now that he is home his main job is to investigate homicides. So he still smokes, but for a while it was all right, a form of divine retribution. He was no longer the killer. He was the seeker, or so it seemed, and for a while he was very good at his job. He liked the-who-done-it of it all, and he was good at distinguishing the different shades of darkness to find the darkest light of all. Sometimes he would find the scumbags, the real criminals, and that made his job worthwhile. But most of the time, the path into the darkest dark led him into the depths of the depression where he only found poverty and despair, just like in Latin America.

Denny turns on the TV, adjusts the size of the picture, and a picture of an excavation site in the midst of a beautiful virgin forest appears on the screen. The camera focuses in on the towering trees, their giant corpses, and then to a warehouse that has been blown up. Debris is splattered all about the site.

A reporter's voice is heard in the background, "Fortunately, nobody was hurt, but we are told by reliable sources that the property damage is estimated to be in the millions."

The picture focuses on several bulldozers that have been torn apart by explosives. The reporter is standing next to one the bulldozers, its blade arm torn from its steel socket. There are military police on the scene. The caption at the bottom of the screen informs us that we are at the Glacier Park Development Site.

The reporter signs off, "And this is John Sully, Vision World News."

"Shit," Denny picks up the phone and touches some keys.

From the other end of the line he hears, "Federal Security Offices, Control Officer Sweeny here."

"Sweeny, this is Denny. What happened at Glacier Park?"

"The Green Peace Warriors blew up the excavation site and all the equipment. That is, we think they did. Someone called Vision World this morning and claimed he was a member of the organization. The same old stuff, Glacier Park is public land and should remain so, and they, the Green Peace Warriors, will oppose with any means available the encroachment by private enterprise on our national heritage. Quote unquote. Do you want to hear more?"

"No, I got the picture, and I don't like it. This attack may be linked up with this big shot I'm supposed to baby-sit. I want a special terrorist unit on red alert, and I want you to double the security forces on Merling's route."

"They requested low visibility."

"I don't give a shit."

"OK, Denny."

Denny is looking through the papers in his brief-case, looking for anything that will give him a clue. "Swee-ny, do they have anything on the agenda about a military exercise?"

"A military exercise?"

"Yeah, I just watched them torch a square mile of wheat over here. I mean real toasty, attack vehicles, air support, the whole package."

"I'll check. You want to hold?"

"Sure."

While Denny is waiting for Sweeny, he watches the television newscast. On screen he sees Cheri Normal. Cheri is Denny's favorite newscaster. It must be the slight over-bite and the eyes that seem slightly crossed, the flaws in the otherwise perfect diamond that makes her seem so ac-cessible. At the corner of the picture is a picture within a picture of the American and Chilean flags coming together - the red, white, and blue of the United States of America merging with the red, white, and blue of Chile - one star about to become the fifty fourth state in the emerging un-ion of North and South America.

Denny listens to Cheri's child-like voice, the slight lisp, the lips touching, almost like a kiss. "The American occupational forces in Chile report that they have nearly eliminated all armed opposition."

The picture switches from Cheri to a picture of American M4 tanks on their way to Santiago, the capital of Chile. Denny hears Cheri's voice as the picture switches again to a high-ranking officer in the United States Army.

"General Ford, how is the liberation going?"

"Very well, we're on our way. And soon..."

Denny turns off the sound on the TV and fills in the lines, "The world will be safe for McDonalds." Denny laughs and then freezes the picture on the face of Cheri Normal and magnifies the view of her cockeyed smile, a smile that seems to say that no matter what the news, good or bad, everything is going to be all right because we're going to have fun. That's the American way. Denny's infatuation with Cheri is interrupted by Sweeny.

"Denny?"

"Yeah."

"There's nothing about any barbecue out there."

"OK Sweeny, I'll keep in touch."

Denny hangs up the phone, and some distance away he spots something in the middle of the road. As they draw closer, he begins to make out what it is. It's small. It has ears.

"Stop!" he shouts.

The driver slams on the breaks and skids to a halt. Denny gets out, walks to the front of the car and looks down at a little rabbit frozen in fear.

"What's the matter, baby," Denny asks in the gentle

voice of a child, then crouches down and looks tenderly at the little rabbit who doesn't respond. Only the gentle movement of its breathing tells Denny that it is alive. The poor little thing is in shock.

Denny gently reaches down, picks the rabbit up, and cradles it in his arms, "There we are, sweetheart. You can't hang out in the middle of the road. You're going to be squished. You better come with Uncle Denny, and I'll find a new home for you. These people are fucked up."

The rabbit makes no effort to resist as Denny returns to the car, and with the rabbit in his lap, they drive off. Denny feels the warmth and strokes the delicate fur like air. He can see where the fire has singed some of the rabbit's fur, and he can feel its little heart beat feverishly as they near the control tower of reinforced concrete surrounded by fortified bunkers that are gray, hard, and angular in form with glass slits for windows like arrow ports.

Chapter Three

When Denny arrives at the control center, he enters the building with the rabbit cradled in his arms. He is greeted by one of the military officers assigned to the installation, and he is then led to the control tower where he is introduced to Brad Merling's chief of security, John Hathaway. Hathaway, who is in his early fifties, is tall and slightly overweight like a former tight end who likes to eat rich food in expensive restaurants then work it off in the gym with only partial success. However, despite the years of self-indulgence and the wear and tear of time, Hathaway still possesses a commanding presence and an air of authority with his military bearing, the short cropped silver gray hair, and the cold hard face of a mercenary who has succumbed to sadism, tailored suits, and expensive rare sports cars.

Hathaway is about to extend his hand, but then he looks down at the rabbit and smiles, "What's this? Pot luck?"

"No, it's a survivor of the ecological holocaust that I just witnessed."

Denny watches the hypocritical smile of a corporate

PR man vanish revealing the corporate mercenary type behind the mask. There you are, Denny says to himself, now I see you, you son of bitch.

Denny extends his hand and formally introduces himself, "I'm Colonel Dennis Martino. I believe you're expecting me." Hathaway's grip is firm and unyielding, the usual Marine bullshit.

The corporate smile returns, "Yes, Colonel, I'm John Hathaway, and it's a pleasure to meet you, but as you can see, we're quite busy. My advice to you is to sit back and relax." He winks at Denny in a conspiratorial way, "Easy duty."

Hathaway turns his back on Denny and is about to sit down again at the control panel. Denny realizes that he has been dismissed and he says, "My orders from my commanding officer were to report immediately to Mr. Merling, personally."

Hathaway turns to square off again, and Denny is amused once more as he looks into the hard stare of an ex-major general, a front-line officer, and the one time head of the anti-terrorist Special Forces Command in Washington. Oh, yes, he knows who John Hathaway is. He's been dancing around with guys like him ever since he joined the army, but now things are different. Hathaway has no rank. He's a civilian and that look of superiority is going to buy him a boloney sandwich.

The electromagnetic force created between John Hathaway and Denny is very interesting because they are opposites, yet, they're very much the same. They come from the same place. They have experienced the same things. They understand each other's language, each gesture, the slightest body movement or expression. That is why when Hathaway reads the disdain on Denny's face, the hard stare fades, and it is replaced by the glint of the black market of the soul and the ironic smile of a man who makes three times as much as Denny makes doing basically the same thing.

"Very well, Colonel. Follow me and bring the rabbit." Hathaway laughs and says, "This may turn out to be interesting."

As they walk to the elevator, nearly everyone they pass stares at the little creature in Denny's arms as if it were an alien. Denny strokes its ears, and he can see that it is still quite frightened as it breathes in all the cold calculation of the place.

Denny stops and says to the lieutenant who is accompanying him, "With all the big game hunting going on around here, there must be a kitchen."

"Yes, sir."

"Good, then I want you to take Bugs Bunny here and find a box for him and some lettuce, maybe some carrots, some water. You know what I mean."

The lieutenant's face is animated, "Yes, sir. I had a rabbit for a pet when I was a kid."

"Good. Bugs Bunny here is an endangered species, and I'm taking him in custody as a ward of the state. And when I leave this place, I want to see him in the back seat of my car, in a secure box with lots of air and lots of food or your ass is mine." Denny smiles pleasantly so as to undercut the threat, "Got it?"

The lieutenant smiles and nods to Denny indicating that he understands very well the message. He's part of the joke, and he's been ordered to make everyone kiss Bugs Bunny's ass.

Denny tries to get a firm hold on Bugs with both hands so that he can hand him over to the lieutenant, but Bugs resists, and he attempts to burrow under Denny's coat. A good sign, Denny thinks to himself. First he wants to hide, and then he'll struggle to be free. Just like me.

"Now, don't worry." Denny says, "The lieutenant here is going to take good care of you, Bugs. Trust me." Denny pulls Bugs out from his burrow and hands him over to the lieutenant then enters the elevator. Hathaway and he are alone together, and as they descend into the depths of the complex, Denny observes that they both look like they're urinating into a latrine, shoulder to shoulder, legs spread apart, looking up at the descending numbers, feeling the weight of gravity as they descend into the bowels of the system.

Finally, as if he had just shaken the last drop off his dick and zipped up his fly, Hathaway turns to Denny and says, "To be perfectly honest with you, Colonel, I don't know why you're here. For that matter, I don't know why we need this elaborate security network you have set up for the tour. As you know, Mr. Merling has his own security team, and we're quite capable of protecting the Chairman. And... we can do it, Martino, without being conspicuous. Mr. Merling is selling paradise to the Chinese, not a military police state. Am I making myself clear?"

"Oh, yes, sir, in triplicate. But if you don't want me to be here and you don't like the security measures that we have taken, then call my commanding officer and complain to him, Mister Hathaway." Denny gets a great deal of pleasure emphasizing the "Mister" and Hathaway's loss of rank.

"I did, Colonel."

"And?"

As the door to the elevator slides open and they enter a reception room paneled in dark walnut, Hathaway says, "It's the same old story, Colonel. It is his job and his ass." Hathaway laughs, "And since shit rolls downhill, it's your job and your ass."

"You got that right." Denny is relieved that he may have come to an understanding with this prick. They approach two large smoked glass doors.

"The only problem with this scenario, Colonel, is..." Hathaway opens one of the doors for Denny and gestures for him to go in first, and then says, "It's my job, and you're in my shit."

The door closes behind Denny, and he realizes that he has walked right into the middle of a presentation by the head of Vision World. Denny reaches behind him for the doorknob. He tries to open the door. It's locked. He sees Hathaway smiling at him from the other side of the smoked glass. I'm fucked, he says to himself, and I've only been on the job for a couple of hours. God Damn it, Martino. What an asshole you are. With his back pressed against the cold concrete walls, Denny tries to hide behind the holographic images of the fields.

Merling glances over at Denny then ignores him completely and continues his presentation, "So, ladies and gentlemen, in essence, we are offering you a good part of two states, Montana and North Dakota for development and 50,000 acres of prime farm land to feed your starving masses, for what? For simply offering us the same trade concessions that you have given the Japanese. Think about it. We can do for you, now, what will take the Japanese years to accomplish. We can give you the food surplus that you need, and at the same time, offer you investment opportunities in America."

Merling presses some buttons and the holograms disappear leaving the room bathed in a pleasant light. "Well, that's it. There are touring buses outside, and when we get back, the venison will be ready to serve with an All American menu, copies of which you will find on the table before you."

Brad watches the Chinese devour the printed words, and he is amused by the obvious pleasure and eager approval of born again gluttons. Merling laughs. His voice is congenial, "Well, ladies and gentlemen, or should I

say, fellow Americans, let's go take a look at the neighborhood, and when we get back, we'll have dinner then continue our conference and discuss my proposal in some detail."

The applause is genuine, and the delegates are impressed. Denny makes his way through the laughter, the
good cheer, and the strange sounds of a foreign language.
He makes his way to Merling who is shaking hands with
one of the delegates. Merling turns toward Denny. First
Denny sees the corporate mask that Cheri, then Hathaway,
and now Merling wears. He sees the ubiquitous smile, but
then Merling recognizes Denny and the smile seriously
depreciates.

Denny snaps to attention and salutes the head of
Vision World. "Colonel Dennis Martino, sir. I've been assigned by General Shea to take charge of all security forces
while you and your delegates are here. I'm personally responsible for your safety, sir."

Merling smiles and says, "Tell me Captain, do you
usually barge into meetings like that?"

"No, sir, but your man, Hathaway, has a weird sense
of humor."

"Yes, he does, but I don't."

Denny listens to the voice of a man who can command a satellite in space to strike down a fawn with a
lightning bold, "And, Colonel," the voice says. "If you ever
step on my lines again, you will be peeling frozen potatoes
in the Arctic."

"Yes, sir."

"Good, then we understand one another." The mask appears again, the smile that gives off no heat.

Merling extends his hand, "Well, Colonel, it's been a pleasure, and I do hope you will be a little more un-obtrusive in the future."

Denny smiles, "Yes, sir."

Merling sees John Hathaway approaching, "And you two have already met."

Denny turns and sees Hathaway. There's a broad smile on Hathaway's face. Merling watches the interplay between Denny and Hathaway with amusement. Then he says to Hathaway, "I want you two to work together." The tone is there again.

As Ms. Yuong passes by, Merling gently grabs her by the arm, excuses himself, and begins a conversation with her as he ushers her to the exit. When the delegates leave the center and enter the tour bus that is awaiting them, Denny walks over to his staff car, and he tells his driver that he is going to ride with Hathaway in the surveil-lance vehicle owned by Vision World. He orders his driver to follow them then looks in the back seat. Bugs Bunny is in the box chewing on some lettuce. Denny turns to the driver and says, "He looks normal."

"Yes, sir. He's perked right up. I think he's OK."
Denny's relieved. Now he has to find a place for him. Not here. Maybe tomorrow he can take him to one of the national parks and set him free there. Denny takes

one last look at Bugs. Bugs can't wait to get out of the box. It dawns on Denny. That's what makes animals superior to humans. We love the box.

Denny enters the surveillance vehicle owned by Vision World. It is similar to the mobile units used by the military police, but far more elaborate, far more sophisticated. Hathaway hands him a head set then presses some buttons, types out some code numbers, and at his command the video screens that wall the interior of the vehicle and beyond light up revealing the many eyes that guard the way.

Denny is amazed by what he sees. It's as if they were not in the vehicle. The interior extends out into space, projecting high definition three-dimensional views of the route they are taking. Hathaway presses several more buttons and the perspective changes completely. Now, it seems like Denny is in the tour bus with Merling and the Chinese. He watches Hathaway manipulate the laser grid, and he can see that by manipulating the grid, he can monitor the eye movement of anyone on the bus and see what they see. Hathaway makes one final adjustment then focuses the camera, and Denny can see what Brad Merling is seeing.

The vast wheat fields pass by as they cruise onto Route 36. Soon the fields give way to grassland, cattle behind barbed wire, and the plains sloping upward to the misty peaks of the mountains that disappear into the distant blue sky, parallel bands of reality. In the background,

Brad Merling can hear one of his assistants giving a guided tour to the Chinese delegates, transforming what they see into dollars and cents.

He hears Ms. Yuong who is seated next to Merling ask, "How did Vision World get started?"

Merling chuckles and looks at his own shadowy image in the window of the bus. It seems to float timelessly in the glass as the exterior world passes by, "Oh, dear," he says. "Many years ago, when I was a young man, I had started out in advertising and then made the switch to television production. Like most young men my age I was always plotting, plotting to make money, plotting to get ahead, plotting to get laid. Plotting to plot, but I worked hard, and I tried to understand the phenomenon of TV. I tried to understand its essence. What it really is. Then one day it dawned on me. I was at my summer home in the Hamptons, and I was drinking with a house guest of mine, Bob Baker, a friend from work. We were talking about what makes an actor an actor and why most TV actors are bad actors. Are you familiar with the history of TV?"

"Oh, yes, I'm a dedicated student." Ms. Yuong's eyes flutter, "I don't want to make too much of myself, but it was my admiration of your work that brought me here. And it was I who insisted you be involved in the land deal. I want you to bring Vision World to China. Are you pleased?"

"Yes, and quite flattered." Merling is embarrassed by the intimacy, so he quickly returns to the subject. "Well, then, if you have studied the history of American TV, you're probably familiar with Tom Resnick."

"Oh, yes, I've seen everything he's done."

"Good, that's who we were talking about. Tom is an excellent example of a very bad actor that was a very big success. And as we were talking about him, it occurred to me why Jim Colt, Tom Resnick's character, was so appealing. Jim Colt's a big strong guy who kills people. But, he's got a little boy's voice. Women want to mother him. He's a big baby. He's Tom Resnick. There's no acting there. Tom is one of the biggest babies I ever met, and he naturally has a little boy's voice. That's why he got the part. He didn't have to act."

"And, as Jim Colt, he's totally dependent on the rich," Ms. Yuong says. Her voice is accusatorial.

"Yes, he's sort of a night watchman, caretaker, and, uh, security guard, who sidelines as a detective, but he spends most of his time fuckin' around on the beach and driving a red Ferrari that he doesn't own."

Ms. Yuong laughs, "He's not too bright."

"No, but he figures things out eventually. Actually, he's just an average guy who fell into a cushy job working for the rich. Look at his war buddies, JP, the big black guy who is a little over weight and has a one-man helicopter service, and then there is Fred the bartender. They're both average guys, like Colt, living off the land, not really settled down, playing out their youth for all its worth as if tomorrow may never come, lucky to have survived Vietnam. Fits a lot of guys, don't it?"

"Yes."

"Another thing that I recognized as I studied the characters in the show was that Colt's girlfriends are never really knock outs. Any girl's got a real chance with him."

Ms. Yuong smiles and says, "You're right, of course. Even I fantasized."

"So you see. Anyone can identify with him, and he's within reach. That was the first key. Now take Mr. B. You're familiar with him?"

"Yes."

"Bottom line, Mr. B was a loud mouth, no talent bouncer that they literally picked off the streets and made a star. It was like he won the lottery, and he proved that anyone could make it. That was the second key. Bob and I went on and on with example after example, filling in the picture, but in the end, Bob missed the point, and I knew what I had to do. I had to create a show in which the audience feels like they are walking into the TV, into the show, the character, and the character is walking out of the TV and is alive in their living rooms, the two become one, the viewer and the viewed. That was the secret. That was the formula for *Windows*, my first major success. In *Windows* I filmed a real live family on location in Manhattan. Day and night we filmed the Labelle family, and because the camera was always on them, they began to play to it. And as they played to it, the camera brought out the extra in the ordinary, until, finally, they were extraordinary.

"Mr. Labelle was a modestly successful entertainment agent who became more successful as we filmed him. His eldest daughter, Jan, who worked for him, had an over developed libido, and she turned into a bombshell under the lights. Ms. Labelle, his ex-wife, was a plain looking fat woman who also grew under the lights. She became brighter. As we turned her inside out, she became very articulate and humorous, so we made her a talk show host. And Miranda, the youngest daughter, was a crazy teenager who played to the cameras naturally. We didn't have to do anything with her except convince her that she could do anything that she wanted to do, anything that came into her mind. And she did.

"Everything was coming together. We combined the elements of a modern soap, a variety show, and a talk show. It was great, but in the end something was still missing. I decided that it was the advertising breaks. They broke the tapestry of fantasy and reality that I had woven together as a seamless whole. That's when I discovered what I thought to be the final key. I made the ads a part of the show. The products sold the show, and the show sold the products. The ads were reinforced by the story, by subtle gestures, images and colors that would repeat themselves until they climaxed once again in the ad that became the story and the story that became the ad."

"And *Windows*," Ms. Yuong says, "revolutionized the industry."

"Yes, it did. I had one success after another, and I

became the head of the network. I thought I was on top of the world. But it's curious though how destiny and chance seem to conspire. Right when I thought that I had reached the peak of my success, Averill Reed discovered how to turn an electron particle into a wave and then back into a particle again, and we developed vision board, a wall board that makes every wall a camera and projector and every room a holographic grid that produces high definition three-dimensional images that are so real you cannot distinguish the real from the images.

"Then Roland Marchant invented the quantum supercomputer, and we now had the capability of processing the quantum nature of human consciousness and the billions of alternative universes that collectively dwell in each of our minds, the billions of stories in which each of us is the main character, the focal point of the camera. Now everyone is on TV or can be, and everyone can be spied on. This is the carrot and the stick. This is the plugged in, turned on society where everyone can substitute themselves for the main character or sports hero in any story or game. Everyone can alter their appearance, lose weight, enlarge their breasts or penises, change their shape and the color of their hair or eyes and buff themselves up with just the push of a button and the turn of the knob, and every day, every minute, anyone can audition for a part in the main story that brings all these alternative universes, these individual focal points, into one story that expresses most completely our collective consciousness and the

American Dream."

Ms. Yuong touches Merling's hand, "And we want to be part of that dream."

Merling laughs, "Well, first you better buy yourself some real property."

They both burst out laughing then Ms. Yuong says, "You married one of the stars of *Windows*, didn't you?"

"Yes, I married Jan Labelle. In fact, my sister-in-law, Miranda, is hosting an opening of a project that I helped fund and organize." Merling leans forward towards Ms. Young in a false gesture of intimacy and says, "That's one of the reasons I was willing to come out here to Montana. I want to see it, and I think you'll enjoy the exhibit as well. In fact, it should be one of our first scheduled stops."

Merling consults his notebook computer and is puzzled. "That's curious." He touches a button on the communications panel, "John?"

"Yes, sir."

"John, I don't see Miranda's opening here on my agenda."

"You never indicated that you wanted to stop there, sir."

"Well, I'll be damned. I thought..." Merling paused for a moment, puzzled, then he said, "You do know what I'm talking about?"

"Yes, sir, the supermarket."

"Well, my mistake. I guess I forgot."

He reaches for his computer notebook and uploads

a map of the local area and directs the computer to locate the exhibit. "John, the address is 362 Green St., the old Route 13. From the map it seems to me that we can make a short detour and make it our first stop."

"But that area has not been secured, sir."

"Well, do your job, John."

Merling turns to Ms. Yuong and says, "You'll enjoy this." Merling looks out the window of the bus, and he can see that they are approaching the foothills of the Rockies and entering the walled suburbs of Helena that are guarded by a private security force. The walls are made of artificially aged red brick, and they are covered with ivy. The entranceway gate is made of ornate wrought iron and gives the impression that you are entering Paradise, or at least an upper middle class version of paradise that is decidedly Victorian with its peaked rooftops, pillared porches, tall windows, carriage houses, and stately shadows and flower gardens.

Brad sees children playing on one lawn, and he wonders why he married Jan. Probably he married her because she was his first creation, the first creature of the New Age to emerge from Zeus's mind. It was like falling in love with himself.

Chapter Four

"**G**od damn it!" Hathaway shouts when Merling cuts him off. "Why do we have to go to that god damned exhibit now?" He turns to Denny, "Martino, can you get your people over there?"

Denny taps into the communication lines. "I can if you can buy me some time. How about the scenic route?"

"You got it." Hathaway presses some buttons and the map of the route and the surrounding area appears.

Denny points to a route on the map, "There, the scenic loop."

"I got you." Hathaway contacts the driver and gives him the alternative route. He then turns to Denny who is dispatching a security unit to the site of the exhibit and says, "Martino, clear the area. I don't want to see a civilian."

Denny taps in a number on the phone, and as he's doing so, he says to Hathaway, "We're in luck. The opening isn't until later this afternoon."

Denny speaks to the director of the exhibit who at first is not very cooperative. But then Denny explains to the director how gravity works and what will happen if a guy like Merling, who lives on the top floor, decides to take a shit.

"We don't want any leaky pipes here, do we, sir?" The director agrees, and Denny orders a computer link up. He wants names and addresses of all employees and personnel directly or indirectly involved in any way with this exhibit. Denny hangs up the phone, and he watches the personnel data that the director is feeding into the system. He then runs the list of employees through the computer banks to see if there is anyone on the staff with a criminal record or known affiliations with a radical political or environmental group. He finds nothing that would indicate to him that there is any danger there.

Denny sits back in his chair. There's really not much more for him to do until they reach the red zone. He becomes curious, "Hathaway, why are we selling all this land to the Chinese?"

"Because the Chinese and the Japanese are about to sign a treaty that will eliminate all trade barriers between the two countries."

"That's bad?"

Hathaway rolls his eyes at the stupidity of the question. "You're god damned right it's bad. We're in a trade war here. And the three main combatants are the United States, Western Europe, China, and Japan, right?"

"Right."

"Well, figure it out. We control the Americas. The Western Europeans control Eastern Europe, Russia, and most of the old Soviet Union. The Middle East has been sucked dry. We are all cutting up Africa for whatever is left there, and the Chinese and the Japanese control all of Southeastern Asia. Now what do you think will happen if China allies itself with Japan?"

Denny pauses for a moment. He's thoughtful, and then he says, "China and Japan will control the Far East. So we have to keep the China door open, or we're in deep shit. It's trade for land."

Hathaway aims his index finger at Denny as if it is a gun and fires one off, "You got it."

Denny thinks about this, and he still doesn't like it. It doesn't seem right. We shouldn't be able to sell our country the way we do, but he doesn't say anything to Hathaway because Hathaway is a mercenary, and he would probably laugh in his face. Denny returns to casually monitoring the route they are taking. He can see that they are passing through Apple Grove, a replica town for tourists and retired middle level management personnel owned by Disney World. They still have a long way to go.

On Main Street, they pass by a 50's theater with a neon starburst of orange and blue and flowing electronic script that spells out the name of the theater. Across the street from The Star Theater is the Red Robin, a chrome wrap-around dinner reflecting the colors of the neon sign and the colors and images of the street and the russet tones of Hancock's, a forties hardware store that stands next to The Red and White Drug Store from the same era. In the middle of the town stands a courthouse with classic

Roman columns guarded by the symbol of the American Revolution, a bronze eagle perched upon its dome. The oak and walnut trees shadow quiet lawns, and the "Real Estate for Sale" signs on many of the lawns arouse the curiosity of the Chinese on the tour bus.

At the other end of town the shapes flatten out into low slanted rooftops, extended eaves, and the elongated planes of the brown brick ranch homes of the fifties that open up to a world of picture windows, hedges, dogwood trees, and neatly mowed lawns and flower beds. This is the section of Helena where Denny lives.

Denny decides to see what his wife is doing. He taps some keys that access the surveillance system, and his wife, Heather, appears in their bedroom. She is shopping at one of the Vision World home fashion stores. With her remote control, she is able to turn the room into a mirror of cameras that reveal from every angle what she looks like as she tries on one thing after another with just the touch of a the buttons that float in the air like pretty colored bubbles.

At the moment she is trying on a black cashmere dress that shows off her legs and ass as she gracefully swirls her skirt and watches the flow of fabric as if she were caressing herself, but then with the touch of a button, the cashmere dress changes into a paper dress made like a cutout for a doll. With another touch of a button, she changes the color, length, and style of her hair. Her hair is no longer blond, flowing over her shoulder, but bobbed, jet black to match her long black lashes, sky blue eyes, deep red lips, and rouged child-like cheeks.

Heather is smiling at the walls, the cameras, the millions of eyes she believes to be there. She whispers the lines that Vision World has fed her in hopes that she will be picked up for a live ad, the dream of every housewife. This is not an unrealistic dream for Heather. Vision World seems to like her, and she's been picked up for a spot-ad quite frequently. Probably because, from the beginning, Heather was a TV baby, nurtured by the Tube, fed with images of the perfect upper middle class housewife to grow into, the perfect illusion, nothing too big, nothing too small, attractive, agreeable, pleasant, always smiling, bubbly, full of life, enthusiastic. Yet, she was iron hard and willful in her relentless pursuit of the American Dream, and she was willing to ignore all the suffering in the world, the babies starving, bellies bulging pregnant with death if, for one moment, that vision endangered her picture of the perfect home. Otherwise, she's caring, concerned, charitable in a tax deductible way, willing to give of her time in token gestures of good will that she wears like precious earrings, attuned to the sound of praise, a good woman, totally out of touch with reality, the perfect subordinate, secretary, or assistant, a dream on paper and frigid in bed. She's what every lower class woman wants to be and a role model for her peers. She's Miss America without the measurements. Most women can identify with her. Most men would like to marry her and, with the proper makeup, she's within reach for most women in the mirror.

Heather presses another button, and her hair turns sapphire blue, straight, shoulder length, long dark sapphire lashes, and green eyes. Her candy necklace turns into a silver thread with a blue sapphire stone. She whirls about, and her paper dress changes into silver polymer that clings to her skin.

The phone rings.

Heather steps naked out of the hologram. She orders the baby doll dress and the accessories to be delivered later that day then puts on a cotton robe and presses a button on the control panel. A print out appears on the screen informing her that her mother-in-law is calling. Heather instructs the system to put her mother-in-law on hold.

Denny watches Heather leave the bedroom and enter a kitchen fashioned into soft edges, pleasant symmetry, bright primary colors offsetting black enamel and a white linoleum floor. She takes out a can of crushed tomatoes, a couple of bell peppers, an onion, and cilantro from the vegetable bin, and then she arranges the ingredients on the worktable. She makes sure that all the labels are showing. Denny knows exactly what she is doing. She's setting the stage for a home kitchen show in hopes that her mother-in-law will want to play.

Heather turns on the telephone channel for the TV, and Denny's mother appears on the TV screen. She is in her room at the state home for the aged, but she is surrounded by holographic images of her past. Her room, at this moment, looks like the kitchen they had when Denny's dad was alive. Denny can see the old kitchen cabinets with the oak veneer, the old coffee machine standing alone like a dinosaur of early plastique. He can even see the old refrigerator, a big block of pink enamel. Pasted on the door of the refrigerator is a decal of the sun, a yellow circle with black dots for eyes and one curved line for a smile. He had put that decal on the refrigerator when he was a child right next to the little choo-choo train magnet that still holds in place a shopping list. "Candy" is written in the scribble of a child at the bottom of the list. Mom's hair is gray, and she has warm brown eyes and a pleasant smile. She touches her hair, and Heather picks up the cue.

"Oh, mother, you've been to the beautician."

"Yes, dear, do you like it?"

"Very much."

Denny's mother poses for a moment. She has that pleasing appearance of a woman who has worked hard all her life, but not too hard, who has suffered, but not too much, who has lived, but not excessively. Denny's mother was a schoolteacher, and she believes in good, but she also believes in life insurance, old age benefits, health insurance, and counting your change. These days she lives out her memories, drinks tea, watches TV, and worries about her grandchild. Denny's mother is perfectly normal, and he loves her.

Denny's mother's eyes wander around the room,

37

looking for something new to talk about, a new appliance, a new look, there is nothing, but then she spots the food on the work table and asks, "Are you making dinner, dear?"

"Yes, mother, I'm trying out a new chili recipe that I got from our housekeeper. She's from Guatemala. And look." Heather reaches into the cabinet and brings out some dried chili peppers. "I got these and the cilantro from the Latin Quarter yesterday."

"Oh that should be nice, Heather. Can I see the recipe?"

The cameras have been programmed by Heather for a cooking show, so they first focus on the recipe, then on Heather, then the gloss of the green pepper, the voluptuous shapes she is cutting as she explains the recipe, step by step. Then the camera focuses on the yellow label in the background and the brand name, Cora, and the holographic picture on the label of bright red plum tomatoes and the rustic brown and earthen yellow color of the onions in the background, a perfect commercial still-life.

Denny's mother is smiling as she intently devours the directions into the hot spicy flavors and mysteries of Latin America, but then something very strange happens that shocks Denny. Vision World is turned off. The kitchen loses all its color, its lines, the décor, and his mother's room turns into an empty space with just a bed, a table, and a chair.

He looks at the screens. Everywhere the illusion is

gone. His wife looks catatonic, as if she were in a still frame. His mother puts her hands over her eyes and cries, "Oh, Heather, sometimes I feel so empty."

For a split second Denny gets a glimpse of what is behind Vision World, the living being that tries to pull him into the void and then is gone. Vision World goes on again, and Heather and Denny's mother go on again as if nothing has happened.

Denny turns to Hathaway and says, "What was that?"

"It's a brown out. You've never seen one before?"

"No."

"It's not common, but in areas like this where the system is expanding so much, sometimes there just isn't enough juice."

Hathaway turns Denny's wife off, the screen goes blank, and he says, "Let's get back to work Martino. We're getting close to the exit."

Chapter Five

Denny watches the tour bus pass through the geometry of the sixties and seventies, cubes transposed one upon the other like an atonal musical scale ascending to the floating tiers of Helena's modern skyscrapers that circle the parks, the bicycle paths, the ponds, the squares of the inner city with their historical shops and trolley cars, and the 1880's train station where the magnetic commuter trains speed to a stop. Out over the city, Denny can see where the terrorists struck, the gouge in the mountain. Far below the site of the explosion are the shantytowns that have grown up along the mountainside, a necklace of poverty strangling Helena.

The bus makes a turn onto the exit and descends into the inner city. This section of Helena is where luxury autos are sold to the very rich, and posh restaurants serve food that no one else can afford. For some reason the surveillance cameras and the computer surveillance system focuses on the Peugeot Cafe, a glass and chrome tube construction where a customer can dine, lounge, sip cocktails, and buy a car. In the cocktail lounge, chrome automobile bumpers artistically welded and sculpted together form a circular bar. At the center of the bar, a futuristic prototype automobile rotates slowly so as to highlight its features, the sweeping lines, and the flow of air and light that generates energy and causes the photo-sensitive skin of the car to glow and change colors with the change of light, fire red at sunset, midnight black at night. Beyond the bar, the seating is casual, leather lounge chairs and couches with chrome frames. The floor is surfaced with re-fractive glass, like the lens of an old fashioned automobile headlight.

"Hold it right there," Denny says.

Hathaway freezes the picture.

"No, back a little bit," Denny says

The camera tracks back.

"There. Who's that?" Denny asks. He points to a woman sitting with two men at one of the tables.

"That's Miranda Labelle, Merling's sister-in-law."

"I thought so."

Yes, he says to himself. I do remember her from the hit show, *Windows*. She was much younger then, but she still has those beautifully shaded eyes, the shy look, and the girlish gestures that are more artful now, graceful. She is deeply involved with the conversation, animated.

Denny turns to Hathaway, "Do you recognize the two men?"

"No, but it's obvious that they're all there for the opening."

"Let's listen in."

"No, we don't have time," Hathaway says, "But I'll program the computers to monitor the conversation and take some close ups of the men with Labelle. I'll do a make on them later." Hathaway gives the computers the appropriate commands then switches the focus of the cameras to Merling.

Denny hears Brad Merling say, "Twenty five years ago, the Art Council and the American Historic Commission bought the supermarket with all its contents. We also bought every car in the parking lot. Then we sealed the supermarket and the parking lot in a vacuum shell to be opened today. Gentlemen, welcome to the Grand Opening of the Super Shopper Food Market."

Denny scans the parking lot, and he sees that the parking lot is a historical museum of cars. He smiles at the old familiar faces, the steel giants from the past with chrome teeth, life-like eyes, and wide gaping mouths that gobble up air and turn it into fire, 400 cubic inches of pure power and muscle. In between the monsters, he can see the little bugs with their hard little shells that replaced these fiery reptiles and the fierce mammals, the Cobras, the Broncos, the Mustangs, the Scorpions, the Cougars, and the Thunderbirds that roamed America's roads when men were free, long before we ran out of fire, and long after the skies darkened and the dinosaurs died.

The vehicle that Denny and Hathaway are riding in pulls to a stop, and Hathaway turns to Denny and says, "Let's go."

They hurry out of the communications vehicle and make their way to Merling who is leading the delegation into the super market. As they approach the entranceway, the doors of the supermarket slide open, and Denny moves quickly through the door so as to take a defensive position in front of Merling, but as he does so he almost bumps into a shopping cart being pushed by a man leaving the store.

"Excuse..." Denny stops in mid-sentence. He is looking into the face of a man whose eyes are staring beyond him, through him, to the parking lot and the monster that waits. Denny looks beyond the man and sees that the market is full of people frozen in time, people coming and going, pushing their grocery cart before them, all motion stopped, still lives.

As Denny steps around the life-like figure, he hears Merling say, "We took pictures of everyone in the store, and then we made the most characteristic of them all come back and did plaster casting of them, exactly as they were. This is how they dressed, this is how they looked."

The phantom people spook Denny. They're just too damned real. And the supermarket, the total vision, is awesome. It's like it was before the depression, before the food shortages and the starvation. The room is immense. The meat section and vegetable section extend beyond belief, and there are so many things, so many colors and shapes - flowers, rows and rows of candy, canned goods, walls of soda pop.

Denny is impressed with how many overweight people there are. He looks at a woman who is blown up with fat. Her children are overweight too. The woman is dressed in a simple cotton dress, athletic socks, and nameless brown loafers. The two boys are wearing sweatshirts that advertise products in bright bold letters, jeans that have a large label on the back pocket, and sneakers that advertise with bold logos and letters the product of the maker. Nobody, however, wears price tags like they do today. Denny looks into the cart and sees that it is filled with half gallon bottles of Pepsi, boxes upon boxes of cookies, TV dinners, a large box of sugared corn flakes, ice cream, huge gobs of ground beef wrapped in clear plastic that clings to the red meat.

Denny then looks into the mother's eyes, the eyes of the children, the eyes of the people in the store. They all have blank mindless stares. They seem to be in a trance, intent on their consumption of the vast amount of food being offered to them, devouring with their eyes the labels, the greens, the bloody meat, bumping into one another, forming traffic jams of shopping carts full of food.

These people were junkies, Denny thinks to himself, and the exhibit captures that era for what it was, an era of mindless consumption. They consumed anything and everything, until they consumed themselves and sold out their birth right for a handful of beads, a couple of Japanese toys, Pepsi Cola, a cart full of TV dinners, and an image of America that didn't exist. They all sold out for chump change, even the smart ones and the thin ones who bought fresh vegetables and fruit, good cheeses, and low cholesterol meat. That's as smart as they got. They're the ones with the Porches and the BMW's in the lot. And now they're riding the bus with everyone else.

As he passes into the fresh fish section of the store, Denny observes the fresh fish piled one on top of the other, all varieties from everywhere in the world featuring dead eyes, lips puckered out, all colors, dead rainbows. Even the big predators have been slaughtered, the Mako shark cut up into slices, the tentacles of an octopus all mashed together. On the far side of the counter he notices a couple with a child who is riding in the shopping cart. The man is looking down the aisle. He seems to be staring at Denny. The woman is pointing at a fish item, and the counter person seems to be intent on pleasing. Denny notices that the man has a stain between his legs. A thought flashes through Denny's mind.

Statues don't piss their pants.

Denny reacts immediately. In one single movement he pushes Merling aside and reaches for his pistol. The apparition erupts into reality and plaster shatters everywhere as Denny sees beyond the illusion to the man, the gun. The man fires wildly. Denny hears screams. He hits the man, once, twice, three times in the chest and then another apparition erupts, the woman.

A burst of fire rips into the woman, then the child. The woman crashes into the piles of fish and the fish shatter into fragments, eyeballs roll across the floor like marbles.

Denny shouts to the security guards, "Cover Merling!" Then he swings his gun around looking for another assassin to break out of the life-like figures. The supermarket has erupted. The security guards are firing at all the still lives, the shoppers, the vegetables, the meat, the rows of boxes and cans. They're terrified by the phantoms, terrified that something could be alive in here, that it could kill them, and that it could be anywhere.

Finally, the fire subsides, and the tension drains into an empty silence. Denny looks around and sees that the exhibit is destroyed, reduced to fragments of plaster of Paris, papier-mâché, cans riddled with bullets, boxes torn apart, empty. All that remains is the real horror of death. Denny stares at the man and woman torn apart by bullets, and then he panics. Was there really a child? He stares down into the horror, and he sees the child's head, cracked. The hand is still intact, the box, the label, the eyes. Denny is relieved to see that there is no real person inside the illusion.

Denny feels a hand on his shoulder. He hears Hathaway's voice, "Martino, it's all over. Great job."

Denny hears himself say, "Merling?"

"He's all right. But the Yuong woman ate it. That's it for this fuckin deal. Come on. You need some fresh air, soldier."

Hathaway turns Denny away from the death scene, and he walks him out of the supermarket.

Denny hears himself say, "Did anyone else get

hurt?"

"Another Chink bought it, and a security guard got it bad. A couple of other people got nicked. There was a lot of loose fire in there."

"Too many ghosts."

Hathaway studies Denny for a moment, "Listen, Martino, are you all right? I've got to get the rest of the Chinese out of here."

"I'm all right."

Hathaway studies Denny for a moment more, and there's a smile on his face when he says, "Dennis Martino, you're a real live motherfucker."

Denny doesn't respond, but he feels the lack of Hathaway's presence as he walks past the cars, the stare of the monsters. He stops in front of a Volvo station wagon. He touches the hard cold steel, the silver gray. He walks around to the driver's side and touches the door handle. It's not locked. Denny opens the door and slides into the driver's seat. He looks at the dash, the gauges, and feels the sense of being in a cockpit. The key is in the ignition. Denny starts the car and listens to the soothing throb of the motor. Those were the days when the roads were open to everyone, not just the elites. He remembers when Heather and he were young, driving a car just like this across country, free to go wherever they wanted, stop when they wanted to, camping along the way in the national parks. He remembers one night how they danced around the campfire, the doors of the car wide open, the music from the car stereo filling the empty park, drifting through the tree tops to the stars, two high notes en-twined like the strings of a guitar, vibrating, making love to the sound of the falls, gravity pulling them down into the core of the fire, the silent sleep.

They woke the next day to the sound of birds chirping, and they were on the road again, the open road to freedom. How he loved this car. Denny puts his hand on the gearshift. Reverse.

Chapter Six

Denny is sitting in the antique Volvo staring out into the past when the car door opens. It's Hathaway. "Come on, Denny. Merling wants to see you."

Hathaway leads Denny to the surveillance vehicle where Merling is inside sitting comfortably in front of the control panel. He gestures for Denny and Hathaway to sit down, and then he turns to Hathaway and says, "Do you know who those people were?"

"Not yet."

Merling turns to Denny and smiles. "Nice job, Colonel. We were fortunate to have you along. I owe you my life."

"I was just doing my job, sir."

Merling looks at Denny, and he studies him for a moment. Denny's features are rounded, relaxed. His movements flow, and even when he is at attention, he seems at ease. He has an understated athleticism that Merling likes, and judging by the action shots that Merling has just gone through of the firefight, Denny photographs well. The camera seems to like him.

Merling has learned from glancing through Denny's records that Denny was awarded the Silver Star for bravery in action, and he was made a full colonel at twenty-eight years old. But then one day he just refused to fight any-more, so they shipped him back home. First they put him in a counterterrorist division, and then he was demoted to homicide. The rap on him is that he is burnt out. But that doesn't square with what Merling saw today. No, Martino is not burnt out, Merling decides, but there is a look of wariness to him, an expression in his eyes that gives Mer-ling the impression that Dennis Martino is looking for something that he doesn't want to find. Merling likes that look. It makes Martino look vulnerable, sympathetic. Even Hathaway likes him, and Hathaway doesn't like anybody.

Merling decides that he likes what he sees. Martino has star qualities, but he needs to be pushed back into the spotlight. He needs to act. Merling is convinced that, given the opportunity, Martino will perform, and he will play his part well.

Merling smiles and says, "Colonel, I want you to come to work for me. I want you and Hathaway to find out who these people were and what they were up to. I want to know if there is anyone behind this. And if there is, I want you to get them."

"But sir, I'm in the army, and I don't determine my assignments. I was just assigned to you for the day."

"I'll take care of that. I think that you can safely as-sume that you have been subcontracted to me for twice the pay, that is, if you agree."

Denny thinks for a moment about the proposition, and he realizes that for the last few years he's been sleep walking through his job, just going through the motions day after day. First he stopped fighting, then he stopped looking, and now... He's got to wake up or he's going to end up as just another ghost, just like the ghosts back there in the supermarket, a monument to his own folly.

"I would like to come to work for you, sir," Denny says. "Thank you for the opportunity."

"Well, it's settled then. See what you can find out here, and I'll expect you in Washington with a report. Then we'll see." Merling extends his hand and says, "Welcome to Vision World."

Denny leaves the surveillance vehicle, and he returns to the scene of the crime and begins to direct the investigation. As they search through the broken images for clues and evidence, the two assassins are being carried away in body bags. According to their IDs they are Robert and Melissa Hewitt. They have a local address. Denny orders two teams of surveillance specialists to work all night editing surveillance information that they may have on this couple. This may mean going over several years of data, but the computer will aid the search by reading emotional levels, fear, key words, and associational patterns. It will also cross reference names and places. Denny takes one final look at the exhibit. What a waste. They may never be able to put it back together again.

He turns and walks away from the shattered illusion, finds his car, and orders his driver to take him home then sits back and relaxes. He is really tired. He feels the energy drain out of him, but then he looks down.

"Bugs, I almost forgot about you." Denny reaches down into the box and picks the rabbit up, "How you doing? You look pretty lively to me. And look. You ate your lettuce. What a good boy. Tomorrow we'll find a nice home for you, and everything will be all right. No more boxes, no more humans for you, buddy. Free at last."

Denny places the rabbit in his lap and he strokes it absent-mindedly. He reviews the case, what he has, which isn't much. He tries to sort out all the possible motives.

When he gets home, Heather is waiting for him, and she is wearing the baby doll dress. Her hair is jet black, bobbed. Her eyes are sky blue, just like in the hologram. She's very excited. She saw Denny on TV, and now she has dreams of a new life for them. She sees Denny as the hero of a new TV series, and for herself she sees infinite possibilities. Then she sees the rabbit and orders him out of the house. He's dirty. He can't be controlled. He'll shit all over everything. Denny tries to remind Heather of when they used to go camping, how much she liked nature. But that's ancient history to Heather. This is now. Bugs Bunny is definitely not in fashion, so Denny puts him in the garage. Poor Bugs, Denny thinks as he finds some good vegetables in the refrigerator and bottled spring water for the poor little rabbit, and he promises him that tomorrow things will be better.

When Denny returns to the house, the stage is set in their dining room. The chili from the food show is ready.

After dinner, Heather leads Denny to the bedroom, and they make love. Heather is really hot, but Denny realizes that it isn't him who is making her so excited. It's her belief that they are being watched. When he looks into Heather's eyes, he sees that she is wide-awake dreaming of Vision World. It is entering her every cell. Her whole body is an orifice filled with electronic impulses that have turned her on.

As she begins to climax, she whispers, "Oh God. I want you. I love you. I'll be anything you want me to be, anything."

Once again, Denny realizes that she is not talking to him. Denny closes his eyes and makes believe that she is Cheri Normal, and he tries to fuck her blind. But why Cheri, why does she turn him on? Is it because she is the Goddess of News and Everything New? After all, that's what America is all about. Isn't it? To be forever new, to be born again every day, to never look back, to have no past, no history, to always look forward to an empty future, to be filled by what?

Denny opens his eyes and gets out of bed. He has tears in his eyes.

"Where are you going?" Heather asks.

Confused, Denny says, "For once in my life, I'm going to find out what the hell is going on. I'm tired of being a character in someone else's story.

Chapter Seven

The next day, Hathaway walks into Denny's office at the regional headquarters for the national military police, and he is amused to see that Merling has programmed Denny's office to look like a private eye's office in a 1960s version of a 1940s film noire detective story. He smiles at Merling's sense of humor and attention to detail, the scratched and stained dark walnut desk and swivel chair, the burgundy and gray faded Persian rug, the antique coat stand with polished brass hooks, and the two burgundy leather chairs with decorative brass tacks along the seams and cracks in the upholstery where tuffs of cotton filling stick out giving the furnishings the appearance of being left there by the last occupant who purchased them at a Salvation Army furniture sale.

On Denny's desk, next to a clear glass ashtray that looks like it was stolen from the neighborhood bar is a pack of non-filter Camel cigarettes and a brass desk lamp with a green glass shade and an old fashioned light bulb that infuses the desk with yellow light and an emerald glow. A red flickering light from a neon sign can be seen through a tear in the old fashioned pull down shade yellowed with age.

Hathaway tugs on an embroidered ring at the end of a string attached to the bottom of the shade and the shade rolls up with a flapping sound that is romantic in its mechanical imperfection. The scene outside is a three dimensional life-like projection of Chinatown in Los Angeles at night during the 1940s. Hathaway can only see the **H** and the **O** and part of the **T** of the red neon hotel sign, and below he can see a trolley car, shoppers and tenement dwellers, tourists and peddlers, and the sound of two languages merging together with the constant drone of tires against asphalt. He hears the clang of the trolley car bell, and he can see the green neon sign of the Peking Restaurant and the orange, yellow, green, and blue glow of Chinese paper lanterns reflecting off of the black polished mirror- like-surfaces of the cars and the street glistening from a recent rain.

Hathaway pulls down the shade that acts like the volume control knob on a radio and the sounds from the street disappear. The only remaining sound in the room is the pleasant whispers of steam from a cast iron Victorian radiator.

Hathaway laughs then says, "OK, Philip Marlow, where's the bottle?"

Denny smiles and points to the bottom drawer of his desk and says, "Compliments of Brad Merling."

Hathaway pulls out the drawer and sees a bottle of Four Roses Whiskey, two highball glasses, and a Gideon Bible. "Perfect," he says as he pulls the bottle of whiskey and the two highball glasses out of the drawer, and he pours Denny and himself a double shot of whiskey, straight, no ice.

Denny, who is looking at the computer screen image suspended above his desk pours some of the whiskey into the cup of coffee he is holding in his hand and says, "He's also linked me up to your database. Is there anything you guys can't see or hear?"

"Not much," Hathaway says. "And when we finish the Zeus Project, we'll be able to hear an ant shit and make you think you're in Heaven when you're living in a garbage can."

Hathaway takes a sip from his own glass, "Not bad," he says as he picks up a picture of Heather from Denny's desk. Heather looks like the girl next door who left the blinds open so that Denny could see her undress at night. From the file that he has on Denny and his wife, he knows that they have no children, and they probably won't have any in the near future, not until Heather losses her figure and she is too old to play the ingénue. Only then will she consider doing baby ads and playing the stay-at-home soccer mom desperate for an affair or a family tragedy that would catch the camera eye.

As Hathaway puts down the picture of Heather, he hears a strange crunching sound, "What the hell is that? You got rats in here?"

Denny pulls back his chair and slides out an old cardboard box from underneath the desk. Bugs Bunny is inside chewing on a carrot and some lettuce.

Hathaway laughs and says, "You still haven't got rid of that fuckin rabbit?"

Denny shrugs and says, "It's a long story," as he slides the cardboard box back under the desk. Denny then leans forward and enlarges the screen on the computer, "Here, take a look at this."

Hathaway looks over Denny's shoulder at the pictures of the two assassins who attempted to murder Brad Merling. "Who are they?" Hathaway asks.

Denny points the cursor at the man, taps in a command, and the image is magnified. The man is tall, thin with light brown hair and fading blue eyes. "His name is Robert Hewitt," Denny says, "A typical victim of the depression, upper middle class background, good education, some military service, a computer programmer, unemployed for the last five years. He became active in the ecology movement early on. Joined the Green Peace Party two years ago. On the surface, he appears to be a seemingly innocent pinko, but, in fact, the CIA file on this guy tells us that he and his wife are suspected members of the People's Army, a new terrorist group that has appeared in the United States recently but originates in Brazil."

Denny magnifies the picture of the woman. She is short, dumpy, with mousy brown hair. "Her name is Melissa. She's another average sort. Comes from a well-to-do family. They met in college, Stanford. She's an anthropologist, or was, until the funding and grants disappeared and the family money ran out. There's no indication that she even knew how to fire a gun. As far as I can see, this was a suicide mission. These two had no hope of coming out of the assassination attempt alive."

Hathaway studies the pictures of the two assassins for a moment then he walks out of the room and returns with a cup of coffee. "What else do we have?"

"They took a trip to Brazil, and while they were there..." Denny taps another key and a picture appears of a man in uniform.

Hathaway recognizes the man, "General Pastanoz."

Another picture appears of a car blown apart. Denny lights another cigarette and says, "They were in Rio when Pastanoz was blown away."

"Where did you get this from?" Hathaway asks.

"A Central Intelligence Agency file. They've had these two under surveillance for a year now."

"Do they figure the Hewitts are connected to the Pastanoz assassination?"

"Maybe."

"So what does the CIA have on the People's Army?" Hathaway asks.

"Nothing, no names, no informants, they don't seem to have a clear picture of who these people are, and that bothers me."

"Why? Do you think that they're stone walling you?"

"I don't know, but they've been watching these two

for a year, and they've comes up with essentially nothing. I went through the Vision World surveillance tapes in one night and come up with this."

Denny picks up a disc and places it in the recorder, presses a button, and Hathaway sees Robert Hewitt, the dead assassin, sitting down in his living room. Hewitt is watching a baseball game on TV that Hewitt has programmed so that it transposes his own image on that of the pitcher for the Mets. It is Hewitt who is on the mound in uniform, leaning over, concentrating on the signals from the catcher, feeling the ball in his hands, the strings.

He winds up and there is a knock on his door.

He pitches. The batter swings. Strike one.

"Yes," Hewitt says as he pumps his fist, and he watches himself on TV kick dust off the mound after he has struck out the batter. There's another knock at his door, "Damn!" Robert Hewitt says as he gets up from the couch and walks into the kitchen. There's a third knock, harsher. Hewitt opens the door, and he sees a man standing before him.

Hathaway sees what Hewitt sees. He sees a man at the door that looks like the typical vegetarian, average height, average built, an overly sensitive face, slightly underweight, needs some meat. Hathaway notes that the man seems intent. There's perspiration on his brow, and he seems nervous.

The man speaks in a rather placid tone, "I need to talk to you, Robert. I hope you don't mind me stopping by?"

Hewitt at first seems confused then casually says, "No, not at all, but do you mind if we walk and talk? I've been in the house all day, and I could use some fresh air."

"Good idea. It's a perfect day." The man says and smiles warmly.

As the door closes Hathaway hears Hewitt, cheerfully say, "It's good to see you."

Denny presses the stop action button and turns to Hathaway and says, "We had the computer monitor the voices and the body language." Denny points to the man talking to Robert Hewitt and says, "He is very nervous, afraid. Robert Hewitt is confused, angry, and very nervous."

"I can see that, Denny, so what?"

Denny plays back the disc to where Robert Hewitt opens the door, and then he focuses closely on the face of the man at the door.

He looks at Hathaway and smiles, "You don't recognize him?"

Hathaway looks closer. "No."

Denny smiles triumphantly. "As soon as I saw him, I knew I'd seen him before." To extend the suspense, Denny taps the desk with his finger to indicate that Hathaway is on the clock.

"Come on, God damn it," Hathaway says. "Let's cut the bullshit and get to the chase. Who the fuck is it?"

Denny touches the screen and a picture appears on the screen of Miranda and two men seated at a table in the Peugeot Cafe.

Hathaway leans closer to get a better look. Finally, he says, "That's from yesterday's surveillance tapes. We were coming into the exhibit."

"Right."

Hathaway is looking at the man who came to Robert Hewitt's door. "Who is that asshole?" Hathaway asks.

"Greg Barnes, he's the editor in chief for the magazine the Green Peace Party publishes called *The Globe*."

Hathaway now focuses on Miranda who is intent as she listens to Greg Barnes. Hathaway listens to the drivel about the ecology, the death of the grizzly, the loss of our forests primeval. The other man at the table is just sitting there watching them. He looks Latin American, possibly European, maybe Mid-Eastern. His features are blurred by a beard, but he has the eyes of a predator.

"Who is he?" Hathaway asks.

Denny shrugs, "I sent his face through the computer, nothing."

Hathaway aims at the man with his finger as if it were a gun, "That's our man. He points to the editor for *The Globe*, but he's our lead. Have you interrogated him yet?"

"No. I've been waiting for you."

"Where is he now?"

"In his office, he's been there since early this morning. I ordered my men to detain him if he tries to leave the building."

"Good, let's go."

Denny begins to shut off the computer, but then he pauses. He looks at the faces of Melissa and Robert Hewitt. They're smiling back at him. He looks at the picture of General Pastanoz, the blown up car, the picture of Melissa and Robert Hewitt wasted amidst the debris of a dead dream, the two men with Miranda Labelle. Then he points out the sequence of pictures to Hathaway, "There's something wrong with this," Denny says.

"What?"

"I don't know. The footprint seems too clear. I don't think I'm that smart."

"Maybe they're just that stupid."

Denny shrugs. He puts on his coat and throws up the collar and looks into the screen once more. He exhales and then watches the smoke swirl around the death scenes, the leads. "There's another thing that bothers me," he says. "How do two average Americans get from here to there?" He points to the smiling faces and then to their bullet torn bodies, "What went wrong?"

Hathaway grows impatient, "Come on, Martino. We don't have time to pick over dead meat. We've got a live lead. Let's follow it."

Chapter Eight

Denny and Hathaway take an elevator to the rooftop where a gray and black metallic Raptor helicopter with dragonfly wings is waiting for them. Denny enters the beast, and as he straps himself into his seat, he can hear and feel the turbines turn over, the jets ignite, and the high tech creature with a prehistoric form blast off, a predator in search of its prey. As they fly over the countryside, Denny sees the traces of all the old highways and roadways that were at one time an intricate network of arteries and veins, now varicose. All the public roads and highways have been replaced by private turnpikes for commercial traffic, high-speed luxury automobiles, and overcrowded magnetic trains that buzz like beehives. For the average citizen, travel is restricted to walking, biking, or commuting by train to and from work or traveling by train to resort and recreational areas managed by the Disney World branch of Vision World.

Denny has seen so many things in the last few days - the selling of America's countryside to foreigners, the supermarket museum of the consuming dream that devoured America, the bullet ridden bodies of two average middle class unemployed suburbanites turned terrorists, and, now, through the canopy of the raptor, he sees thousands upon thousands of people who are demonstrating for The True Democracy Movement, flooding the streets of Helena and the central plaza. Thousands more are standing on the tiers of the sky-scrapers that form an amphitheater around the inner city, the vast plaza, and the mall. Denny knew about the scheduled demonstration. He had seen old fashioned paper flyers, posters, and banners. There was even an invasion of Vision World by hackers who had scrolled an announcement of the coming demonstration across the screen during a Vision World newscast that was totally ignoring the upcoming event. This caused a big stir at headquarters, and it caused pages upon pages of intelligence reports to come across his desk, most of which he had seen before.

Denny was quite familiar with The True Democracy Movement and its goals because he had to research it in conjunction with a murder case not long ago. He knew that it is a grassroots movement that is attempting to surround Washington with an alternative government based on the initiative, referendum, and recall process as a check and balance again an imperial presidency and a representative government that does not represent the will of the people. However, it wasn't the idea of direct and participatory democracy at all levels of government or the concept of citizen lawmakers that frightened the power elite the most. From the intelligence reports that he read, the media moguls like Merling felt that they could control public opinion because they controlled information in America, but more importantly, they controlled the story.

No, it wasn't political democracy that frightened them the most. What really scared them was that The True Democracy Movement also demanded economic democracy. They argued that democracy could not end at the workplace door where we work for eight hours or more in what is essential a totalitarian state run by bosses, so they advocated employee managed and owned businesses and a national banking and currency system that determined investments and was democratically controlled. Essentially they were eliminating Wall Street, the stock market, and making money off of money, and the one-dollar-one-vote political system. Denny recalls Miranda's and Senator Lorenz's conversation at the Plaza and the Senator's speech, and the movement is beginning to make more sense to him.

The experts on Vision World argued that the concept of economic democracy was a disastrous concept that would destroy the American economy and that America was never a democracy. It was a republic, and from its inception the Constitution was constructed to protect America from majority rule and the passions of the masses. However, according to the intelligence reports, the concept of citizen lawmakers and economic democracy is becoming quite popular, and it is spreading like an uncontrollable "disease of the mind" throughout the nation, but recently the global corporate barons who control fortress America decided to strike back against what they called the "excesses of democracy."

Four months ago a federal district court reversed two hundred years of precedent and ruled that the initiative, referendum, and recall are unconstitutional, and that when the American people delegated legislative powers to their representatives in the Constitution, they did so completely and irrevocably. Two months ago, Senator James Barr announced that he was going to introduce a bill in the Senate that would make the advocacy of extreme democracy a criminal offense and those advocating it would be subject to imprisonment as enemies of the state. Three weeks ago, the President announced that he was going to propose a constiutional amendment that would abolish the House of Representatives and replace it with a Corporate Assembly.

In response to these attacks, The True Democracy Movement called for a nation-wide assembly of the people. They were calling for a simple response from the American people. "No."

"No," to a Supreme Court that is considering a case that will make democracy unconstitutional. "No," to a Congress that is considering a law that will make the advocacy of democracy a criminal offense, and, "No," to a President that wants the whole country to consider a constitutional amendment that would turn America into a Corporate State.

Denny wonders if in fact there is a nationwide demonstration going on, so he turns to Hathaway and says, "There's got to be at least two hundred thousand people down there, John. What is going on in the rest of the country?"

Hathaway touches a key on the control panel, and he and Denny now appear to be in the middle of a three-dimensional image of the Vision World command center. From this perspective, Hathaway can access the whole network, and when he touches another key, Denny can see real time three-dimensional scenes from The True Democracy Movement demonstrations occurring simultaneously in all the major cities in the country. Denny is surrounded by millions upon millions of people.

"My God, John, we're in the middle of a fuckin' revolution!"

Hathaway laughs and then says, "No, Martino, what we have here is an interesting question. If a tree falls in the woods, and you can't hear it or see it, does it exist?"

"What's that supposed to mean?"

"It means, Martino, that here is what the majority of the American people are seeing who have enough sense to stay at home and watch TV."

Hathaway touches a key on the control panel, and all the people disappear, and they are replaced by a sitcom and a joke that Denny can't hear because of the roar of the masses of people down below. "That's a lie," Denny says.

"No, Martino, that's entertainment." Hathaway

laughs then motions to the pilot to bring them down, and the raptor lands on the rooftop of the Public Safety Building. The co-pilot throws open the door of the heli-copter and Denny hears the sound of the whirling blades of the helicopter cutting through the voice of the people. "To know, to know," are the words that beat the air like the sound of ancient warriors banging their swords against their shields in a plebiscite for war.

Hathaway and Denny rush from the helicopter, and they hurry down the stairs to the station below that is in chaos. As they pass through the control room, Denny glances at the bank of surveillance screens that view the city, and he sees that the demonstration is larger than it looked like from above. The whole city has come out for this.

Denny spots one of his men waiting for him, and he asks, "Is my car ready?"

"Yes, sir, it is outside in the parking lot. I reserved a traffic patrol vehicle programmed for your use. Look for the number four parking space. You'll find it there."

Denny and Hathaway leave the building and Denny spots the toad-like green and khaki car with bug eyes for headlights. Denny gets in the driver's seat, punches in his identification number, and they speed away. He presses a button, the headlights flash red, and the siren comes to life as they race along an emergency road that has been kept clear by the security forces. As they pass through a tunnel, Denny sees the image of the vehicle cast upon the walls in a stream of red. It looks like an animal screaming in pursuit of its own shadow growing larger and larger then disappearing as they emerge at the other end.

Denny slows down and then stops for a roadblock of armored cars that form a wall to protect the access way. He sees troops standing in lines along the perimeter of the roadway to the plaza. They are wearing battle gear with armored vests, riot shields, clubs, and helmets with visors to protect their faces and their identities. Denny rolls down the window for one of the security men. He flashes his ID then shouts, "We have to get to Charles Street."

The officer salutes then shouts back, "You're not going to get through here, sir. It's impossible."

Deny turns to Hathaway and says, "We have to walk, John."

Denny and Hathaway get out of the car, and they begin to work their way through the mass of people. When they get to the plaza, Denny sees that the organizers have placed close circuit giant TV screens around the plaza so as to undermine Vision World's efforts to black out the event. They must have hacked into someone's corporate satellite because they are filming in real time and projecting primitive but effective two-dimensional images showing the demonstrations from across the county, showing everyone everywhere that they are not alone.

In a single moment he is seeing and hearing millions and millions of Americans throughout the country simultaneously shouting in unison, "Power to the People."

As Denny moves through the mass of people the chants grow louder and louder, almost lifting him off the ground, weightless in the sound, he feels a part of the mass, a part of some being that has taken away his individual identity, his isolation, and turned him into a giant.

Denny and Hathaway make it to the other side of the plaza, and they walk down Charles Street into the old city below the tiers, a part of the city that only the poor know. It is the city of darkened streets in daylight, buildings falling apart or fallen down into rabble, shafts of light highlighting garbage, broken windows, and a stairway to nowhere. The streets are strewn with broken bottles, discarded bags, scraps of life swirling down a side street that they take as they move away from the sounds of freedom, the echoes fading into the nothingness of abandoned warehouses where the homeless live in the shadows of the city.

A pile of crushed boxes begins to rise amidst a growling noise.

Both Denny and Hathaway freeze in fear, weapons in hand, aiming at the boxes that rise then fall away revealing a man in rags who towers over them, arms spread as he mouths wordless words. The man has a bottle of liquor in one hand. He smiles a toothless smile and takes a swig out of his bottle then staggers away, stops, turns, smiles again, then in a voice that seems to come out of a grave, he forms words that he surrounds with laughter. "Arise ye wretched of the world, you have nothing to lose but your chains."

Denny and Hathaway watch the man return to the shadows then disappear. The laughter lingers then follows the lone man into the echoes, the chants. They holster their KKB automatic pistols, and Denny looks at Hathaway's face. Gone is the amused corporate mask. Denny sighs and says to himself, Oh, Christ, here we go. He is in a battle zone again. They enter a shaft of light, a square with buildings intact and stores here and there. The signs are mostly in Spanish, and there is a cracked marble fountain at the center of the square, the marble green with moss, molded, and the cherubs that once were fat and plump now lack arms and limbs. Across the street Denny sees a car parked near the office of *The Globe*. Inside the car are two of his men. He walks up to the car and taps on the window. The window rolls down. Denny puts his arm on the roof of the car and leans over to speak, "Is he still in there?"

"Yes, sir."

"This is the only way out?"

"No, sir, there's a rear exit, but we have two men covering that."

"Good." Denny straightens up and for the first time he realizes how tired he is. He turns to Hathaway, "Are you ready?"

Hathaway looks about the street. The street is empty of life. "Something's wrong."

Denny frowns, and as he walks toward the building

he says, "I know."

They pass through a wrought iron gate, and they reach the entranceway to the building, but they don't immediately enter. The building is an old well-kept colonial brick townhouse. Hathaway carefully checks the door for anything that would indicate a bomb, a trap. Denny peers inside, but he only sees a rocking chair, a coat rack and an embroidered message woven out of colorful yarn in an old fashioned wood picture frame hanging from the wall - Home Sweet Home.

Denny draws his gun and motions for Hathaway to cover him as he enters. The door flies open with a bang and then there is silence as they pass through the vestibule into a room crowded with desks, desk top computers, pictures decorating the wall, and a bulletin board filled with memos. On one wall is a hologram of the Rocky Mountains that looks like a picture window looking out into the sunset, pastels darkening into brilliant greens and glacier peaks, snow against a purple sky with bands of orange.

Below the picture, slumped over her desk, is the receptionist.

Dead.

A bullet through the back of her head.

Denny, weapon in hand, lifts the girl's head. She is young, twenty-two, maybe more. A clean shot. He touches her cashmere sweater, and it feels like soft fur, but her body is stiff and cold.

Hathaway motions to the stairs that lead upward to the second floor. They move slowly across the polished wood floors. The floor squeaks in warning. Denny stops dead and stares at eyes staring at him, eyes hiding behind thickets, barely seen, eyes afraid, brown fur blending into the limbs of trees, the shades of green and the shadows. The eyes are alert, almost alive in the holographic images, the pictures on the walls.

In one picture he spots a ruddy fox hiding behind autumn leaves, furtive. In another, an eagle is hidden high up in a tree. Denny realizes the walls are full of eyes peering at him, and as he looks deeper and deeper into the camouflage, he sees more eyes, and he wishes that he could hide too. Humans suck.

Denny follows Hathaway step by step up the stairway, the brass rail feels cold to his touch. His feet feel heavy, and he feels all tangled up in his clothing. Hathaway's topcoat looks like a shroud as he hunches over, and Denny hears a sound from above, a sound of something slipping, slipping, over and over again.

The sound grows louder and louder as they reach the top of the stairs. Hathaway motions for him to check the editor's office. As Denny turns on the laser sight to his automatic pistol, he moves quickly. He can feel the tension in his body releasing as he becomes weightless with adrenaline, the red beam of his laser sight slashes across the room cutting through the air as he bursts through the doorway, his weapon aimed, scanning the room.

What he sees causes him to lower his gun and rest himself against the frame of the door to the hallway. It's over. Hathaway appears behind him after having checked the other rooms. They both stand at the entranceway looking into the office, looking at the man slung backward in his chair.

Denny and Hathaway holster their weapons and walk casually into the room. Denny stands in front of the copy machine, the sound. The copy machine is throwing sheets of paper out onto the floor. The floor is strewn with the copies that have formed mounds then fallen away forming new mounds of paper. Denny touches a button, and the machine stops.

He picks up a sheet and reads it. It's the lyrics from a song.

This land is your land.
This land is my land,
From California to the New York islands.
From the redwood forest to the...'

Denny vaguely remembers the song, but he can't remember the melody. He looks at the sheet in his hand then at the pile of papers on the floor. That poor dead bastard at the desk was probably printing these up to pass out at the demonstration so that everyone could sing in unison this old song of freedom, but this is one song that will never get sung. Denny drops the sheet of paper, and he joins Hathaway who is examining the body.

Hathaway turns to Denny and says, "Well, there

goes one lead. It had to be a silencer. He was shot before the girl downstairs."

Denny idly looks through the papers on the man's desk and says, "The only lead we have now is the Labelle girl."

Hathaway is also shopping through the dead man's things. He nods his head in agreement. He thinks for a moment then says, "Denny, I think you ought to go interrogate Miranda Labelle, alone."

Denny looks up, puzzled.

"We know one another, and she doesn't like me at all," Hathaway says. "I think you'll have better luck without me."

Denny puts down the papers, "OK, when should I go?"

"Now."

"Now?"

Hathaway gestures indicating the mess about them, the body, "I can take care of this. Your men can help me, and maybe I can find a lead on the other man in the cafe."

"You think he's our man?"

Hathaway walks around the desk and opens a drawer. He begins to look through it as he says, "My gut feeling is, yes. Take the car and use the raptor. By the time we get done here the rally should be over."

Denny is at the door, then he pauses. He thinks of Bugs. "Doesn't she live in the mountains?" Denny asks.

"Yes. And Martino..." Hathaway looks up and says, "Be gentle. Remember, she's an Olympian Goddess of Vision World and Merling's sister-in-law. If you think there is anything suspicious or that she is involved, it's for our ears only. If you feel that she is in any danger, stay with her and call for backup."

Denny smiles and casually salutes. As he is leaving, he passes by the staring eyes, the woman dead at the reception desk. Outside, he takes a deep breath of fresh air then orders his men to help Hathaway. Denny gets in the car and drives away past the huge steel beams that support the tiers of the city and makes his way through the darkness, the labyrinth of streets below the city above, the labyrinth that will hide the crime, the mystery of what happened today deep down below the peeks of the towering buildings that catch the light.

Chapter Nine

Denny flies back to the base and picks up a five man tactical combat unit to help him protect and secure the potential suspect and/or victim, Miranda Labelle. He also picks up Bugs Bunny thinking that he will finally find a home for him in the mountains. On his way to the Labelle estate, he goes through Miranda's file.

Miranda Juliet Labelle grew up in Manhattan, went to Stanford as an undergraduate, and then went on to Yale for a Masters in Theater and Art. She won a Guggenheim Scholarship, and she was a recipient of two Ford Foundation Grants for the Arts and one Alpha Foundation Award. She won three Emmys by the time she was twenty-one. She is twenty-eight years old, and two years ago her net worth was estimated at one and a half billion dollars, but in the past few years she has spent a good part of her fortune trying to stop the sale of national park land to private developers. She bought the land when it went up for sale, and then she returned it to the government, retaining ownership rights in trust so that it couldn't be sold again, but, judging from the records, it has been a hopeless cause for her. As fast as she buys the land, more land goes up for sale.

She has also tried to keep major works of art out of private hands by purchasing pieces that the museums have been forced to sell because of the depression. Once more, she has returned the property to the seller retaining ownership rights in trust, but once again her efforts have been frustrated by the number of museums that are closing all around the country. Miranda Labelle has lost a fortune putting her finger in the leak of a dike beyond repair, and Denny likes her for it.

Denny reaches into his briefcase and pulls out a digital recording of one of the first episodes of *Windows*, the reality TV series that made Miranda Labelle a star and a household name. Denny looks at the date of the recording and estimates that Miranda was sixteen then. Her sister, Jan Labelle, who was also a star in the show, must have been around Miranda's age now, twenty-eight, maybe younger. He's curious about her too. What sort of woman would Brad Merling marry? Denny inserts the video.

Windows flows across the TV screen in a sensuous script as Jan Labelle reaches for an egg shaped bar of *Caress* soap. The camera focuses on the label, the smooth oval shape, the creamy foam, and the sexual satisfaction on Jan's face as she takes a shower, the water messaging her breasts, the foam coming on her hands, the cream running down her legs.

The music ends when Jan turns off the water and throws open the shower curtain revealing flashes of nudity as she reaches for a towel.

Jan's mother, Susan Labelle, is in the kitchen of their New York City apartment cooking Italian link sausage in a frying pan. Her kitchen seems much used by a lover of food, a gourmet with a commercial stove and French copperware. The camera focuses for a moment on the brand names of the cookware and the appliances, and then on Susan who is an opulent women with gay brown eyes and light brown hair who looks like she enjoys being fat, enjoys wearing long loose fitting hand painted dresses with an abundance of flowers and big old basketball sneakers with their tongues hanging out.

Susan walks to the bathroom door and shouts over the sound of the hair dryer, "Jan, are you going to eat with us?"

Jan, who is sitting in front of a mirror giving her hair some final touches, shouts, "No." She then turns off the hair dryer and begins to make herself up. Once more the scene becomes a subtle advertisement, this time for Paradise cosmetics. The camera focuses on the shades, the shapes, the labels, the forming of Jan's face as she reveals the mysteries and power of illusion to teenage girls and women who follow every move, every week as Jan makes herself up, over and over again, each week a new face, a new look, a new woman, a new life.

They watch her pick up a brush and put a final touch on her eye shadow then smooth out her black shear nylon stockings. She slips on her dress, a moment in the mirror - straight long black hair, bangs, slender curves in black, gray and silver silk, black high heels.

She leaves the bathroom and walks into the kitchen. Her mother is sitting at the serving counter drinking a glass of wine. Susan looks her daughter over then smiles and says, "Dazzling."

She scrutinizes her daughter once again, "Maybe stupefying, definitely awesome. Where are you going tonight?"

"Dad and I are going to see a rock band tonight, Huey Long and The Goodies. Dad might sign them. He thinks that this Huey guy may have rock star potential. I think he wants me to manage him."

Jan sits down on a stool across from her mother, pours herself a glass of wine from the bottle, appraises the label then asks, "Where's Randy?"

"I sent her to the store."

"Mom, Doris is pregnant. She's going to have a baby."

"Really?"

Jan gets up from the stool and walks into the living room that is separated from the kitchen by the serving counter. Both she and her mother are thoughtful. The living room is a tasteful blend of quiet modern with Bohemian touches and American antiques from the Colonial period, obviously inherited. Over the fireplace hangs a colorful quilt bed cover, circa 1815.

Jan is casually stroking the head of an old antique rocking horse made of maple now darkened with age.

"How do you think Randy is going to take this, Mom?"

Susan gets up from where she is seated at the counter and pours herself another glass of wine. "She's going to be heartbroken. Randy thinks her father doesn't love her anymore, and this, of course, will prove it, the bastard. Any man who falls in love with his secretary then makes her his partner is an asshole. The woman's a moron. Can you imagine it? He's got her handling the writers. Good God, if it were up to her, they would publish novels on toilet paper. That's how practical she is. Who would have thought that your father would go banging around in a genetic junk yard to find his heir apparent?"

"Mom, don't start."

Susan adjusts the flame on the fire to a very low simmer then walks into the living room and sits down on a white linen sofa that faces the fireplace. The warm color of a Persian rug is muted by the lack of light. She turns on a light to cheer up the room. "It's his fault that Randy is so messed up," Susan says. "You should watch my show tomorrow. I'm featuring Susan Blake, the Chairman of the President's Commission on Family Life, and Barbara Stills, the author of the bestselling book, *Why Do Our Children Hate Us?* We're talking about broken homes."

Susan hears the outside door opening, and she puts her finger to her lips, "Quiet, don't mention anything about the baby." Susan gets up and returns to the kitchen. She turns off the burner and reaches for a pot.

Miranda walks in carrying groceries that she places

on the counter. Even though she is wearing overalls, a plaid flannel shirt, and sneakers, Miranda appears soft, sweet, almost fluffy except for her beautiful silky hair and her eyes that have an oriental touch accented by mascara and long dark lashes. She seems nervous and frazzled, "I know. I know," she says. "Don't say it. I'm late. But Agostino's was the pits."

Susan goes through the bag, "Limes, I wanted lemons. OK, we can do it with limes." She holds up a bottle of grated cheese for inspection then puts it aside, "Parmesan cheese, I wanted Romano. All right, Randy, we'll have Parmesan even though you know I like Romano better." She holds up a jar of Spaghetti sauce. "What is this?"

"Spaghetti sauce."

"I said *Ragu*." She hands the jar to her daughter.

"Go."

"But Mom."

"Randy, some things by the same name..."

Miranda takes the jar and says, "I know. I know. Some things by the same name are not the same thing." She turns, and she begins to walk out the door. "*Ragu*," she says.

"*Ragu*," Susan echoes to brand the viewer with the name of the product they are selling, and Miranda leaves.

Susan turns to Jan and says in a conspirator's way, "Come with me. I want to show you something."

They enter Miranda's room. A rag doll and a teddy bear are propped against a pillow on an early American colonial poster bed. One wall of the room is covered with photographs. Susan points to an enlarged photograph of the antique rocking horse that is in the living room. "Look."

From a variety of angles, Jan sees that the horse is half buried in snow somewhere in a desolate forest of barren trees, some fallen and dead. The horse's front hooves are raised in a pathetic attempt to rock itself out of the snow.

Mixed in with the photographs of the rocking horse, are photographs of a golden doll hanging from an abandoned Christmas tree that has been thrown in the garbage. Snow and a few strands of glistening tinsel hang from the dying branches. A pin is stuck in the doll. The eyes are two black holes. Jan appraises the pictures, "Did Randy take these, Mom?"

"Yes."

"They're very good."

"I know that, but that's not why I wanted you to see them. Look at the theme: desolation and abandonment." Susan's eyes are tearing up, "What is she telling us about her own childhood, her own dreams?"

"Have you talked to her about this, Mom?"

"No, but that's not all." She opens the drawer to a dresser and pulls out Miranda's diary. "She'll kill me if she finds out I've been reading this."

"What is it?"

"Her diary, listen to this. 'Yesterday, Jessica came

over to the house with a vibrator. Can you believe that! We played with each other all day. It got really slobbery, and Jessica got really excited. I don't know. I felt kind of funny. Jessica called today, and she said she wanted to come over again. She said she wanted to fuck me really bad. Said a lot of dirty things. I got a little hot, but I said, no. I'm tired of playing let's pretend. I want a real man. I want to get laid! Maybe I'll go down by the docks where the truckers park their rigs to pick up prostitutes and transvestites. I wonder what it would be like to have a trucker for a lover. After all, trucker rhymes with fucker. It's got to be good. Ha, Ha. Well that's all for now, Mr. Higher Up, signing off. PS Heather came over anyway, and do you know what we did?' Susan stops, "I won't go on. We have to get out of here." She carefully puts Miranda's diary back into the drawer, and they leave the room.

"My God, Jan, what does it all mean? What is she thinking of? What is she doing?"

"Mom, it's just a young girl's fantasy."

"I hope so, but I'm worried about her. She seems so unhappy." The doorbell rings. Susan looks at her daughter in surprise, "Who's that?"

"It's Dad. He's come to pick me up."

"He can't come in here." Susan is quite upset.

"He knows that. He said he'd just buzz and wait in the car." Jan grabs her coat, "Mom, I got to go." She kisses her mother, and she is about to leave when Miranda come in.

"Dad's outside," Miranda says. "What's Dad doing outside?" She's all frazzled again.

"He came to pick me up," Jan says as she reaches for her diamond studded purse.

"Where are you going?" Randy asks.

"To meet a client, Randy, I have to go." She kisses Miranda on the cheek and leaves.

Miranda holds out the jar. The camera focuses in on the jar, the label, *Ragu.*

Susan grabs the jar and says, "Good, let's eat."

Miranda rubs her hands, "Oh, boy."

Chapter Ten

The *Windows* episode cuts from the interior of the Labelle home to the exterior of the townhouse where a red coupe is parked. The camera pans the car. It glistens in the night light, its lines set off against the darkness, light reflecting off the chrome, the hood, the parking lights glowing orange, and the name of the car, *Starfire*.

Jan opens the door. The camera focuses on her legs and the shear silk slipping across soft rich leather, her legs exposed to the warmth of the interior, the colorful glow of the dashboard.

At the wheel of the car is her father, Victor Labelle, a striking man, who is elegantly dressed and has swept back highly stylized salt and pepper hair, gray eyes like Jan, high cheek bones, a sharp nose, and thin lips. He is tall, slim, and fit for a man in his early fifties. Jan is excited, "Dad, where did you get this car?"

"I just bought it. Do you like it?"

"I love it!"

Victor touches the stereo controls and the interior fills with sound. The scene changes to an exterior view of the car taking off into the night lights of the city, into the music as Victor Labelle tells his daughter all about his new car, its features, its virtues, where he bought it, and how much it cost, a real bargain.

The car pulls up to the International Club. There are several limousines parked outside and a long line of people waiting to get in. Jan and Victor get out of the car, and they go to the head of the line where they are ushered in and seated at a table with a good view of the stage. In the center of the room is a large oval bar made of blue neon lights and glass. Over the bar is a digital read-out of airline departures and arrivals, stock market quotes, and Vision World news from around the world. Beyond the bar is the dance floor and the stage suspended in darkness, waiting. In the background large flowing neon letters spell out: *The International Presents.*

A waitress immediately comes to the table. She, like all the waitresses, is a fashion model, and she is showing a new line of clothing at the club. The waitress is tall, thin, and perky, with long straight blond hair, blue eyes, and a cheerleader's face. She is wearing a dress made of soft milky rubber, like a prophylactic, skin tight except for the short skirt that is filled with air like a balloon.

Jan likes it. It's cute, bouncy. She looks at the price tag attached to the dress. The camera focuses on the price, the name of the designer, the store, but then the room darkens, and she hears a voice say, "Ladies and gentlemen, tonight we present for the first time on stage at the International Club, Huey Long and the All-Night Goodies."

The lights go on over the dance floor, the stage. Above the dance floor, hanging from the ceiling, is a full-scale model of an eight passenger supersonic corporate Lear jet. The dance floor is lit up like an airstrip, and behind the bandstand is a holographic view of the New York City skyline, The Rome of the World. On stage are a lead singer, Huey Long, and his band. The air is filled with the sound of rock and roll, upbeat but still down and dirty. Dancers move rhythmically into the lights and the hard beat of city life. The lead singer is good-looking but not pretty, his lyrics are poetic but street wise, intellectual in a bawdy way.

During a transitional point in the music, Victor turns to Jan and says, "What do you think?"

"I think we can get two good albums out of them, maybe more. Definitely two top of the pops."

"I think you're right."

They settle in to listening to the music, and the camera focuses on the performance. When the set is over, Victor turns to his daughter and touches her on the hand, gently. "Jan, Huey's going to be coming to the table. I want you to handle him." He smiles, "Seduce him if you have to, but get those contracts signed."

"What are you saying, Dad? Do you want me to tangle him up in my panty hose?"

"If you're asking me that question as your father, no, of course not, but if you're asking me that as your boss... Victor's face turns hard, cynical. I want commercial spots. I want ads. I want tour. I want the second album in two months. These guys will die without exposure. That's what I want, sweetie, and I don't care how you do it."

Jan salutes, "OK Boss."

A new performer is introduced. It's Cornelia Sica, a singer from Italy. One stage disappears into the floor and another emerges from the hologram. A formal orchestra is playing, and the music is sophisticated, romantic. The singer is beautiful, tall with long red hair, dazzling green eyes. Her voice is wonderfully sensual, clear. The tone of the room changes into warm intimacy, love.

Huey comes to the table, and Huey and Victor Labelle exchange greetings. Jan is introduced to Huey, and the look they give one another is flirtatious. Huey sits down, and Victor pours Huey a glass of champagne as Huey sits back in his chair, casually, self-contained, one leg crossed, his foot resting on his knee, a glass of champagne in one hand. His hair is stylishly unkempt, and he is wearing a silver sports jacket, casual and loose, the sleeves pushed back. His pants are full, comfortable, held up by suspenders, no shirt, no socks, and loafers. He casually exposes the room to his stinky feet, his hairy chest, and his easy smile.

"Huey," Victor says, "I'm going to have my daughter handle you. Believe me when I tell you this." He leans over as if to secretly confide in Huey, "Don't let the good looks fool you. When it comes to the music part of our business, she's the best."

Jan looks on, closing her eyes for a moment like a cat bored with the spectators on the other side of the bars. She picks at her salad with her fork then stares at Huey.

Victor sits back in his chair and gives Jan his final benediction, "She's better than me."

Jan smiles at Huey, "My father, as usual, is being very modest, Huey. But it is true. I do feel I can handle your career." She looks at her glass of champagne and then she looks at Huey, "Do you have any problems with this?"

"No."

"Are you certain? If you have any doubts, this is the time to talk it over."

"No, not at all, everyone knows that you handled The Sex Tubes. You've got a very good reputation in the business, and the Labelle Agency is the best." He looks from Jan to Victor and spreads his arms in a gesture of abundance, spilling some of the champagne on his hand, the floor, "How can I go wrong?"

Jan looks at Huey, amused. Then she looks at her father, smiles, and says, "Dad, beat it."

Victor's gesture is one of surrender as he says, "She's right. She's right. I have to go." Victor extends his hand, "Huey, Jan has the papers that I want you to sign. Trust her." He kisses his daughter on the cheek and is about to leave.

Jan opens her hand, "The keys, Dad."

"You're kidding."

"No, I'm in the driver's seat now, right?"

Jan enjoys the pained expression on her father's face as he hands over the keys, his feeble attempts at being gracious. He's pissed. Dad doesn't like sharing his toys. She's ruined his evening, and he'll punish her some-how, but she's enjoying the moment. Jan watches her fa-ther leave, and then she studies Huey for a moment. He is listening intently to the singer. At moments, Cornelia's voice is so clear it sounds like a clarinet, high, sonorous, flowing over the low masculine voice of the saxophone, soaring over the full bodied sound and rising one octave, two octaves, three, suspended...

Huey turns to Jan, "She's great isn't she?"

Jan smiles, "She's one of ours. I just signed her for her first record contract in America. I have the digital re-cording in the car. Huey, have you eaten dinner?"

"No."

"Why don't we drive out to Connecticut? I know an old country inn out there that serves wonderful French provincial. We can talk on the way. That is if you don't mind me taking you for a ride?"

"Is that a figure of speech, Jan?"

"Of course it is." She gets up, "But... if you don't want to become a millionaire. You can stay here."

Huey laughs, "I'm coming. I'm coming."

As they exit the club, Denny remembers how the Jan Labelle story goes. She makes herself up new all the time, but the story is always the same. She makes all the men she handles into lovers, makes them into stars. But then she turns them into whores, makes them prostitute their art for money, and go down on it for greed. Then she dumps them and takes on a new comer, and she does it all for Daddy.

    Denny watches Jan get behind the wheel, turn the engine on, caress the knob of the gear shift, and then slide it into gear.

Chapter Eleven

In the next scene of *Windows,* Jan is racing through the streets of New York in her father's sports car with Huey, their faces aglow with expectation. The camera pulls away to an exterior shot of the rear lights of the *Starfire* disappearing into the neon scroll and collage of lights and signs and brand names, the golden theater lights and billboards of Broadway that promise action, drama, adventure, and a way out of your life.

The scene dissolves into darkness, and Denny hears the repeated click of a camera. With each click the darkness takes form, and Denny sees Miranda Labelle taking pictures of steam pouring out of a steel manhole cover like a ghostly spirit escaping the dark caverns of New York's subterranean mind. He then watches her walk down a street along the Hudson River and the old docks of New York City. Miranda is not like her sister who turns life into herself then gets rid of the remains. Miranda is more like the camera that she loves. She is the aperture that lets in the light, the shadows, and the darkness. She has been blessed with wonderment, and she wants to know what everything is like, what it is like to be everyone she sees and captures in her little box. She wants to know what it is like to open herself up and make love to a man. Miranda is bound and determined to lose her virginity tonight.

Miranda hears someone moan in a darkened doorway, and she takes a picture of the genderless shadows that seem to meld into one another as abstract spirits of desire sucking up all the light. As she walks across the street, a yellow cab races by nearly running her over. She gives the cab driver the finger and walks to where the trucks are parked and peers between two tractor-trailers into the darkness and opens her aperture wide to draw in what little light there is and takes a picture of a used rubber and torn panties in a mud puddle next to the giant teeth-like-treads of a tire on a tractor-trailer truck. Walking further into the darkness down the rows of trucks, past the metallic creatures and the tires as big as she, Miranda takes a picture of a monster tractor-trailer that gleams midnight black with towering chrome smokestack lightning like exhaust pipes rising into the moonlight. The motor throbs idly to the sound of slam-dance music in the distance and the laughter of the crowd hanging around the front of the Ram Rod Bar and Grill. In the background is an abandoned pier and warehouse. The warehouse is in ruins with broken windows, a collapsed wall revealing bare steel girders, broken glass, and debris.

She is about to focus on the monster's face, the square jaw, the large gaping chrome mouth, and the steel teeth when she hears someone say, "It's one hell of a truck, ain't it?"

Miranda turns around, startled. A tall lanky young man in his mid-twenties with a boyish smile is leaning against a truck with a cup of coffee in his hand. Her eye immediately goes to his crotch. The young trucker is wearing *Super Fly Levi Jeans.* They are traditional button fly Levis except one of the buttons is always unbuttoned, and what button you buy to unbutton is a matter of self-expression at a price. The young trucker is wearing the deluxe model. The button is a diamond that sparkles in the dark like a star.

Denny knows from the director's notes that this is the first time that this product has been introduced to the public, and the product is doing what the manufacturers intended it to do. Miranda can't take her eye off of the young man's crotch.

"I saw you take a picture of it. It's mine," the young man says.

His voice breaks the spell for a moment, and Miranda raises the camera to her eye to take a picture of him. He has faded blue eyes and even features with a shadow of a beard that gives him a rugged look. The look is reinforced by a green and gold John Deere cap tilted back with his dirty blond hair sticking out, semi wild. His black and white plaid wool hunting shirt is unbuttoned and open revealing his bare chest, trim waistline, low hung Super Fly jeans, and the open invitation.

Miranda takes one last shot and lowers her camera, and says, "Yes, it is really cool." She then pushes her hair away from her face to reveal her eyes, the shadowy long eye lashes with silver sparkles on the tips.

Denny can see what the trucker sees as he looks Miranda up and down. Her jet black hair is cut in a page boy style, and her lips are painted pink tonight. She is wearing old style Levi overalls fashioned for a teenage girl to show off her cute ass. The camera focuses on her straps that are attached with clasps to oversized embossed Levi logo buttons. Behind the buttons her breasts peek out of a plum colored skin tight ballet pull over shirt, and the tongues of her partially tied calf skin work boots stick out over the cuffs of her overalls. To top off the look that she has created, she is wearing a dark blue Yankee baseball cap. There are no hard edges to Miranda. She is like a free form pillow that God shaped into a beautiful girl that you can dream upon, embrace, and bury yourself in as she gives to your every touch. Denny realizes that he has a hard-on when he hears the trucker ask, "Do you want to see what's inside?"

Miranda looks nervous and excited at the same time. She nods her head.

The young man walks over to the cabin of the truck and opens the passenger side door, "Be careful. It's a long way up. Grab that handle there."

He helps her up into the cab and then walks around to the driver's side, opens the door, and leisurely swings himself up behind the wheel. The dashboard is full of gauges, lights, buttons, a computer screen, and an electronic communications device. It's a high tech space age machine with a rabbit's foot dangling from the rear-view mirror.

The young man presses a button and a country western song comes on. It is Don Williams singing, "Ain't it Amazing."

"What's your name?" the young man asks.

"Randy."

The young trucker smiles, "Hi, Randy, I'm Steve."

"Does your truck have a name?"

"Yep, Big Mac"

"I bet Big Mac has been around."

"Yep, we been to most parts of the country, probably places that you never heard of. Amarillo, Texas, ever heard of that?"

"Amarillo, Texas," Miranda says. "That sounds so poetic. I want to go there."

Steve puts his arm around her and says, "You want to go with me?"

"Maybe," she says then raises her face so that Steve can kiss her.

He is about to kiss her, but he pauses and says, "Randy, can I ask you something without you taking offense?"

"Sure."

"Are you a girl?"

Miranda sits up. "Of course I am."

"No offense, but around here you never know. I've

97

heard a lot of stories." There is a twinkle in his eye when he says, "Do you mind if I feel to make sure?"

Miranda opens her mouth in surprise and then looks away. There is a moment of embarrassed silence where all Denny can hear is the motor of the engine idling and Don Williams singing, "Ain't it amazing that there's still dreamers."

Miranda whispers, "Yes," and puts her head on Steve's lap and stretches her body out across the couch like seat, her legs curled up so that she can fit.

The camera focuses on her logo buttons being unclasped, her nipples swelling up, and her Levis slipping down revealing her Victoria Secret silk panties. Labels caress labels as Steve slips his fingers underneath her panties and pulls her pants down and feels her up. When she gets wet, he smears her juices all over her pussy, her thighs, and ass. She is wet all over when he pulls her pants completely off and she gets up on her knees and buries her face in his crotch smelling his sex, her hands unbuttoning each Levi logo button until he is in her mouth.

Denny can hear her sucking. He can hear the monster truck throbbing, growling, and growing more powerful as Steve plays with the gas petal like a musical instrument she's playing with her lips.

Miranda slips Steve's cock out of her mouth. She is out of breath. Her lips are moist and wet, hot. Her pussy is liquid fire. She has to have him now. She breathlessly straddles Steve and comes down on his penis screaming both in ecstasy and pain then pumping to the sound of the motor banging away, her pussy bursting open wider and wider from the thousands of mini explosions, his cock like a cylinder head driving her on and on, going faster and faster, until they both come to the sound of the monster's horn that causes her to scream and raise up off of Steve's penis as he comes all over her pussy. He reaches up and pushes her back down deep, her aperture now fully open to take in all the light, all the darkness.

For a while she just stays there taking it all in, hugging Steve, listening to the music, feeling the last few buds pop open like the sparks from a fire going out, and when it is all over, she laughs. They both laugh as Miranda slips off of Steve and says, "God, so that is what all the fuss is about."

Steve smiles and says, "Did you enjoy the ride?"

"Oh, yes."

"Do you want to do it again?"

"Oh God, no," Miranda says as she looks at the clock on the dashboard and begins to dress. "I have to get home, Steve. I've got school tomorrow. Can you give me a ride?"

"Sure. Buckle up."

Steve pulls the big tractor and trailer out of its parking space, and he moves down the road to the sound of country music, the twang of the guitar on liquid air and Willie Nelson singing, "With no place to hide, I looked in your eyes, and I found myself in you."

Miranda peers out the window and watches a transvestite wearing a tight fitting dress walking across the street with her gay boyfriend as if weightless on the way to the ruins where they will find warmth and heat in their fantasy selves. Even the steel spikes, the leather pants, and the fist fuckers across the street at The Ram Rod Bar and Grill look airy from the interior of the giant cab that towers over the scene that can't swallow her up anymore.

She directs Steve down narrow Village streets lined with old brick townhouses with wrought iron bars across the windows and stoops that rise above the night walkers, the cars packed bumper to bumper. Denny can see from Miranda's face that she is loving it, being so high up and powerful that the taxicabs that she hates have to give way to her. She can even see into the second story windows of a townhouse where a classmate of hers lives. She can see the tall ceilings, bookcases filled with books, a Steinway piano, and Charlie in his bedroom doing his homework. Miranda directs Steve to sound his horn, and Charlie looks up and out the window at Miranda waving at him enjoying the incredulous look on his face.

A few moments later she points and says, "There," That's where I live."

Steve stops and says, "Will I see you again?"

"Will you be coming back to New York?"

"Sure, I come to New York at least once a month."

"Would you like to take me out?"

"Sure, what do you like to do?"

"Shop, but don't worry, I don't expect you to like it. I'll show you the town. I'm a real New Yorker, you know."

"It's a date," Steve says. "And maybe someday Big Mac and me can take you to Amarillo."

"Oh, I'd like that, and you and I can make it in the back of a pickup truck in the parking lot of the Amarillo Dinner to the smell of hamburgers, French fries, and beer. Budweiser I think. Sounds yummy, doesn't it?"

Steve smiles and says, "Sounds like a country western song to me."

Miranda smiles enigmatically and then she digs into her pocket and pulls out a card and hands it to Steve. "Here's my card. Call me when you're back in town."

The card says, *Miranda Labelle – Young Adult.* On the back is her phone number. Steve feels Miranda kiss him on the cheek, and when he looks up he sees that Miranda is out the door. She waves goodbye, and Steve smiles and waves back at her, blows his horn, and then heads down the street. Miranda raises her camera to her eye and takes a picture of the truck, the big black box that seems to take up all the space and block out the city skyline then get smaller and smaller until it looks like a child's toy that disappears into the night.

Denny turns off the video of *Windows.* Wow, he thinks to himself. No wonder every guy in this country wanted to be in her pants. He wants to be in her pants. He wants to be the one to fuck her in the back of a pickup truck, and he wants to be the one who she gives it all up for, but he realizes that he will have to be very careful with her. Miranda Labelle is full of surprises. That is what she does for a living, and Denny is doing exactly what Miranda wants him to do after watching *Windows.* He wants her, and he is wondering what she will do next and what she is doing now.

Chapter Twelve

Miranda is in the woods sitting next to a stream near her home painting in watercolors. Her feet are in the water, the canvas is on her lap, and the palette is lying beside her on the grass. Miranda, who is wearing a flowery summer dress and a wide brimmed straw gardener's hat, dips her brush into the stream and mixes it with dabs of paint that touch the light and turn into flowers - yellow and orange and red fire bursts. Miranda dips her brush into the water again then dots the brush with blue and green, and a stream forms on her canvas, the colors flowing into the still life. She adds a dot of darkness for depth and it expands into the nothingness that moves. She dips her brush in the stream again, and a flash of rainbow leaps out of the water, startling her. She laughs when she sees the trout disappear back into the water, and she wonders if she conjured it up. Did he really exist before she imagined him, or was it the rainbow that thought him up, an ugly little gnome that lives on the tip of her brush, a ball of water and colored mud, a dot composed of many dots, each dot the complete whole of all that is and was before.

Miranda cleans her brushes in the stream and puts

her painting tools away. She decides to call it quits for the day and walks up the pathway back to her home that is constructed of redwood and stone in harmony with vast expanses of light and glass. She walks through terraced gardens, up steps that lead to a balcony that extends over the falls, and she enters a kitchen that is open and warm, comfy like her Mom's.

Miranda places the box of painting equipment and the canvas she is carrying on a counter, opens the refrigerator, takes out a pitcher of fresh orange juice, and pours the juice into a large glass. She refreshes herself as she sorts out her mail. Most of her mail comes through a fax machine or telecommunications, but some people still send letters, usually for the effect, the personal touch on birthdays and holidays, often formal invitations to one thing or another that she usually rejects or ignores.

The letters on the counter have been lying here for two weeks, unopened. She's about to throw them all away, but then she recognizes a familiar name on a return address. Tom Williams, she says to herself. I haven't heard from or seen Tom in ten years. I wonder what he wants. Miranda opens the envelope and sees that it is an invitation to a dinner that will feature a debate between the President and Senator Arthur Lorenz, the leading challenger for the Presidency in the November elections. The event is being sponsored by the New York City Women's League, and it will be held at the Plaza Hotel. At the bottom of the invitation is a scrawled note - *Please come, Love. Banana*

Man.

She smiles. She remembers back to when she first met Tom at Stuyvescent High School in the Village. They were in a philosophy class, and the teacher had asked them to write an essay. The question was, What Is Life? She had tried to answer the question as she thought Plato would - that life is an idea. She muddled through Plato's idea that reason and logic are the crowning disciplines that will reveal the composition of the universe, the music of the spheres, and the scales of justice.

What is an object but a shadow of?

Her paper was full of eraser marks, smudges on the perfect, drawings on a cave wall. Is our body chained together by a logic that dances to the right tune?

She couldn't remember exactly what she had written, but at the end of class when she placed her paper on top of Tom's, she burst out laughing when she read that "life is a banana. You can do three things with it. You can hold it in your hand, put it in your mouth, or shove it up your ass."

Miranda looks over the invitation again - the time, the date, the man. Arthur Lorenz, the man who is causing all hell to break loose in American politics today. Yes, I am interested. Let's see... I have to be in Washington Thursday. She's about to make a decision, when she hears the sound of a helioplane nearing. She looks out the window and sees that it is descending onto her landing platform. The security system activates, and the shields close down over the windows blocking all access to the building. Laser guns and an electronic net enclose the helioplane in a target zone.

She watches the blades turn and turn more slowly rocking the plane to a rest. A good-looking young man in his early thirties emerges from the helioplane with four heavily armed soldiers. He is wearing jeans, a blue polo shirt, running shoes, and a knee length tan field jacket that is loose and open. In his hands, he is carrying an old brown cardboard box.

Denny reaches into his pocket and pulls out his identification badge and holds it up so that the security system can photograph it and clear him. A few moments later the defensive shields are retracted, and he walks to the door. It opens. Miranda Labelle is standing at the door. Her feet are bare, and Denny is surprised by how normal she looks. She's a pretty little thing, he thinks to himself, but then he cautions himself again. She is also one of the wealthiest and powerful women in America, and the hair trigger security system that she has surrounded herself with leaves a clear message. You don't come to visit Miranda Labelle uninvited. If you do, you just might get your ass blown off, no questions asked.

He's about to introduce himself, but Miranda looks into the box, sees Bugs, and immediately reaches for him and hugs him to her breasts.

"Where did you get him? He's such a darling."

"He was burned out of his home."

"Oh, the poor baby, look, you can see where his hair has been singed."

"I know. Do you think it would be safe to let him loose here in the woods?"

"Sure."

She kisses Bugs on the nose, "He'll be fine here." She then turns to Denny and says, "Come in."

Denny enters an immense room with very high ceilings with light flooding in from all angles.

Miranda sets the rabbit back down in the box and gently says to Bugs, "Now, you stay here, and I'll get some food for you." She turns to Denny. "I'll be right back, Colonel. Make yourself at home." She runs off leaving Denny alone.

Denny walks across a black slate floor. It's a cool day, and logs are burning in a large fireplace. The room is bathed in color. There are paintings hanging everywhere. He pauses to look at a painting of points of balance playing with threads of light in a negative space.

Next to that painting is another of swirling lines, earth and rock, threads and fibers unraveling into primary colors, the dynamics of flow over vibrant waves of static matter.

He hears Miranda say, "Do you like them?"

"Yes, very much."

Miranda is pleased. "I painted them."

"They're very abstract."

"Not really. The bible says that we can only see God

through the eyes of a child. So in these paintings, I'm trying to achieve a level of perception that existed before we are programmed by society. They're from a series of paintings entitled, *A View from the Crib.*"

Denny smiles, "So this is what the world looked like when I was nearer to God."

"I think so."

"Very interesting," Denny looks at two other paintings that look vaguely familiar to him. One is a very large painting of abstract geometric forms contorted, a bull raging amidst straight lines, gaping triangles.

The other picture is of two women with beautifully exposed breasts amidst tropical leaves, vivid colors, a platter of bright red fruit touching her nipples.

"Did you do these?" Denny asks.

Miranda laughs and says, "Oh, God, no. I wish I did. Don't you recognize them?"

"No I don't."

Miranda looks at Denny curiously, sadly, "They're famous paintings. The big one is by Picasso. I bought it from the Metropolitan Museum of Art when it closed. I have to find a new home for it."

"What's it about?"

Miranda smiles and says, "I think it's about line and form, humans being reduced to a colorless outline of themselves, captured in the dynamics of modern warfare, the Spanish Civil War and the murderous geometry of the industrial age. We are seeing humanity being shaped into automatons, reduced to squares, rectangles, circles, mechanical shapes suffering the cruelty of the industrial age, trying to free themselves from reason gone mad. The bull is the rage of nature tangled up in the straight lines of linear thinking, the gaping triangles of horror in which all harmony and balance and the free flowing lines of life are destroyed. It's about the United States today."

Miranda sees the confusion on Denny's face, and she laughs then points to a Gauguin painting of Two Tahitian Women. "Do you like this?" she asks

"It's beautiful," Denny says.

"Do you like the boobs?"

Denny laughs, "Very much."

"Why?"

Denny looks at Miranda, amused. He looks at the breasts again. "I like the way they look, the way they feel."

"Generous?"

Denny smiles, "Very."

"Full?"

"Yes."

"Life giving?"

Denny nods his head.

"Well that's what the paintings about."

"Boobs?"

"No, Silly, nature, but you're not here to discuss art, are you?"

"No, I'm afraid not," Denny says, "I need to ask you some questions related to the assassination attempt on your brother-in-law, Mr. Brad Merling."

"I see. Sit down, Colonel, and tell me what it is you want to know." She gestures towards a very old couch with white canvas upholstery that has been painted with splashes of color, finger prints, and food stains. Denny realizes that the couch is an art piece, and he is leery of sitting on it.

Miranda smiles and says, "Don't worry. It's dry."

Denny sits down, and Miranda sits across from him on a similar couch. Sitting between them are a stuffed elephant and a stuffed donkey that are playing monopoly on the coffee table. Their pockets are stuffed with money. Their pieces have both landed on, *Go to Jail.* Lying next to Miranda is a giant stuffed lizard that is brown with pink polka dots, squinty green eyes, and a huge mouth.

"This is Herbert Mudpuppy." She pats him on the head. "He will eat anything, logs, nuts, bolts, rocks, and fiberglass. You name it. The only things that he finds indigestible are human beings. Mudpuppies are noted for their good taste, but it's a sad story because he had a brother who was very bad. Adolf wanted to consume the world, and one day he just set out to do it. Just like that. And he got pretty far too. He ate fifteen cars, a dump truck, a garbage truck, twenty-five parking meters, and two blocks of asphalt. Then he just rolled over, burped, and died. He's over there."

Denny looks over to an alcove where there are bookcases filled with books and a leather chair. Near the chair, Denny notices the antique rocking horse that he saw in the video. At the foot of the chair is a truly stuffed Adolf, belly extended, lying on his back with a parking meter in one hand and a piece of asphalt in the other. The asphalt is covered with whip cream, a cherry on top. Adolf died with a smile on his face.

Denny laughs and then looks at Miranda who is smiling at him. Oh, those eyes of hers. They are so open. She is taking him all in, and he wants her to do it, swallow him up. Once more he has the desire to be inside of her, to see life from her eyes, but then he realizes that he is staring at her. He is embarrassed.

He clears his throat, smiles awkwardly, then reaches into a pocket and pulls out some pictures. He shows her one, "Have you ever seen this man before?"

"Yes, that's Greg Barnes, the editor of *The Globe.*"

Denny places the picture on the coffee table so that it faces Miranda, and then he shows her a picture of the mystery man. "And this man, do you recognize him?"

Miranda looks at the picture of the man and, at first, seems not to recognize him, but then she takes a closer look and says, "Oh, yes, of course. I met him with Greg. We had lunch together."

"When?"

"The day of the exhibit, the day that an attempt was made on Brad's life. But..."

Denny raises his hand to stop her before she starts. "Please be patient Ms. Labelle and allow me to ask the questions. When I'm done, I'll try to explain as much of this as I can. OK?"

Miranda's face expresses exasperation and impatience, but she seems to resign herself as she sits back on the couch and tucks one leg up under the other, "All right."

Denny shows Miranda a picture of Robert Hewitt and says, "Did you ever see this man before, or this woman?"

"No I haven't." Miranda is nervously biting on a finger. "OK, now I've been patient. What's this all about?"

"Please, just a few more questions."

Miranda continues to look exasperated but she smiles and says, "OK."

"Why did you go to lunch with these two men?"

"We went to lunch prior to the opening. *The Globe* was doing a special feature on the exhibit."

"At any time, did either of these men or both have access to the exhibit prior to the opening?"

"Yes, I showed them the exhibit the night before. They wanted to take pictures of it before the opening."

"Did you find that strange?"

Miranda stops to think for a moment. "Yes and no, I sent them quite a few pictures of the exhibit two weeks prior to the opening when Greg expressed interest. I thought they were adequate for his needs, but for some reason he didn't."

"Was there a picture of a man and woman and child

in a shopping cart at the meat counter? Do you know the scene that I'm referring to?"

"Yes, of course." Miranda thinks for a moment. "Yes, there was."

"You're sure?"

"Yes."

"At any time did you leave them alone at the exhibit?"

"What do you mean?"

"Out of sight."

"Oh, yes, there were a lot of final touches to do. It's a big store. I pretty much left them alone to do what they needed to do while I worked on a few pieces."

Miranda has lost all patience with him, and her stare is quite pointed as she says, "You still haven't answered my question, Colonel, what's this all about?"

Denny points to the pictures of Robert Hewitt and his wife and says, "They are the two who attempted to assassinate Mr. Merling. They both died in the attempt."

"But I don't understand." Miranda stares thoughtfully at Denny and asks, "Why are you asking me all these question? What does Greg Barnes have to do with this?"

Denny realizes that he can't hold her off any longer. He puts the picture of the male assassin next to the editor's. "This man's name is Robert Hewitt, and we have made a connection between him and your friend Greg Barnes. And, this is the kicker. Greg Barnes was found murdered this afternoon in his office."

Miranda puts her hands to her mouth, "Oh, my God!"

Denny notes to himself that when he defined Greg Barnes as a friend, Miranda did not correct him. Denny decided to leave that one dangling. He points to the mystery man. "Can you remember anything about this man that may help us, distinguishing marks, any peculiarities, character traits? For example, does he walk with a limp?"

Miranda smiles, she likes this game, "No, quite the opposite. He's very light on his feet. I realized that when we were at the exhibit, the night before the opening. I was working on a piece, and he walked up to me without my knowing that he was there."

"Good. You got the idea. Is there anything else?"

Miranda stops to think for a moment, "He had a beard and mustache, but I remember thinking as I studied his face that he would be better looking without one. I thought he might have a complexion problem and that was why he has a beard."

She pauses then says, "He was very calm, very quiet. He said he was from El Salvador, and when he did speak, he had quite a heavy accent. Several times I had to ask him to repeat what he had said. He was very polite, but I could tell, he didn't like that. I assumed that he was reticent to speak because he was embarrassed by his lack of fluency in the language. Some people are like that. Don't you think?"

Denny nods his head in agreement, "Sometimes,

but in this man's case it could have been a put on."

"Oh." Miranda is disappointed. She fiddles with her hands, wrings them. She's nervous now, "Oh dear, I can't think. This is so awful."

"I know, but you don't have to give it all to me now. Sometimes these things take time. Is there anything else?"

Miranda shakes her hands in exasperation, "Oh, dear, I'm usually so good at this."

"Ms. Labelle, did you know that Brad Merling would come to your exhibit?"

She pauses then settles down and says, "No, but I thought he might. He comes to most of my exhibits. And when he can, he usually comes to the opening."

She pauses again, digests what she just said then looks up quite surprised, shocked, "They used me?"

"Yes, so it seems. They took a chance that he would be there. It was a good guess, a shot, so to speak."

"But how did the assassins get in? Did they sneak in and hide?"

"No, it's not as simple as that. If they merely hid, my people would have found them when they inspected the exhibit prior to his arrival. No, what they did was far more clever. From the pictures that you sent them they duplicated those papier-mâché figures of the man and woman at the meat counter, but they did it with real people inside. Is that difficult?"

Miranda pauses to think the question through, "No,

that's how you create the original mold."

Miranda thinks for another moment. An expression of amazement comes across her face. "I see. You're saying that they had the assassins molded into the figures, and the night before the exhibit, they switched them for the originals."

"That's the way it looks. Does it make sense to you?"

"They had a van."

"But did they have time?"

"Yes, but how did you discover them?"

"We were lucky there. The man pissed his pants. They probably had a catheter and a bag taped to his leg, but it probably came loose, and luckily I spotted it."

She looks more closely at Denny, "You're the man who saved Brad's life. I saw you on TV. You work for Brad."

"Yes and no, I'm on loan. Now just a few more questions." Denny gives Miranda some examples of words, each with a specific accent, and he asks her how the mystery man pronounced those words. Finally, he picks up the pictures and puts them in his pocket.

She looks at him puzzled, "We're done?"

Denny smiles and says, "For the time being?"

Miranda face registers relief, sadness, and then excitement as she says, "Am I a suspect?"

He lies, "No, of course not."

"Oh," She seems disappointed.

"May I make a phone call?" Denny asks.

"Of course," She looks at him slyly, "I suppose you want to be alone? Secrets."

"Yes, too many, I'm afraid."

She picks up a remote control that is on the floor next to the couch, and she presses a button, and a control panel emerges from beneath the coffee table.

"I'll leave you alone," she says then she gets up, disappears, and reappears with Bugs in her arms. She walks across the room, sits down on a stool in front of a grand piano that is painted pink and begins to pet Bugs as she says, "You've been on quite an adventure, haven't you?"

Denny punches in Hathaway's code number. He hears Hathaway's voice on the other end. "It's Martino," Denny says. "I'm here with Ms. Labelle."

"Has she been helpful?"

"It's what I thought. The editor and the mystery man told her they were doing a feature article on the exhibit. They got access to the exhibition the night before. She did not recognize the two assassins, and she doesn't know anything about the mystery man, except that he claimed to be from El Salvador. She was helpful with the accent. I think he's from Brazil."

"You may be right, Denny. He ain't who he's supposed to be. From the records at *The Globe* and from the people we talked to, he's supposed to be a freelance correspondent from El Salvador named Enrico Ferte, but, in fact, the picture of Enrico Ferte that the Salvadoran government sent us is not a picture of the same man that we saw at the cafe. Nor is it a picture of the man who has been walking around here calling himself Enrico Ferte. My guess is that Ferte has become a missing person, and our man... I don't know. We have his picture out worldwide, but my guess is that he had his escape route well planned."

"What do you want me to do?"

There's a pause, then Hathaway says, "Is Miranda secured there?"

"I don't know. She has super high tech security around her home, but I don't know much beyond that."

"Do you know what her plans are for the next few days?"

"No."

"Ask her."

"Hold on." Denny gets up and approaches Miranda, "Ms. Labelle, excuse me, but could you tell me what your plans are for the next few days?"

"Why?"

"I don't want to alarm you, but you could be in danger."

"Why?"

"Anyone connected with this incident is potentially in danger. These people obviously don't like loose ends."

Miranda looks down at the rabbit, "Does he have a name?"

"Bugs."

She smiles and says, "Of course. Men always think of the obvious."

Denny's voice is soft, "It's really unlikely from what you told me, but we do have to take precautions."

Miranda thinks for a moment and then smiles. Denny notes something mischievous about her smile, "I'm going to New York City for the debate between the President and Arthur Lorenz, and then I'm going to Washington to see Brad."

"How long will you be in New York?"

"A day or two."

"Thank you." Denny returns to the phone and tells Hathaway what Miranda's plans are.

"Martino, I want you to stay with her until she gets to Washington. Can you do that?"

Denny looks up, and he sees that Miranda is sitting across from him. She smiles, "I suppose you're talking about me," she says.

Denny nods.

"Well, then, it's the God given right of any woman to listen in." She sits back and hugs Bugs.

"They want me to stay with you until you get to Washington," Denny says. "Can I do that?"

"Who are you talking to?"

"John Hathaway."

Miranda makes a face and shakes her head negatively like a schoolteacher that has just heard the name of a little boy who she knows very well. "Bad. Bad. Bad."

Hathaway says, "What did she say?"

"She said you're bad."

Hathaway laughs, "Let me talk to her."

Denny hands Miranda the phone. She responds to Hathaway cautiously, but they seem to be on friendly terms, that is, until Hathaway asks her a question to which she responds, "It's none of your god damned business." She hands the phone back to Denny.

"She's agreed to allow you to accompany her," Hathaway says. "But remember don't get caught up in the lights. You're there to observe, not be observed. You're just a bit actor in this story, Martino. Got it?"

"Don't worry, Hathaway. I'm just here trying to do my job."

"Good, I know I can rely on you. And, Denny, I want to know what the hell she is up to when she goes to New York City. Arthur Lorenz is what I think she is up to, and Brad is going to shit when he finds this out."

"Right."

Hathaway laughs and says, "She's something, isn't she?

Denny looks at Miranda, and she is smiling smugly, "Yes, she is," he says.

"Well, don't underestimate her. She's sharp as a whip and a determined little girl when she gets her mind set on something, totally irresponsible." Hathaway hangs up.

Denny turns to Miranda and says, "Excuse me for a

moment. I'm going to send the helioplane home."

"And the guys with all the guns?"

Denny thinks for a moment. There is no reason for the assassin to come after her. He knows everything that she knows, and this place is as safe as a vault. "Yes, and the guys with the guns."

Denny leaves the house, and when he returns Miranda is still sitting on the couch. She is sitting back looking quite comfortable. "So, it seems that you're going to take care of me," she says.

"I'm going to try to."

"And you have to do everything I say."

Denny laughs, "Not quite. My job is to protect you."

Miranda laughs too, "Oh good I do love to be protected. So what's next?"

Denny looks at the rabbit and says, "I think I should do right by Bugs and let him go. What do you think?"

"You're right. I'm being selfish." Miranda gets up and hands Bugs over to Denny.

"Where should I take him?" Denny asks.

Miranda leads Denny into the kitchen and gives him directions that will lead him down the same path that she followed earlier, to the same spot.

"He'll find his buddies there," she says.

Chapter Thirteen

Denny hears the sound of rushing water fill the air as he walks out onto a platform that is suspended over the falls. He walks down a floating stairway, crosses a stone bridge and follows the flow of the water down the pathway that Miranda had taken earlier in the day to a spot where she was painting a landscape. Denny finds it hard to let go of Bugs, the fantasy rabbit he always wanted as a child. When he takes him out of the box, he feels the simple warmth and heartbeat of life, and he sets him on the ground and then watches him disappear into forest where he belongs. He's about to go back to the house, but he stops to take a look at the view from the spot where Miranda had been painting the landscape. The palette of colors is still on the ground, but the canvas is gone, and, yet, the picture is still all around him. Denny tries to imagine the landscape like Miranda described the Gauguin - the sensuous breasts, the sloping curves, the rising thighs, and the silky slip of cascading water that forms a pool below the falls that reflects the trees in full bloom and the blue sky peeking through the forest, playing tricks with the light like jeweled earrings.

Denny smiles when he thinks about how much fun

he had with Miranda today. Then he thinks about how little he laughs anymore, how depressed he has become. One of the reasons he is so depressed, he thinks, is that, like most Americans, he doesn't go anywhere anymore. All he does is change the picture on the three-dimensional virtual reality picture window that really isn't there, and he thinks he is in the fuckin' Bahamas, but he never leaves home except for work. Somehow he's forgotten what it is like to be alive and be a part of this. He listens to the birds, the buzz of the insects charging the air, and then it stops, first the insects, then the birds.

Silence.

Denny slowly reaches inside his coat for his automatic pistol. As his hand grasps the handle, he feels cold steel on the back of his neck, and he turns to find himself facing a shotgun.

Behind the barrel of the shotgun is a very tall bearded man wearing old fashioned horn rim glasses, a hunting shirt, and jeans. A very large working boot is propped against a rock. The man smiles and says, "Friend or foe?"

Denny raises his hands, "I'm a friend."

The man speaks to someone else, "What do you think, Jake? Says he's a friend. But he looks like a federale to me."

Out of the forest appears a heavyset man wearing an old combat jacket and carrying a M60 machine gun with a cartridge belt. "Yep, he looks like a federale to me too, Ned." He pokes Denny with the barrel of his M60, "What ya doin hangin around the Label house?"

"I'm here to see Ms. Labelle."

Ned steps closer so that he and Denny are face to face. "You're not here to hurt the little lady, are you?"

"No, I'm here to protect her."

Ned and Jake break into a fit of laughter, and then Ned says, "You're doin a fuck of a good job of it, aren't you, Mr. Federale." Ned holds out his hand, "Let's see your ID."

Denny begins to reach into his coat, but Jake pokes him again with the barrel of the M60 and says, "The other hand."

Denny is getting pissed off. He looks at Jake's cold, stupid, resolute stare, and he can feel his adrenaline flowing as he hands his identification to Ned.

Ned looks at the ID then smiles at Jake, "Well lookie here, we got ourselves a Colonel in the National Security Force."

"Don't say. Maybe we ought to shoot the pig."

That's it for Denny. He turns on Ned and Jake and says, "Let me tell you two assholes what the story is here. I didn't get any sleep last night. Yesterday, I had to shoot two people who read the wrong flyers, and, today, I figured out my life sucks. But for a moment here..." Denny's voice begins to rise. "I'm just beginning to feel good..."

Denny pushes the barrel of Ned's shotgun aside and shouts, "When some honky mother fuckin red neck cock suckers like you come around and bust my balls."

Ned laughs, "You know something, Jake? I think we got him pissed off."

"You're god damned right I'm pissed off, and I want to know if we got a problem here or what?"

Ned lowers his shotgun and smiles. His teeth are bad from lack of care. "Nope, we just thought we'd let you know that the little lady is never alone. We watch over her."

Denny stares at Ned, "That's it?"

"Yep."

Denny takes a close look at Ned and Jake, and he decides that they are ex-army, and that they are probably not alone. It also dawns on him that he's probably talking to two Green Peace Warriors.

Denny laughs at the absurdity of his situation and says, "Well, that's really nice, Ned. It makes my job a lot easier."

Ned lowers his shotgun and says, "Want some shine?"

For a moment, Denny doesn't understand, but then he says, "Are you asking me if I want a drink?"

"Yep, come on, and I'll show you the terrain."

Denny decides that he needs to know more about who these people are and what is going on around here so he says, "Sure, why not?"

Ned turns to Jake and says, "You stay here, and I'll take the Colonel to the ranchero for a swig of real whiskey.

Come on, Colonel. Follow me."

Ned walks off, and Denny follows him through the woods to a path that leads to a dirt road. On the road Denny sees a 1951 one half ton F-1 Ford pick-up truck, another monster from the past with prehistoric chrome gills on the side of the engine hood. The truck is a patchwork of colors made up of different body parts that have been replaced but never painted over to match one another.

Denny opens the squeaking door to the passenger's side and climbs in. Beer cans are strewn on the floor, and the ashtray is full of butts. There are some tears in the vinyl upholstery; and just when Denny is wondering if the old relic will run, it roars to life.

Denny listens to the motor, "Are those four barrel carbs?" Denny asks.

"Yep."

"That's not the original motor?"

"Nope," Ned smiles, and then peels out to the sound of gravel and dirt flying in the air and steel banging against steel. They drive through the forest for a mile or two. Along the road he can see that many log cabins have been built on the mountainside.

"How many people live here?" Denny asks.

"About a hundred families."

"And you all live on her land?"

"Yep."

"For free?"

"Yes and no. When we have the money, we pay rent and that goes towards our share in the estate. Otherwise we take care of the land."

They turns up a side road and drive past several more log cabins until they get to a log cabin that overlooks a valley and the mountain range on the other side. Ned pulls to a stop next to a woodpile. Beyond the woodpile Denny sees a garden with stakes sticking out of the ground with spindly string beans growing from drooping limbs. There are rows of tomatoes and lettuce and what looks to him to be cucumbers, and some dark green vegetables in the background.

Denny and Ned get out of the truck and as they walk to the cabin, a woman walks out to meet them. The woman is wearing a T-shirt and blue jeans. She's a large woman who probably was overweight much of her life, but now seems shriveled up from dieting or the lack of food. Denny can see suspicion in her deep-set eyes, fear.

Ned points to Denny and says, "This here's Colonel Martino, Margaret. He's visiting up at the Label house."

Margaret extends her hand to Denny, and Ned continues on into the cabin. Denny is left standing there with Margaret who seems uneasy.

"Nice place, "Denny says.

"We like it." She gestures to a wood bench on the front porch. "Would you like to sit down?"

"Yes, please."

Denny notices that her voice is cultivated and that

she moves quite gracefully for a big woman. He would guess that she's from a middle class background, a fact that belies her appearance, her unkempt hair. But she's probably just another product of bad times.

They walk to the porch, and Denny sits down, but Ned's wife remains standing. "How did you meet?" she asks.

Denny laughs. "We met in the woods."

He watches her fiddle nervously with her hands as she says, "Oh, I see." She looks behind her for Ned and then turns to Denny and smiles, "I bet he brought you up here to taste some of his home-brew? He brings everyone up here for that. It's quite good, but you be careful not to drink too much." She smiles and says, "They don't call it 'white lightning' for nothing."

Denny smiles and says, "Thanks for the warning."

"These are dangerous times. It's not safe to be alone in the woods."

"I know."

She studies Denny for a moment. "God, you must think we're a bunch of hicks, but we're not, Colonel. We lived in the city. I had a job working for the social services. Ned was in the army before he met me, and then he got a job as a mechanic when he got out. He specialized in antique cars, but bad times came, so we came here. Minimalism, I think you call it. Ned is an outdoor man, hunting and fishing and all that stuff." She smiles, "Person-ally, I love TV, a soft sofa, and indoor plumbing, but I've grown to love it out here. It really is God's country."

Ned walks out with a jug in his hand, "I see that you're getting acquainted with the little woman here." He puts his arm around her, "She's not so little, but..." He winks at Denny and says, "You gotta have your women strong." He winks at her, "And beautiful."

Margaret is embarrassed, "Stop that Ned." She pulls away, but Denny can see that she is pleased.

Ned hands Denny the jug. "Here, take a swig of this."

Denny grabs the jug. It's ice cold. He curls his finger around the handle and rests the jug on his arm as he lifts it and takes a big swig. The alcohol hits him like a charge of electricity. He looks at Ned who is smiling, "Jesus, this stuff is great. What is it?"

"Apple brandy, I made it from seven kinds of apples and fermented them in an old barrel that I got from the old Jack Daniel's factory. Then I distilled it real fine. Take another swig."

"My ass isn't gonna fall off, is it?"

Ned laughs, "Nope. Not if you don't stand up."

Denny lifts the jug again, and as he does, he sees two children flash by him, a girl in her early teens chasing a boy a bit younger. They run through the wash that is hanging on the line.

Denny hears Margaret shout, "Slow down, you two." Then he hears her say, "Damn." Denny sees the same soiled hand prints on the white sheet that Margaret sees.

Ned laughs and says, "Them's mine. The boy's a bit of a pain in the ass. Stubborn like his mom. He's twelve and goin through what Margaret calls... What is it, that stuff you say he's got?"

Margaret turns to Denny and says with the wisp of an ironic smile on her face, "Hormonal dysfunction."

Ned laughs, "He's got something hard down there between his legs, and he don't know what to do with it yet. That's his problem."

Margaret says, "Men," as if that explains everything. She extends her hand to Denny then excuses herself. Denny watches her walk towards the garden as Ned sits down next to him. The sun is setting on the garden, the forest. The log cabin overlooks a valley, the mountain range on the other side. It's a magnificent view. Not very far above is where the tree line ends and the snow and ice begin, ice blue and evergreen, the clouds creating moving shadows across the peaks and cliffs and falls that cut deep into a the valley and the life that surges upward, life reaching for the light everywhere.

"It's nice here, Ned."

"Yep, but don't let her fool you. She's cold as a witch's tit in winter." Ned takes a swig of the moonshine. "Brr," He shakes off the cold with another jolt of white lightning then hands the jug to Denny and says, "But the game's comin back and there's fish in the stream. It's not easy and sometimes..."

Ned doesn't complete the sentence. He just stares into the darkness of his thoughts for a moment and then goes on. "But what's the alternative? Working at the dumps? That's where they force the homeless and unemployed to work. There's a valley near here we call The Pit. You ever seen it?"

"No, but I heard of it"

Ned eyes Denny for a moment then says, "Maybe ya should. You'll get a better idea of what we're all about around here."

"OK."

Ned gets up and goes into the cabin, and he returns in a few moments with the jug in a cooler packed with ice and pair of binoculars strapped to his shoulder. "Come on," he says."

"Wait a minute," Denny says. "I want to say goodby to your wife."

Denny approaches the garden. Margaret, who has been picking string beans, gets up and meets him at the edge of the tomato patch. Denny extends his hand, "Thank you for your hospitality."

She smiles, "Well, thank you for coming." She looks into Denny's eyes, "Ned's a good man, Colonel Martino. I hope you realize that. If someone else had found you out there alone... Well, it may have been a different story."

"I understand that Margaret. If there is anything that I can do for you, let me know." Denny hands Margaret his card.

She looks at it as if she hasn't seen anything like it in a long time. She seems pleased as she puts it in her pouch with the string beans. She smiles and says, "Thank you, Colonel."

Margaret turns away and returns to her garden, and Denny joins Ned who is waiting in his crazy quilt patched up antique Ford pickup truck with its broken tooth grill smiling at him. The picture would be comical except for the similarly antique but seriously deadly weapons he carries in the gun rack and the World War II vintage 45 automatic he carries in a shoulder holster underneath his arm.

Denny gets in the truck, and they peal out, stones and dirt flying everywhere as Ned races down an old logging road, the 4-speed-gear-shift sticking out of the floor bending like a fly rod as Ned changes gears, and they listen to an old country western song about how the bank took the farm away. Despite the break-neck-speed, the drive is quite pleasant. The sun is setting and the mountains are beautiful in this light, but then they drive over a ridge, and Denny sees the horror.

Ned pulls to a stop, and they get out of the truck. From where they are, they overlook a valley and a mountainside that has been totally stripped of trees. In many places the topsoil has been washed away baring rocks that look like bones sticking out of a dead skin. Below, the vast valley is being filled with garbage.

Ned hands Denny the binoculars. He adjusts the

132

focus, and he sees men, women, and children from the concentration camps working in the dump, condemned here because they have committed the crime of being un-employed or homeless. Under the watchful supervision of armed guards and the overseers, they are sorting through the garbage separating out all that can be salvaged or re-cycled. For the most part, they are doing it by hand as a continuous stream of trucks dump more garbage and the bulldozers plow it over and spread the garbage around.

At the end of the dump is a colossal pyramid of burnt out tires, a monument to the dead end that we have become. Black clouds pour out of the recycling plant into a red sky, and the sun descends on the valley that was once a part of America the beautiful but is now being filled up with the refuge of our dreams and our own disposable people.

Denny hears Ned say, "I'll die before I work there."

Denny finds himself saying, "Me too."

Ned hands Denny the jug of moonshine, and he takes a swig of Mother Nature's solution to a depressed economy. Ned takes a swig of the shine and then belches loud and deep, corks the jug, and then stands up and says, "Well, Colonel Martino. I better get you back, or the little lady will give me a lot of shit for getting one of her white knights all fucked up."

Ned walks away without saying another word, and Denny follows him to the truck. On the way back to Miran-da Labelle's house, Ned is quiet as he negotiates a dirt road through a forest that has turned to darkness and shadows. There's also a lot of darkness between them, and even though Denny likes Ned, he has to do his job. He has to ask questions and determine if Ned is a security risk.

"Ned, are you a member of the Green Peace Party?"

"Yep."

"What's the Green Peace Party about?"

"We're for standing up against corporate fascism and the pricks that are turning this country into a garbage can. That's why we support Senator Lorenz for President. We're for a national initiative, referendum, and recall voting system. We're for economic democracy, and we're for turning America back into a land of farmers."

Ned sounds like one of those flyers that Denny read in the dead editor's office, but he keeps that to himself and asks, "How's he going to do that?"

"Do what?"

"Turn America back into a land of farmers?"

"He's gonna buy back at fair market value all the land that the foreigners have bought up, and he's gonna give it back to the people by creating small and medium size farms and networking them into cooperatives like we use to have in the old days."

Denny remembers the mega-farm that he saw yesterday, the vastness of it all and the high tech automated machinery. "How are you going to compete against the mega-farms? They're so big."

"There's the myth, "Ned says. "Bigger is not better. Why do you think they're selling the fuckin things to foreign countries like China that are starving for crop producing land? They can't make money on them, and the bald ass fact is that the scientists have discovered what working farmers have known all along. Small and medium diversified farms can out produce mega-farms. They can grow food that is healthier for you, and they don't rely on pesticides and oil-based fertilizer that pollutes the water and depletes the soil."

Denny finds the idea interesting. He listens to Ned talk about how small and medium sized farms are local, and they spend their money in the community where they live, and they save fuel by relying less on long distance shipping. Then Ned goes on and on about fertilizer and the virtues of cow shit, chicken shit, horseshit, and bullshit until Denny realizes that Ned is controlling the interrogation and that if he doesn't change the subject soon he will never learn anything about what the hell is going on around here, so he decides to cut to the chase.

"So, Ned, how do the Green Peace Warriors fit into this? They claim that they are the military arm of the Green Peace Party."

"Wait a minute, Colonel. You know damned well that the Green Peace Warriors have been declared a terror-ist organization, and we have made it quite clear that we don't support the violent overthrow of the government, and we deny any affiliation with the Green Peace

Warriors."

"There are a lot a people out there, Ned, who think that's bullshit. They say that the only reason the Party denies any affiliation with the Green Peace Warriors is that if it were proven that they are the militant arm of the party, you too will be declared a terrorist organization and be outlawed as a political party."

"Oh, come on, Colonel. Do you know how many people vote for the Green Peace Party? Millions. Are they all terrorists? And what about Senator Lorenz? He has accepted the support of the Green Peace Party. Does that make him a terrorist and guilty of treason? And what if he gets elected? Does that make the majority of the American people guilty of treason?"

"No," Denny says. "That's a peaceful revolution, and that's what America's all about, but you guys want your cake and eat it too."

"No, Colonel, we just want a fair and honest election. Do you think that we're gonna get it?"

Denny shrugs and says, "Ned, I don't know. I'm just a homicide detective who got stuck with a security detail, and now I've been assigned to find out who took a shot at Brad Merling."

Ned pulls up to the gateway to Miranda Labelle's estate and says, "Well, here you are, Colonel. Hope you enjoyed the tour."

"Thanks for the hospitality, Ned."

Denny is about to get out of the truck, but Ned

reaches into the glove compartment and pulls out an electronic device, clicks it, and the invisible electronic defense system shuts down.

"Fuck," Denny says. "You work for her."

As Ned drives through the gateway, he says, "I told you that we look out for the little lady."

"So who are you? Are you a part of a security unit? Do you work for us?"

Ned pulls up to the stairway leading to Miranda's home and says, "Colonel, no disrespect, but you are way over your head here. Don't misunderstand my meaning. I'm sure you're damned good at what you do. For a fact, you remind me of an old red bone hound I use to have. If he got a whiff of an asshole that didn't smell right to him, he'd track it down until he got to the truth of the matter. But, Colonel, when Brad Merling picked you, you stopped being just a detective doing his job. You became part of Vision World."

"What the hell does that mean?"

"Well, I'm gonna give you a clue, Colonel. It means you're a part of the story now."

"What if I don't want to be a part of the story? What if I only want to do my job?"

Ned laughs and says, "Well then, Colonel, just be boring, and they will lose interest in you."

Denny laughs and then gets out of the truck. He offers Ned his card and says, "Thanks for the hospitality and the advice, but if you hear anything or know anything, here is my personal cell number. Give me a call. Ms. Labelle may be at risk."

Ned takes the card, laughs, and says, "Just like a said, a damned red bone hound. I think that Merling may have underestimated you, Colonel. You may be what Vision World can't digest."

"What's that, Ned?"

Ned smiles and says, "An honest man in search of the truth."

Ned waves goodbye and drives off leaving Denny standing at the stairway leading to the main entrance to Miranda's home. He watches the old Ford pickup truck fade into the darkness and the silence. The red taillights and the roar of the engine are swallowed up by the shadows, the woods, the crickets chirping, and he notes to himself that when he used the word "you" in reference to the Green Peace Warriors and used it again in reference to the connection between the Green Peace Warriors and the Green Peace Party, Ned did not correct him.

Denny stops for a moment and takes a deep breath. He looks around once more at the only reality. It is a beautiful night. The stars fill the sky, and they are quite bright in the clear mountain air. The evergreens loom all around him like giant specters of shadowed beauty that veil a mystery. The tranquility and the solitude frightens him, and he marvels at how Miranda can live out here alone in her cantilevered glass bullet proof castle with terraces overlooking the falls and a stream that has been channeled so as to act as a moat around an architectural masterpiece that seems to float in the air, its vertical and horizontal lines penetrating one another so as to make it hard to determine what is inside and out.

As Denny walks up the stairway, the door to the main entrance opens, and a flood of light pours through like a spot in a theatrical stage set. Miranda is standing at the door waiting for Denny. She is upset, "Where have you been?"

"I've been visiting with your friends."

"Ned?"

"Yes Ned and Jake. Ms. Labelle, you might have told me that you are surrounded by Green Peace Warriors, and they work for you."

"They're just people who want a place to live modestly and in tune with nature."

"Ms. Labelle, do you realize that those nice people out there are probably the same people who blew up that development!"

Miranda shouts back, "Good, they shouldn't be building that fuckin' development up here!"

Miranda pauses then smiles, "Oh, look. We're having our first fight, and it's all my fault. I should have told you that I have bodyguards, and they don't like strangers."

"They're...your bodyguards?"

"Yes."

"But, Ms. Labelle, those people are dangerous."

"Colonel, don't be naïve," Miranda says, "All my

friends are dangerous. And except for Ned and the people who live on this land, all my friends are members of the power elite. Do you really think I can trust them?"

She's right, Denny thinks. You don't look to the most ambitious, most avaricious people in the world to protect you. But how deeply involved is she with the Green Peace Warriors? Is she involved with what happened yesterday? Would she off her brother-in-law for the sake of America the Beautiful? Denny looks into those devilish eyes, and he finds himself saying, "In a flash."

Miranda takes Denny's hand in hers, "Now, about tomorrow, I made a call to my producers. In the morning they'll all be here. We'll be in New York City by evening." She smiles at him, "I've arranged everything for you, clothing too. I want you to look good for the cameras." Miranda pauses. She seems to be tracing the lines of his face with her eyes, "Colonel, when was the last time that you had any sleep?"

"I've been up for about forty-eight-hours."

"I thought so. Come on. You need your rest. Tomorrow is going to be a big day."

The sympathy in her voice draws out his real feelings. Yes, he is tired. He looks at the couch. It looks reasonably comfortable. "I'll rest here," he says.

"All right," Miranda leads him to the couch and takes off his coat for him. She stares at his gun strapped to his shoulder, and when he takes it off and puts it on the coffee table, she picks it up. "My God, this is a nasty looking little weapon. What is it?"

Denny is taking off his shoes. "It's a PK40. It's relatively new. The laser beam is actually the barrel of the gun. The beam creates an electrical magnetic field that forms a vacuum. The explosive pellet is pulled through the vacuum and explodes once it penetrates the target. It's incredibly accurate because no matter how far away the target is... you're always firing at point blank range."

Miranda turns the weapon over in her hand studying it from every angle. "How many rounds?" she asks.

"A hundred."

"Nasty."

Miranda places the weapon back down on the coffee table and sits down near Denny. She tucks in her legs and studies Denny for a moment, and then says, "Where are you from, Colonel?"

Denny lies back on the couch and props his head against a pillow. "I come from around here."

Miranda studies his features for a moment more, his eyes, his nose, his mouth, and his cheekbones. She likes what she sees, but she's curious. "Your last name is Italian. But you're African American too, right?"

"Yes. My mother is an African American."

"How interesting, back then racial intermarriage wasn't so common. How was it for them?"

"To tell you the truth, my mother wasn't very black, and my father wasn't very Italian. They were schoolteachers who lived life out of a textbook. They wanted to be good people and do the right thing. They wanted to belong, and they did. They were good Americans, but I think my mom was right."

"About what, Colonel?"

"She told me once that she felt sorry for me. She said that when colored people finally make it in this country, there won't be anything left of the American pie."

Miranda's face expresses sadness, "She might be right." Miranda smiles, "And of course you were a good boy?"

Denny laughs, "Oh yes, a good student, a good athlete, a good worker. I was so good that I was accepted to West Point, and I've been taking orders ever since."

"Don't you ever want to rebel?"

"Sometimes a voice inside me wants to shout, "No," but I don't know what I would be shouting, no, for. I don't know what I believe in."

"Brad says that conformity is the only thing that is holding this country together anymore. That's one of the reasons Vision World is so important. It defines what we believe, and it makes us all a part of the story."

Denny smiles at Miranda and says, "He may be right, but I envy you. You can do anything you want to do and be anything you want to be."

"Only if I'm trivial and entertaining, Colonel, but I'm going to change that."

"How?"

"I don't know yet."

"Are you involved with the Green Peace Warriors or the People's Army?"

Miranda stares at Denny for a moment and then smiles mischievously. "So I am a suspect."

"Yes."

"Good. That means you have to really get to know me, isn't that so?"

Denny smiles, "Yes."

"Isn't that dangerous?" Miranda asks.

"How's that?"

"You may get to like me".

"I already do."

Miranda smiles coyly, "And more?"

Denny can see a clear outline of Miranda's bare breasts underneath the light cotton fabric of the oversized white T-shirt that she has changed into.

"Miranda, are we on TV?"

"We're always on TV, Denny. That's what Vision World is all about."

"But doesn't it bother you...having everyone watch you?"

"No, Vision World is sort of like God. You know God is always watching you, but you ignore him. However, at the same time, you're glad he's there because you're not alone and everything matters."

Denny notices that she isn't wearing anything underneath the T-shirt except a pair of white bikini panties. Denny sighs. He wants desperately to make love to this woman. But over 400 million people are watching him, including his wife who would probably love the ratings. Denny closes his eyes. It's too much for him.

He can hear Miranda get up. He can feel her sit down next to him on the couch. He can feel her warmth, and he can smell the sweet smell of Caress soap as he feels her lips touch his ear, and she whispers, "Do you want to be alone with me?"

"Yes."

"Then we'll have to kill God," she says then kisses him and is gone.

Denny sighs and stares at the walls. He wonders if anyone is really watching. He wonders if it really matters. He thinks about Miranda's sister, the many women in the mirror, his wife making herself up into every other woman in the world, and Cheri, forever new. He wonders if they're all one woman behind many alluring masks, the thing beyond the wall when the power goes off. He continues to wonder as he slips off into sleep away from the walls, the eyes, the creature sucking in the heat, the light. He slips down, down into the water, the depth. But he finds no rest there as he sinks slowly towards an octopus with TV screens for suckers. In the TV screens, he sees the deer being zapped, the papier-mâché people with their empty stares exploding into blood. He sees the cracked head of the child, an empty jar. He sees Miranda going down on the trucker's cock, swallowing him alive, and he feels himself being drawn into the TV screen too. He tries to

scream.   But in the end he disappears into nothingness.
Peace.

Chapter Fourteen

The next morning Denny wakes up fully clothed on Miranda's couch. He sits up and tries to gather his thoughts, but then he smells the scent of fresh coffee brewing, and he follows the scent into Miranda's kitchen. Miranda's kitchen looks like a cubist abstract painting composed of clear-cut geometric planes and shades of blue and green. The cabinets and kitchen appliances appear and disappear with a touch of a finger, and the electronically controlled shades on the picture windows control the rays of the sun so as to create beautiful still-lives of real objects - a polished stainless steel soup pot radiating light on the stove, a floral arrangement of mountain flowers in a cut crystal vase, a coffee maker, cream and sugar, breakfast rolls, and a note that reads, Denny, I couldn't pick you up last night and carry you to bed. The fresh orange juice is in the refrigerator.

Denny opens the refrigerator, finds the orange juice, then grabs a honey bun, and walks back into the living room. He's about to turn on the TV to watch the morning news when he hears the sound of vehicles outside, voices, a stampede of feet. The front door flies open, and the house is invaded by Miranda's production team. There are so many people in the house, so many voices that Denny can't figure out who they all are. Miranda appears in her T-shirt and panties, and she is immediately descended upon. Denny is pushed into the background, but he continues to observe Miranda who is conferring at every moment with someone or another, going over possible situations, plots and lines as the make-up people, hairdressers, and fashion designers work on a progression of looks and what she will wear. Closets and drawers are thrown open, fabrics are draped all about. Everyone is talking all at once, and a travel secretary shouts over the phone making arrangements for the flight. Denny is able to make one phone call to his wife and another to Hathaway who promises him that he will have men and equipment waiting for him in New York City. When Denny gets off the phone, hands grab at him. His clothes are cleaned, his hair is cut, and he is even given a few make-up tips. A lawyer for Vision World shoves papers at him to sign, and an advertising agent shows him what labels to show as a costume designer shoves one hand up his crotch and another down his leg measuring him for new clothing.

Four hours later, he is flying over New York City in a supersonic jet with Ned sitting across from him wearing a tuxedo, black tie, and size thirteen work boots polished for the dance. Denny is reading a file on Ned, and he discovers that Ned grew up in Huntsville, Georgia and that his father was a Baptist minister, the town justice, and a used car salesman. Ned was a good student in high school, played varsity basketball, and scored high on his Math SATs. He went to Georgia Tech as an engineer major, and according to his college application, he wanted to be an automotive engineer, but then the depression came, and he had to drop out of school at the end of his sophomore year. Soon after that, he joined the Army believing that when he finished his tour of duty, the government would pay for his continued education.

Ned's service records indicate that he was part of a search and destroy unit, and because of his size, he got to carry the heavy Gatlin gun and rocket launcher. The records also indicate that half way through his tour of duty he was awarded the Bronze Star for bravery and promoted to the rank of master sergeant. Up to that point, Ned's military records indicate that he was the model soldier, but then the Santa Rosa Massacre happened.

Santa Rosa was a small farming village in Chile that had been designated by army intelligence as a village sympathetic to the terrorist rebels, and it was believed that they were supplying the rebel cause with foodstuffs and recruits. Based on the notes taken from the military court hearing convened to determine what happened at Santa Rosa, Ned's unit had been ordered to burn down the village in retaliation for an attack on an American military unit earlier in the month. It was believed that the villagers had provided the guerillas with information that enabled them to ambush the Americans.

According to the testimony of several soldiers who were there, the lieutenant in command of the unit had given the order to kill everyone. One soldier testified that he saw Ned shoot the lieutenant with a revolver and then put the gun in the hand of a dead farmer, but several other soldiers swore that they saw the farmer shoot the lieutenant. Private Anthony Rodrigues, the soldier who originally reported the massacre, testified that it was Ned who stopped the slaughter. He took command.

The court, after hearing all the evidence, concluded that there was not sufficient evidence to charge Ned with a crime, but Ned was busted from master sergeant to private, and soon after that he was discharged from the army as unfit for duty.

Denny puts down the report, "Have you read this?"

Ned takes the folder with the report in it and leafs through it, "Yep."

"What do you think about it?"

Ned lets go with a huge fart that is followed by a chorus of moans and laughter that suggests to Denny that this is not the first time that Ned has aired his views.

His suspicions are confirmed when he hears Miranda say, "Ned, what did I say about your rights to free speech in a confined space?"

"Burps, yes. Farts, no," Ned says.

"You got it."

Ned hands the folder back to Denny and says, "Sorry, Colonel. I got carried away."

"That's all right, Ned. It just makes it easier for me to follow your trail." Denny points to the folder and says, "You don't mind me asking a few questions. I'm confused about a few things in this report."

"Smell away, Colonel."

Denny smiles and says, "Is it true that your father was a Baptist minister, the justice of the peace, and a used car dealer? How did that work?"

Ned laughs and says, "Damned good for everyone. If you bought your car from him and you went to church every Sunday and you contributed to the Baptist mission, you were forgiven for all your traffic and parking violations by God and General Motors."

"What about Santa Rosa? What happened there?"

There is a time lapse where Ned seems to be traveling back into his past and then out of the darkness emerges one word, "Madness."

Denny points to the report and says, "At the hearing, the ballistics report stated that the gun that killed the lieutenant was a Colt 38 Special." Denny points to Ned's right ankle, "What kind of gun do you have in that ankle holster of yours, Ned?"

Ned smiles and says, "A Colt 38 Special."

"Why did they let that go?" Denny asked. "The soldier that accused you said that you carried a 38 Colt Special in an ankle holster and everyone in the unit knew it."

"What do you think, Colonel? You read the report."

Denny leafs through the pages and then stops. "It

says here that the soldier who was the satellite communications operator testified that he was there when the lieutenant received a call from command headquarters, and after that call, the lieutenant told him that he had just been given an order to kill everyone in the village. When the soldier asked the lieutenant who gave the order, he just pointed to the sky. I don't' think the court wanted to know where that order came from. I don't think they wanted to trace that order up the chain of command, so they swept it all under the table and cashed you out."

'Well, there you go," Ned says. "You found the asshole. Good job, Redbone."

"No benefits, no college fund, no Georgia Tech.'

"Nope."

"That's a sad story, Ned."

"You missed something there, Colonel."

"What's that?"

"The psychiatrist who evaluated me said I might be a borderline sociopath. What do you think of that?"

Denny thinks for a minute then says. "Ned, I've been a soldier much longer than I've been a detective, so, as a soldier, I've only got one question for you."

"Shoot."

"Can I go to sleep next to you in a foxhole?"

"Yep."

Denny shrugs and says, "Case closed."

Ned gets up and says, "You want a drink?"

"Do they have Coca Cola?"

"Yep."

Denny thanks Ned, and he goes back to work. He reaches down into his briefcase and pulls out the file on Senator Arthur Lorenz, and he reads that the Senator was born in New York City over his father's Italian restaurant. His mother was Jewish. Lorenz claims that his parents taught him to believe in all religions. They also taught him to believe in education. He went to Amherst then the University of Chicago for graduate school. He was considered a brilliant scholar, but then he got involved in politics. He started the New Democratic Party in Ithaca, New York where he was teaching political science at Cornell University. The party grew from a grassroots political movement into a national force in American politics. Three years ago, Arthur Lorenz was elected to the United States Senate, and today he is considered a major contender for the Presidency. He's fifty-nine years old, a widower who has three children, two boys and a girl. He's written three books: *The Citizen Lawmaker, Democracy: The Economic System of the 21 Century,* and *Jefferson Revisited.*

Denny is reading the summaries and reviews of Arthur Lorenz's books when he feels the airplane descending, and he hears the pilot announce over the intercom that they are flying over New York City. He looks out the window and sees the skyline at sunset and a spectacular view of the bridges and the walkways that connect the rooftops of the old city to the floor of the new city like a glistening spider web. The modern skyscrapers, surfaced in metallic glass and potter's glaze, look brilliant in the setting sun, dwarfing the old Empire State Building that stands in the middle of a park like an obelisk, a single point to mark where the Leviathan that once was America lived. But now the city is in decline. Large segments of Brooklyn, Queens, and the Bronx have been plowed over, and at the edge of the barren land, Denny sees what seems to be a scene from a World War II movie. Whole sections of the city look like they have been bombed out with only fragments of buildings still standing amidst rubble, exposed walls, interiors, and stairways to nowhere.

"Here you go, Redbone," Ned says, and he hands Denny a bottle of Coca Cola as Denny continues to look out the window. The light is fading and the scene is becoming darker and darker, then blurs as the plane approaches the runway and touches ground, the jets slowing down to a whisper, the condor shaped plane falling back on its haunches, it's head and large beak high above the runway, silent.

Denny disembarks, moving quickly through the crowd to the exit. The door to the exit way slides open, and Denny immediately spots the Vision World logo on the surveillance van parked nearby. As he approaches the van, he is met by a tall well-built young man wearing a business suit and the corporate smile that Denny is now becoming familiar with when dealing with Vision World and its corporate security team. The young man introduces himself as Andrew Zelko, the communications aid assigned to him. They shake hands, and Denny notices that the young man's hand is small and soft. It's the hand of someone who spends most of his time pressing buttons.

"How many men do I have?" Denny asks.

"Ten, sir, five agents have already been positioned at the Plaza Hotel and two cars are in place."

Denny spots the lead car and the trailer, the usual nondescript sedans. He watches the production crew entering their vans, and he hears a jet take off, the thrust of the engines compressing time and place.

He turns to Zelko and says, "Let's go to work."

They enter the van, and Denny sits down at the control panel. He looks at the switches and buttons. The screens are alive with images, and the set-up looks very similar to the system that he and Hathaway worked with in Helena.

"I worked with an AQ-10 like this in Montana," Denny says. "Is there anything different about this system that I should know about?"

"Oh yes, sir, we're hooked up to the production crew and their computers and satellite system, which means that they can give us any exterior or interior view we want."

"How do they do that?"

"They seed the area they're shooting in with micro-particles that act like mirrors. They spread like floating spores and cling to everything, so the production crew can shoot in any light, any place, anywhere."

"Neat."

"That's not all, sir. We can also feed your data into their computer, and it will incorporate that material into their story line. Which means it will feed us any images that may be of danger to Ms. Labelle and alert us to any plots that develop around the story line."

"Great. How do I do it?"

Zelko presses some buttons and points to the keyboard in front of Denny. "Just type it in. There's no particular format."

Denny types out the information that he has put together, the names of the characters, the question marks. When he is finished, he presses a key, and he can see into the interior of one of the production vans. The crew is working with the data that the computer is feeding them. Thousands of TV screens projecting holographic images are floating in space as the computer sorts out, blanks out, and merges images into the composite picture that the viewers will see.

The Director looks at the time and says, "We have one minute". Then she says, "Miranda, can you hear me?"

"Yes."

"We're going on air."

The Director begins her count down. The activity around her intensifies, a red light begins to flash, and the Director shouts, "Lights, cameras, action," and Miranda appears.

Chapter Fifteen

Miranda is wearing a white gown that flows like water about her figure. To Denny she's a vision of beauty, statuesque in her high heels, a princess crowned with a garland of diamond dust shaped into star bursts that are woven through her jet black hair dappled with flakes of gold.

She enters the limousine, and she is alone except for the driver and Ned who is sitting in the front seat. The sleek black limousine leaves the airport and passes along the highway. Miranda looks out the window into the distance, and she sees that where there were once beautiful wealthy homes and cozy suburbs there are now homes abandoned and in disrepair with shattered windows and lawns full of weeds. Dead playthings are strewn here and there. A swing-set lays belly up, its legs straight up in the air.

On the monitors Denny can both see what Miranda sees and what the Vision World audience sees as the studio cuts to an interior view of an early colonial mansion and a room stripped of all its furniture, the walls barren and cracked with plaster torn away revealing the skeleton of a dead house. Men, women, and children are sleeping on the floor, ragged squatters who live in the abandoned home. One child is tied to a post so that it will not crawl off and fall through one of the holes in the floor.

They all seem to be buried in a death-like sleep that is their only escape from the wretchedness about them. The sole source of light and heat is a fire burning in an old fireplace, the marble mantelpiece and facing veined and cracked exposing the raw stone and the crumbling bricks. Over the fire a beat-up old kettle is suspended on a rod, and a young girl wearing a down coat torn in many places is kneeling on one knee tending the kettle of watery soup.

Denny can hear the girl counting as she places beans in separate piles, and he realizes that the girl can't count past ten. She merely repeats the first ten numbers over and over again until she gets confused. Then she tries to even out the piles by sight as the shadows of the fire dance across the floor and the kettle forms a bulbous caldron of despair that consumes the room in darkness.

Out of the darkness a star burst of consumer images filled the screen as a prelude to *The Super Shopper Quiz Show* that takes place in a shopping mall. The contestants ask questions that anyone who watches Vision World, day after day, hour by hour, would know. The contestants are Cynthia Cordoza, a physician, Lisa Bloom, a housewife, and Martha Green, a vagrant. They have taken the money that they have won and piled it into their shopping carts, and now they are racing at breakneck speeds through the shopping mall, a labyrinth of stores. They are racing against time as they convert money into things, images mostly that they touch with their magic wands causing the images to disappear then reappear in their shopping carts.

Sometimes, however, the things they touch are real. Cynthia has touched a real refrigerator, and if she wants it, Super Shopper will ship it to her home immediately. But Cynthia doesn't need new refrigeration because her old box still works just fine. What she needs is a new image to cover over the cheap materials of her mass produced generic refrigerator with the illusion of luxury, so she decides against the real thing and touches the image of another refrigerator, and the image appears on the pile in her cart, balanced on top of the image of a new couch to shroud the old frame.

Cynthia, excited by her good fortune, races off driven onward by the voice of the host in the background who is rattling off the names of the products, the prices, and where she stands in the race against time as she careens around a counter, drawn by the passionate colors of want and the cool colors of possession.

Lisa Bloom's cart is also filled with colorful images. She has gone to the electronics store where she has exchanged her money for a black box that, when hooked up to her Vision World system, will turn her home into a fashion store. She will have designer packages and whole wardrobes to wear, and she can wear her new images around the house, at parties, or in any other box that has the same system. She can go from box to box with her illusion, but she can never go out.

Now that Lisa has her black box, she is heading for *The Danger Zone* where she will find the ultimate dream box, a new home.

Martha Green, a vagrant, is heading for *The Danger Zone* too. *The Danger Zone* is where the high priced luxury items are. But the rules of the game change there. In *The Danger Zone* you can pick from anything regardless of the price, but if you don't pick the real thing, you lose everything, all your money, all your hopes, all your dreams, all your images. For Martha, the vagrant, *The Danger Zone* poses no real threat. She has nothing to lose. She has no home, she has no Vision World, and she has no box to put her images in. She must find something real, so she stands at the entranceway to *Auto Paradise* ready to go into a room filled with the latest model cars that no one can afford but the very rich.

Martha hears wheels squeaking behind her, and when she turns toward the sound, she finds that Lisa has entered *The Danger Zone* too. She is heading for *The Model Home Show.* She's going to take a chance. Martha admires Lisa who has so much more to lose. She's a very brave girl. Martha smiles at Lisa and shouts, "Good luck, Lisa."

Lisa smiles back, but Martha can see fear in her eyes.

Martha turns and enters the showroom. She moves cautiously about the room looking at the cars, trying to find some indication of what is real or not, but she can't, so she decides to pick the one she really likes - a mobile home made of a plastic that changes colors with the light and can become a beautiful see-through bubble that she can lounge in and see the stars at night.

This is it.

She takes a deep breath then strikes the van with her wand. She can hear and feel the familiar thud of reality.

The applause is deafening. "She got it!" someone shouts.

Martha opens the door, gets into the driver's seat, and plays with the controls that change the interior into a living room, a bedroom, a dining room, and back again. Then she sees the starter button, presses it, and hears the gentle hum of the electric motor.

As Martha puts the van in gear, Lisa is facing her model home, the one she wants - a concrete box. It's the latest fashion, with no windows, only hologram picture windows inside that gives you the impression that you are living in a beautiful glass house open to everything and any scene or view that you want. It's the perfect home for dangerous times because it has no openings to the outside world except a steel door, but it has a flower garden on the rooftop and is part of a complex of beautifully arranged boxes that are stacked up like the stairways of an

Inca temple overlooking Oyster Bay on the Long Island shore.

Lisa walks up to the door, and the music in the background keeps beat to her heart rate. She is very frightened as she reaches for the doorknob. She touches it, and the door flies open. A gust of wind smelling of decay and corruption blows her dream house away, and Lisa finds herself at the edge of a vast disposal area, in a valley stripped of trees, The Pit.

All her dreams have turned into junk being plowed over or turned into molten liquid and fumes. She can hear the disposal units crunching up her dreams, crunching up her home. Lisa screams and runs out of *The Model Home Show* into the mall. Her eyes are full of tears. Her cart is empty. Everything is gone. She sits down on the floor of the exit way and cries hysterically.

Martha, who is driving her van back to where the game started, sees Lisa sitting at the exit way, her face in her hands. She knows immediately what has happened.

She stops, gets out of the van and runs to where Lisa is seated. She kneels down and puts her arms around Lisa to comfort her. "Oh, darling, don't cry. Come with me. You don't want to walk all the way back looking like this, do you?"

Lisa tries to smile but continues to cry as she allows Martha to help her into the van. Comfortably seated in a lap of luxury, Lisa stops crying and looks around the van at all the add-ons. "You won this?"

"Yes. Isn't it great?"

Lisa starts crying all over again.

Martha puts the van back in gear, drives off and says, "Oh, Lisa, don't be like that. You have to look at the bright side of things. You have a home, a good husband, and children too, right?"

Lisa wipes her eyes, "Yes."

"Well, there, don't you see? I lived in a cardboard box on 42nd Street before today. You have to count your blessings."

Lisa smiles and she tries to put on a good face, "I suppose so," she says as Martha pulls up to where the game started.

Martha gets out of her van and the studio audience applauds and cheers. She gives the victory sign to the audience and Lisa smiles bravely.

Bob Holly, the host of the show approaches Martha and congratulates her, then quizzes her on where she will go, what she will see.

"Everywhere," Martha shouts.

Bob turns to Lisa and says in his most sympathetic voice, "Lisa we're so very sorry. But..."

The audience shouts and gestures wildly. They give her the thumbs up sign like ancient Romans at the Coliseum.

Bob smiles broadly, "As you know, it is within my power to give you a reprieve. And you've been so lovely..." He motions to an assistant who appears with the black box that Lisa wanted, and he hands it to her.

Lisa jumps up and down. She is ecstatic. Martha hugs her, overjoyed by Lisa's good fortune.

There's a moment's lull, but then the audience begins to cheer again. Here comes Cynthia with a cart filled with mere air piled up to the ceiling, a cart full of dreams. She is smiling, overjoyed, triumphant.

The cheers and screams of joy are transformed into the sound of a police siren as *The Super Shopper Quiz Show* recedes back into the galaxy of dots that for a moment became a story then fragmented and became a new galaxy of dots that make up a new story, the TV show, *Help Line*, a show that follows police calls as they happen throughout New York City.

On the monitor Denny watches a patrol car racing through the caverns of the old city far below the colossal skyscrapers that ascend into a perspective that only the Gods can see. The patrol car passes by the Cooper Union Building with its Italianate motif, layers upon layers of classical lines, one generation building upon another until all the windows were broken by vandals and the building was abandoned, the first free institution of education in America where Abraham Lincoln gave a speech that launched his career, gutted, the walls falling, an interior studio exposed where art students worked and painted, drew up new lines, frontiers in space reduced to shredded canvas, forms torn from their frames, paints and chalks and dark charcoal lines crushed into faded visions of the future.

The siren of the patrol car screams and echoes through the dark caverns of the unlit streets, its emergency lights flashing wildly as the patrol car passes building after building, its light reflecting blood red off rusted cast iron Romanesque pillars and cast iron panels that have fallen to the street amidst the rubble of early Federal with its simple straight lines and elegant curves and balance reduced to rot.

This section of New York City, The Village, was part of a project begun three years ago. Most of The Village was to be bulldozed over except for the historical sections that were selected for preservation. One stupendous sky-scraper was to be built around this section forming a wall of suspended cubes and massive voids of light and air. It was to be a monumental art piece of murals and shape, colors that would vibrate in the light. But the depression came and the project was abandoned leaving the area framed in by the skeleton of the future. Within the corpse, amidst the wasteland, some historical landmark buildings and neighborhoods survive behind barbed wire fences like concentration camps of culture and civilization.

Fred and Carlos, the two patrolmen assigned to this district, are oblivious to the scene. Fred is a heavy set man of African descent, and Carlos is a Latino, slight of built, with yellow Indian eyes that are alert to the debris in the road that could blow out a tire. For Fred and Carlos, being on *Help Line* is easy duty because the criminals, like everyone else, want to be on TV, and they will do anything to get on the show. Over the years Fred and Carlos have watched the crimes and the criminals get weirder and weirder as one psychopath after another competes to get the attention of the cameras. What makes their job easy is that most of them don't care if they get caught. They'd rather be caught and be a star than be nothing like everyone else.

On the virtual reality viewer in the patrol car, Fred and Carlos are watching two of the biggest stars of *Help Line*, The Nightmare Brothers. The Nightmare Brothers are holding up a liquor store in their sector.

Fred turns to Carlos and says, "We're primetime tonight, Carlos," and then he steps on the accelerator and races through the wasteland to the scene of the crime.

The liquor store is brightly lit with neon lights that eliminate all shadows. The two shopkeepers, who are an elderly couple, look like characters in a surrealistic dream. Their faces are distorted by Nodada, an antidepressant drug that makes them smile while facing terror. The two hold-up men are wearing make-up, lipstick and rouge so that their features will be clear to the TV cameras. One of the holdup men looks into one of the cameras that he knows is there. His lips are twisted into a crooked smile. His eyes are dilated into large black holes that have eclipsed his brain leaving only shadows that prowl amidst the need and rage that consumes anything in its way. His face is bony, and his lips are full. His chest is bare except for words of hate scribbled all over his flesh. He begins to open his mouth but then he pauses. His eyes blink as if he is trying to remember his lines.

"Hell, ya all know me," he says. "I'm Bob and over dar is my brother, Bill."

Bill is in the background. In one hand he has a shotgun that is pointed at the shopkeepers, and in the other hand, he is holding a portable disc player with huge speakers that he is resting on his shoulder. Bill waves his shotgun and smiles at the audience. Several teeth are broken.

The camera shifts back to Bob, the crooked smile. "We're the music, man. And we're here to play our favorite instruments to the music that ya all request."

Bob holds up his favorite instrument, a 380-magnum revolver, smiles, and then says, "So yah all just write down the songs yah all want on the sidewalk in front of the Village Cigar Store. It's on the corner of Sixth Avenue and West Fourth. Just like ya always do. Yeah, ya all know where I mean. And, me and Bob, we'll play it for ya, for sure. And if ya got any messages for the folks out dar, ya write em down too. OK?"

Bob pushes his long greasy hair back and smiles more broadly and steps forward for a close-up. "Tonight, we got a request by Mary Jo. Hi, Mary Jo, here's your song. And I bet ya never heard it played like this." He's about to turn away from the camera, but then he stops, "Oh yeah, and Mary Jo says, 'Fuck you.' "

Bill turns on the disc player, and it blasts out

sounds and words that are jumbled up with a metallic screech and steel chords that are trying to break the sound barrier while the singer screams, "I'm gonna get ya. Yes, I am."

Bob and Bill fire their guns in rhythm to the music, blowing away the two old shopkeepers, spraying the walls and the bottles with blood, shattering glass. The spirits mingle as the drums bang out a machine gun solo. They stop firing but the music continues to play as Bill reaches into the cash register and pulls out some money, and Bob opens up two bottles of Vodka. They both take a swig and raise their bottles in triumph as Bob shouts, "We're da Nightmare Brothers playin your tunes. So hello Mary Jo and good-bye mother fuckers."

Back in the patrol car, Fred is watching the scene. He turns to his partner and says, "Son of a bitch. Those fucks have been on air for three weeks now. You know they got a fuckin album out?"

"No, shit, what's it called?"

"*Boogie Till Ya Die*. They even got the sound effects of the shootings, and I heard they're gonna put out a video, *Bob and Bill's Greatest Hits*. Can you believe this shit?"

Carlos glances over at the radar screen, and he can see two other patrol cars converging on the same target. The computer directs each car so that they will converge on the target simultaneously.

"They ain't going to make it, Fred. I think we got

those pricks tonight."

The three patrol cars pull up to the liquor store, just as Bob and Bill are walking out the front door. In the gun battle, the music continues to play as one policeman goes down and the two holdup men get blown away. Millions of people are watching as the cameras focus in on the action, the expressions on the men's face as they get hit, the rage, and then the deadly calm amidst the pulsing red lights that slowly dim.

The Bob and Bill show has been terminated.

When Fred and Carlos get back to the car, Carlos pulls out two Budweiser's and hands one to Fred. The camera focuses in on the cold amber bottle, the label, the Budweiser logo. Inside the bottle there is an image of America to be consumed. It's a holographic video built into the bottle, and when you twist the top off the bottle, the video begins to play.

Fred and Carlos take a swig of the American flag waving, the stars and stripes dissolving into a cowboy herding in some unruly cattle, the rope cast out into the setting sun that fades into a campfire, the stars, a moment of rest at the end of the day, the light of the fire going out with the final swig. Carlos and Fred throw the bottles away as offerings to the God of Waste, and get back in their car. A red light is flashing that there is another *Help Line* call. Fred looks at the viewing screen and says, "Oh, shit, Carlos, we got another one."

On screen, a man in his mid-thirties is sitting on a

plywood box covered with dirty pillows, and he is talking to a blank TV screen, blank walls, and a blank room where all the images are going or gone and all that is left is the skeletal remains of his base model illusion. The man is telling his life story and pleading with Vision World not to cut him off. Even as he talks, things disappear, and with every loss, his face expresses the pain, the grief, the effort to find the pathos in his life, things that people will sympathize with, understand. There must have been something he did that made him worthwhile.

He shouts at the TV screen, "I'll kill them! I'll kill them!" He is holding a gun, and he gets up from where he is sitting and walks into a back room where his wife and children are huddled on a bed crying.

The wife clutches the children and pleads with her husband. "John, don't do this. Please darling. Things are going to be all right."

"Things are not going to be all right!" he shouts, and as he does so, the stylish bed disappears leaving only a mattress on top of a wooden frame made of two by fours and a cheap organic foam that has been shaped, shaved, and sculpted to fill in the illusion and give the illusion a feeling of substance like a stage set put together by an amateur carpenter from a do-it-your-self kit.

"Oh no," he can't stand to look at the horrible poverty behind the illusion, and he rushes out of the room. There are tears in his eyes as he sits down and begins to talk to the television again, the lifeless blank screen that once was a portal to God.

"You got to help us. I've worked hard all my life. I'm the best god damned painter in this town. I worked on all the old historical buildings. I used real paint! Two coats of primer, two coats of the best paint, that's the trick."

He pauses. He wishes he had a bottle of beer, the one with a picture in it of workers finishing a day's work and dipping into the cooler packed with ice, pulling out a cold bottle of America's best beer, having a party, joking about who did what and who fucked up.

He puts his face in his hands and says, "God, help me. I don't want to kill my family, but what can I do? Oh, God, is anybody listening to me?"

Through his hands, through his tears, John sees a beam of light fill the room. He looks up, and to his astonishment he sees himself, he sees that the TV is alive. It's back on, and he is staring into his own image in the box.

He shouts into the bedroom, "Mary, come look. We're on TV!"

Mary and the children peer into the living room from the bedroom. Slowly, their eyes are transfixed. They walk to where John is sitting, and they sit beside him. John puts his arm around his wife and draws his children to him. He smiles into the screen and says, "This is my family."

On screen Bob Holly, the host of *The Super Shopper Quiz Show,* appears. "Welcome John and Mary," Bob Holly says. "Welcome children to *The Super Shopper Quiz*

Show. Our audience has chosen you and your family as contestants to be on our show next week."

The audience is cheering and applauding. A woman in the audience has tears of joy in her eyes. Fred, his wife, and his children are hugging each other.

Bob Holly appears again on the screen and says, "Fred?"

"Yes?"

"Remember, now, Fred, you have one week, so do your homework."

"Oh, we will."

He turns to his wife and says, "We have to work day and night, Mary."

Mary nods her head in agreement, "We can work in shifts, dear."

The children bounce up and down in joy, "We can help too."

They all stare at the television and smile. It is a family portrait of hope that then dissolves and disappears into the darkness to become part of the starlet night and the glow of the New York City skyline.

Chapter Sixteen

From the surveillance van, Denny watches Manhattan loom larger and larger, and he observes that this is not the Manhattan that he visited with his mother and father as a child. The city that Denny remembers was ablaze with lights, but what he sees now are dark silhouettes of the massive towers, some luminescent, the glazed surfaces of the newer and more massive towers glowing in the dark. Deep down in the caverns of the new city is the old city where the streets are lit with security lights that form a mist the penetrates all the shadows with a ghostly hue and gives the impression of being in a dream where nothing is clear until you turn on your TV set.

In the old city most of the first and second floors of the buildings have been walled up and the old entrance-ways have been replaced by reinforced steel waterproof doors that are now only used as emergency exits and de-livery doors. The streets now are a matrix of rooftops that are connected by bridges and walkways, rooftop gardens and stores or walk-down restaurants. Five fortress-like-skyscrapers in the massive style of Gothic Modern form the pylons for the new city that floats in a ring around the old. It is here in the part of the city known as The Ring that glows golden in the night that the affluent live amidst expensive stores and restaurants and a continuous mall. It is here where real things are sold that can't be seen down below where ghostly illusions dwell behind walled up windows and locked steel doors where the sounds of *Super Shopper* can be heard, and the host Bob Holly is shouting, "You won! You won! You're one of us now!"

The surveillance van turns onto Fifth Avenue and Central Park, and as they pass by the boarded up Metropolitan Museum of Art, Denny can see that the park has been fenced off. It is now a squatter's village filled with people living in tents and shacks made of cardboard boxes, wood, cinder blocks, odd pieces of plastic, sheet metal, and any other type of industrial waste that can be picked up or stolen from a building site or found in a garbage can for free.

On one of the screens Denny sees a large bronze statue of Alice in Wonderland and the Mad Hatter glowing red from the dancing flames of a bonfire the poor gather around to keep them warm in the hellish fairytale.

On another screen, Denny can see Miranda exit the limousine, and as she smiles and waves to the crowds of people who have gathered to see the celebrities, Denny scans the faces, filtering them through the computer database for known suspects, anyone who could be of danger. He then focuses on the homeless people behind the chain link fences who have gathered to watch the rich and famous. As the cameras scan the faces, he stops, adjusts the focus, and zooms in for a close up of a ten year old girl who, like many of the people in the park, is fearful of having her clothes stolen, so she wears all her clothes in tattered and torn layers. She is wearing an orange dress over a green and pink flowered skirt that is being worn over blue jeans tucked into bright red rain boots. A brown wool army blanket is worn like a cape to give her the appearance of a gypsy street urchin from the middle ages.

Her small and frail hands grip the wire mesh of the fence, and she looks wide eyed at the glamorous gowns and the diamonds that glitter like stars and the splendor of the Plaza Hotel with its marble entranceway lit up by four tall bronze torchers. The building towers upward and she sees hundreds of windows glowing like molten gold, a masterpiece of Baroque architecture crowned with a peaked mansard rooftop from the French Second Empire decorated with miniature towers and round recessed windows that looked like portals for ghosts who look down on her in her wonderment. She is oblivious to the two heavily armored tanks stationed near the entranceway to the park, the muzzles of their cannons aimed at her.

Denny turns to Zelko and asks, "Are all those people locked in there?"

"Not really, but if they want to stay in the park, they have to be there by sunset or they don't get in, and once they're in, they don't get out until daylight."

Denny orders the computer to scan the park, and hundreds of screens flash into view. The computer quickly sorts through these different points of view, and a few screens remain. On the main screen Denny sees a three-dimensional image of the pathway leading to the Central Park Zoo. Denny magnifies the picture so that it gives him the feeling that he is on the path, and he sees that where there were once rows of benches along the pathway, there are now only twisted wrought iron frames stripped of their wood. Another view of the same scene shows that some of the forest has been hacked down for firewood. A fallen sign spells out in an ancient language long forgotten, *Euonymus kiautschovica et Ligustrum vulare.*

The computer picks up the sound of something moving through the bushes, and Denny gets a glimpse of fur. At first he thinks that it is an animal, but when the cameras zooms in to get a closer view, he sees that it's a man in a full-length fur coat whose hair is dyed green and shaped into long spikes. His eyes are wild, and he has a large gold earring through his nose. Denny watches the man crouch like an animal behind a cluster of bushes called witch's broom. Denny hears footsteps that grow louder and louder until a young man appears walking down the pathway. In the background, above the treetops that form a spider web of moonlight, is a silhouette of Belvedere Castle, a miniature Gothic castle that was built of stone as a lookout for tourists, but now it reinforces Denny's feeling of being in the Dark Ages.

The young man walking down the road is carrying a metal lid to a garbage can for a shield, and in his other hand he is carrying a machete that he is casually swinging to the beat of the music playing on his portable music pod. He is wearing headphones, and his mouth is full of words to a song that no one but he can hear.

Denny wants to shout, "Watch out!" but he knows the boy can't hear him when the man rushes out of the bushes and smashes the boy in the head with a baseball bat. The lid of the garbage can slams against the concrete, and the boy lies sprawled out, his legs twitching.

The man takes the music pod and headphones off the boy's body, and then he rifles through the boy's torn pockets. He pulls out a cheese sandwich that he quickly shoves into his own pocket, and then he reaches into another pocket and pulls out a slip of paper and smiles. The camera zooms in closer, and Denny can see that the slip of paper is a lottery ticket for today's drawing that hasn't been drawn yet.

Denny watches the man pick up the bat and whack the boy one more time. Denny can hear the skull crack just as he sees Miranda enters the Plaza through a crystal and bronze revolving door that opens up into the great violet marble foyer crowned with a Tiffany stained glass dome. She then passes through the lobby that is furnished and decorated with gelded Louis XVI furniture, French Renaissance tapestries, Savonnerie rugs, marble columns, and magnificent crystal chandeliers.

Denny watches the mugger run down the pathway and enter the zoo. He passes by abandoned cages with tall wrought iron bars that look like spears. The cages are filled with people living like animals who have locked themselves in for their own protection. The man opens the door to one of the largest cages, and he walks around a deep pool of water and enters a stone cave where a bonfire is burning, the flame reflecting off the wall revealing graffiti and primitive wall paintings of figures that are part man, part animal, part machine struggling for the light as the flames flicker across the walls of the cave then disappear back into the shadows to emerge once again as phantom figures, forming bloated words, one upon the other, all jumbled up with the colors of hate, love, islands of pink flowers in a sea of red, and black tires flaming.

"Jose loves Anita" has been written on one wall, and they are being swallowed by a cloud of florescent green snakes turning into dollar signs, black swastikas mating with purple and orange pentagrams. *The Devil is God's Right Hand Man* is scribbled over a symbol of the Cross of Jesus on another wall, and a star burst sprays out of chaos then disappears back into the flames.

The mugger who murdered the young man approaches the fire and kneels before a heavy-set man with a red beard and long red hair who is sitting on a throne-like-chair and wearing a golden crown. Behind him stand what seem to be his bodyguards, two giant black men wearing black leather pants and boots and black leather armbands and collars with steel spikes. Their chests and arms are tattooed with the some of the same images that are on the wall, creatures that are half men half beast, half human, grotesque mismatched mutations armed with baseball bats.

Next to the man with the crown is seated another man in a ragged topcoat wearing torn jeans, a black knit sweater, and sneakers. He has clean features, dark jet-black hair, sleepy eyes, and a large aquiline nose. He looks Latin American to Denny, Spanish with a touch of Indian blood.

The mugger holds his hands out as if in prayer and says, "My Lord, King of Debris, I have a gift for you, Sire." He opens his hands and reveals the blood stained lottery ticket.

The King, who has a black fur coat draped over his shoulders like a cape, takes the lottery ticket from the man's hand. His eyes reflect the fire and his eagerness when he asks, "Was he still alive when you took it?"

"Yes, Sire."

"He was dying?"

"Yes."

The King stares at the numbers, the numerology of a man whose number was up, and says, "You took it. Then you killed him?"

"Yes."

"You're sure?"

"Yes, look!" The murderer holds out his bloody hands.

The King grabs hold of the man's hands and sniffs

the blood. He smiles and says, "Yes, a lottery ticket taken from the hands of a dying man."

He shows the lottery ticket to the man sitting next to him and says, "This is truly lucky."

The man stares with utter contempt at the servant and his king and then slowly blinks like a cat bored with a meal he can't eat, not now.

The King reaches into a bag and pulls out a bottle of whiskey and hands it to the servant, "You've earned this. Now go and keep whatever else you stole free of tribute to me."

The man seated next to the king watches the bringer of fortune leave and he says, "Let's finish our business, now." He reaches into a knapsack and pulls out a stack of one hundred dollar bills and hands them to the King. The King begins to count them, and the man says, "I want you to have your people bust out of the park tonight, ten o'clock to be exact."

"Why?"

"We want to disrupt the debate. Can you do it?"

"No problem," the King says. "I'll just tell them that the army will be here in the morning to herd them into a work camp. They'll believe me." He smiles and says, "Then I'll tell them that dinner is being served at the Plaza Hotel and everyone is invited."

The man stands up, "Good, then I can rely on you."

"Yes."

The man picks up his knapsack and throws it over

his shoulder. As he reaches the exit way from the cave he turns. His form is haloed in a darker darkness as he says, "Everything depends on you, and we do not tolerate failure. Do we understand each other?" The man smiles sadistically and reveals a cruelty that lurks far beyond the borders of nature and dwells in the realm of evil.

The King puts the money in a pocket of his fur coat. He stares at the man for a moment then says, "I rule here. If you want a riot, you'll get one. Now get the hell out of my cave."

Denny watches the man leave the cave. He's certain he's seen the man before, but he's racked his brain, and he can't figure out where. He turns to Zelko and says, "Can you track that guy?"

"I think so."

"Good. I want pictures of him from every angle. I want you to run him through the computer. I want to know who that son of a bitch is."

"Yes, sir, but what are we going to do about the riot their planning?"

"Good question," Denny says. He pauses to figure out what is going on. Are they merely trying to disrupt the debate, or is there something else going on here? Denny turns to Zelko and says, "Contact the military police. Tell them what we saw here and ask for additional protection for the Plaza, then instruct your men to stay close to Miranda."

He pauses to think through the problem again, and

then says, "Have your men instruct all the security forces at the Plaza to be on guard for anything, and I mean anything. Double-check all personnel at the Plaza, guests, employees, everyone. We may have an assassination plot here."

"Yes, sir."

Denny watches the king and his bodyguards leave the cave, and they walk to the center of the zoo to where there was once a large pool where the seals swam and played to the amusement of the tourists, but now the seals are gone and the pool is full of firewood. One of the king's bodyguards pours several cans of kerosene over the piles of wood that fill the empty pool, and the other bodyguard lights a torch and throws it into the pyre causing it to explode into a blazing ring of fire that lights up the zoo.

It must be a signal for the people to gather because on multiple screens Denny sees the homeless converging on the pyre from cardboard shacks and makeshift tents, cages and animal shelters. They come pouring out of the tunnels underneath the bridges and pathways, and even the earth itself seems to be moving as the branches and leaves of fallen trees and bushes and dirt are pushed aside to reveal tunnels and rooms dug underground.

The king orders some of his minions to bring out cases of wine, whiskey, and beer that are passed out free to eager hands. Music plays, and the vast number of people gathered around the fire in the central plaza of the zoo begin to drink and dance to a salsa beat and the sound of horns and guitars hitting high notes, their shadows and figures weaving in and out of the flames that light up the toy soldiers and animals that used to march around the zoo clock, on the hour. They now lie dead and twisted backwards into another time in tune with the primordial chants, cymbals clashing, a guitar screaming, one note reaching the end of its lifeline.

The King of Debris climbs a ladder that ascends to the top of the cages that once housed the lions and tigers. He stands there and smiles at the turnout. He has what he wanted, a massive army of discontents. He motions to a minion who produces a bugle from underneath his black wool topcoat, and he commences to call reveille. The sound carries over the bedlam, and all the other sounds begin to dim until only the horn can be heard.

When the bugler has ceased playing the call to arms, the king shouts, "Denizens of Hell." His voice is full, and it carries through the zoo to every corner of his domain, "I bring ya ill news from the outside. Tomorrow they will come for us and take us from our homes. They will take us to the work camps." Individual words of protest merge together in a single roar of rage and then joy as he shouts, "We're busting out of here!"

The king waits for the cheers to subside, and then he continues, "Right now the fat cats are over at the Plaza Hotel stuffing themselves with food while our children starve. Right now the fat cats and their wives are in the Grand Ballroom dancing on our graves indifferent to our suffering. Well, it's coming to an end, Brothers and Sisters, it is our turn to dance, and we are going to dance the dance of the American rattlesnake and strike at our oppressors. Are you with me?"

There is a roar of approval, and the king motions to one of his subordinates to unfurl a Revolutionary War Navy Jack with thirteen red and white strips to symbolize the original thirteen states with a coiled rattlesnake in the center of the flag. Across the bottom of the flag is the motto, *Don't Tread on Me.*

Amidst the cheers, two standard American flags are also unfurled, and the three flag bearers position themselves to lead the march down the pathway to the main exit. All the music boom boxes are tuned to the same song as the people form a line behind the flag bearers, and like a giant snake they begin to undulate down the pathway to the main entrance, the sound of the music growing louder and louder, the rhythms pounding at the gates of sound, the hiss of flames, torches lighting up the limbs of trees with dancing shadows, shouting, a drum pounding like a giant heartbeat, chants of freedom emerging from the darkness calling for revolution as the music weaves itself into another tune, the heavy beat receding into strings lightly touching, vibrating gently, forming the notes of a waltz as the picture dissolves into a picture of the Grand Ballroom at the Plaza Hotel, pure white with gilded gold, magnificent crystal chandeliers, and Greek and Roman gods and goddesses floating above the brilliant lighting on billowing clouds and music gently soaring.

Chapter Seventeen

Miranda looks around the Grand Ballroom of the Plaza Hotel, and she remembers the last time that she was here. She was a young debutante attending the Mayflower Ball, and on the walls and ceiling were the same old pictures of gods and goddesses and cherubim emerging from sperm-like clouds into the celestial light.

Back then it seemed as if they had all emerged from the pictures to dance the dance that never changes, to dance upon the same marble floors that their parents and their parents before them had danced upon below the same magnificent chandeliers, flowers who had come out to be plucked by young men of all shapes and sizes who sniffed their perfume and pecked at their cheeks and necks as mothers clucked and moved about like hens in the grand barnyard of metamorphous.

And now, it's as if the ball had never stopped. It's still the same old dance of power and flowers, and the band is the same old band, playing the same old tunes, the partners changing from time to time with new players appearing here and there, everyone growing old in each other's arms, reproducing the dance from one generation to the next.

Miranda hears someone call her name. She looks around the room and sees Franklin and Brenda Peters at a distant table waving at her to join them. Miranda looks for Tom, but he is nowhere in sight. Franklin gives her his All American smile, stands up, and the cameras and the lights lock on to the two of them, Miranda and Frank. There is no escape. She smiles and waves back. And as she walks through the dancers to Frank and Brenda's table, she thinks back to when she first met Frank.

Franklin Peters was another of Brad Merling's creations, another of Dr. Frankenstein's children. Early in his career he was considered a real comer, a football star and then a war hero. Vision World had even followed him off the football field into war and made a series out of his exploits on the battlefield.

When he came home, Brad coupled Franklin's series to her series. At first, being a sucker for good looks, she bought the package, and there was talk of a pending marriage of the two stars, but once she got to know the model man, she couldn't stand him. In fact, she found him the perfect counterpart to the model woman. Where the model woman finds escape in change, her counterpart, the model man, can never change. He's always the rock, the unmovable force, the willful perpetrator of permanency who finds escape in law and order, a prison cell of violently suppressed feelings that will never be liberated because in order to free the man he will have to give up the power to control that which is not him.

Franklin, as long as she has known him, has always been in control. Franklin has always been right, and he has always been dangerous. He was and is the perfect model of the one-dimensional-male who will kill you rather than expose himself for what he is, a stupid blockhead.

Fortunately for Miranda, Franklin Peters had a fatal flaw. He was boring, and to Brad Merling that is an unforgivable sin. So Brad gave up on the marriage of the two series, and Frank was relegated to a supporting role. It seemed that the model man was condemned to oblivion, but when Miranda asked Brad what was to become of Frank, he just smiled and said, "Not to worry. I have plans for Frank."

It was then that Brad introduced Brenda Jackson into Franklin Peter's life. Brenda Jackson-Peters was and is now a morning talk show host and a professional singer and dancer who is cute as hell, the girl next door who never closed the blinds on her bedroom window and goes to church every Sunday. Brad was sure that they would fall in love and get married because, in his words, "Brenda determines the size of a man's dick and his desirability by the ratings he can conjure up in the womb of her ambition, and Franklin has no other choice except oblivion and shrinking expectations."

Everything went as planned. First Brad created the perfect picture of the ideal couple, then the perfect marriage, and finally the perfect home. Brad brought them along slowly featuring Frank and Brenda in spot ads and holiday specials. Franklin became a featured sports commentator and a model for the myth of fair play and competition. He was the winner who got the beautiful cheerleader who could dance and sing and talk forever the prattle of everyday life that filled the void between commercials. All and all they were nothing special in the big picture of Vision World, but then out of the blue where Brad Merling loves to live, President Dickson picked Franklin as his running mate. Now the idiot is running for Vice President of the United State, and he is a star again.

"Darling," Franklin Peters says as he embraces her then introduces Miranda to his wife who gives her a warm hug and a kiss on the cheek. He then introduces her to his campaign advisor, David Balsam, and his wife, Cory.

Frank pulls out a seat for Miranda to sit in and says, "I'm surprised you're here, Miranda. I never thought that this was your sort of thing."

"It's not, but this race is so interesting, I thought I'd get a closer look at the combatants. Where's the President?"

"He canceled out of the debate at the last moment. The Boss is a very busy man and ..."

David Balsam breaks in, "And to be quite honest, Ms. Labelle, it's very dangerous for the President to be out among the people with all these radicals at large. Almost every day we receive a threat against his life. We certainly can't afford to lose a President who is engineering the greatest economic comeback in American history."

Balsam pats Frank on the back, "That's where Frank comes in. We need a young warrior. We need someone with courage and youth that can go to the front lines and take the heat."

Frank smiles, "I guess I'm carrying the ball again. I got the call yesterday to come here and give our side of the story."

A waiter comes to the table and is about to serve Miranda, but she sees the leftover Chicken Kiev and strawberry shortcake on the table, and it is obvious that everyone has eaten, so she turns to the waiter and smiles graciously and says, "Oh, no, I'm sorry I'm so late, but a glass of white wine will do just fine. Thank you."

She then turns to Frank and asks, "So what is your side of the story, Frank? Are you behind the Boss's push for a constitutional amendment that will eliminate the House of Representatives and replace it with a Corporate Assembly?"

"Yes, certainly, it's our only hope of getting out of the disastrous economic situation that we're in now."

"But, Frank, we elected Theodore Dickson because he promised to get us out of the recession that we were in. And the only thing he's done is lead us into a depression."

"That's not true, Miranda. It was Congress's inability to act, except to block the President's plan for economic recovery that led to the depression."

Miranda can see that Frank is being fed his lines through a transmitter in his ear, but she knows Frank, she knows how to press his buttons, and maybe she can get through the party line to the real man.

"So then," she says, "You're telling me what we need is a real boss with real power?"

Frank smiles, "Yes Miranda."

There, she says to herself. There's the smug smile of a man who believes that power is knowledge. That's what she wants people to see, but whoever is on the other side of the party line must see it too because Frank immediately changes his tune.

"What I mean to say is that we're in an economic war, Miranda. We're being challenged by strong corporate states, and if we want to compete, we have to complete the incorporation of America. Business is the business of America, as the old saying goes."

"So we're to become Corporate America to compete with Corporate Japan and Corporate China and Corporate Europe. Is that it?"

David Balsam breaks in, "Miranda we're not talking about a radical change here. We're talking about streamlining the American government to meet the economic challenges of the future. We still have a Senate."

"A Billionaire's Club," Miranda retorts.

David Balsam shrugs and says, "And we have a President elected by the people"

"One man," Miranda says, "whose image is easily

manipulated by the media, a potential demagogue."

"Miranda," Brenda says, "Why are you being so negative. Frank is here to help us. And the President is not really the boss. It's a term of endearment for a wise old man who has tried to give us the benefit of his many years of experience. He's just trying to make America work."

"Really, Brenda, then what is that dear old man doing about all those poor people who are living in abandoned homes or living in Central Park like caged animals? What I saw coming in from the airport was awful. Frank, how do you explain that?"

Miranda sees Frank look up. Someone is behind her. She turns and sees a short man with a beard smiling at her. She observes the eyes and the face behind the beard. She recognizes him, "Tom!"

Miranda stands up and embraces Tom Williams, her old friend from high school. They stand there for a moment, their arms around each other. Miranda introduces Tom to everyone at the table, and Frank offers Tom a chair that he declines.

"Miranda and I haven't seen each other for years. Do you mind if I waltz her off to the dance floor?"

Tom smiles at Miranda and says, "Would you do me the honor, Madam?"

Miranda curtsies, "I'd be charmed."

She takes his arm, and as they are about to walk away, Franklin Peters says, "Miranda, ask Senator Lorenz the questions you asked me. It's his state and his mess."

Miranda smiles and says, "You mean New York State is not a subsidiary of Corporate America yet?"

She walks away before Frank can respond, and when she gets on the dance floor she says, "God, I hate that man. He's such an asshole."

Tom laughs, and Miranda smiles at him. She's so excited to see her old friend. She has so many questions, "How have you been? Where have you been? What have you been doing with your life? Tell me everything."

Tom and Miranda are standing on the dance floor. Tom smiles and says, "Everything. Yes, everything. Isn't it incredible that as we get older, if we're really successful, all our dreams, our lives, can be reduced to a page or two in a resume?"

Tom takes Miranda's hand, and they begin to dance the dance. He spins her around in a grand fashion and begins to read off his resume. As Tom tells his story, the ballroom music is woven into the music coming from the park, and the picture of Tom and Miranda waltzing dissolves into the procession of homeless people chanting above the violins, "Power to the People."

Denny watches the military police begin to ring the park. Two attack vehicles join the two tanks stationed outside the Plaza Hotel. He looks at another screen that is tracking the Latin American man who met with the king in the cave. Denny decides that he can't just sit here and watch whatever is happening unfold. He has to do something. He turns to Zelko and says, "I'm going after that son of a bitch."

"Who?"

Denny points to the Latin American, "Him."

"I'll go with you"

"No, you stay here and guide me through the park to my target. Get someone in here to help you."

"Yes, sir."

In the background Denny can hear Miranda say, "You got married!"

"Is it so unbelievable?' Tom reaches into his pocket and pulls out his wallet. "I just happen to have..." He flips open his wallet and shows Miranda a picture of his wife. She has a sweet face, a compassionate smile, and thoughtful eyes that stare out at Miranda behind wire rim glasses and make her feel guilty but she doesn't know why.

Denny, checks his gun and leaves the van. On the street, he stops a bum, hands him some money, exchanges his expensive field jacket for the bum's tattered topcoat and battered hat, and then heads for the entrance to the park. He shows his identification to the military police, and they allow him to enter the park where he disappears into the darkness.

On screen, Miranda says, "Oh, she's pretty, Tom."

"I know, but look at this." Tom flips over the pictures in his wallet and shows Miranda a picture of his son.

Miranda smiles and says, "He looks just like you. He even has that same serious, determined look."

Tom looks fondly at the picture of his son and says,

"A link off the old man's sausage, I guess." He then flips the wallet closed, "But where was I... Oh, yes, Thomas Ascot Williams goes to Yale for graduate school, majors in political science, and specializes in American Social and Political Behavior. That's where I meet Professor Arthur Lorenz. He becomes my mentor and my sponsor for a Fulbright Scholarship, and, to my surprise, when Professor Lorenz goes into politics, he hires me as a political analyst and researcher."

"You work for him?" Miranda asks, but she already knows that Tom works for Lorenz. Her staff gave her a run down on Tom. He's Senator Lorenz's top researcher, and he spends most of his time with a small staff of young bright workers, who like him, are dedicated to the movement.

Tom smiles guiltily like a young boy who reveals that he has a rubber in his wallet.

Miranda pauses in the dance, and she looks at Tom suspiciously. "So that's why you invited me here."

"Yes, you're the First Lady of Television. When you come all America comes with you."

"Tom!"

"It's true."

"You little pimp, you," she says.

Tom smiles and whispers in her ear, "He's good looking, a widower, brilliant, moderately wealthy, and he's going to be the next President of the United States. Aren't you just a little bit interested?"

"Well."

"He watches your show whenever he can, and he thinks you're wonderful, 'absolutely fascinating,' quote unquote."

Miranda puts her arm in Tom's arm and smiles as she says, "Maybe just a peek."

Miranda and Tom walk across the room to where Senator Lorenz is seated with four other people. Senator Lorenz looks up as Tom and Miranda approach the table, and he stands to meet them.

"Arthur, I would like to introduce you to..."

"Tom, everyone knows who this is. It's a pleasure to meet you, Ms. Labelle. I've been looking forward to this."

Miranda is struck by how tall he is. He has to be at least six foot four, and if she was to take each element of his face and analyze it, she might judge the man to be ugly. But, in fact, all the parts fit together, a curious trait of men like this who you have to judge finally as attractive, much like you would a phenomenon that you might see in nature like falls that have sculpted caverns and gorges through glacial rock or trees that have been knurled by gusty hard winds.

As Senator Lorenz seats Miranda, he begins to introduce his companions. The first person he introduces is a man in his sixties with white wavy hair and patrician features. "Senator Justin Bradley is a colleague of mine," Senator Lorenz says, "And one of the most dedicated men I've ever met. Justin is seriously hard headed, however. Over

and over again he asks me, 'Arthur, are you against capitalism and private property?' Over and over again I say, No
Justin, I am not against capitalism and private property.
Unlike the President, who wants us to choose between
democracy and capitalism, I've turned capitalism on its
head and created a synthesis of capitalism and democracy
that will enable us to evolve to new levels of freedom and
prosperity, and I call it America Incorporated."

Justin Bradley whispers in Miranda's ear so that
everyone can hear him, "Socialism by another name," and
the other man seated at the table that Miranda doesn't
recognize says, "Worse, its bad economics."

Arthur Lorenz laughs then says, "As you can see,
Miranda, I don't surround myself with yes-men. But now
let me introduce you to Justin's better half. Madeline Ar-
rington-Bradley is an excellent novelist and a wonderful
hostess, one of the best cooks in Washington. Believe me,
when I finish a meal in her home, I will agree to anything."

Senator Lorenz whispers in Miranda's ear, but everyone can hear. "She's the real brains in the family, and
she's the only one that can get through that hard head of
his. She does it the old fashioned way. She nags the hell
out of him."

Madeline Bradley, who is a tall lean elegant looking
woman who highlights her gray hairs to accent her age,
protests, "Oh, Arthur, you're terrible. This poor girl is going
to get the wrong impression of Justin. He's not hard-
headed. He's just a little..."

196

"Dense is the word, Madeline," Senator Lorenz says, and he has everyone laughing now.

Senator Bradley turns to his wife. "He'll change his tune Monday, Madeline, when he wants my vote. Monday, the word for me will be shrewd, practical, not easily swayed by the ephemeral."

Senator Lorenz laughs and says, "Maybe so, Justin, times change, minute by minute"

Senator Lorenz then introduces the heavy-set man in his early sixties who is seated across the table. His name is Roger Baines, and he's the President of World Bank, the largest single banking network in the world and a member of the Commission.

"Roger is one of the few enlightened minds in banking today," Senator Lorenz says. "And do you know what's so enlightened about him? He's one of those rare bankers who still believes that he is spending other people's money. The woman next to him, for a change, is his wife, Elizabeth, who is the source of all his enlightenment. She won't let him spend a dime of his own money, not unless she approves, and that is almost never."

Elizabeth, who reminds Miranda of her mother, protests. "That's not true."

"What's not true Beth, that he doesn't cheat on you or that you haven't let him buy a new car in the last twenty years?"

"Neither, I don't let that man out of my sight and..."

Arthur turns to Miranda and says, "Roger still drives

the old Ford that he first kissed Beth in. And she's still holding the same purse strings that she was holding that big night when they went parking for the first time. And, I'll tell you one thing she didn't have in that purse, that night or any other night for that matter." Senator Lorenz winks at Miranda and says, "They have five wonderful children."

Miranda notes what a charmer he is. He has everyone laughing, everyone at ease. She watches him pour her a glass of champagne without asking, but it's exactly what she wants. Senator Bradley explains to her that they have been grilling Senator Lorenz to warm him up for the debate. Everyone encourages her to ask him some questions.

"And remember," Senator Bradley says, "This is hard ball, Miranda."

Tom laughs then says, "You don't have to worry about that, Senator. She just fried Franklin Peters."

"Go ahead, Miranda," Elizabeth Baines says," It's Arthur's turn. Let him have it too."

Miranda studies the Senator for a moment. He knows, and she knows that they're on TV and that this has all been set up by Tom so that the Senator could get more TV time and possibly an endorsement by her. She can also see that he doesn't have a transmitter in his ear. There's nobody feeding the Senator his lines. She likes that. She likes him, and she is really interested in what he has to say, so she decides to throw the first pitch right down the middle of the plate.

"Senator, I don't understand what you mean by *America Incorporated*. Are you talking about 'socialism by another name' as Senator Bradley suggests?"

"No, Miranda, I'm talking about democracy at work, and at the heart of my campaign are three major reforms of our political and economic system. One, an initiative, referendum, and recall voting process at all levels of government that will create a nation of citizen lawmakers as a check and balance against a representative system of government that does not represent the will of the people. Two, we will create a truly democratic society by extending our Bill of Rights and our civil liberties to the workplace. We have to put an end to a system where we work day to day in an authoritarian workplace, and we only vote every two to four to six years so as to delegate all our sovereign power to our so-called representatives who have been bought and paid for by the same people that we work for day to day. And, three, I propose that We the People of the United States, collectively, go into business with ourselves by investing in employee owned businesses and, thereby, form a fifty-fifty partnership with American labor where each and every citizen will share in the profits. But, unlike many socialist models of the past, the profits and interest from our investments will not go directly to the government, who will then decide what to do with the money. The money will go directly to the people and be deposited in their own private capital fund."

"But Senator," Miranda asks, "do you really think the American people are capable of making their own laws?"

Senator Lorenz smiles, but it is not the ingratiating smile of a politician but the smile of a college professor who is about to instruct a student who has stopped him in the hallway after class. "Miranda, for two thousand years, the power elite as they have mutated through time in one form or another from the right to the left or to the middle and back again have used every persuasive device at their disposal to convince the vast majority of the people that they cannot make decisions for themselves and that majority rule is mob rule.

"However, the truth of the matter is that the initiative, referendum, and recall have been a part of the American political system for over two hundred years, and today we have at least twenty four states that have instituted one form or another of the initiative, referendum, and recall process, and there has recently been a flood of localities and states where amendments to state constitutions and city and county charters have been proposed and supported by the vast majority of the people. Democracy is the wave of the future and it is happening now. Furthermore, it has been studied thoroughly over time, and from these studies and the data accumulated over the last two hundred years, it is perfectly clear that when the American people are given the power to legislate, they show a great deal of restraint and a sense of public responsibility.

"For example, over time, when we break down the voting in initiatives, referendums, and recalls by race, gender, economic class, and party affiliations to see who the winners and losers are, we discover an amazing fact. Everyone wins about fifty percent of the time. That's a damned good batting average considering that, in our present system of government, we don't even get up to the plate. Another fact that emerges from the data is that the American people have a wonderful instinct for smelling big money interests behind an initiative or a referendum, and over eighty percent of the time they will vote that initiative or referendum down.

"No, Miranda, if you are looking for the mob, you will not find it by looking at the history of democracy in America. You will find the mob in the boardrooms of the major global corporations and the financial institutions that feast on the common wealth and break our laws with impunity. You will find the mob in Washington where every day they sell out the promise of American. No, Miranda, the American people are not the problem. We are the solution."

Miranda is thoughtful. She looks around the table. Everyone is sitting back, listening. They know that this is the Senator's and her show. She decides that she has to choose her words carefully. She has been careful not to overcommit until she fully understands what this man is up to, but at the same time she feel like she should be supportive.

"Senator, the political reforms that you are advocating seems to me to be in the finest American tradition, but your advocacy of economic democracy seems to me to be far more problematic. Do you really think that American workers in partnership with the American people can run a large scale corporation? Will they have the expertise? And I'm not clear on this. Are you talking about equal wages?"

"No, Miranda, I'm not talking about equal wages. I'm talking about a system where the workers and the American people will determine who gets paid and how much, and given our value system and the economic system that we will implement, I believe the American worker and the American people will vote for salaries that will be competitive, but at the same time they will be more equitable, and we will not have the gross and obscene differences in wealth and incomes that we have today.

"As for whether or not the American worker and the American people can run a large scale corporation, we have sufficient evidence to indicate that large scale employ owned and managed businesses are far more efficient and productive than private large scale corporations, and when you factor in the public element we insure that the employee owned and managed businesses will be more socially responsible and responsive to the common good and add significantly to the common wealth.

"As for expertise, we will still have experts and CEOs, but they will be working for us, and they will be

202

chosen by the people who know best who is most quali-
fied to lead the company for the benefit of all, the workers
themselves who are involved in every aspect of the business day to day."

Senator Lorenz pauses then says, "No, I'm not making myself clear enough nor am I describing the true hor-
rors of our present economic system. Miranda, once you
recognize that the United States is a biomechanical organ-
ism and that money is blood to that system, it becomes
perfectly clear what sort of economic system we live in today. It is a virulent form of vampire capitalism where the
very few are sucking off the life blood of each and every
one of us. America is dying, Miranda. Our very life blood
is being sucked away, and when the vampires of global
capitalism have sucked us dry, they will leave us drained of
our commonwealth and move on to another host nation.
They are doing that globally now. Brazil is a prime example. But, what is truly horrific about this is that it is not just
about us being sucked dry and left to die. By its nature,
vampire capitalism requires continuous growth, and, therefore, at this stage of its development, it has become a can-
cerous growth destroying the very planet upon which it
depends, and in the end it will kill us all, capitalist and poor
alike.

"What we need to do," he says, "Is rid ourselves of
the vampires who feed off of the body politic, this cancer-
ous growth that is killing us all. We need to get rid of Wall
Street and casino economics, and we need to get rid of

compound interest where it is a critical factor in the need of capitalism to continuously grow. We also need to rid ourselves of the blood banks that only feeds the few. I will do this by nationalizing the banking system in America so that the banks will function as they should in a healthy society and money will circulate through the body politic nurturing and bringing sustenance to every individual, every cell, so as to ensure the good health and wellbeing of each and every one of us and the wellbeing of us all.

"For example, we will channel investment money into employee owned and managed businesses because study after study has proven that economic democracy and employee owned and managed businesses, overall, out produce and are more efficient than your traditional large scale capitalist enterprise. In addition, employee owned and managed business will ensure equitable distribution of the burdens and benefits of social labor, and develop human potentials for creativity, cooperation, and empathy. With equal citizen representation on the board of directors, employee owned and managed businesses in partnership with the American people will also ensure that the enterprise is responsive to the general wellbeing of the community, the environment, and the society at large. So, in answer your question as to whether or not American workers in partnership with the American people can make the critical economic decisions that affect their lives, the answer is a categorical, yes. Democracy works."

"Arthur," Miranda says, "it's a wonderful vision, very

inspiring, but, of course, the devil is in the details, and I have so many other questions that I'm sure we don't have time for here. For example, you claim to retain the entrepreneurial spirit of capitalism, but how? I don't quite see it, and I'm not quite sure what you mean when you say that compound interest is a critical factor in the need of capitalism to continually grow, or what you mean when you say that you are going to get rid of Wall Street and casino economics? What about the private sector? Have you eliminated it all together?"

"Miranda, you're right. We are running out of time here, but I'm sure if we sat down with the experts on this and the data, I could convince you that this works. But I have a question for you." Senator Lorenz pauses for affect then says, "Miranda, will you be my running mate?"

Madeline Bradley shouts, "Oh, my God, Arthur, you're right. She's perfect."

Miranda is shocked. She never expected this, but she's pleased. She loves surprises, plot twists. "You're joking," she says.

"No, I'm not. You have led the fight to protect and preserve our public lands and parks, and you have led the fight for land reform. You have also been a leader in saving and preserving museums and public libraries, and you have spent most of your fortune on helping the poor. If I'm elected, I will need to focus on the political and economic reformation of this country. I want you to head a committee that will draft land reform legislation that will repatriate farm land owned by foreign entities and break up large corporate mega-farms. I want a new Homestead Act. I also want you to lead the movement for a cultural Renaissance in America, and, finally, I want you to create public spaces that will nurture our sense of community and our oneness with nature. I want you to create a masterpiece of beauty and love. I want you to be you. What do you say?"

"Senator, I don't know what to say."

Senator Lorenz touches her hand as a gesture of endearment and says, "Don't say anything now. Think about it. We'll..."

Senator Lorenz is cut off in mid-sentence. He hears someone say, "Good evening ladies and gentlemen and welcome to the Presidential debates sponsored by the New York City Junior League."

Miranda turns to see a woman standing at the podium for the speakers. Behind the woman on the wall is an explosion of sunbeams from which a large American bald eagle appears, wings outstretched. Upon its breast is the red, white, and blue shield of the United States of America.

As the room quiets the woman says, "Tonight we have with us Senator Arthur Lorenz and the Vice Presidential nominee, Franklin Peters, who is standing in for President Dickson. The format of the debate is that each speaker will be given fifteen minutes for an opening address. Then we will accept questions from the audience giving each candidate five minutes to respond with an additional three minutes for rebuttal. The order of the questions asked will be determined by a computer that will randomly select participants from the audience seated here. That said, I would like to thank all the members of the Junior League who made this wonderful event possible, and without any further ado, as the Chairwoman of The League, I am proud to introduce our first speaker, the presidential candidate, Senator Arthur Lorenz."

Arthur smiles, "Here I go."

He rises from the table and walks to the podium while the audience cheers and applauds. He acknowledges the warm greeting then waits for the room to quiet then says, "Fellow Citizens, there are many issues in this campaign, but when you break down this election to its essential points, you are left with one critical issue, one critical choice that will determine the fate of the United States of America. The choice that the President is asking you to make is a choice between capitalism and democracy. Quite simply, the President sees democracy as being bad for business, so he wants to get rid of it. He wants to get rid of the House of Representatives and replace it with a non-elected Corporate Assembly, and where I promise you a land of citizen lawmakers and economic democracy, he promises you a New Dark Ages of corporate feudalism where America is a franchise ruled by a hereditary aristocracy, exactly what we fought against in the American Revolution. Make no mistake, if you make the wrong choice in this election, it may be..."

Denny is in the middle of the masses of people in the park, and he is following the man that he saw in the cave. The music is growing louder and louder, filling the forest, swallowing Denny up as he struggles against the waves of people marching to the beat of the beast, each an individual note, an individual cell that has formed a larger body with a life of its own, a composition of words and voices that entwines itself with the words of Senator Lorenz who Denny can hear through the receiver in his ear.

"So, in the end, we have no choice but to join together as a united people because you and I, alone, can never hope to beat the Leviathan of Corporate Power, but, together, we the people of the United States can become a Colossus of Liberty."

The Senator's voice weaves itself through the music, the forest, the fire forming tongues of flame in the cauldron of chaos amidst the chants, the heartbeat of the beast, the gods looking down from the ceiling of the ballroom.

"Together, we can take back our government, our farmlands that are now being sold to foreigners, the homes we lost to usury, the factories and businesses that have been exported in pursuit of child and slave labor. Together, we can rebuild our industrial and technological base and become once again the Dynamo that made America great. We can rebuild our cities and build new monuments to our aspirations as a people, tributes to the human spirit. We can restore America the Beautiful, and we can become once again the guiding light of freedom for generations to come, the modern Athens of a New Golden Age of Enlightenment.

Senator Lorenz pauses then says, "My fellow Citizens, we are at the threshold of one the greatest moments in human history, and this is the truth beyond any other truth that I have spoken tonight. Democracy is a revolution that has never been won, but our time has come."

At that moment, a horn penetrates the music and the chants. Denny hears shouts of joy, release, and he realizes that it is the signal for the mob to charge the main exit from the park. Denny is afraid he's going to lose the man he's been following, so he begins to push his way through the mob, but the man must sense him. Denny watches him turn and scans the mob looking for his pursuer. He makes eye contact with Denny and quickens his pace. Denny loses him for a moment then sees him further away. Denny moves quickly to narrow the gap. They make eye contact again. This time he's certain the man has made him.

A pistol appears in the man's hand, and Denny ducks using the mob for a shield. But the man fires anyway. He hits the man in front of Denny. Denny sees the man's head explode, and then he sees a woman go down disappearing in the surging mass of people. The man tries to fire again, but everyone is running now, and he is caught up in the stampeding herd. He must keep up or be trampled down. Denny is running too. He's loses sight of the man, but there's nothing he can do about it. He's part of the herd now that is bound together for protection and strength as they surge forward.

Someone shouts, "Arise ye wretched of the world you have nothing to lose but your chains."

The birds that have gathered in the trees for their fall voyage fill the air with their screams, thousands of wings flapping as the doors of hell fly open and the air explodes with fire.

"Jesus Christ." The troops have opened fire on the people. He sees bodies upon bodies being ripped apart. Thousands of people are being shot down in front of him. He sees brain matter splatter a child's face like a creature from a horror movie. The screams are horrible. Denny dives for the ground as people are being hit all about him, but they keep coming, rushing into the mouth of death as the attack vehicles and the tanks open up creating a wall of fire to impale the screams upon. One body falls upon Denny and then another. Denny is looking into the face of a dead woman who is lying in front of him, her eyes expressing the fact that life is not here. It is someplace else.

Finally, the fire stops. It seems to be over. Denny pushes away the bodies that he has been buried under and stands up. The topcoat that he bought from the bum is covered with blood and gore. He takes it off and throws it over the woman then speaks into the transmitter, "Zelko, are you there?"

"Yes, sir."

"Where's that bastard that I was following?"

"I'm sorry sir, but I lost him. Things got pretty hectic here, and Ms. Labelle is my first priority. Did I act correctly?"

"Yes you did. How is she?"

"She's still in the ballroom, sir. I have all of our security people around her."

"Good," Denny says. "Get the limousine ready and tell our security people that I'm coming in, and I'm going to get her out of there."

"Yes, sir."

Denny walks quickly to the exit from the park. He pulls out his badge so that it is visible, and he triggers an electronic device in the badge. The electronic device sends out an identification signal, a signal that should be picked up by the riot troops so that Denny will be recognized as one of their own. As Denny looks at the slaughter, he wonders who ordered them to fire. This whole thing looks like a set up orchestrated by an agent provocateur, but why, he asks himself as he exits the park.

On the street he can see that many people have escaped the park by climbing the fences, and now they are running in every direction to escape the clubs of the riot police. As he approaches the entranceway to the hotel, two soldiers come up to him. He is targeted by two beams of light. Denny hold up his badge for them to see, and the soldiers begin to move away

"Hold it," Denny says. "I have something for you

211

two to do. I'm bringing out a VIP. There'll be a limousine pulling up to the front of the door, license number ML1. I want you to stay here and protect the vehicle. That's an order. Do you understand me?"

"Yes, sir."

Denny takes a closer look at the two soldiers. He looks beyond the riot gear and the bulky bullet proof armor. Jesus, he says to himself, they're just teenagers. Denny then takes a close look at their identification numbers and writes them down then says as he is walking away, "OK, boys, don't fuck up, or I'll have your ass."

He enters the Plaza Hotel. The lobby is a mad house. A man and woman who are obviously from the park are being dragged out of the hotel like two sacks of garbage while another man is being clubbed into submission. As Denny climbs the steps to the ballroom, a man in rags runs past him. The man is large and bulky and he is able to burst through the two security guards who try to stop him. Denny sees the crown and realizes that it is the King of Debris, and he races up the stairs after him followed by several soldiers. The King runs into the Ball room and stops, stunned by the riches, the crystal gods alight in the sky, the white silken women with the shadow men, tables full of food.

He growls and runs to a table, picks up food with both hands and waves the food at the jewels, the breasts, the...

He is shot in the temple and he collapses into the

table then crashes to the floor amidst screams, the food. The man's face is buried in fish eggs and chicken breast, salmon steak and plums squashed red in the flambé.

Standing on the other side of the room is Franklin Peters with a gun in his hand. Denny looks at the expression on Frank's face and he knows who fired the shot.

Denny turns and sees Senator Lorenz standing next to him. "Is he dead?" the Senator asks.

"Yes."

Tom Williams approaches Senator Lorenz, and the Senator says, "Come on Tom, I'm going down there and see if I can stop this."

The Senator turns to Denny, "Who are you?"

"Colonel Denise Martino, I'm here with Ms. Labelle, sir."

He grabs Denny's arm, "Get her the hell out of here."

"I plan to."

"Good, do it."

The Senator walks away, and Denny looks about the room and spots Miranda standing nearby. Ned is standing next to her holding his 45 automatic in his hand, an old but very effective stopper. There are so many body guards and secret service agents with guns drawn that it is hard to distinguish who is what and it's a wonder that they haven't started firing at each other.

Denny walks to where Miranda is standing. She is staring at the dead man, her hands over her mouth. She is crying.

Denny touches her gently and says, "Come on, Ms. Labelle. I'm going to take you out of here."

Miranda looks across the room at Franklin Peters who is smiling as he shakes a man's hand. "I've got to do something before I go," she says, then strides over to Franklin Peters and hauls off and slaps him in the face as hard as she can and says, "Congratulations, Frank, you just saved the leftover chicken Kiev from the starving masses."

She turns away and walks back to where Denny is standing and says, "O.K. we can go now." But then she looks at the dead body, and she starts crying again. Denny puts his arm around her, and she clutches his arm with both hands and leans against him for support as he leads her away.

Denny speaks into the transmitter, "Zelko, we're coming out. I want men at the door. I want a lead and trailer car."

They make their way down the stairway to the lobby with Ned leading the way, pushing everyone and anyone aside. As Denny exits the Plaza through the revolving doors, he sees the merging images of stained glass, bronze torchlights, and marble stairs. It's as if reality has become a kaleidoscope. He spots the limousine parked near the Fountain of Abundance, a statue of a nude woman holding a basket full of fruit, water pouring down one marble basin after another, the water turning into the blood of dead bodies strewn around the base of the broken fountain.

As he rushes Miranda into the car, Denny calls Zelko for backup. Ned jumps into the front seat, and as Denny gets into the back seat, he sees Senator Lorenz standing near the car.

The Senator sees him as well and gestures to Denny indicating that he wants him to wait. He is arguing with a high-ranking officer, and Denny hears him say, "What the hell happened here? That park was opened up to those people to give them shelter. It's not supposed to be a prison."

"Someone fired at us."

"Who fired at you?"

"We don't know."

"Someone fired at you, and this is your response?"

The sirens drown out their voices, and Denny doubts that either man can hear the other one speak. The Senator turns away from the officer and walks toward the car leaving Tom Williams to bark at the officer who is now barking back.

Denny opens the window to the car, and the Senator leans down and looks at Miranda who is leaning against Denny's shoulder with her face buried in her hands. "Miranda, are you all right?" The Senator asks.

Miranda raises her head. She is mad now, and with tears in her eyes she says, "Am I all right? Are you all right, Arthur?"

Senator Lorenz shakes his head, "No, Miranda, I'm

not all right. I'm barely holding it together, but someone has to take charge here."

"What can I do to help?" Miranda asks, determined. "I know first aid."

Denny, alarmed, says, "No, Ms. Labelle, I can't protect you. Our security is completely broken down. I need to get you out of here."

Senator Lorenz says, "The Colonel is right, Miranda. I'm a presidential candidate. I have Secret Service agents all around me now, but you... We have professional people pouring in here from every hospital. I know you want to help, but you would be exposing yourself needlessly, and there is too much at stake."

Senator Lorenz turns to Denny and says, "Do you know where you're going?"

"No, sir, but we're going now!" Denny sees Zelko in the surveillance van pull up behind the limousine, and a lead car pulls up in front of the limousine, its motor racing. They are all plugged into what Denny will do next.

Denny is about to give the order to head for the airport and Vision World's private jet, when Arthur Lorenz says, "Wait a minute."

Senator Lorenz takes out an old fashioned pen and a pad of paper and writes something on it. "Take her to my place," he says. "I'm going to be here most of the night trying to straighten this mess out. I can stay here at the hotel. I'll arrange for her staff to meet her there."

He hands Denny the sheet of paper, "Here's my

address. I'll call ahead. My people will be expecting you."

Denny thinks about it. He doesn't have a clue what awaits them at the airport so he hands the driver the slip of paper with the address on it and shouts, "Go!"

Chapter Eighteen

The driver burns rubber as he peels away from the Plaza Hotel and tears down Sixth Avenue. Someone throws a bottle at the limousine, and Denny can hear the glass shatter against its armored skin. Soon, however, they are in normal traffic, and the streets seem relatively quiet. The people who have escaped the park have scattered into the darkness of the cavernous streets or have become part of the misty haze of people who look like ghosts in the white light of the avenues.

Denny speaks into a transmitter. He checks with the lead car and the trailer then turns to the driver and says, "You can slow down now. I think we're alright."

Denny relaxes. He feels the crisis is over. He looks over at Miranda who is now looking out the window into the darkness deep in thought. God, what she must be going through, Denny thinks. He's been through this before. This is what he ran away from to become a homicide detective. One murder is quite different than the mass murder of men, women, and children. It tears away your view of reality, what you believe in, who you are, and what you are fighting for. The word quantification smacks you in the face and blurs out all human meaning. Denny looks out the window into the darkness, and he can see that they're passing through ruins, abandoned buildings, a hopeless waste, and then they pass into the remnants of The Village where Senator Lorenz lives.

They pull up to an old red brick apartment building with Gothic touches and stone trim, and they are immediately met by the Senator's security people. They usher them into the building and into a private elevator that will take them to the Senator's penthouse apartment. One of the Senator's security men hands Denny a scheme of the building, and Denny sees that it is quite secure. Denny also sees from the building plans that Senator Lorenz took the structure built around an old water tower on the rooftop, a structure that was built to look like a Gothic castle, and turned it into an apartment, a castle for himself with French doors opening up to a garden along the rooftop.

The door of the elevator slides open, and Denny walks into a room with cathedral sized stained glass windows and a vaulted ceiling that towers above. The room is essentially a library and study walled with book-shelves filled with leather bound books. A fire is burning in the hearth of a carved stone fireplace the size of a garage door, and a dark antique mahogany and leather mission style couch and two chairs are situated in front of the fireplace for warmth. On the end tables are two antique stained glass Tiffany lamps that sparkle like gemstones. The glow from the Tiffany lamps and the fire seems to dance across the black marble floor and weave itself like threads of light into a beautiful dark burgundy Persian rug and a medieval tapestry of a captive unicorn that hangs above the fireplace and is woven with fine wool, silk, and gilded threads of silver and gold. The unicorn is surrounded by a short circular fence that it can easily leap, and it is tethered loosely to a pomegranate tree that it can easily escape. It is a prisoner of love and beauty

Denny looks for Miranda and sees that the Senator's valet has taken Miranda in hand and is showing her about the apartment. He is leading her up a black wrought iron winding stairway to the loft above that seems to be the Senator's bedroom. Denny sits down on the couch in front of the fireplace and confers with the security people. When they settle on who will be responsible for what, everyone leaves, and Denny is left alone with Miranda who is in the garden out on the rooftop.

Denny speaks into the transmitter, "Zelko, are you there?"

"Yes, sir, I'm parked outside the apartment."

"Good, I have a question for you. Do I have access to all classified files and records?"

Zelko hesitates then says, "Yes, sir, Vision World controls all communications and information, and you have top clearance. You have access to all data bases, sir."

Denny decides that he doesn't want Zelko looking over his shoulder, so he says, "Good. I'm going to be working with the computer through most of the night. All you need to do is set it up so that I can work with it alone.

Can you do that?"

"Yes, sir. I'll set it up for easy access. You ask the questions and the computer will give you the answers, and it will help you through any problem that you have. But, sir, I can help you with this. That's what I'm here for."

"No, the way I figure it, I have you, Ned, the driver, and the two security agents from the lead car, right?"

"Right, but we can call in more men."

"No need. Lorenz has four security people here, and there is enough room on the first floor to sleep a small army. Let's make this easy, four men on, four men off. You arrange it with Ned and their security chief. Then set up the computer for me and go to sleep."

"But sir..."

"No buts. I'm going to need you to be wide awake in the morning because it's your show when she wakes up and smells the coffee, and I don't want to know about anything until that plane hits the ground in Washington."

"Yes, sir."

Denny turns off the transmitter and then walks out into the garden. He finds Miranda at the edge of the parapet looking through a telescope down onto the city streets below. "I want to show you something," Miranda says, and she turns the telescope south towards the end of the island, then adjusts the focus and says, "Look."

As he steps in front of her and she steps back to make room for him, he accidently touches the bareness of her shoulder, and it feels as if he's touched a woman for

221

the first time. He smells the perfume in her hair, and it smells like freesia and baby's breath flowers

"Can you see?" Miranda asks.

Denny looks through the telescope, and he can see the Statue of Liberty. Two years ago, terrorists had badly damaged the statue when they tried to blow it up, and now it has scaffolding all around it. And the torch is gone.

He hears Miranda say, "Lady Liberty looks like she's in prison. Doesn't she?"

"Yes, she does."

"Now take a look at this." She takes the telescope from him and aims it down to where she was looking before, adjusts the focus again, and invites Denny to share another vision and to see life through her eyes.

Denny looks through the telescope, and he sees an endless line of people. But what are they in line for? He follows the line to its source and then he sees a sign for the New York State Lottery, *A Dollar a Dream*.

The street is strewn with losers, false hope. There's a bum lying on the curb next to where the lottery tickets are sold. Is he dead, Denny wonders, or is he dreaming? Next to the bum's feet is a lottery ticket sticking out of a pile of shit like the missing torch of the Statue of Liberty.

Miranda puts her arms around Denny's waist and leans her head against his back. He can feel her breasts. "Isn't it awful," she says. "That's what the American dream has turned into, a 400 million to one shot."

Denny turns around and looks into her eyes, and it

is like standing at the edge of the ocean on a beautiful sunny day, the perfectly white sand glittering with diamond dust slipping out from underneath his feet as the tide tries to pull him into her depth. Denny desperately wants to kiss Miranda. He desperately wants to be inside of her, but he can't. He's the man on the wall. He is here to protect her, and if he kisses her, Vision World will swallow her up because she is a potential danger to them now, and they would love to trivialize her in this moment of weakness where amidst this horror story they are both in desperate need of love.

Denny feels the tide disappear below his feet. He sways but then regains his balance and says, "You need to say yes, Miranda."

Miranda looks puzzled, "Yes to what, Denny?"

It is the first time that she has called him by his first name. "You have to say yes, to Senator Lorenz. You have to be his running mate. This country desperately needs you."

Miranda shakes her head, "I don't know, Denny, there is so much that I don't understand."

"Miranda, you're brilliant. You'll figure this all out. You'll figure out Senator Lorenz, but that is not why you should say, yes. Sure, Lorenz is brilliant too. He may even be a great man, but he's vain and full of himself and his vision for America. Look at this." Denny waves his hand to take in Lorenz's penthouse. "He sees himself as a Renaissance prince who will lead us out of the Dark Ages, and maybe he can, but he can't do it without you. You have what this country needs more than anything, a great heart. Miranda, this country needs a mother; it needs to be nurtured back to life."

Miranda smiles and says, "Oh, dear, and I have such small breasts."

They both laugh and then Miranda says, "There is certainly a lot to think about, but it is getting late, and I need to get some sleep." She gently kisses him on the cheek then turns around and leaves the garden through the French doors.

Denny watches her through the windows of the doors ascend the winding stairs to the bedroom, and he takes one last look at Lady Liberty in a cage then enters the penthouse. He sighs and realizes that he has just experienced one of those moments in a person's life where he will always wonder if he did the right thing, but it's time to go back to work, and there is a man he has to track down, and he has to take advantage of the Vision World computers in the surveillance van while he still has access tonight. He may not get another chance again to use the Vision World computers. He may not get another chance at Miranda again. Denny smiles at the irony, and wonders if he made the right choice or is he what Ned claimed him to be, just a dumb bloodhound.

Denny takes the elevator to the lobby, exits the building, and enters the communications vehicle. He finds his travel bag, takes a shower, changes his clothes, and sits down in front of the computer and says, "All right, Snoopy, show me what you can do."

Denny types out some questions on the keyboard. He wants to know why the computer made the decisions that it did because if the computer selects data and scenes around a plot line, then its choice of the man in the cave wasn't arbitrary. But what criteria did it use when it selected the scene? Did it overhear the conversation between the king and the man in the cave and determine that they were dangerous? Did it recognize the king as the leader of the people in the park? Or was it something else?

Denny goes over the data that the computer is feeding him. He listens to the conversation between the king and the man in the fur coat who clubbed the boy to death in the park. This is a scene that Denny hasn't seen before. It's a scene where the king first gives his minion an order to take a lottery ticket off a dying man. It's this story that the computer seemed to be following, and it was this story that leads back to the cave. But as Denny studies more thoroughly the information that the computer is giving, it's obvious that it was responding to other data as well. Denny sorts through this data, and it all seems to lead to one source. Denny shakes his head in disbelief.

On the screen is a copy of a report that he, Dennis Martino, wrote. Eight years ago he wrote it when he was a lieutenant stationed in Mexico City. In the report is a picture of a man with a beard. His name is Pepe Gomez, and he's the same man that was in the cave, the same man that he chased through the park. The computer has dug up Denny's own past for him.

The memory is so clear to him now. He is back in Mexico City at the Aztec ruins. It is night, and the sky is bursting forth with fireworks that light up the monster faces of the gods of the Aztec pyramids that eat people with their stone teeth. Steps lead to the sun, the moon, the stars, and to an altar where innocent hearts are torn out and fed to the gods as the night sky lights up with orgasmic fireworks.

Denny is looking at the face of a dead woman, her child, her husband, her son. He is looking at an old man who had come to the festival merely to watch the fireworks, and an old woman who probably came every year to the festival of the lights celebrating Mexico's liberation from their ancient conquerors. All the dead are victims of a terrorist bomb.

A Mexican policeman comes up to Denny and says, "We've caught one, Lieutenant Martino."

"Where is he?"

The Sergeant points to the pyramid and a door into the inner sanctums. The entranceway leads down a flight of stairs. A torch is burning for effect, lighting up hieroglyphics of a serpent god and a man on a voyage across a sea in an ark with wings. At the bottom of the stairs is a room that looks like a room where a watchman might rest. There's a table, a hot plate, a desk. A bulb at the end of a cord swings gently back and forth through swirling cigarette smoke and the shadows of men talking, laughter.

As Denny enters, the room goes quiet, and the laughter trickles off into silence. Seated at the table smoking a cigarette is a young man with dark pool like eyes that show no sign of human feelings. Seated across from him are the Chief of Police, and a man Denny recognizes as Bill Mayo. Denny doesn't know Mayo, but he does know of him from the file that he keeps on CIA operatives. He knows from his file that Mayo is into heavy duty shit, deep cover crap.

Mayo sees Denny then turns to the Chief of Police and says, "Get him out of here."

The Chief of Police gets up from the table and walks towards Denny. Denny can see that the man with the deadly pool like eyes is smiling at him. The Chief whispers into Denny's ear, "Come with me, Lieutenant. This one is out of our hands."

Denny feels a flare of anger, but he allows the Chief of Police to lead him out of the room. As they walk up the stairs past the hieroglyphics, the secret messages to the stars, Denny asks, "What the hell is going on there?"

"Evil shit."

"But aren't we going to question that guy. I was told that he's the terrorist that did all this shit."

"He's one of ours."

"You mean he's not a terrorist?"

"No, he's a terrorist, all right. And he's probably the one who blew up those people."

"Then what the fuck are you talking about?"

The Chief of Police whispers, "He's a terrorist, but he's one of us."

"You mean he works for the CIA?"

"No, I think he works for the Alpha Commission."

Denny is surprised. He didn't know much about it, but he thought that the Commission was a board of national and global corporate leaders that the President appointed to advise him on economic policy. "Are you saying that the Commission is a player in this?"

"Yes."

"Why do you say that?"

"We intercepted a phone call to Mayo from a Commission agent. They want that prick in there released. Mother of God, what is this world coming to?"

"And what about these people?" Denny points to the bodies and the body parts strewn all over the street.

The Chief of Police shrugs, "Casualties of war."

The Chief of Police gets into his Jeep, and he orders a subordinate to get rid of the bodies then turns to Denny and says, "Denny, what are you surprised by? That the Commission has an intelligence force of its own, or that the predator should appear to be something else so that it can get close to its prey?"

"To infiltrate the National Liberation Army?" Denny asks.

The Chief laughs, "The Commission set up the NLA to discredit terrorists and infiltrate the revolutionary movements in this country. Jesus, Mary, and Joseph, wake up, Lieutenant, that bombing out there is bad press. It's as simple as that."

The Chief drives off, and Denny is left standing in the middle of the fireworks flinching with every explosion not knowing what is real. But does it matter in a world where men pray to gods that prey on man?

Denny returns from his memories of the past and adjusts the monitor so that he can get a close up picture of Pepe Gomez. He compares the pictures in the park to the picture he has in the file of Gomez. There is no doubt. The terrorist he saw in the tomb in Mexico is the same man he saw in the cave. Denny orders the computer to give him access to the Commission's files on covert actions, and the computer responds immediately. He's in.

Boy, Denny thinks, would I like to have this thing for a few days. He's just been let into the inner sanctums of power. Denny types out National Liberation Army, and the computer begins to search.

Several hours later, after he has gone through all the data the computer has fed him, he is staring at a picture of the members of the National Liberation Army. It's a group shot, twelve men, taken some years back, taken somewhere in the jungle. It's a shot like many shots that he has seen of soldiers trying to remember a moment in their life when they were together with other men, bound by a friendship that only living near death can bring. He himself has been in many such shots, and sometimes when he gets drunk and he has a sympathetic listener, Denny will take out his scrapbook and begin to reminisce. There is, however, a big difference between his pictures and this picture.

In this picture, Denny is staring at Pepe Gomez, and next to him is standing the man who Denny believes was behind the assassination attempt on Brad Merling, the man who is the prime suspect in the murder of the editor and his secretary. Did these two men work for the Commission back when Gomez set off the terrorist bomb in Mexico City? Do they work for them now? Why would they want to kill Brad Merling, the head of the Commission? Is this some kind of corporate coup? What is the truth behind this labyrinth of lies, duplicity, plots, and counter-plots?

Denny looks at the clock and sees that it is five o'clock in the morning. He has to get some sleep, so he lies down on the bed in the van and looks up at the stars that Vision World becomes when he puts it on standby.

In his dream Denny hears Miranda say, "They killed thousands of them."

Denny holds Miranda in his arms. She's feverish. She looks up to him and says, "Make love to me Denny. Please."

He kisses her tears, they're like fire, and her lips are burning. She leads him to a bed of flowers in the garden atop of Senator Lorenz's penthouse castle and slips out of her white silk gown that is like flowing water. She lies down nude in the flower bed and draws him down into her as she whispers, "I want babies, Denny, hundreds of them. Give me babies, Denny, babies."

She's on fire, and Denny, who is taking his clothes off, realizes why she's so hot. For a woman to see so much death, every cell in her body must be crying out to survive, to reproduce, to destroy death with life. He realizes that she's right. They are in a life and death struggle, and he wants what she wants. He wants her eggs. He wants to pour his life into her. He wants to multiply.

Miranda grabs his cock and puts it inside her. She's so open he feels like he's in her womb. He feels like he is planting her in the garden, planting his seed that explodes inside her as they come together for what seems to be forever going deeper and deeper into the sea until he sees a one eyed octopus with TV screen for suckers pulling her away. He tries to pull her back, but he too is caught up in one of the suckers, and he cannot move. He shouts, "Miranda. Miranda! I love you," only to wake up in the van staring at the Vision World screen, a new episode.

Chapter Nineteen

President Theodore Dickson is looking out a window of the White House at the Washington Monument. He loves the white marble, the immortal calm in contrast to the eternally changing seasons, the green that will soon change to red and orange then brown then dead.

There is nothing reliable about nature, the President observes. The blue sky could darken over at any moment into a dismal gray. Even the fountain is a futile joke about the nature of gravity, and the flowers are a tragic reminder that everything dies. The President prefers the winter when everything is blanketed in snow. He loves the stillness, the purity of white. White is immortal, never changing, the uncorrupted spirit. White means a new start, a blank canvas, a pure soul. The President loves white, and he hates the forever shifting colors of time and history that always ends in darkness.

He picks up his spray gun and looks at his masterpiece. He has painted the East Room all white, everything - the floor, the walls, the ceiling, the cornices decorated with Greek palmettes, the furniture, and even the golden drapes and the mahogany piano supported by gilded eagles. He has one final touch to put on his masterpiece, but the President has a problem. He has painted himself into a corner, and for two hours he has been standing in front of the window waiting for the floor to dry.

The President takes one step and then another. He looks behind, nothing. He isn't being followed. Laughing at his joke on fate, he walks across the floor to where a portrait of Martha Washington is hanging, and he pulls the trigger on his spray gun covering the portrait from top to bottom with a white mist, leaving only the brush strokes and the ghost of Martha Washington who emerges from the painting, all white.

The President takes her hand, and he dances with her across the room into the whiteness, the purity of spirit. When he has danced her into the middle of the blankness, he lets go of her, and she falls away and disappears into the white floor. To make certain that she is gone for good, he sprays the spot where she disappeared so that she will never appear again, and then he turns his gun on a portrait of George Washington by Gilbert Stuart. The portrait by Stuart is the only piece in the White House that remains from the time that the White House was originally occupied in 1800.

The President stares at the portrait, and it seems to him that George Washington is alive and standing in front of him. He is wearing a black morning coat and black boots, black on black that dreadful color that absorbs all other colors, all other light. It's as if only his hands and his

233

face are all that remains of the image that forged a nation. All else is hidden in the darkness surrounded by red storm clouds that shroud the ancient columns of the Republic.

President Dickson is shaking. He is losing nerve, but he must do it. He must blank out history and return America to its immortal purity. He pulls the trigger, and the hand in which George Washington is holding a sword disappears. He cuts a white swath across the darkness to the other hand that is suspended above a table that contains a quill and scrolls of papers. He pulls the trigger, and as the scrolls of paper turn blank, the President recites the words on one of the scrolls before they disappear forever.

"We the people of the United States," he says, "in order to form a more perfect union, establish justice, insure domestic tranquility, provide for the common defense, promote the general welfare, and secure the blessings of liberty to ourselves and our posterity, do ordain and establish this constitution for the United States..." He stops. All is gone. He's wiped out all traces of the Word, the American Bible, and all that remains of George Washington are the brush strokes and the ghost that stares back at him through the blankness. He gives the canvas one final coat, and his work is completed. The President walks to the door and turns around to take one final look at his masterpiece. All is white, but he still can see the pure forms cleansed of shadows and darkness, death. He is pleased, but there is more to do, more rooms to cleanse.

He leaves the room and quietly moves down the

hallway to where he can hear children laughing. It sounds like the Kennedy children. Now he has them. He can finally put an end to the laughter, the ridicule. He bursts through the door, his gun ready. But the laughter has stopped, and there are no children to be seen. They're gone, or are they?

He is in the Green Room that is green no more. Gone is the moss green wallpaper that seemed to suck him up in that quagmire of nature and its water silk vapors. Gone are the dead browns, the mahogany with satinwood inlay, and the cream and green silk that you could slip on never to get up again, lost in the profusion of chaos. Where could they be, he asks himself. He looks behind the furniture, but they are not there. He's puzzled. Where could they hide clothed in the colors of original sin? Then he realizes that everything has been painted white except for one painting - *Matinee sur la Seine, beau temps*, by the French Impressionist Claude Monet. On a small plaque in golden print it says, "In loving memory of John Fitzgerald Kennedy, 35th President of the United States from his family."

Now he has them, he thinks. Now he will be done with this room for good. He peers into the watery colors that flow into one another, light transforming nature into a dream about to disappear, to be washed away. He listens for the laughter beyond the water to the shoreline on the other side of the vanishing point, but what he hears are footsteps coming down the hall. He turns in fear and listens. Could it be Abraham?

There's a gentle knock at the door, and the President recognizes his valet's voice, "Sir, you're on in a half hour."

"Yes, I'll be there in a minute. Thank you, Robert."

The President reaches into his pocket, and he takes out a container of pills. At seventy-three years old he has pills for everything. They keep him alive. The pill that he drops into his mouth is a pill that will stimulate his memory. Recently, he has been blanking out and forgetting who he is. When it happens, oblivion comes to him as a pure white light, and then he is nothing. But, in those moments, when he isn't there, his body and mind are taken over by the spirits of presidents from the past, and he becomes possessed.

The President takes one last look at the Monet. They are there, somewhere. He whispers, "I'll be back."

President Dickson leaves the room and walks down the Grand Hallway. The Grand Hallway is lined with Roman columns and each set of pillars frames a portrait of a president, or so they did before he blanked them all out. Some of the portraits have six or seven coats of paint on them, and yet they still return to possess him. Even now he feels like he is being watched. He approaches one of the blank canvases and looks deeply into the blankness, deeper and deeper to see if anyone is there. At first there doesn't seem to be anyone, but then he sees the ruddy hair, the square jaw and that benign smile, the eminently reasonable mocking eyes of that hateful man. He steps back and sprays the canvas with a new coat of white paint then peers into the canvas again. He's gone.

God, he hates Thomas Jefferson. At one time, he was possessed by him, and he began to invite cabinet members and their wives to dinner. He drank expensive French wine and talked about Hume, Locke, and Hobbes, debating the nature of man. Good or evil? What nonsense. Man is neither good nor evil. Man is a producer and a consumer of goods and his value is determined by the amount of money that he makes. It's as simple as that. How much are you worth? That is the question.

The President walks through the door to the Oval Office, and his aids, the make-up staff, and the camera crew converge on him. One aid takes away his spray gun, and another hands him his speech. The make-up people begin to work on him as a barber trims his hair. He gives himself up completely to the makeover as he studies his script.

The make-up man applies one last touch to his face, steps back, and says, "There."

The director says, "Go."

The President is sitting at the elaborately carved oak desk that is made out of timbers from the H.M.S. Resolute. The Presidential flag and the flag of the United States of America stand like sentinels in the background framing a view of the Rose Garden. On TV the President of the United States looks like he has always looked to the

American people. He's a short man, not particularly good looking. In fact, he's quite plain, a self-made-man. In his own words, he's a common man who has achieved un-common goals. He's living proof that the American dream works, and he speaks slowly and simply so that everyone can understand his common sense approach to life.

"Folks, I have good news for you. America is on the rise again, and, on the home front, the wheels of industry are beginning to turn once more. Americans are off to work with lunch pails in hand, and our children are safely tucked away in schools where they belong.

"In the new states and territories of Latin America, freedom and liberty is the business of the day bringing in-vestment opportunities and jobs for those who want to work, homes for those who are willing to save and sacri-fice. This is the American way, a way of life that the people of Latin America are embracing with the fervor of patriots. It is the way of life that has made America great.

"North and South alike, we believe that no matter how humble your beginnings, that with hard work and tal-ent you can reach the top and be rewarded with success. This is what a socialist like Senator Lorenz doesn't under-stand. He doesn't understand that we don't want to give up the heights and peaks of monetary success and materi-al well-being for the flat lifeless plains of communism. We don't want to eliminate millionaires. We want to be mil-lionaires. And we can be. We don't want to give up the power to mold our own individual destinies and shape our own future. We don't want to eliminate bosses. We want to be the boss. And we can be, by gosh, every one of us. But damn it, you have to earn it. There are no free lunches in America, and, yet, Arthur Lorenz would have us give away everything that we have worked for, and he calls it democracy. That's just old fashion bull biscuits, folks."

The President smiles the knowing smile of a patient father then says, "Senator Lorenz is full of a lot of foolish ideas like that. But you and I, we don't live in an ivory tower with our heads up in the clouds. We're a practical people. And we learned early in our history on the frontiers of America how to change and adapt so as to survive. If something doesn't work, we try to fix it. If it still doesn't work, we try to change it. And if it still doesn't work, we throw it away as useless.

"Now, we're not much for pretty words and dreams of a far distant future where nobody works. We're practical people with common sense. We know what works and what doesn't work. That is why the American people will vote for a constitutional amendment to eliminate the House of Representatives and replace it with a Corporate Assembly that represents the best and the finest in our society."

The President nods his head expecting everyone watching him to nod their heads as well in the mirror of television. Confirming the affirmation that he knows is there, he says, "The American people have no problem with this amendment because they know that we have tried to fix the House of Representatives. We have tried to fix it again and again. But it still doesn't work. The House of Representatives has degenerated into a house rotten at its core filled with self-serving narrow-minded representatives of petty private interests. They have stood in the way of progress in America, and they are responsible through incompetence and mismanagement for the problems we have today."

The President now takes on the posture and the expression of a determined leader of the Free World and says, "What I am proposing is a more efficient Congress, a streamlined body politic for a fast moving quickly changing competitive world, a body politic that will work in cooperation with American business, a Corporate America that will compete with Corporate Japan, China, India, and Europe in the world market and win. This I promise you. If you vote for me, America will work, and America will be number one again because the American spirit never dies. It's alive in me."

With those words, he realizes that he has conjured up the ghosts again, but it's too late. He sees the white light coming, and then he's gone. He is possessed by someone else who says, "Talking about the American spirit reminds me of when I played for Knute Rockney, before I got sick and died. One day, the Rock threw a football out onto the field and said, 'play ball,' and we went at it. The ball got lost in the pile-up, but who cared. Then it trickled out of the pile, but nobody noticed. We still went at it.

We loved it. The Rock, he showed us how to play the game, to play ball and excel individually and still be part of a team, to play by the rules, and when you won, you really won. And that lesson, the courage that we were taught carried over into later life and into war. In the Second World War, when I was a bomber pilot, and we lost two engines over the Atlantic..."

At Vision World's central headquarters, the key members of the Commission are sitting at the conference table in the boardroom watching the President on television. The boardroom is an enormous glass globe and the conference table is a monolithic block of pure white marble suspended in space. The glass floor is a dark cobalt blue, and it remains stable as a global map of Vision World and its subsidiaries, constellations, and satellites, revolve around the conference table like stars and planets in the Vision World universe.

William Lowe, who is watching the President on TV, turns to Merling and says, "What the hell is he talking about?"

Merling shrugs then rolls his eyes, "He thinks he's Ronald Reagan." Merling laughs again, "No, he thinks he's Ronald Reagan who thinks he's one of the mythological heroes that he played in the movies."

William Lowe shakes his head in disbelief, "Is it true that he has painted the White House white?"

Merling nods in ascent.

"All of it, everything?"

241

Merling nods again and says, "Almost all of it."

William Lowe continues to listen to the President go on and on about how he had to clear the mountain, how he had his crew bail out so that they would be safe, how he had to do it alone. William Lowe looks around the room at the other members of the Commission and says, "We have to get rid of him!"

"I agree." Jacob Hess says, "But first we have to win the election then the President can step down for health reasons."

"But are we going to win the election?" Sam Brinton asks. He is looking to Merling for a response.

Merling casually shrugs and says, "It's going to be very close, Sam."

Lowe is livid, "If it's that damn close, why are you giving Lorenz prime time TV coverage? And why was Miranda Labelle there? My God, is she really going to accept Lorenz's offer to make her his running mate. This could be disastrous for us, Arthur, and who is this Martino nobody who is sticking his nose in our business."

Merling closes his eyes and rubs them with the palms of his hands. Sometimes he feels like he's seen too much, and he wants to close his eyes forever, but the feeling passes and he opens his eyes and stares at William Lowe, a man he doesn't like. Merling remembers William Lowe before the makeover. Bill was five foot six inches tall with short legs and a disproportionally oversized torso. He walked like his hands were paddles, his chest out, chin up to accentuate his height. He had bulging featureless eyes and a bulbous nose and big meaty lips, but now after reconstructive plastic surgery he was made to look more proportional with four inches added to his height, and his face was reconstructed to make him look less like a toad. Now he had a more attractive manly look, a square jaw, high cheekbones, and steel blue eyes that perpetually squint like a Western gunslinger facing the sun in a gun duel. He even enlarged his penis, Merling was told.

However, despite the makeover, for years William Lowes's only claim to fame was that he inherited billions of dollars and patents worth billions of dollars more, but recently, in the last few years, he has bought up most of the defense industry, and he has led the movement to privatize the military. More recently he has been going around lecturing businessmen and professional associations about Social Darwinism and how America is a meritocracy and needs to be ruled by the best and the finest. More publicly he had been lobbying for better pay for the military police so that they can live well in comparison to the poverty that most Americans must bear, and at the same time he has been invited to large gatherings of the federal and state police associations to give speeches on how they are the Guardians of the American Way of Life. Brad also learned from one of his own agents, who is an ex-CIA operative that Lowe is secretly funding eugenic research that promises to make smart people smarter, strong people stronger, and weak people weaker. The founder of the company has boasted that he will be able to create a new super race of heroes to rule the masses at a price that only they can pay.

Merling wants to call William Lowe a dickless dildo, but he merely puts on his corporate mask and smiles showing none of his feelings. He can't tell him that Vision World focuses on Miranda precisely because she can't be controlled, nor can he tell him that he did not pick Dennis Martino, Vision World picked him in its experiments with randomness and creativity, and he just went along for the ride. Nor can he ever reveal his deepest and darkest secret. He has very little control of Vision World anymore. It has taken on a life of its own, and it has gone beyond the pat plots and propaganda that he and his staff of writers and producers were feeding it. Something special is happening, something spectacular. How can he explain that to these fools who do not have a clue about the true nature of power. He can't, so he will do what he is very good at. He will lie to them.

"Bill, I did not want to give Lorenz prime time," he says, "But the attempt on my life, Miranda's involvement, her decision to meet Lorenz, this caught us by surprise. We had no choice but to follow the story line."

"You could have cut and gone to something else."

"No, if you think that, you don't understand Vision World. The illusion has to be seamless. If we cut arbitrarily, we create a glitch, a bump that will wake up our viewer, and break the hypnotic spell. Even when we change channels, we have to change channels within the context of the story, or the viewer will realize that there is really only one channel and they have no real choices. That realization is far more dangerous to us than anything that they could have heard or seen yesterday in New York."

Sam Brinton is somewhat alarmed when he says, "Are you telling us, Brad, that you have lost control of the system?"

"Oh, no," Merling says. "We still control the story. We just don't control every detail and specific event. Sam, you need to know how Vision World works. We don't determine all the intricacies of the story, the millions upon millions of lives that Vision World observes and absorbs and singles out day to day to make a part of the story. Essentially we program the plot and define the end game, and then we edit and snip, enhance, and add and subtract to make certain that Vision World sticks to the story line, and we get the results we want."

"Well, god damn it," William Lowe says, " You better do some snipping and editing fast, Brad, and get this fuckin story straight because it seems to me that we could lose this election, and if we do we, we'll be doing some snipping and editing of our own."

"You can start by phasing out Miranda Labelle," Sam Brinton says. "One way or another she has to go."

There is a general murmuring and agreement at the table and Merling is alarmed. He didn't think it would come to this so fast. "Hold it," he says, "Let's not press the panic button yet. The President is still ahead in the polls, and we can win this election, but as you can see, we can't focus on the President. We need to focus on Franklin Peters, his successor. A vote for the President has to be a vote for Frank."

"How are you going to accomplished that?" Lowe asks.

"Frank is going prime time. We've created a new TV show that will revolve around him."

"What's the angle?"

Brad is staring at the screen. The President is smiling into the camera. He is signing off with a little quip about his home life, a family he never had in a place he'd never been, another movie from the dark recesses of his mind full of mythological movie characters who have come to life forming the fabric of his reality, the reality of his followers who believe in him and believe that he is the embodiment of all these spirits that possess him.

God, he wishes he had a Ronald Reagan, Brad thinks. What he could have done with him, but Franklin Peters will have to do.

William Lowe is waiting for his answer, but Merling continues to stare at the television. Finally William Lowe explodes, "God damn it, Brad. I asked you a question, and all you do is watch television!"

Merling turns from the TV and says simply, "I'm sorry, Bill, but this is my business, and I think I've found an answer to our problem."

"What's that?" Lowe asks.

"Turn your TV on tonight at 8:00 o'clock. We're showing the pilot then."

"Is the show that good?" Sam Brinton asks.

"It's not just good, Sam. It's great."

"What's it about?"

"It's a sitcom with Franklin Peters playing Dad. I have his whole family in on it, Brenda and the kids, and it will be shot from their home. The show will be a metaphor for the solution to all our problems, and Frank, the father of our country, is the answer. He will be the voice of reason and moderation solving the problems of his misbehaving and misdirected children."

Jay Brunelli is enthralled with the idea, "What's the name of the show?"

"Father Knows Best."

Chapter Twenty

Brad Merling leaves the meeting with the Commission, and he enters his office, a virtual reality fantasy of imperial power with black marble Doric columns that dwarf the human. The black marble floors with web like veins extend into the inner sanctums of Vision World where power seems to have no beginning and end, and darkness is the essence of space.

Hathaway and Denny are seated in front of Brad's desk that is composed of geometrically balanced rectangular planes of titanium, platinum, onyx, and gold suspended from silver threads that are like glistening dewdrops that disappear into the ceiling less ceiling. They are sitting in two matching black leather chairs trimmed with titanium, and they are both looking at a computer screen that is floating above the desk like an apparition. The only other source of light is coming from the towering columns of sheer silk curtains that glow ochre in the sunlight.

Merling notes that Denny's suit looks like he slept in it and his hair looks like he just got out of bed. Merling is impressed with the job his wardrobe staff and hairstylist have done on Denny. They have picked out fabrics, clothing styles, and a haircut that would make Denny look good despite his total lack of care for his appearance. Brad especially likes the worn calfskin moccasins with no socks. What Denny doesn't realize is that his self-conscious effort not to be a product has made him the anti-product product. Merling smiles as he approaches Denny and says, "Martino, it is good to see you. When did you get back?"

"A couple of hours ago, sir."

Merling sits at his desk, "Hathaway tells me that we have a problem."

"Yes, sir." Denny opens his briefcase, takes out a data retriever, and slips it into the computer terminal. A computer-enhanced copy of a photograph appears on the screen.

Brad Merling looks at the picture on the screen and says, "So what am I looking at?"

"I pulled a file on the National Liberation Army, and I came up with this picture. It's a group picture of the members of the National Liberation Army taken about eight years ago in the Yucatan."

Denny points to one of the men in the picture, "This is the man I chased in the park. Eight years ago I encountered the same man in Mexico City. His name is Pepe Gomez, and he is the agent provocateur who blew up men, woman, and children to give terrorism a bad name. I was also informed back then by the Police Chief of Mexico City that Gomez was an ex-CIA agent working as a private contractor. According to the Police Chief, Gomez was hired by the Commission to set up the National Liberation Army

as a pseudo terrorist organization for the purposes of infil-
trating the revolutionary movement. Do you know anything about that, Mr. Merling?"

"No, I don't."

"But, sir, you are the head of the Commission."

Brad Merling laughs at Denny's naiveté and then
says, "We're not as monolithic as we seem, Colonel. We all
have our territory, and we come together when it serves
our interests. We all have our own private security forces,
and we often initiate our own private covert actions when
we feel it is necessary. More often than not, we work together, and we all recruit from just about every military
and intelligence service in the world. We're global corporations that do business all over the world, and we have
security interests that extend far beyond the nation state.
Basically, we recruit wherever we can to find good men
who want to get paid more. Men like you, Colonel. So
what is the point to all of this?"

Denny points to the man standing next to Pepe
Gomez in the picture and says, "This is the man we believe
was behind the assassination attempt on your life, the man
who is the prime suspect in the murder of the editor and
his secretary. His name is Charles Ramon. He was born in
Brazil, educated in the United States, and trained by the
CIA as an agent. He was dropped from the CIA payroll
about nine years ago, and soon after, he appears on the
security records of several Latin American countries as a
terrorist. There is no indication that any of these countries

250

knew of his CIA affiliation except in Mexico where, like Gomez, he was identified as a Commission operative. Now it seems that the National Liberation Army has mutated into the People's Army, a terrorist group located in Brazil. And, it would seem, Gomez and Ramon are soldiers in that army. Are they still working for some unknown member of the Commission? Is this a pseudo terrorist group, or is this the real thing? We don't know. But, we are quite certain that Gomez, Ramon, and the People's Army are responsible for the attempt on your life, the murder of the editor and his secretary, and the riot in the park. The rest is conjecture."

Merling studies the faces of the two men who want to be his executioners. One is deadly somber, resolute, and the other looks like he's having a hell of a lot of fun killing people. He is mesmerized by the fact that they both seem to be looking at him. He turns to Hathaway and says, "John, have you talked to anyone at the agency?"

"I talked to Bob at the agency today. He confirms that Gomez was believed back then to be working for Jacob Hess. However, Bob thinks that he may be a rogue agent who has gone wacko. I tend to agree."

Jacob Hess, Merling thinks. Jacob Hess was and is now a member of the Commission, and he and his board control most of the agro-business in the Americas. "I can see how Jake would use an agent like Gomez back then, but I don't see him having the balls to pull something off like this. Does Bob know of any connection between them now?"

"No," Hathaway says, "Nothing that he knows about. As I said, he thinks that the more likely scenario is that Gomez is a rogue agent who has gone wacko, and I tend to agree with him. Listen, Boss, all we have is this connection, but anybody could be behind this. It could be the Chinese or even the European Union. Or, both these guys are off the farm. Terrorism is big business these days."

"Very well, so what is our plan?" Merling asks.

"Martino is our point man on this, and he has a good idea. I approve."

Denny picks up the cue from Hathaway to begin his presentation, "I worked with a Colonel Valasques when I was stationed in Brazil. We got to know one another pretty well. I guess you would call him a friend, if you could call a snake a friend. Anyway, he's a very high-ranking intelligence officer down there, and there are two things that I can say for certain about Valasques. He is fearless, and he can be bought. I want to go to Brazil, contact him, and see what I can come up with on Gomez, Ramon, and the People's Army."

"Good," Merling says. He reaches into his desk and pulls out a coded electric checkbook. He taps some buttons, sets some codes, and then hands the checkbook to Denny and says, "You have unlimited resources. Hathaway will show you how to use it. You can transfer funds into and out of this account instantaneously." He pauses for a moment then says, "Well then that's it. John will keep me informed. When will you be leaving?"

"This evening, sir."

"Well then, good luck Martino. You and Hathaway can work out whatever needs to be done. Now you will have to excuse me. I have to turn the lights out on a star. Where's Miranda?"

"She's in the reception lounge," Hathaway says.

Merling extends his hand to Denny, "We're relying on you, Martino."

"Yes, sir, but about Ms. Labelle, I feel like I'm still responsible for her security. She may still be in danger."

Merling smiles warily and says, "The only one who is going to be in danger, Martino, is me when I tell her that I'm taking her off prime time TV. So don't worry about Miranda. She will be with me most of the time working in a very secure environment, and we will continue to keep a tight security net about her. Is that correct Hathaway?"

"Yes, sir."

"Well then, that's it," Merling says. Denny is dismissed from his mind, and he turns to Hathaway and says, "Send Miranda in on your way out."

Hathaway and Denny leave Merling's office and soon after Miranda enters. Miranda and Brad embrace, and he leads her to the couch facing a view of Washington that they both like. From the window, they can see the Potomac River, the patches of color that turn into sailboats playing in the light, the tree lined parks, magnolias and elms that add a Dionysian touch to the Imperial style of Rome, the columns, the domes, and the stone giants, Washington Monument pierces the sky, thrusting upward into a needle's point, a dot to mark the spot for the Gods to see when the planets align.

Merling kisses Miranda on the cheek, "Randy, it's so good to see you."

He loves the perfume she is using. It smells like sugar doughnuts. "Would you like something?" he asks as he releases her from his tender grasp.

"Yes, make me one of your wonderful martinis."

Merling gets up from the couch and walks to the control panel. He presses a button and a side panel in the wall slide open, and a cocktail bar emerges that is composed of clear glass geometric planes that look like a twentieth century cubist sculpture. Brad reaches into the chrome-faced refrigerator, and he takes out a crystal bowl of ice made from natural spring water.

Merling places some ice cubes in the shaker then reaches for a crystal bottle filled with dry vermouth. He splashes the ice cubes with the vermouth, stirs it around then pours the vermouth out. "Miranda, I want you to work for me."

Miranda looks at Merling quizzically.

"On what?"

Merling gestures about with his hand and says, "Everything." He grabs another crystal bottle and pours in the gin, raising the bottle slowly upward, extending the pour, the flow of pure spirits. He's fascinated by the way that the colorless liquid flows over the colorless ice in a colorless glass. It seems to absorb the room, the light, forming formless forms that ring when he touches the potion with the silver spoon.

"I want you to be my assistant director," he says. "I want you to be ready to take my place if anything happens to me."

Miranda looks up from the glass, alarmed by what she just heard, "What are you talking about, Brad?"

"Miranda, they're trying to kill me." He watches the gin and the ice with the fragrance of dry vermouth swirl into each other. "And it's quite possible that the 'they' is the Commission or some members of the Commission who feel that I've become too powerful."

Miranda looks shocked and frightened for Brad, "What are you going to do?"

Merling reaches for two crystal glasses, tall, thin stemmed, fluted and flaked with delicate lines like cracked ice. He pours the spirits into the glasses and hands one to Miranda. "I'm going to fuck them." Merling laughs at the pure joy of the word, a word he seldom uses. It's nice to save a word for special occasions, to savor it with your martini.

Merling hands Miranda her martini, and they both raise their glasses lightly touching rims that ring as they meet and then they drink. Miranda licks her lips, "Oh, my god that tastes good. You make the best martini, Brad."

Miranda is thoughtful for a moment then says, "Of course, I'll help you if I can, but why me?"

"I need someone I can trust, someone who can understand the full scope of Vision World." Merling leans forward. There's urgency in his voice, "Vision World must go on no matter what."

"Why don't you have Jan help you?"

"She's not interested. You may not know this Miranda, but your sister is the First Lady of Washington Society. If you're not invited to her parties, you're one of the walking dead in Washington. She doesn't want to give that up. In fact, I need her right where she is. If anyone can find out what's going on in Washington, she can. At her parties all the secrets are learned. They're spilled out on bed sheets and in dark rooms, in closets and behind bushes." Merling laughs, "She knows more about domestic affairs then the CIA or the FBI put together."

"But what about my show?" Miranda asks.

"Miranda, if you accept Senator Lorenz's offer, and I continue giving you prime time coverage, they may kill both of us."

Merling sits down on the couch beside Miranda, and he puts his arm around her and says softly, "I need you by my side." He gently brushes his lips against her hair, "God, I miss you. Jan and I both do. Will you do it?"

Miranda thinks for a moment and says, "Under two conditions".

"What are they?"

"You're asking me to give up a lot for you, Brad, and if I'm going to do it, I don't want to work for you. I want to work with you. No orders".

"Agreed."

"The second condition is that I want a talk show."

"A talk show?"

"Yes, I'm going to socialize while I'm here. Invite people to dinner, interesting people. It will be a casual talk show."

"I don't know, Miranda. Maybe you should just shoot me now and put me out of my misery."

"Brad, it's perfectly harmless. And there's no way that I can get in trouble. It will be low key, not prime time, and it will only appeal to a literate audience, which is nearly nobody."

Merling doesn't quite believe her, but he can't resist another subplot. It may prove interesting, "All right, but I have the right to pull the plug if I think it is getting dangerous."

Miranda extends her hand, "It's a deal."

They shake hands, and Merling says, "Let's be bad and have another martini."

"Definitely."

Brad is about to make another martini when the phone rings and Jan appears on the screen. She asks if Miranda is there, and when Brad informs her that she is, she says, "Oh, good, tell her that I'm waiting for her out front."

"She'll be right down," Brad turns to Miranda and says, "You better go. She's very excited about seeing you." He smiles, "We'll have our martini shootout, later."

Merling hugs Miranda warmly and says, "Thank you, Randy. I knew I could count on you."

Miranda leaves, and he smiles to himself. Miranda is so easy to seduce. All you have to do is play her heartstrings. On the surveillance screens, he watches her walk down the hall to the elevator. As she approaches the elevators, Denny exits Hathaway's office.

Miranda waits for him, links arms, and says, "Where are you going? With me?"

"No, I'm not," He says then smile, "But I wish I was. I'm going to Brazil."

The elevator door opens, and they enter.

"When?"

"Today."

"Oh." Miranda is disappointed. "Why?"

"I have to follow up a lead. It seems that what happened last night in New York may be linked up with the attempt on Merling's life somehow."

Miranda is concerned, "Is it going to be dangerous?"

"It may be. I don't know."

"Are you going alone?"

"Yes."

Miranda thinks for a moment and says, "Why don't you take Ned with you. If I ask him, he'll go."

Denny hesitates, "No, you need him with you."

"No, I don't. I can get Jake if I want to, and Brad has his people around me. Denny, you want him. I can tell."

"I could use a back-up man, but I don't know anyone here that I could ask or trust."

"I'll ask Ned."

"OK, but let him make up his own mind."

"Oh, Darling, don't be silly. Nobody makes up their own mind around me. Haven't you noticed?"

Denny laughs, "All right, but tell him it is double pay for combat duty."

"Oh, he'll like that." Miranda smiles and then she puts her arms around him and says, "I'm going to miss you. Are you going to miss me?"

"Very much, Miranda." He is about to blurt out that he loves her when the elevator stops, and the doors slide open.

They enter the vaulted reception area of the Vision World headquarters and walk out onto the street. Miranda's sister waves frantically at Miranda from her limousine, and her two pink poodles burst out of the limousine and race up to Miranda. They are overwhelmed with joy as they jump up trying to reach her face with their tongues.

Miranda shouts, "Romeo, Juliet, stop it!"

Jan gets out of the car, and Miranda watches her sister walk from the limousine to the entranceway. Jan has the long legs of an haute couture fashion model, the skin of a teenager, and the figure of a female Olympic swimmer with breast implants. Her body is sprayed with diamond dust so as to highlight the sensuous curves of her legs and her breasts that are barely hidden by a micro-dress that is made of silk and an electro-organic fiber that changes color, shade, and tone unperceptively so as to create the illusion of a new and youthful Jan every moment. Miranda is envious. Jan is eight years older than Miranda, but she looks ten years younger. However, there is a price to be paid for Jan's narcissism. Both Jan and Brad are sterile from taking the anti-aging drug, and her only children are Romeo and Juliet.

Jan wags her finger at the dogs, "That's enough, now in the car." She points, and the dogs run then peer out from within, eager for more licks.

Jan turns to Miranda, "They miss you." She hugs Miranda. "I'm so glad you're here."

Jan pauses then looks Denny up and down and says, "Oh, what a nice watch dog, Miranda. Is he coming with us?"

"He's not a dog, Jan." She looks at Denny lovingly and says, "He's very much a man, and his name is Colonel Dennis Martino. Denny this is my sister, Jan Labelle."

Jan extends her hand, "You'll have to excuse me, Colonel, but I always get men and dogs mixed up." She turns to her sister. "But come along, dear, we have to be running." She hugs her again and says, "I haven't had you to myself for such a long time."

They are about to leave, but Miranda turns around

and hugs Denny, kisses him on the lips, and whispers in his ear so that Vision World can't hear, "Denny, don't let them confuse you with their labyrinth of lies. You are the Minotaur, and you will gore them in the end with the truth." She then turns and enters the car, waves goodbye, and they drive off leaving Denny behind with a confused look on his face.

Brad Merling, who has been watching Colonel Martino and Miranda on the viewing screen laughs. He sees a little love affair in the making. He likes the idea; it will add all sorts of nuances to the story. He envies them. He remembers when he first met his wife, Jan. It was a busy night at Odeon's, a cafe bar that he hung out at when he worked in New York City. It had just finished raining and everything glistened in the neon light outside. Even the gutters had an attractive darkness to them, and the limousines parked outside had streaks of light and color flashing across their sleek bodies, the chrome.

Soft black silk, pale white skin, dark red lipstick, and a lot of leg was sitting at the bar, and when she crossed her legs he saw her black silk garters and a glimpse of panties the color of Juniper. He had to meet her. Brad slipped out of the booth, and as he walked through the crowd, he looked around the room looking for someone who might know her, and then he spotted Ted Driscoll. Ted knew everybody.

He passed through the group grope of hands and elbows and asses and chests, silk and wool and flannel suits, all stirred up in a stew of hormones and sexual desire, perfumes and body deodorants, a polymorphic drunken swirl of spirits.

Merling tapped Ted on the shoulder. Ted turned around, and Merling got a whiff of scotch and breath mint as Ted shouted out Brad's name as if he didn't know it. Merling leaned over and shouted in Ted's ear through the laughter, the conversations, and the bedlam of booze, "Ted, who's the girl sitting at the end of the bar, black dress, big juicy lips, great bod...Don't stare...You're still staring."

"Oh, Jan Labelle, Phi Beta Kappa, Wells College, an MBA from Harvard, semi-rich and on the make, a real barracuda."

"What does she do?"

"She did some modeling, mostly ads, now she works for her father as a talent agent, quite good I hear." Ted smiled, "Would be actress."

"Thanks." Brad walked through the crowd and headed straight for the cherry red lips.

"Hi, I'm Brad Merling. Ted Driscoll tells me you do ads."

"So you're Brad Merling," She extended her hand.

"How do you know my name?"

Dark lashes revealed gray eyes, "I always keep track of who can do me and who can't, especially when they're up and coming casting directors, so to speak." Jan showed a slight trace of mockery in her smile.

Brad laughed, "Well, I'm definitely on the rise. What sort of ads have you done?"

"I've done lipstick ads."

"You've got beautiful lips. It was the first thing I noticed." He was totally sincere.

"Do you know why you noticed them, and why they're so magnificent?" She touched her red lips with her pink tongue.

"Why?"

"Because every time I open my mouth I look like I'm sucking cock." She touched him right on the tip of his dick with her finger and smiled, "Don't get too excited, Brad. It's merely a professional affectation. I've also done soap ads, and I can make you come all over your soap... just by holding it. Everything I touch, people want."

She casually ran her hands down her dress, across her hips. Her slip seems to be whispering to him. Buy. Buy. He feels foolish, out of control. He never met a woman before who could be so aggressively seductive. She turned him on. He wanted her to consume him with those blood red lips of hers, but he retreated behind his image as a businessman to buttress up his ego. He had what she wanted. He had to remember that. "I think I've got a part for you in a TV show. Are you interested?"

She took a silver cigarette case out, lit a cigarette, and blew lavender smoke in his face. "Brad, I have to tell you something."

"What's that?"

"You're not going to get to first base with me un-less you come up with a contract."

Brad smiled and said, "Do you have a card? I'll call you tomorrow and set up an appointment."

She opened up his jacket and kissed him on his nipple leaving a perfect lip mark on his perfectly white shirt. Then she reached into her purse, took out a pen, and wrote under the lip mark, By Labelle 272-6749. "Call me tomorrow," she said.

He looked at her calling card, her face, her smile. She had completely blown him away with the unexpected. He laughed, "We'll have lunch."

"We'll have dinner after I signed the contract. Ra-mon's. I don't like surprises."

Desperate to regain control, he played his trump card. He opened his hand to reveal a vial of coke. "Would you like to step into my office and discuss this now? It's pure Columbian, 100% pure."

She eyed the coke then said, "Oh, a surprise, how nice".

"I thought you said that you didn't like surprises."

She got up, linked her arm with his, and said, "I lied."

They passed through the crowd into the coed bath-room decorated in the art deco style, a lot of black and white, sensuously curved chrome, and cream lights. Most of the stalls were filled with couples snorting coke or fuck-ing, but they finally found one that was vacant. Brad took out the vial and spooned out some coke and offered it to her. She leaned over and gently opened her nostril, first one then the other and wanted more.

"Well, Brad, what do you have in mind?"

Brad took a couple of quick snorts for himself. "I'm thinking of blending the ads into the stories until the ads become the story. Do you think you can do it?"

"Let's see. Do you mean something like this?" She consumed him with a kiss. He could feel the wet fire on his lips as she whispered, "Passion's Flame by Avon, $69.95 at Bloomingdale's."

He laughed, "That's exactly what I mean, and something like this." He kissed the nap of her neck, the nakedness, as he inhaled the smell of early morning dew and violets touched with excitement. He sucked the lobe of her ear, "Bloomingdale's?"

"No, my pussy," she said as she loosened his tie.

Label by label she stripped him, getting all the prices right, until she had him stripped down to his underwear. She was about to take him in her mouth, but then she stopped. She looked at the label on his underwear, snapped the waist band so hard that Brad reached down in pain. "Ow, that hurt. What did you do that for?"

Jan got off her knees, and looked at him like she just discovered a bug in her bouillabaisse. "Fruit of the Loom, $6.95? Really Brad." Her voice was dripping with disgust, and she left him standing there in the toilet, his pants down to his ankles, completely exposed, and looking like a fool.

Brad laughs at the memory of her. What a great fuck she was. He couldn't get enough of her back then. But he's not interested in fucking one person at a time anymore. He wants to fuck the whole world, to come in their brains, the orifice of all creation.

Chapter Twenty One

The limousine in which Miranda and Jan are riding pulls away from the curbside leaving Denny behind. Miranda sits back in the plush black leather seat and says to her sister, "So, tell me everything. I haven't seen you in a year."

"My life is a complete bore. I only go shopping so that someone will be nice to me. I pretend to be interested in buying very expensive things so that they will kiss my ass. I get a call from a sales woman, and it goes like this.

"Hi, Jan this is Sally from Rulhoff's."

"Oh, Hi Sally."

"Jan, about the Ferrari that you were interested in buying, this year's model just came in."

"Oh yes," I say. "Why don't you stop by? We'll take a spin. How about lunch, my treat, I say."

Jan shrugs, "So I spend a couple of hundred dollars on lunch, but I still get off cheap. My psychiatrist charges me two hundred dollars just to say hello."

Miranda laughs, "Jan, I can't imagine you as a Victorian spinster."

Jan laughs as well and says, "It's true. I go to a medical doctor and complain about my aches and pains especially of the heart." Jan puts her hand on her sister's breast as if she were a doctor holding a stethoscope, "Now, breathe in and out, dear," she says. "Heave." Jan laughs, "I get hot just thinking about it. What a way to get felt up. It's so scientific and...healthy too. But, alas, I've fucked two heart doctors in the last three months, and I'm still not cured."

They laugh.

"What about Brad?" Miranda asks.

"Oh, Brad isn't turned on by me anymore." She lights a cigarette and stares out the window and studies her own reflection, the perfect features, and the sensuous lips. She's a masterpiece of plastic surgery and chemistry. For a moment, Jan is depressed, but then she makes up a new face, the face of a despondent child. "Oh, Miranda, all my lovers are such a bore, and now when I ask my mirror, who is the fairest of them all. It doesn't say me anymore. It says you."

"Don't be ridiculous, Jan. You're still the most beautiful woman in the world, and I'm still your dumpy little sister."

"That's true. But I wish I had that hunk Lorenz chasing after me."

"Jan, the Senator isn't interested in me. He's interested in the media coverage I bring to him."

"Oh, I don't know, dear. I watched you two on TV. It seems to me that he gave you the look, several times."

Miranda pauses to consider the possibility, "No, I

don't think so, Jan. But even if he were interested in me, it wouldn't matter. I think I'm in love with someone else."

"Not the Colonel?"

Miranda shrugs and smiles, "Maybe."

"Oh, dear, he's so common."

"No, he's not common. He's normal, and I love that about him. Remember the dark blue wool jacket sweater that I used to wear all the time? It was so comfortable and cozy that I often went to sleep in it. It was like my fur. Denny is like that."

"He sounds delicious. That's perfect then. You get Mr. Warm and Cuddly, and I get Lorenz. Oh, believe me. Arthur Lorenz will be easy. I know my men. Just leave him in a room alone with me and..."

"Mr. Warm and Cuddly is married."

"Isn't that always the case? And Arthur Lorenz is probably saving himself for history. Oh, they're all such assholes. They project their own faults on us. They all take it in the ass, but they call it the chain of command and then call themselves good soldiers rather than cock suckers."

Jan laughs then says, "And, when they are on top, when they're finally on top, they can't do it anymore. And the reason that they can't do it anymore is that they have totally deluded themselves all their lives. That's why we will rule in the end, dear. We know what's behind the makeup. They don't have a clue."

"You sound like you hate men, Jan."

"Oh, I don't. I love them. I love to abuse them. And they love to be abused by me because they know that their little egos are a farce, a balloon that they love to have deflated just to get rid of the pressure. Believe me, dear. They want to cut it off, to be passive and receptive, to be like us. They're tired of being dick heads, or at least the best of them are."

"Jan, are you sure that you and Brad can't have babies? Maybe that is what you need, someone to love beyond yourself, someone to care for and love unconditionally. I know I want that someday."

Jan begins to sob, "We can't. Brad and I are sterile. It comes from taking too many anti-aging pills."

"I know, but can't you just give up the pills?"

"And grow old! Oh, God, I couldn't stand it. Besides, I don't even know if the process is reversible now."

"You could try."

"Brad and I have been thinking of another option."

"What's that?"

"We're going to clone ourselves. We'll have a baby girl just like me and baby boy just like him. It's like living our lives all over again."

"You can do that?"

"Oh, yes, it's terribly expensive. But it can be done. It's still experimental, but there is a fifty-fifty chance of success. We'd be experimental models of course, and there are no guarantees, but you have to admit that the possibilities are interesting."

270

Miranda thinks about it. There truly are some interesting possibilities. Jan and Brad would be the mother and father of themselves. Miranda laughs and says, "You and Brad can get married all over again."

Jan laughs, "Yes, isn't that interesting, Miranda? I thought of that. Maybe we could do it right this time."

The limousine passes through the guarded gate to Jan and Brad's estate, and they travel along a roadway lined with giant black oak trees. The limbs embrace one another high above forming an archway of leaves turning multicolored. At the end of the roadway, Miranda can see an artificial lake, Japanese gardens, and a Frank Lloyd Wright house, modern but oriental in form. It's beautiful.

There is one thing that Miranda envies her sister for other than her looks, her body, and maybe her tits, and that is her home. Jan's home is a product of Vision World, and it is constructed along the same lines as Disneyland. In reality it is merely a bunch of building blocks made of vision board that can be arranged in any shape, form, and size. A satellite creates and controls the holographic images for the outside of the house and the grounds, and with some architectural and mechanical changes to the actual structure, they can create any home, any environment that they choose. Miranda would love to have one, but she knows for a fact that Brad paid one hundred million dollars for this set up.

Miranda turns to Jan, "Sour grapes says, so it's Frank Lloyd Wright this month, is it?"

Jan laughs, "Big sister who has everything says, Oh it has been Frank Lloyd Wright this month and last month and the month before that. We've gone through three Frank Lloyd Wright houses in six months. It's a phase that Brad is in."

Jan turns to her sister and says, "Quite frankly, I wish we could settle on one house for a while, but we have the ball coming up just before the elections, and we're planning something spectacular for that. We're going to need... I don't know what you would call them."

"More boxes?"

"Yes, more boxes." She sticks her tongue out at Miranda and continues, "And there is going to be a tremendous amount of landscaping done."

"What's the house going to look like?"

"The palace, my dear, but I can't tell you anymore. It's a surprise, and you're going to have to wait and see. But after that, I'm having Serge Horcutt design an estate house for me in the modern mode. You've heard of him?"

"Sure. He's really hot now."

"Yes he is. And, he's good in bed too. He's going to do something spectacular. He gets very few opportunities like this, where the only limit to what he builds is his imagination. I'm helping him with the plans. We made love on the floor plans already, and where I came, he's making that my bedroom. Isn't that clever and so romantic."

"Jan! "Not really."

"Really, and I must say that he fills the room quite

adequately."

They both laugh like little girls in bed at night telling each other forbidden stories.

Miranda watches the house come into view, the arbors of flowers and plants that form the terraces, the brown brick and green wood that blend into the floral symmetry, casual in harmony. The terraces lead to a rock garden, a pond, and a stream that leads to the lake surrounded by forests and trails.

When they arrive, Miranda goes directly to her bedroom. She is so tired. All she wants to do is to go to sleep. She looks out the window of the bedroom into the Japanese garden. It is so beautiful, but it is not real. Miranda begins to cry. She doesn't know what she is crying about, or what she is crying for. Maybe she is crying for everyone. Maybe she is crying for Brad and Jan. Maybe she is crying for herself. All she knows is that she needs to grow up and get out of this fairy tale turned into a nightmare.

Chapter Twenty Two

Denny and Ned are flying to Rio de Janeiro on a private jet owned by Vision World. Denny looks at his watch, and he sees that it is time for the TV show, *Father Knows Best*, starring Franklin Peters. He switches on the virtual reality TV then turns to Ned and says, "This is the show I was telling you about. This is the show that Merling has created to make Franklin Peters a star again."

On screen appears a picturesque view of Franklin and Brenda Peters' home, a simple two-story farmhouse built in the early 1800s. The house is painted light yellow, and the bright red front door is flanked by two antique colonial lanterns. A giant Japanese maple and a smaller but beautifully formed white oak tree shade the house, and the pathway leading to the front door is lined with beds of violets, blue geraniums, yellow daffodils, white poppies, and herbs. In the background is a red barn, an English maypole, and a blue and gold wooden birdhouse mounted high on a wooden post amidst a bouquet of hyacinth and ivy.

As Frank walks into the house he calls for his wife, Brenda.

"I'm in the kitchen, Frank."

Frank walks through the hallway. The wall opposite

the stair to the second floor is covered with hand painted wallpaper, a mural done in the American primitive style of the colonial and early Republican era. It is a panoramic view of Washington and the Potomac during this early period. There is a cluster of square little houses, and the White House is only partially built.

The only furnishings in the hallway are two banister-backed side chairs with woven wicker seats placed on each side of a maple candle stand decorated with fresh picked marigolds and orange tiger lilies. Frank enters the kitchen that is quite simple, modern, comfortable, and he finds Brenda preparing dinner. Brenda is wearing a light yellow dress and a bright red apron.

He kisses her on the cheek, "How was the show today?"

"You didn't watch it?"

"No, I'm sorry, Brenda, but the President called me in just as it was starting."

"It went well. We had Donny Andrews on from the Repeaters".

"The Repeaters, are they still going?"

"They have a new album out, but basically it's the same old stuff. Remember the song, *You're My Man*?"

Brenda, who was a professional dancer and singer earlier in her career, sings the song and dances suggestively sucking on the vowels as she reaches down and plays with Frank's zipper.

Their ten-year-old daughter, Virginia, who they

have nicknamed, Dumpling, walks into the kitchen, "Hi, Dad." Dumpling looks curiously at her mother and father. Her father has his hand up her mother's dress, and she seems to be feeling his pants.

Frank, embarrassed, steps away from his wife, and Brenda straightens her skirt.

"Hi Dumpling," Frank says.

"Look at what I did in school today, Dad." Dumpling stands next to her father and holds up a picture done in colored pencils of a tree and a stream. It is realistic, well-proportioned, balanced, and done in gay harmonious colors.

"You did that, Dumpling?"

"Yes."

"That's great."

"What about this?" She holds up another picture of a stick tree with dolls, little cars, boxing gloves, and flowers for leaves. The picture is crudely done with an off-colored sun in the background. In the foreground, a stick boy is running past the tree chasing a stick girl dressed in a yellow square and a red triangle for clothes. In his hand, the stick boy is holding what looks to be a sword.

"Hm, that's nice too," Frank says, but there is no enthusiasm in his voice.

"But you like this one better, I bet." She holds up the first picture that she showed him.

"Yes, I do. It looks more like a tree and a stream, and it's beautiful. Like you."

"Mom?" She holds up the two pictures for her mother. Brenda wipes her hands on her apron and looks closely at the pictures. "I agree with your father. I like that one."

"But why do I like this one better?" She holds up the more child-like drawing, "And why do my friends like it better too? Why, when I show these two pictures to adults, including my teacher, you like stuff like this?" She waves the pretty tree and the gaily-colored stream at her parents.

Brenda puts the arugula in the blender to chop it up, "Grown-ups look at things differently, Dumpling."

"How?"

"We like things that look pleasant to the eye."

"Like candy?"

"Yes sort of," Brenda says. She is curious about what her daughter has in mind. She knows she shouldn't, but she just can't resist asking, "Dumpling, what is it that the little boy has in his hand?"

"A rocket."

Brenda is trying to hold back her laughter when Rebecca comes in the kitchen and kisses her dad on the cheek, "Hi, Dad"

"Hi, Sweetie Pie," Frank takes the two pictures and shows them to his daughter, then asks, "Which one do you like, Becky?"

Rebecca picks up one of the sliced carrots that is on the cutting board and puts it in her mouth. She pauses, but only for a moment and casually points to the one that her parents picked out, "That one."

"Ah," Frank says, "That's grown-up stuff, but kids her age like this one better." He holds up the one that Dumpling likes for Rebecca to see.

Rebecca looks at the radish then at the sliced cucumbers. She can't decide which to take. She decides on the radish, looks at the picture, and laughs, "That's because they're polymorphic perverse."

Brenda looks up from her cookbook, "Do you know what that word means?"

"Yes."

"What does it mean?" Dumpling asks.

Rebecca looks to see what her mother is cooking. "It means that you better not show that picture to the school psychiatrist, or Mom and Dad may be getting a call to come to his office for a consultation."

"What does that mean?" Dumpling asks.

Rebecca pats her sister on the head, "It means that you're sick, Pop Tart."

Frank looks more closely at the picture that Dumpling likes. Puzzled, he says, "I don't see anything wrong with this picture."

Dumpling snatches it away from him, furrows her brow and says, "Philistines," then stomps out of the room.

Frank turns to his wife and says, "Does she know the meaning of that word?"

"I don't know," Brenda says as she sautés the garlic

and pancetta then puts the chopped arugula in the pan.

Frank smells the odors. He gets up and looks over his wife's shoulder and kisses her on the cheek. "Brenda, that smells wonderful. What is it?"

"It's a vegetable, herb, and pancetta sauce for pasta, very simple. One bunch of arugula chopped, two cloves of garlic chopped finely, one quarter of a pound of pancetta chopped, and one cup of chicken broth. Sauté the garlic and pancetta in olive oil, add the chicken broth and..." She peeks into the pot to see if the water is boiling, "And when the spaghetti is nearly done, you drain it and add it to the sauce along with the arugula. Cook for a few more minutes and top it off with parmesan cheese and, voile." She pours the spaghetti in the pot. "It will be ready when the pasta is done."

Rebecca puts her arm around her father, "Dad?"

"Yes, Sweetie Pie?"

"David and I want to go to New York this weekend to see the New York Philharmonic. We thought we'd take in a play, shop, and come back Sunday in time for school."

Frank's eyes widen, "What? Becky, you're only seventeen years old. And you want to go to New York for the weekend with your boyfriend?"

"It's an educational adventure, Dad."

"An educational adventure, is that what you call it?" Frank turns to his wife, "Brenda, has she talked to you about this?"

Brenda smiles then says, "Yes, but I told her to talk

to you. I wanted to see the expression on your face."

"Uh...Becky," Frank says, "I know that David is a fine young man, but alone together, in New York for the weekend?"

"Don't you trust me, Dad?"

"Of course I do. It's not that, but...I need to think about this."

"OK Dad, I know you'll come up with the right answer. Mom, can I help you?"

"Yes, dear, you can mix up the salad. I made the dressing. It is on the counter."

"No problem."

Brenda rolls her eyes, and she says to her husband, "Isn't it amazing how perfect they can be when they want something?"

"Mom!" Rebecca shouts.

Buzz walks in the kitchen and immediately smells the food, "Hi Mom, Hi Dad." He looks over his mother's shoulder, "What's for dinner, Mom?"

"Nothing, if you don't set the table".

"No problem, Mom." Buzz takes plates from one of the cabinets. As he is leaving the room, he turns to his sister. "Did you ask him, Becky?"

"Yes, I did."

Buzz mimics his father's expression when he is about to say something serious. "Frankly, Dad, I think it's all an elaborate plot to shack up."

Rebecca turns around and glares at her brother,

"Buzz, shut up!"

Brenda gives her son a warning look then says, "You heard your sister, Buzz. Shut up and set the table."

"Just an opinion," Buzz leaves the room.

Rebecca closes in on her father again, "Dad..."

Frank raises his hand and gestures for her to stop, then says, "I think I'll go watch the news."

Frank walks into the study and sits down in a wing chair upholstered in a light blue fabric speckled with white. Next to his chair is a child's red wicker chair, and in the background is a dark cherry wood colonial table with a Pennbury lamp. On the wall, above the mantle of the fireplace, is a painting framed in gold by the artist who did the canvas wallpaper mural in the hall. The painting is in the same style - a primitive of a village, a road, a horse and carriage, all-child-like. The focal point of the picture is a yellow toy house with a red door and blue squares for windows, the Peters' home in 1806.

On the mantle of the fireplace are Frank's Heisman Trophy, pictures of the team, Frank in action, Frank in a Marine uniform, and a picture of Franklin Peters being given the Medal of Honor by the President of the United States.

Frank turns on the TV, and Cheri Normal appears. Her trademark beauty is made mystical by her cross-eyed stare that seems to be looking inward like a soothsayer or a Vestal Virgin that is looking into the womb of illusion and the reality of Vision World.

She smiles voluptuously and says, "Today at the United Nations the General Assembly once again voted for a resolution that would establish a committee for the purposes of forming a new charter for the United Nations. The new charter would require all member nations to give up the right of self-defense and would establish an international military force composed of the member nations that would be responsible for maintaining world peace.

"The resolution states that it is within the power of the world government to ensure life, liberty, and the pursuit of happiness within the constructs of a bill of rights to be drafted to protect the individual states. In addition, the General Assembly recommended that the United Nations be given the right to tax its member nations and abolish the Security Council or amend the charter so that a two thirds vote of the General Assembly would over-ride a veto by any or all members of the Security Council."

Cheri smiles that smile of hers that is so neutral to life and death, joy and sorrow, "Once again the Security Council vetoed the resolution."

Her co-host Bill Hoch appears on screen and says, "An update on the Presidential election. A recent Gallop poll shows that the President and Senator Arthur Lorenz are in a near dead heat in their race for the presidency." In the background a graphic appears. President Theodore Dickson - 41 percent. Senator Arthur Lorenz - 41 percent. Undecided – 8 percent.

Frank hears Cheri's voice. "And disaster strikes

where we least expect it." On screen, a picture appears of Disneyland. In the picture a giant statue of Mickey Mouse is seen blown apart as are Huey, Dewey, and Louie - the childlike symbols of innocence and pre-pubescent youth, blown away.

Mickey's head is severed and cracked like a big black egg. A single eye looks down at the mangled remains of bodies strewn all about, and in the background is a roller coaster that curves like the Dow Jones chart of a very erratic stock that ascends out of sight into Pow Pow Land.

Dumpling comes into the room and sits in her little chair next to her father. She holds his hand and watches Cheri appear on the screen again and say, "In California a bomb exploded in Disneyland killing twenty people. The left wing terrorist group that has claimed to have planted the bombs is the People's Army. The People's Army is a new group that has made an appearance in the United States recently and is rumored to be behind the attempted assassination of Brad Merling, the President of Vision World and a member of the Commission. Later in the show we will have footage of the explosion at Disneyland as it happened and the moments before. We will hear and see and experience the moments of joy experienced by the victims before their death. Bill?"

Bill Hoch appears beside Cheri, "And, Cheri, later on in the show we will go to Watkins, Ohio. Tom Farr blew a bubble and flew away."

"You're kidding."

"No, I'm not Cheri, and to cap the show off we will be visiting with Professor Harold Stewart who has developed a controversial theory about how the universe was created and where we're going."

Cheri smiles, "Should I pack my bags?"

"According to Professor Steward, yes ..."

Dumpling picks her nose then tugs on her father's sleeve. "Dad, Dad."

"Dumpling, please I want to watch the news"

"But, Dad, I want to ask you something."

"What is it, Dumpling?"

"You know what?"

"What?"

"Well..." Dumpling can't think of anything. She just shrugs then gets up and climbs up on her father's lap. She fills the screen with her face then hugs him.

Frank laughs then says, "You're just like your mother, Dumpling. You can't stand anyone upstaging you."

Brenda appears in the doorway and says, "Dinner time."

Frank and Dumpling go into the dining room and sit down at the dining room table. The dining room is once again early American, primarily done in beige and browns, cinnamon, hazel, and fawn. White lace curtains and an Oriental rug give the room warmth as does the fire burning in the fireplace. Pink flowers decorate the dining table, and everyone joins hands as Brenda leads a short prayer of thanksgiving. Frank tastes the dish and says, "Brenda this is excellent."

Buzz chimes in. "Yeah this is great, Mom."

"I got it from one of the chefs who appeared on my show."

Frank twirls some spaghetti and is about to put it in his mouth when Rebecca says, "Dad, have you thought about it?"

"Yes, I have, Sweetie Pie, and I have a question for you."

Rebecca is weary, "Let's have it, Dad."

"Is David your friend?"

Rebecca looks puzzled, "I don't know what you mean, Dad."

Buzz breaks in, "He means is he your boy-friend, Goofy."

"Buzz," Rebecca says, "I'm going to kill you, if you don't shut up. All you want to do is cause trouble. You wait."

"No, Buzz is right," Frank says. "That is what I'm asking you, but I don't mean it to be flippant or rude." He gives his son a look of disapproval, "Nor do I want to probe into your personal life. But whether or not David is your boy-friend, in the true sense of the word, is important to me. And it should be important to you. Let me explain."

The theme music plays subtly in the background, the violins pulling the heart strings of the audience. "It's obvious that it's the boy in David that you get dressed up for when you go out, and it's the boy in David who gets you all excited when he calls. But what I'm asking you, Sweetie Pie, is more fundamental. Is David also your friend?"

Brenda looks pleased as Frank continues, "Is he a person you like and enjoy being with? Is he a person you trust and confide in, a person who is concerned about your feelings and is there for you when you need him?"

Rebecca is obviously bothered by this intrusion on what she wants. She is bothered by the fact that she has to think about it at all. "God, Dad, I don't know. What difference does it make?"

"I think you should consider these things."

Rebecca is still annoyed, "I will."

Brenda says, "Frank, why don't I call Aunt Lucy in New York and see if Becky and David can stay with her."

Frank turns to his wife and smiles, "That's an excellent idea, Brenda." Frank looks across the table at his daughter expecting to get a positive reaction.

Rebecca throws down her napkin and says, "Oh Mom! Dad!" She gets up from the table. She is near tears as she storms out of the room and climbs the stairs to her room.

Frank turns to his wife, "What's the matter with her, Brenda? I thought that was a good idea."

Buzz looks up from his pasta and says, "Aunt Lucy is a drag, Dad."

Frank is puzzled. He turns to his wife and says, "Should I go upstairs and talk to her?"

"No, Frank, you were right," Brenda says. "She needs to think about her relationship with David, and she has to realize that we're not just going to let her go off to New York without knowing where she is going to be. She has to make plans. I'm not letting her go if I don't think that she's going to be safe."

"I agree." Frank looks at his plate of pasta, forks some spaghetti and is about to put it in his mouth when Dumpling says, "You know what, Dad?"

"What Dumpling?"

"I thought of something."

"What's that?"

"I bet you'd make the best President."

Frank smiles, Brenda smiles too as Frank explains to his daughter, "I'm running for Vice-President, Dumpling."

"I know, but I bet you'd make the best President anyway," she says with certainty.

Frank smiles, "Why Dumpling?"

"Because I bet you are the best Dad."

Frank looks touched by his daughter's vote of confidence, "Thank you, Dumpling," he says then looks at his watch. "Oh, God, look at the time. I've got to get going."

Buzz asks, "Where are you going, Dad?"

"I have to give a speech tonight."

"What's the speech about?"

"It's about the economic war we're in, son and how

we're going to win it."

"How?" Buzz asks

"It's a three pronged strategy of attack, Buzz. First, we reconstruct the government so that it is more responsive to America as a business. Second, we finish the job of uniting North and South America as one economic unit. Third, with the unification of the two continents, we will control the most productive farmland in the world. And with food as a weapon, we will pry open the doors of trade."

"We're going to starve them out, Dad?"

"I don't think we'll have to go that far, Buzz. I think, that once they figure out what side their bread is buttered on, they'll come around."

Dumpling is confused and lost trying to follow the conversation. "What difference does it make what side your bread is buttered on, Dad?"

Frank and Brenda laugh. Then Frank says, "When you're old enough to know, Dumpling, I hope it doesn't matter."

She thinks about that for a moment then says, "When I become President, I'm going to make sure that everyone has cake for breakfast."

Brenda smiles and says, "I'm sure the French will love you. Now eat your salad, dear."

The doorbell rings. Frank excuses himself from the table, looks out the window, and then opens the front door. It's one of the Secret Service men assigned to Frank who says, "The car is ready, sir."

"Thanks Brian, I'll be just a moment." Frank returns to the dining room, and he says to Brenda, "I'm going to talk to Becky."

Frank then walks up the stairs to the second floor of the house. He walks through a hallway in which the walls have been exposed to reveal the original paint, a pale blue that fades in and out of itself and gives a feeling of the true age of the house. He knocks on the door to Rebecca's bedroom.

Rebecca is in her room casually looking through her wardrobe deciding on what she will wear on the trip. She hears the knock on the door, and she quickly jumps on the bed and puts on the look of a child in mourning as she says weakly, "Who is it?"

"It's Dad."

"Come in."

Frank's face expresses pain as he sees how forlorn his daughter looks. He sits on the edge of the dark walnut canopy bed. "Listen, Sweetie Pie, I'm only looking after you. I don't want you to get hurt."

"I know, Dad."

"Do you feel that you can trust David?"

"Yes, Dad, David is my friend. He wouldn't hurt me, not intentionally."

"OK, I'll trust your judgment on this, and if you want to go to New York, you may."

"No Aunt Lucy?"

"No Aunt Lucy, but you must work out with your mother all your travel arrangements, where you will be staying, etc."

"Oh Dad," she hugs him. "I love you."

"I love you too, Sweetie Pie. But you must promise me that you will be careful, and you won't embarrass yourself or us with any foolishness."

"Oh I promise!"

Frank leaves the room and goes down stairs. He hears gunfire from the study and peeks in. Buzz and Dumpling are watching a videotape of *Man of War*, a TV series about their father when he was a marine in Nicaragua. In this scene, Frank is calling in an air strike on his own position. He is in a bunker calling death down on himself and the enemy. Bombs drop all about him. The camera focuses on the enemy being blown apart. And in the midst of the explosions, Buzz shouts, "Remember this, Dad?"

Frank smiles, "I sure do, Son."

Buzz gives his father the thumbs up sign and says, "Kick ass, Dad."

Frank smiles and walks to the door where his wife is waiting for him, and says to Brenda, "I told her she could go."

"I thought you would, and, really, at some point we do have to trust them. My only concern is that New York is dangerous."

"I told her that she has to work with you on all the

travel arrangements, and I'll assign two secret service men to her. They'll be discreet. She won't even know that they are there, but she'll be protected at all times."

Brenda straightens his tie and kisses him on the cheek, "You know best, dear."

Frank leaves his home and walks down the pathway that passes through the garden. He is escorted by two secret service men. Another waits at the door to the limousine, alert, as are the military police that will escort him. The emergency lights on the patrol cars lazily flash red.

Denny turns off the TV, and he thinks about what he has just seen. What's the big deal? Nothing spectacular, just a pleasant sitcom revolving around Frank and his family who are searching for answers to day-to-day problems. Frank is sort of the straight man for the family, the brunt of many jokes, but in the end, the limousine comes for him with the secret service body guards, and you realize that this father, this man, is very important, very powerful. He carries the burdens of state.

Yet, he is still a father, and it is the father who appeals to us, the man who, through life's confusions, seems to stumble and play the fool. But in the end, guided by some very basic principles and common sense, he is able to come up with the answer, the smile, the care, and the direction we all need. This is the third show that Denny has watched, and this is always the theme. In the end - father knows best.

Denny turns to Ned and asks, "What do you think?"

"I think it's Zieg Heil, mother fucker. The Devil is back."

"I think you're right, Ned. But whoever thought he would come back in a sitcom."

"Hey, Cowboy, nobody ever said the son of a bitch didn't have a sense of humor."

Chapter Twenty Three

As the plane approaches for a landing, Denny can see Rio, the bay, the humped back islands that appear from out of the ocean like Leviathans of the deep. The city of white skyscrapers seems to float between air and water. The reflections in glass dazzle like diamonds, and the purple haze of the polluted clouds touch the outstretched hands of an immense statue of Jesus Christ that looks down on the mountains and tropical forests that surround the city and beaches.

When they land, Denny and Ned take a cab through what has to be the worst traffic Denny has ever seen in his life, madmen driving with no regard for any laws, horns blaring. His driver curses and sings his way through the chaos far below the skyscrapers, the immense buildings that have been built in the last fifteen years. Everywhere Denny looks he can see evidence of Yankee presence towering over the indigenous population in newer and higher skyscrapers, some of the highest in the world. They're all here, all the major corporations. Rio is to the new American Empire what Constantinople was to Ancient Rome. It is the new emerging capital, and the

United States is being slowly disserted by the parasites that have bled it dry.

The taxi passes into a winding tunnel that seems to go on forever. Ned, who is sitting in the front seat, has struck up a friendship with Renaldo, the driver. It seems they both have the same passion, cars. Denny hears Renaldo say, "Horses, man, horses. We still got the horses down here, Mr. Ned. I got two hundred and sixty horses under the hood in this piece of shit, man. And I can get you anything you want. You want a Firebird? I can get it. You want a Thunderbird in mint condition? You talk to Renaldo. I fix it."

"Forget the pussy cars, Renaldo," Ned says. "You got a 1969 Bonneville for me?"

"Oh, man, a 1969 Bonneville, very rare. You are certainly an aficionado, Mr. Ned. But if you got the mulla, I got the car, very rare, very beautiful."

They go on and on cubic inch by cubic inch about the virtues of the automobile, and Renaldo races through the narrow caverns passing one car after another, challenging the oncoming lights, the horns. They emerge from the tunnel only to enter another in the underground highway system. Denny reaches into his bag and places a micro-oxygen filter into his nostrils to protect himself from one of the most polluted cities in the world. He hands one to Ned who does the same. Denny notices that the driver has an oxygen mask attached to the dashboard. It looks like a World War II gas mask.

They emerge from a tunnel into the brilliant tropical light and drive along the Copa Cabaña beach swarmed with people, bodies, beautiful chocolate colored girls with blond hair and colorful bikinis. This is the Rio he remembers. The taxi pulls up to the Hilton, a high rise hotel resort of concrete and glass that faces the beach. Balconies and gardens of bougainvillea, passion flowers, and orchids form steps like an Incan temple down to the sandy beach.

Renaldo hands Ned his card and says, "If you want to get somewhere fast, Mr. Ned, I'm your man, anytime anywhere." He winks at Ned then speeds away.

Ned turns to Denny, "I think we got ourselves a wheel man."

"I thought you didn't like spics."

"Oh, I like'em fine in their own country. I just don't like em comin up north and taking jobs away from me and mine. No, I like em right here, where they belong." Ned looks around and smiles, "Nice place isn't it."

Denny and Ned enter the lobby that is modern and spacious with indoor gardens, palm trees, and fountains. They check in at the reception desk, and the bellhop leads them to the top floor and a two-bedroom luxury suite that overlooks the ocean and the beach below.

Denny immediately calls Valasques who sounds delighted to hear from him, and he makes arrangements to meet with Valasques at the hotel bar later in the afternoon. When he hangs up he says, "I'm going to get some sleep, Ned."

"Suit yourself, Redbone. I'm going to order a case of beer to put in the refrigerator."

"Good idea, partner."

Denny walks into the bedroom, closes the door behind him, sets the alarm, and collapses on the king size air mattress that gives him the feeling of sleeping on a cloud. He presses a button, and the glass panel that leads out onto the balcony slides open, and he listens to the roar of the waves hitting the surf and the sound of laughter, music, the samba beat that permeates the air with its undulating rhythms that first gives him a hard-on then puts him to sleep.

The alarm wakes him up several hours later, and he takes a cold shower and dresses in a white, casual, well-tailored suit. He puts on an aqua blue T-shirt of fine cotton and then puts on a pair of casual shoes. He looks in the mirror. Not bad. He likes being back in Brazil. It's vibrant and still wild and free in its chaos.

Denny walks into the living room. Ned is sitting at the couch with a beer in his hand watching TV. He looks Denny over and says, "You look like you belong here."

"It's the suntan, Ned. Come on. We got to meet our man downstairs."

Denny hands Ned a communication device similar to the one he is wearing. Ned puts the receiver in his ear and then hides the sending device underneath the collar of his shirt. "How do I look?"

Denny laughs. Ned is six foot six and lanky in a

powerful way with big feet and big hands. He's wearing antique aviator sunglasses, a crazy tropical shirt full of flowers, baggy jeans, and his work boots. He looks like what he is, an American redneck and the backbone of the American army, the kind of American who has been kicking the shit out of these people forever.

"You look perfect."

Denny and Ned go down to the lobby. They separate. Ned disappears into the shadows, and Denny walks into a lounge that is light and cheery with an abundance of glass, plants, flowers, and white woven bamboo chairs and couches with colorful floral cushions. He sits at the bar, orders a drink and waits, but not for long. Denny spots Valasques walking in the door wearing the uniform of a general in the American Army. He is amused by the fact that the hard and thin colonel he had known in his youth has become fat with age. Denny might not have recognized him at all except for the uniform, the walk, the arrogant casual air, the smile, and the mocking eyes that seem to look at everything and everyone and say, I know more about you than you know about yourself, and it's not good.

Valasques sees Denny and waves.

Soon they are face to face, and Valasques says, "You look wonderful, Dennees. You have grown well." He hugs Denny affectionately and kisses him on both cheeks.

"Valasques, you look good too."

Valasques laughs then says, "You mean I look fat,

Dennees, and so I should be. I'm a general now. We live in the suburbs. My wife is an excellent cook. We have three children, and I try never to leave the office unless I'm going to lunch. I never get my shoes dirty."

"Valasques, my friend, I need some information."

"So then this is a business meeting, not a pleasure trip. As I thought, I said to my wife after you called, why has my friend Dennees called me after all these years? He never calls me or communicates. It must be that I know something that he doesn't know, and once again he comes to his good friend Valasques for a lesson in life. Is this not so?"

Denny laughs and takes out the checkbook that Merling gave him. He punches some numbers into the computer checkbook and shows them to Valasques. The numbers read twenty five thousand dollars.

Denny then hands Valasques a portable phone, "Call your bank and ask them if you have received a deposit of twenty five thousand dollars in the last few seconds."

Valasques takes a long look at Denny then dials his bank. Someone answers on the other end, and Valasques asks, in Portuguese, for the bank manager. There's a pause. Valasques orders a drink. Then he converses on the phone for a moment. He hangs up.

"Dennees!" He reaches over and puts Denny's face in his hands and kisses him full on the lips. "I love you."

Denny smiles, "I thought you would."

Valasques looks out onto the patio where Ned is sitting. Their eyes meet. "I see you have a pistolero with you, Dennees."

"He tells me that you have two men with you. One is in the lobby and another is sitting over there next to the door to the patio."

"Yes, of course, there have been two attempts on my life in the last two years. They're my own personal bodyguards. Very trustworthy, but I can see your point. It's getting too crowded in here. We need to be alone."

Valasques stands up and grabs his drink, "Come, we'll take a walk out on the beach."

Denny picks up his drink, and they leave the lounge that exits onto a patio. The sky is a brilliant diffusion of light caused by the heavy smog. Blue-black clouds form beautiful pillows of pollution and beams of purple and yellow light that disperse in the heat. Denny remembers that the air is poison, and he reaches into his pocket to pull out the micro-oxygen filter. He's about to insert it into his nose, but Valasques stops him and puts it back into Denny's pocket.

"Don't bother. Be a Carioca," Valasques says. "We don't live long but we live well. This is the price of prosperity."

"It doesn't bother you?"

Valasques links his arm with Denny's as they walk onto the beach, "Sure it bothers us, but it is only a stage in our development. We burn everything, Dennees, the

Devil's own brew, and that is what has made Brazil great. When we become rich enough, like you, we will not have to manufacture anything. We will give up our cars for rapid transit. We will cool our homes with the energy from the sun. And we will leave the pollutants and the poisons for some other poor bastards who need a quick fix."

Denny realizes that what Valasques says is true. Brazil is one of the fastest growing countries in the world, and Rio is now larger and more prosperous than New York City, Los Angeles, or Miami, and, yet, despite the human waste, it is still a marvelous place.

Denny walks along the edge of the water and looks up at the line of skyscrapers that tower over the beach and recede back into the mountains where the jungle waits. Ocean waves crash against the shore exploding like a percussion instrument, the bass to the undulating tones that flood the beach with sound. It's a good place to talk, and he can barely hear Valasques' voice when he says, "So then, Dennees, tell me what you need."

Denny takes a folder out of his briefcase and shows it to Valasques, and as Valasques is reading, Denny listens to the water and feels the sand, the sun. He should have worn a hat, he thinks to himself. He reaches into his pocket and puts on a pair of sunglasses.

When Valasques is finished with the material in the folder, he hands it back to Denny. "You're interested in the People's Army."

"Yes and the two men? Do you know who they

are?"

"Well, this one is Pepe Gomez. He is as you say in your report, a CIA plant that went free-lance. And the other is Ramon. He's the leader of the group and the pipeline to the money."

"Do you know where the money comes from?"

"No."

"Is he a plant?"

Valasques shrugs, "They're old time Marxist, or so they claim."

"So you're saying to me that they're a radical left wing terrorist group whose goal is to violently overthrow the capitalist system?"

"No, I'm saying that's their rep, that's how they recruit and indoctrinate. But my hunch is that Ramon and Gomez are entrepreneurs capitalizing on revolution as a good tax dodge and a way to justify bank robbery, kidnapping, murder, and whatever else they may get paid for.

"Where do they work out of?"

"Up north."

"Do you know where?"

"Not exactly, but they work the small villages and towns along the edge of the Amazon."

"Why haven't you gone in after them?"

"It's not that easy. It would take a small army, and they're low on our priority list."

"Valasques, I need to find these guys. I need to know why they have made Brad Merling a target. Who's involved, and who's paying the bills and why."

"I'll see what I can do, Dennees."

"Valasques, if you can give me a hard-on, you can become a very reech man."

Valasques laughs, "Dennees, I'm your man."

He takes Denny's arm again, and as he leads Denny back to the hotel he says, "I won't disappoint you. Contact no one else. Do not go off on your own. You're on vacation here. You understand?"

"Yes."

"You will hear from me when I have something that will cause the proper erection."

Denny and Valasques work out a coded language to communicate the time they will meet. They establish where they will meet. Valasques writes out the address, hands it to Denny then embraces him in farewell.

As Denny watches Valasques walk away, he wonders if Valasques knows more than he has said. Jesus, he has just given that man twenty five thousand dollars for nothing. He really didn't tell him any more than he already knew, but Merling said to spend whatever it takes and not to worry.

Denny walks back up to the hotel, enters the patio, orders a beer, and sits down next to Ned and tells him everything that Valasques told him then says, "What do you think?"

"I think it's a disgrace that a sleaze bag like that is wearing the uniform of an officer in the United States

Army."

"When they became part of the Commonwealth we incorporated their army into ours, so we're stuck with him," Denny says.

"I know that, Redbone, but doesn't it bother you that we got officers like Valasques in our army and that fifty percent of our enlisted men are Latin American nationals now. Doesn't that make you a wee bit nervous?"

"Ned, do you know anything about the Roman Empire?"

"Nope, can't say I do, except I remember they were bad mother fuckers, and they ruled the world."

"That's true, but in latter day Rome when the best Romans got killed off in war and when the rest of the Romans were too lazy or decadent or rich to fight, they began to recruit barbarians, Germans who fought well for them, became good Romans. Some of them even became emperors."

Ned thinks on it for a moment then says, "What are ya tellin me, Redbone, that Lady Liberty has become an old whore who likes to take it in the ass?"

Denny shrugs, "Valasques is all I got to work with down here."

Ned belches in disgust, "What's next?"

"We wait around here for the call, but while we're waiting, we relax and look like we're on vacation. For starters, I'm going to take a swim and get some sun, how about you?"

"Nope, not me, I'm not goin in that water where all those critters live."

Denny laughs, "Ned, are you afraid of the water?"

"Let me put it to you this way, Redbone. If a shark came up to me and said, 'What the fuck do you think you're doing here?' I'd feel kind of foolish because I got no sensible fuckin answer."

Denny laughs again, "So what are you going to do?"

"I'm gonna to sit right here in the shade, drink my beers, and then go upstairs and take a nap in an air conditioned room. Wake me up when it's time for dinner."

"OK."

Denny returns to their room, changes into a bathing suit, and returns to the beach well-oiled. He lies down on the sand to take in the sun and the beach scene, all the shapes and forms, the near naked beautiful women glistening in the blazing sun, the couples embracing and stroking each other to the ever-present music, the beat that compels them to dance and play, to merge then disappear into the blue water and reemerge again in the blazing sun, water pouring over kisses. Butterflies flutter all about the beach, and frigate birds with vast wing spans and forked tails glide upon the winds, over penthouses, and down into the pollution amidst physical fitness and narcissism in 100 degree heat.

An old man jogs by, and down on the other end of the beach, a group of young bathers play volleyball amidst laughter and cheers. Denny gets up and walks into the water, the waves lifting him up, the coolness sending chills through his burning body as he plunges into the green blue depths. The city seems to float in the background. Rio feels fluid, throbbing, swelling with the heat then exploding again in waves, crescendos of laughter, shouts.

Denny stands up in the water and walks toward the beach the water receding, pulling him back as the ground gives way under his feet. It reminds him of Miranda, being alone with her on the balcony and looking into her eyes. He braces himself at this point where yin and yang meet and tries to maintain his balance until the world stands still again.

Chapter Twenty Four

The next day, after Denny receives a phone call from Valasques to meet him that evening, Denny and Ned decide to kill some time and take a tour of the city. Renaldo acts as their tour guide and drives them to a national park where they follow a road that winds its way up a mountain and through a tropical forest. Renaldo pulls into a visitor's parking lot, and they walk up a trail to the summit. It's been a long time since Denny has been in a tropical forest, and he has forgotten how beautiful it can be. The massive trees have roots like giant arms and hands that dig into the soil. Vines and plants wrap themselves about the trunks of the trees climbing up the branches, intertwining, forming a cathedral ceiling of leaves and light beaming in upon bougainvilleas, passion flowers, flamboyances, and spider flowers. An armadillo crosses the path, and a blue, orange, and white parrot is perched in one of the trees. The bed of the forest is quite sparse, shadowed with light dispersed among the leaves, the ferns and bamboo, the sago palms. An orchid lounges at the base of a tree like a beautiful woman.

By the time they reach the summit the sun is setting. Denny sees the colossal statue of Jesus Christ and below his outstretched hands a panoramic view of Rio draped in the purple and orange and gold sunset. Denny finds Rio an interesting mix of primeval forest, geometry, calculus, physics, surging ocean waves, and burning sun. It is like an alchemist's elixir, poisonous but beautifully alive with black vultures soaring over the head of Jesus Christ like a crown.

Denny turns to Ned and says, "Beautiful isn't it?"

"Yah, she's like a beautiful whore that you don't want to marry, but you have to have her no matter how much money she costs you. And...once you have her, she'll ruin your life, man. Destroy your family. Take all your money, swallow you up, and then go on to the next john."

Denny smiles, "She's the jungle, Ned, and she's beautiful and dangerous, and you're right, she will eat you up." Denny smile, "They'll never tame this city."

Denny looks at the time, "Come on, we got a meeting to go to."

Ned and Denny get back into Renaldo's cab, and he drives them back down the mountain to the old part of the city. As they near their destination, Denny can see that amidst all the changes and modernization there still remains a square of buildings that have survived from the colonial period - stucco townhouses with wrought iron balconies, pastel shutters, and terra cotta tiled rooftops. A Baroque cathedral stands at one end of the square, its spires dwarfed by the skyscrapers. The area is dotted with shops and restaurants, galleries and outdoor cafes. The cab pulls up to one of the old townhouses that is painted ochre with lavender shutters that are badly stained with soot from the pollution. A red neon sign reads, *The Red Parrot.*

Denny says to Renaldo, "You stay here with Ned. He'll tell you what to do."

"Yes, sir."

Denny gets out of the cab and enters the cafe. The interior of the Red Parrot is dark and cool with old wooden high-backed booths and art deco murals of jungle scenes, a jaguar that is a dark shadow within dark green, light in the form of tropical flowers, a python coiled about a tree with winged leaves, and a red parrot sitting on a limb watching.

Denny spots Valasques in one of the booths and joins him. Valasques extends his hand, "Dennees, would you like a drink?"

"No, do you have anything for me?"

"Yes, I think so. I have a member of the People's Army that is willing to talk to us. He's passed on information before, and usually the information is quite reliable."

"Then what are we waiting for? Let's go talk to him."

"Patience, Dennees. It is probably no surprise to you that there are many people here in Rio who would like to know what you are doing here. It is fortunate that I am a loyal friend."

"How much?"

"Oh, Dennees, you are my kind of man. I risk my position, my life, my sources for you, and immediately you want to reward me."

Denny takes out the checkbook, "Valasques, this better be good because..."

"Dennees, you don't need to remind me whose money I'm taking, but you've got to keep reminding yourself that you are here, alone, with no one to guide you but me. We've got a lead, a good one, but this is dangerous business, very dangerous business. And I'm not leaving the comfort of my office and risking the safety of my children for twenty five thousand dollars. It's not half enough."

Denny takes out the computer checkbook, taps in twenty five thousand dollars, and hands the phone to Valasques, "Call your bank."

"No need Dennees." Valasques smiles showing his bad teeth, the product of an early childhood of poverty that no dentist can mask. "I trust you," Valasques says. "Now we can go."

"Where are we going?"

"To one of the favelas up in the mountains. Do you have a gun?"

"Yes."

"Good. Let's go."

Denny and Valasques leave the cafe and get into

Valasques' car. He has his two bodyguards with him. One is driving. The other bodyguard is riding shotgun. Denny glances out the rear window to see if he can see Renaldo and Ned. He can't. That could be good or bad. Either Renaldo knows what he's doing, or he's fucked up already.

Denny sits back and looks out the window. They move quickly through downtown Rio. The sun has nearly set when they enter a tunnel and then finally emerge into the darker sky and a road leading up a mountainside into the slums. The road becomes narrow, muddy. Even with a four-wheel drive, the driver is having difficulties maintaining the car on a road that finally ends on a bluff overlooking the city. The driver turns the car around so that it is facing down the mountain, and then he stops. Valasques says to Denny, "We'll walk from here."

They get out of the car, and Valasques points to the view of the city far below. The dots of light that are appearing everywhere look like a diamond necklace ringing the bay that is now a dark lavender blue in a black background with sprays of orange and red.

"Only in Rio do the poor live in the best part of town," Valasques says.

One of Valasques's men stays with the car. The other disappears into the darkness as Valasques and Denny walk up a pathway past houses built of planks and brick, stone and mud, tin cans, plastic bottles, corrugated steel, anything that will hold together the junk pile of dwellings that are stacked one upon the other.

It is becoming increasingly more difficult to see as the sky darkens. Denny realizes that he is walking down a dark pathway with Valasques with no idea where he is going. This could be a trap. What a fool he is to have allowed himself to get caught up in this case. Denny takes the safety off his gun as they approach a shack made from bricks and planks. It's built up on stilts so as to free itself of the garbage and trash below and the mudslide that this hillside must become when it rains. They walk up onto a porch and brush aside damp wash hanging on a line.

Valasques knocks on the door. A man answers and lets them into what, surprisingly, is a comfortable living room furnished with handmade furniture made simply but well. There's an old high intensity color TV and an old fashioned stereo, a simple little black box with knobs and a few lights. The walls are filled with shelves and shelves of books. Something Denny hasn't seen in years except in the homes of the very rich.

The man is medium build with deep-set eyes, dark features, and chocolate colored skin. Denny notices what may be a trace of Indian blood in the high cheekbones, and when the man speaks his voice seems refined, educated. He asks Valasques if Denny speaks Portuguese.

Denny responses in Portuguese, "Yes I do."

"Good, we can speak directly. What do you want to know?"

"I want to know who's behind the attempted assassination plot of Brad Merling, and what they're up to. I want to know whatever you can tell me about the People's Army."

The man studies Denny for a moment. "You mean the big network guy they tried to knock off recently."

"Yes."

"Do you have any identification that will prove that you are who the General says you are?"

"Who does he say that I am?"

"He says that you're a high ranking detective in the military police."

Denny reaches into his coat and shows the man his ID. The man studies it for a moment and hands it back to Denny.

It's Denny's turn to ask a question, "Who are you?"

The man reaches for a bottle of what seems to be homemade brew and pours himself a shot. He gestures toward Valasques who declines, as does Denny. The man sips the drink then gets up and opens the refrigerator. "I'm a member of the People's Army." The light from the refrigerator pours across the room as the man pulls out a bottle of water and takes a swig from it then returns to the table, bottle in hand.

Denny asks, "Then why are you willing to talk to us?"

The man sits down and says, "I'm also a member of the Union Party. Are you familiar with us?"

"Yes, social democrats who want to see a unified South America independent of the United States. What are you doing in bed with the PA?"

"I was ordered to infiltrate the organization, which I did."

"Why are you willing to help me?"

"We feel that Senator Lorenz's survival is important to our cause."

Denny is taken completely by surprise. "Wait a minute. Lorenz? What does this have to do with Arthur Lorenz?"

"We know that there is a death squad in the United States right now. We know they have a hit list, and Arthur Lorenz we believe is the main target."

Now Denny is really confused, "Arthur Lorenz and Brad Merling? What do they have to do with one another? It doesn't make sense."

Valasques breaks in, "It does if you want to look like a radical terrorist group but you're something else."

"So you target the Chairman of the Commission? That's over doing it a little bit, don't you think?"

Valasques shrugs, "Maybe Senor Merling is out of favor, and they figure that they can kill two birds with one stone."

"Who's they?"

Valasques turns to the man, "Who do you think is behind this?"

The man shrugs, "There are people here that would like to see Lorenz dead rather than be elected President of the United States. In his books he has supported a United

States of South America. He sees it as a necessary stage in the development of Latin America and a prerequisite to our joining a Federation of Western States. He has a large following here. We believe in his democratic vision. Many people do. We believe that if he is elected President, it will mean the end of the corporate state, both here and in your country. The man has many enemies."

"Who?" Denny asks.

The man smiles and says, "The status quo."

"Does the People's Army have any connection with the Commission?"

"I don't know."

"I wouldn't discount Merling," Valasques says. "The attempt on him may have been bogus. He may be behind all of this."

Denny face expresses doubt, "That's stretching it, isn't it?

Valasques smiles and says, "Dennees, my friend, we're dealing with spiders here who build complex webs. Anything is possible."

Denny turns to the man again, "Can you tell me where the central command headquarters is?"

"Yes, I can." The man gets up and goes to a desk that is merely an old door standing on crates painted in bright colors. He returns with a map, spreads it out on the table, and with a pencil circles an area. The area is up north near the edge of the Amazon jungle.

Denny turns to Valasques, "Do you know the area?"

"Yes, the town is named, Saint Gregory, and it is one of many towns that have sprouted up near the mining projects. The People's Army is known to control the area. They control the union that represents the mine workers."

The man interjects, "They take bribes from the owners, keep labor in line, throw them a crumb from time to time, and if anyone complains, they disappear."

"Where is the operation's headquarters?" Denny asks.

"In a farmhouse outside of town within easy access to the jungle." The man marks the precise location of the farmhouse.

"Do you think that we will find a clue to what is going on there?" Denny asks.

"You might."

"Do you think there is anyone left there who knows what they're up too?"

"There may be."

The beeper on Denny's phone goes off causing Denny to nearly jump out of his skin. He takes the phone out of his pocket and answers the call. It's Ned. He listens to the voice on the other end. "Do you know who they are?" Denny asks. "How many? Where are the bodyguards?" He listens then ends the communication and turns to Valasques, "We're in deep shit. My man has spotted a squad of men coming up the path."

"What about my bodyguards?"

"They're dead. Let's get out of here!"

The man is in a panic. He begins to scoop up the maps. Valesques takes out his gun and shoots the man in the head sending him sprawling backwards, killing him instantly. Denny looks at the man, the blood pouring out.

Valasques grabs the maps and shouts at Denny, "Let's go!"

Denny pulls out his own gun and follows Valasques. They leave the house on the run, plunging into the darkness, running in-between the shacks and splotches of life. They hear a tremendous roar. They look back to see that the shack has exploded into a ball of fire.

"A rocket," Valasques says as they continue to scramble downhill.

Valasques seems to know where he is going as the fire caused by the explosion ignites the neighboring shacks. Denny can hear screams and shouts. Lights are going on everywhere as Denny and Valasques continue to slip and slide down the hill. Denny grabs on to whatever he can, clothes on the line, a plank siding to a shack that comes loose. A nail cuts into Denny's hand. Denny falls over a bicycle and puts his wounded hand through the spokes and the wheel, and the bike collapses on his leg.

"Jesus Christ! Son of a bitch!" he shouts. A dog is barking. A door opens and a man appears in the light.

Denny shouts at the man, "Get the fuck back in there, or I'll blow your fuckin brains out!"

The man immediately ducks back into his house. The lights go off, but the dog continues to bark.

Valasques, who is breathing very heavily, helps Denny up. He can hardly speak as he says, "Only a little farther Dennees."

They can see that the explosion has set fire to many of the shacks. The sky is bright with the fire. They keep going until they reach the road. They pause using the bushes near the roadside as cover.

"Give me your communicator," Valasques says. Denny hands it to Valasques, and he calls in for help.

Denny looks back into the darkness, "Maybe we should keep on moving down the road," he says.

"No, we got good cover here Dennees, and either a fire truck or the police or my men should be coming up that road soon. It's the only road to the favelas. And besides, I'm too fuckin tired to move."

Valasques sits down on the hillside, and when he gets his breath, he looks up at Denny, laughs and says, "You have nearly got me killed Dennees. Look at my shoes! They are filthy. Never, never did I think this would happen to me again."

Denny sits next to Valasques, "Can you arrange a raid on the People's Army base of operations?"

"I alone? No, I will need the cooperation of an Air Force General that is a good friend of mine. The ordinance, the men, the planning, the security, especially the security, one leak and... The men cannot know where they will be going, not until the last moment. It will be very difficult."

"Can you do it?"

317

"I can do anything for the right price, Dennees."

"How much?"

Denny and Valasques hear a car coming down the road, and they duck down into the bushes. Denny has his gun ready. Where are the fire trucks? Where are the cops, the sirens? Where are Valasques's men? Come on, damn it, get here, he says to himself, as he clicks the safety off.

The car stops about fifty yards up the road.

The headlights of the car blind him. He hears a door open, but he still can't see. Should he fire now while he still has some sort of target? Jesus Christ, we got shit for cover here. Denny thinks about moving back into the woods, but then he hears what sounds like a bullhorn.

"What the fuck is that?" Valasques asks.

Denny laughs, "That's a fart." Denny stands up and shouts. "Over here, Ned."

He hears a door slam and the car races down the road and pulls up in front of them. Denny sees Renaldo at the wheel, and he hears Ned say, "Want a lift, girls?"

Valasques and Denny race for the car, get in the back seat, and the car speeds away. Denny slaps Renaldo on the shoulder and says, Renaldo, I love your cubic inches. Then he turns to Ned and says, "What happened?"

"I was hiding in the woods. Renaldo and I got some guy down the road to let us park the car in his garage. I love the people around here. They'll do any-thing for money, no questions asked. Anyway, these guys come on real slick, no car, nothing. They waste his two guys real easy. I was impressed. That's when I called you."

"Did you get a look at them?"

"Nope, they were dressed in black, wore face masks, the whole bit."

Valasques gives Renaldo directions, and Denny can see from Renaldo's face in the rear view mirror that he knows who Valasques is, and he's scared to death. There's no talking, no laughing.

Valasques turns to Denny and says, "You can't go back to the hotel. It's not safe. I've got a place for you. We'll go there." Without a word of gratitude to Ned and Renaldo who have just saved his life, Valasques, in a gesture of dismissal, slides the bulletproof panel closed to give Denny and himself privacy.

"Why did you shoot that man?" Denny asks. "There were a lot of other questions that I would have liked to ask him. He was a valuable informant."

"Dennees we are probing into the affairs of the most powerful men in the world. And, somebody, whoever they are, does not want us nosing into their business. When you're playing big time ball like this Dennees, the operational order is, no loose ends and no witnesses."

"Our man in the shack was a loose end?"

"Oh, most definitely, he would have gone back to his people and told them what we were after. The People's Army may have a plant in their organization. One phone call and we would be dead men."

Denny thinks about what Valasques said. He may

be right, but Denny doesn't feel good about himself. He doesn't feel good about being just another one of the animals in the jungle trying to survive. For what? For Merling or Lorenz? Are they worth it? He doubts it.

Denny slides the protective panel open and says, "Listen, Renaldo, I want you to get the Bonneville for Ned. There should be a nice commission in it for you, right?"

Renaldo smiles broadly, "Yes Senor Martino."

"Hey, Redbone, wait a minute I can't afford that car."

"No problem, Vision World is paying for it. You just saved our lives, buddy, and this is the pay back."

"But Senor, we might have problems getting it out of the country. They have strict restrictions," Renaldo says.

"Don't worry about that," Denny says. "The General here is appreciative, and he will smooth the way for you. Isn't that right, Antonio?"

Valasques nods indifferently.

Denny smiles, "See. No problem."

Denny slides the panel closed, and he watches Ned and Renaldo. They are like two little kids as they talk about Ned's new toy and Renaldo's newfound riches.

Valasques pats Denny on the knee. "You spend other people's money very well, Dennees. You're a born leader."

Chapter Twenty Five

The car pulls into a building complex that looks like a fortress from the outside, solid walls. But when they pass through the guard gate, the interior reveals large expanses of glass and asymmetrical clusters of condos bonded together by a large pool, a shopping mall, and tree lined walkways.

Renaldo pulls to a stop in the parking lot, and Valasques points out the way to Denny and Ned and says, "Go ahead. I need to talk to Renaldo for a moment."

As Denny and Ned walk along a pathway, Denny looks back, and he sees the fear on Renaldo's face as he listens to Valasques. Valasques gets out of the cab, and Renaldo drives away. When Valasques joins them, Denny asks, "What did you say to him?"

"All these cab drivers sell information, but, Renaldo and I understand each other. He will keep his mouth shut."

"Where are we going?"

"I keep an apartment here for my little amusements." He smiles, "Even my wife doesn't know of my little nest, so that means nobody knows."

Valasques walks up one of the narrow paths that

separates the condos, stops at one of the doorways, unlocks the door, and then gestures for Denny and Ned to
enter. They walk into the condo, and Denny is surprised at
how tasteful the condo looks. It's a three-story condo with
a winding staircase. The bright red, orange, and yellow
staircase seems to float in the air, and blue and green neon lines and dashes of light weave their way up the stair-
well to a circular skylight. The walls and ceilings are white
on white with bleached white oak floors with shadows of
blue from the neon glow. In the living room, the chairs and
couch are black leather and chrome. The coffee table and
end tables are swirls of colors that geometrically balance
planes of glass.

Denny sits down on the couch, and Valasques
leaves the living room, enters the elevated dining room,
and then disappears into what seems to be the kitchen.
Denny yawns. He stares drowsily at the asymmetrical
marble fireplace and a stone inscribed with ancient Indian
hieroglyphs that hangs above the mantle. On one wall is a
large painting composed of strips of color vibrating in contrast to one another, red and orange, green and purple,
black and white.

Valasques returns with two bottles of beer. He
hands one to Denny and the other to Ned and says, "I will
have someone pick up your clothes and things and deliver
them to you tomorrow." Valesques smiles, "How do you
like it?"

Denny is confused for a moment. He doesn't know

what Valasques means then he realizes that he is talking about the apartment, "Very tasteful, Antonio. You surprise me. I never knew that you were a lover of art. To be honest with you, I always thought you were a tasteless son of a bitch."

Valasques laughs, "You're right, Dennees. It was my mistress that hired the designer. She loves it. And to tell you the truth, I do too. I feel like I got some class when I come in here. No?"

Denny smile, "Yes."

"Ah, but let me show you my masterpiece."

He walks over to a glass table supported by a white ball and a black cone. On the desk are a computer and a picture framed in gold. He picks up the picture and returns with it. "Is this not beauty, Dennees, or am I a fool?"

The picture is a composite of shots of a girl who is probably in her early twenties. She has dark short-cropped hair, chocolate skin, dark brown oval shaped eyes, a pert nose, and full lips. Her body is nymph-like with small breasts and tight tummy, pretty fawn-like legs and a buttock that is shaped like an apple. She is in that wonderful stage of growth between sunrise and sunset, half girl, half woman.

Denny teases Valesques, "This is your girlfriend? No way."

Denny hands the picture to Ned who looks at the girl, belches quietly, then says, "Tasty."

Valasques grimaces with disapproval, and he grabs

the picture out of Ned's hands. For a moment the two men lock stares and what passes between them is absolute hatred.

"She's beautiful," Denny says.

"Yes." Valasques says. He returns to the picture and looks with fondness on his masterpiece. I found her when she was fourteen in a rebel camp that we raided. Her parents had been killed, so I brought her back here with me, paid for her care, her education. And when she was ripe, I plucked her. And now she's mine." Valesques handles the picture tenderly. He seems to be reminiscing upon moments that he has had with the girl. He is obviously in love.

Denny is anxious to get back to business, "Valesques, will you arrange a raid on the People's Army command headquarters?"

Valesques looks up from the picture. He seems to muse over the question for a moment, and then he places the girl's picture down tenderly upon the table and says, "Dennees, quite seriously, we almost got killed tonight, and I'm not as young as I used to be. And, as you can see, I have a good life here. What you paid me was very nice, but I can blow that in the Disneyland casinos in one weekend."

Valesques pauses for a moment to think, to calculate, then says, "It will cost you a million dollars for me alone. I don't know what my friend in the air force will want, probably more, he is a very greedy man. There will be many people to grease. Everyone will have to be paid in order to insure their loyalty and silence."

I need him, Denny thinks. He's my only shot at solving this mystery, "I will give you five hundred thousand dollars up front for your expenses and one million dollars upon satisfactory completion of the mission. I will cut your friend the air force general the same deal. I can't believe anybody is more greedy than you, Valesques."

Valesques laughs, "But what about operational expenses, ordinance, and personnel?"

Between you and your general, you have a million dollars in seed money to cut up and piece out anyway you want, and the remainder in hell if you don't give us our money's worth. That's the deal. Take it or leave it."

"It's done. I will make the necessary arrangements."

"How soon?"

"Soon," Valaques gets up. "You're tired and probably would like to take a shower and go to bed. You should feel perfectly safe here. There is excellent security, and..." He reaches into his pocket and pulls out a card, writes on it, and hands it to Denny, "If you want to go anywhere, call this number. I will have a man available with a car to take you anywhere you want to go. Renaldo has been useful to you, but he is too risky. He knows too much already."

Denny takes the card and sets it on the coffee table. "Thank you."

Valesques extends his hand, "What was it you used

to say when we went out on a mission? Let's..."

Denny smiles, "Rock and Roll."

"Yes, that was it. Well, Dennees, it looks like we are going to lock and loll. How do you feel about it?"

"Scared."

Valasques whispers in Denny's ear as if he were giving him a kiss, "Me too. But to tell you the truth, I would have probably done this for free. It gives me a hard-on just thinking about it. How about you Dennees?   Did I give you a hard-on?" He pulls Dennis closer. "Yes?"

Denny gives Valesques a friendly shove, "Get the fuck out of here you old pervert. I have to get some sleep."

Valasques laughs then extends his hand to Ned and says quite pleasantly, "Pleasure meeting you, Mr. Ned."

Ned glares down at Valasques then turns his back on him and walks away.

Denny says, "He doesn't like you, Valasques."

"He's a pig," Valasques whispers. "Where did you get him, Dennees?"

"Home grown, Valasques, made in the USA. He's why nobody's ever tried to invade the United States. We got a lot of them left up there. Come on up, and I'll intro-duce you to his friend Jake. Jake will cut off your hand, shove it up your ass, and shake hands with your dick."

"Dennees, nobody wants your fuckin country any-more. You can keep it." Valasques smiles and slaps Denny on the back, "I must go now. Fear not. I will arrange everything."

Valesques leaves and Denny sits down. Ned is looking at him in an accusatory fashion. "What's the matter with you?" Denny asks.

"You gave that sleaze-bag all that money?"

"I didn't give that sleaze-bag all that money. I bought an army."

"Some army," Ned looks around the room and says, "Being in here is like being inside a pussy."

"It's safe."

"Maybe," Ned says as he gets up and goes to the kitchen for another beer. When he comes back he stands near the stairway and says, "You know, Denny, some people think I'm dumb. I can't understand some things, but that's because my mind don't like all the little kinks and wormy turns. You know what I mean. Some things aren't meant to be understood. To understand Valasques, for example, you have to have a mind like a snake, and if you got a mind like a snake, you are a snake. No, the best idea is not to understand Valasques. The best idea is to kill him. Do you understand what I'm saying, Redbone?"

"I'm not a fool, nor a snake, Ned."

Ned smiles, "I know. I wouldn't be here if I thought so. But just remember, when in doubt...don't hesitate. Kill that mother fucker."

"Got it," Denny yawns, "Listen I'm beat. Where do you want to sleep? There's got to be a bedroom upstairs."

"I looked, only his and his whore."

"You can have it," Denny says. "I'll sleep here on the couch."

"No way, I'm not sleeping in his bedroom."

Denny shrugs and gets up from the couch. "All right, Ned, whatever makes you comfortable. Get some sleep, and I'll see you tomorrow."

Denny goes into the kitchen, gets another beer, and ascends the stairway to a bedroom. The bedroom has a balcony that overlooks the plaza and the pool. The bed is large and comfortable. Denny sits down on the edge of the bed, takes out his phone, and calls his wife. There is no answer. He gets undressed, enters the bathroom and takes a long shower then returns to the bedroom and lies down on the bed. He can smell the girl, and it makes him think of Miranda.

"Damn," he says. He forgot that the premier of Miranda's talk show is tonight. He looks at the time. He's late, but he may be able to catch some of it live. He looks for the controls and finds the control panel for all the bedroom functions on the night stand. He taps the icon for the TV, and he is not surprised to see that Valasques has all the latest Vision World technology.

Miranda's talk show is taking place at her home in Georgetown, a white brick colonial townhouse with dark navy blue shutters and a delicately pillared doorway. The format for the talk show is a dinner party, and Miranda is seated at the head of an English mahogany dining table, circa 1776. At the opposite end of the table is Senator

Arthur Lorenz who is obviously her co-host. Denny laughs. What made Brad Merling think that he could exile Miranda to TV Elba? Denny touches the screen where each of her guests are seated, and a pop up appears telling him that seated about the table are Karem Gupta, the Ambassador of India to the United Nations; Cheri Normal, Denny's favorite TV newscaster and sex symbol; Roger Baines, the head of World Bank and a member of the Commission; and Serge Solkov, the Russian Ambassador to the United States.

The table is set with cream colored china that has a simple border of olive green and gold, a pattern reminiscent of ancient Greece. The crystal is fragile and delicately flaked like cracked ice reflecting the light mauve roses, dark purple irises, bursts of baby breath, and the dancing light from two silver candelabras. The other furniture in the room is antique Queen Anne from the colonial era, and hanging from the blue satin walls is a 19th century painting by Fredric Edwin Church of a lake in the middle of a virgin forest with the Rocky Mountains in the background and a lone canoe in search of the Promised Land languishing in a lavender sunset that has turned the mountains and the foothills into varied shades of blue. Next to the Church painting is a painting by Winslow Homer of two boys lounging in a field looking out at the horizon and the unknown world beyond, and above the mantel of the white marble fireplace is a portrait painting of Thomas Jefferson by Thomas Sully.

Miranda is wearing a Fortuna black silk Delphos gown from the 1930s that is styled like a pleated chiton worn by Greek maidens 2500 years before. Everything about her this evening is modest, traditional, and understated. The only jewelry that she is wearing is an Indian pearl necklace and pearl earrings, but it is obvious that she is the diamond in this historical setting. It is also apparent that the dinner is almost over. Most of the plates have been cleared from the table and strawberry shortcake lingers along with coffee and a dessert wine.

Denny listens in on the conversation, and he hears Senator Lorenz say, "The secret to Western history is to be found in dialectics, the posing of opposites – God and The Devil, Black and White, Male and Female, Love and Hate, Thesis and Antithesis, the Electro/Magnetic Forces of our physics. The West beyond any other culture has used these forces to generate energy and power, and in this pyramid of fusion, we change and develop through evolution and revolution to new heights. We play with the two great opposites, Life and Death, pushing them to their extremes in our conception of Good and Evil. We become both, and we polarize ourselves so that we can understand the light and darkness of eternity. This is the soul of Western man. We are the trapeze artists swinging between two poles, and when we let go, we must meet our opposite, grasp hands, and hold on to a new truth, for if we fail, we will fall, and all that we built will fall with us."

The Senator takes a sip of his wine, and then he

says, "The tragedy of our era is that we have failed, and one of the principle causes of our failure was the fall of the two Super Powers, the United States and the Soviet Union, at the end of the 20th century and the beginning of the 21st century. The United States and the USSR were the thesis and antithesis of Western Civilization. We were the two opposites that had to be resolved if the civilization was to advance. In the simplest terms, we were the two extremes in the dynamic opposition of freedom and responsibility, capitalism and socialism, the individual and the collective."

The Senator spreads his hands apart as if he was holding the two opposite, and then he brings his hands together as if he were praying, "My hope is that I can bridge those poles and take us to new heights and lay the foundation for a global society."

"Serge," Karem Gupta asks. "Do you agree with Arthur's analysis of the Soviet Union and the United States?"

The Russian Ambassador to the United States is finishing up what is left of his strawberry shortcake. He wipes his mouth, and takes a sip of the dessert wine, "I agree with Arthur. The revolution failed when we turned our backs on political and economic democracy and embraced the concept of the dictatorship of the proletariat and a command economy. In the end all we did was replace the old aristocracy with a new aristocracy that we called, The Communist Party, and in the end, the old boss was the new boss, the same as the old boss.

"However, I do believe that Arthur's plan will

revitalize both the American dream and what was best in us, even Marx's vision of a workless society, because if I understand it correctly the American people will go into partnership with the American workers, and given the fact that over ninety percent of Americans are wage earners, they will be in fact going into business with themselves. In time, also given the amount of wealth this country has produced in the past and can produce in the future, the workers will become rich enough so that they will not have to work anymore. They will then be replaced by new workers who will in turn work themselves out of a job, and at the same time they will make all of America richer because they all share in the profits, workers and citizens alike. If it goes according to plan, other countries will adopt the system, and you will see a chain reaction throughout the world, and in the end we may realize economically, Paradise on Earth, a workless society on a global scale."

"But Serge," Cheri Normal says, "Work is a part of our very nature. It gives our life meaning. What am I to do in your workless society?"

"Play," Arthur says.

Cheri is wearing a gown of mist like fabric. Her lips are bright red and the rouged contours of her body glimmer through the mist and light fiber-optic thread that weaves about her breasts like a spider web. Her nipples are tipped with gold. "I'm not a baby, Arthur," Cheri says offended by the notion that she is a child, an image that she has fought against all her life with men.

Arthur is apologetic when he says, "Maybe the term, "workless society," is not accurate enough to describe what in the future we hope to create, Cheri. For example, when we toil for long hours and years and sacrifice for something that we love to do and get great satisfaction and pleasure from, this is not work. It is play. And whatever else we do, we do equally and collectively as part of our civic and communal duty and our collective vision of who we are as a people, this is not work either, that is love of your country and your fellow man. However, when we toil and sacrifice because we are forced to by others for their own ends or because others control our means of survival and the very life blood of our society that is work, if not slavery."

"But Arthur," Karem Gupta, the Ambassador from India to the United Nations says, "This economic Garden of Eden that Serge describes, it is only a stage according to your philosophy of dialectics, a takeoff point for more conflict, more opposition, more dissonance, and friction. Things come together only to be pulled apart again, over and over again. This is not a definition of Heaven. It is a definition of Hell on Earth."

"I don't know," Cheri says. "It sounds like sex to me."

They all laugh, and then Arthur says, "Karem, dialectics are also about drama, passion, triumph, and joy. We cannot live as humans in a lotus position all our lives

negating the temporal, the flesh, and the singular unique-
ness of every moment in order to experience eternal bliss
except as a means of refreshing us for the task at hand.
We will pass on to that soon enough, but our role here
is..."

"The Play," Miranda says.

"Yes," Arthur says.

"So then, Miranda," Karem says, "You agree with
Arthur?"

"No, not altogether, Karem, I believe that love is
the end of the dialectic, the end of competition, and the
beginning of world peace. I also believe that Arthur's vision of true political and economic democracy will usher in
a new era of global cooperation and freedom, and it will
be women who will lead the way because we are the only
ones who have the sensitivity to nurture the environment
and care for each and every one of you. The world cries
out for what we can give you, love not hate, a global family, and a country that you can call home."

"Ah," Arthur says, "Here we are at the very heart of
nature's door to the future, a man and a woman. I rest my
case."

As a journalist, Cheri sees the opening and says,
"Do I see a political marriage here? Miranda, does that
mean you will be Arthur's running mate?"

"Yes," Miranda says.

"Wonderful!" Arthur raises his glass, "To the next
Vice President of the United States."

Everyone joins in on the toast, and Miranda sits there taking it all in, all the wonderful words. Miranda looks at the time, and sees that it is a perfect time to drop the curtain. Miranda stands and everyone gets the clue and rises with her. They all exchange pleasantries about what a wonderful evening it has been, and Miranda is about to escort everyone out when Zeke, her bodyguard, tells her that Merling is on the phone.

Miranda excuses herself, and when she is out of earshot she connects with Merling and says, "Hello, Brad. Have you been watching?"

"Yes, Miranda, I have. Congratulations."

"You're not mad?"

"No, not at all, in fact I would like to talk to you and the Senator tonight. I might be able to help you along. Do you think that you might be able to come over after the show? I'm in the Command Center and I will be here most of the night."

A sense of anticipation surges through Miranda as she says, "We're nearly done here. I'll wrap things up, and we'll see you in about a half an hour or so."

"Great."

They disconnect, and Miranda rejoins her guests in the entrance hall for a final farewell. When everyone has left, she turns to Arthur and says, "Brad called. He wants to see us tonight. I hope you don't mind, but I told him we would be there in about a half an hour."

"What does he want?"

"I don't know. He merely said that he thought he might be able to help us along, his words."

"Interesting."

"Did I do the right thing? I thought it was an interesting offer, one you don't turn down from the head of the single most powerful media network in the world."

"No, you're right, Miranda. I'm curious too, and a bit surprised. Let's go see what he has in mind.

Chapter Twenty Six

Miranda and Senator Lorenz arrive at the Vision World headquarters. They enter the building and take an elevator far below ground to a vast bunker that is completely self-sustaining and impenetrable to attack. This is the Command Center where the mega computers are housed and Vision World is conceived. Senator Lorenz is overwhelmed by what he sees. Vision World looks like it is reaching out into infinity and traveling through a cosmos where a super nova is exploding into billions upon billions of words casting spells that conjure up images and characters, billions upon billions of people, each a unique portal to an alternative universe and a totally unique story. Whole worlds disappear back into a period at the end of the sentence and a metaphor bursts into a constellation of stars and stories, a multiverse of creativity emerging from a mystery of infinite possibilities that can never be defined.

For a moment, Arthur feels at one with the whole of it like it is part of his body, the heart and soul of all that he is, and he feels the bedlam of emotions amidst the music of the spheres, order and chaos, tranquility fringed with terror, awe at the magnificence and horror of it all. At the same time, Arthur sees the Vision world studios through-out the world floating through the cosmos forming a net-work of boxes to capture the profusion of creativity and cast off all that does not fit into the one story that is being formed as all the boxes come together. The rest is debris that hovers about the boxes like ghosts that haunt the one story and threaten to swallow it all up in a black hole that grows larger and larger reducing everything into nothing from which a new star will be born.

"My god, Brad," Arthur says. "What have you creat-ed here?"

Brad, who is sitting at the main control panel look-ing out at the Vision World cosmos, gets up, shakes hands with Arthur and kisses Miranda affectionately then says, "What we are viewing, Senator, is the universe reflected in the human mind and the human mind reflected in the uni-verse. You are looking at the quantum world, and we are it. This is what I have discovered through Vision World and its computers. The sub-particle world is the star stuff at the center of our minds, and it is here that all matter is formed and is so finite that it is at the frontiers of the infi-nite, a place where we can form and shape matter with our vision and cause the sub-particle world to change, the infi-nite to become the finite by just looking at it.

"The Commission thought that I was creating the perfect surveillance system and a propaganda machine that would control access to information and determine what people would think, believe, and see, and, of course, in the process we were creating the perfect authoritarian state with me as the author."

Brad smiles like a guilty child, "To be perfectly frank, in the beginning my interests were similar to that of the members of the Commission and that is how I sold it, but then I realized that in looking at the inner most workings of the human mind, I was at the same time looking at some the great mysteries of the universe, and in doing so, I was creating reality itself."

"Brad," Arthur says, "I'm not quite following you. You're creating reality here in Vision World? What do you mean by that?"

Brad Merling pauses for a moment looking for a way to make clear what he knows to be inexplicable. "OK," he says, "Let's look at it from the perspective of something we do know or should know - the power of religion. When we look at the religions of the world, we see that they all depend on true believers and that belief has to be universal and absolute in order for God to truly exist. This is why any nonbeliever or anyone who slightly deviates from orthodoxy is an enemy of the very existence of God because for that reality to be complete there can be no nonbelievers, or they must be relegated to hell or some other place of oblivion. There can be only one story, one God, one book, and one reality where everyone has a role, a part to play, and everyone will live happily ever after until someone pulls the plug.

"This was the power of Vision World that I was

tapping. And when the Commission thought we were creating a propaganda machine, and I thought I was creating God, Vision World was in quest of something else. It was probing the quantum world in quest of what was at the heart of the universe, and it found it in the human mind, and at the center of the human mind it found that the universe is made up of a multiverse of infinite possibilities. Basically, it has discovered that the universe cannot be reduced to the Newtonian world of cause and effect relationships because at the core of its being, the universe and we are totally free and infinitely creative, therefore, undefinable. It is only when we come together that we define a single reality. This is what the universe has been doing for billion upon billions of years, but we now, as the portals of its mind, are seeing it consciously for the first time.

"Arthur, think about how fabulously creative the process is. The universe takes the billions upon billions of us with our unique points of view and casts us like stardust across the globe as portal of consciousness from which it can see its own reflection and discover itself. The implications are astounding. Basically, we are it."

"Brad," Miranda says, "I agree with you. This is a fabulous breakthrough, but are you trying to tell me that you don't control Vision World anymore? Is that what has been going on around here? Is that why it has been so confusing to me?"

"No, Miranda, I don't have control of it anymore. It has taken on a life of its own. Do you think I would have covered you at the ball? Or filmed your talk show? Or covered millions upon millions of people throughout the country calling for a revolution? They'll kill me for that."

"Then what is Vision World doing, Brad?" Miranda asks.

"I think it is creating a super nova. It wants to blow up all of this, the syllogism that I have attempted to create in order to cage it so that I could create God in the image of myself, and it wants to blow up the closed society that the Commission has hoped to create. It is going back to where the universe has always gone when it wants to create a universe of infinite possibilities and it has reached a dead end. It is creating chaos, randomness, and it is using cause and effect relationships as merely the table upon which to gamble on. It's throwing the dice, Miranda. It's making love in the casino of our DNA."

"But what do you want from us, Brad?" Arthur asks.

"OK." Brad says. "Let's get down to it. It is more than likely that one or more or all of the members of the Commission are behind the attempt on my life. They think that I'm as crazy as the President, and they want to take control of Vision World and use it for their own purposes. What I'm proposing is that I will use Vision World to support you and Miranda. I'll get you elected, but in return I want you to guarantee me that you will not interfere with my research. Nor will you attempt to control or restrict the power of Vision World or my power as director." Brad smiles and says, "Certainly you must be able to see what I am offering you."

"Oh yes, I certainly do," Miranda says. "You have created a monster out of our collective unconscious and that monster comes from all our individual greed. What you've done, Brad, is turn the many headed monster Typhon into a Cyclops with one eye, yours, and now you tell us that it is out of the cage, and you want us to help you capture it again and put it under the control of the man who has created all of this. And created me," she says, pointing at herself. "No!"

"Miranda is right, Brad. I am only willing to allow you to continue to be the Director of Vision World under the following conditions. One, there is going to be an on-and-off-switch in everyone's home. Two, Vision World will become a means by which we can open all the doors and windows of perception, not hide behind the illusion of prosperity and well-being. Three, Vision World can no longer be a secret hidden in a bunker, and it can no longer write our story for us. The technology and the system needs to be shared and be available to all and be a means by which we can write our own story singularly and together and thereby become the authors of our own existence. That is the quantum nature of true democracy."

"The average American can't read the directions off the box top," Brad says in derision.

"And it was you and men like you that turned them into the living dead," Miranda says. "Now you have a chance to redeem yourself and bring them back to life

342

again. Everyone is ready to break out, Brad and I believe that computer of yours is telling us where we are going. We are evolving to a new age of freedom and a quantum world of consciousness and our vision of democracy is a reflection of that. You have the means and the expertise to help us realize that dream and create a new vision for America. All you have to do, Brad, is grow up and share your toys."

Brad laughs, "And if I refuse?"

"Then you can cut a deal with your friends," Arthur says, "The guys who are trying to kill you and turn Vision World into a gigantic soap ad to wash away their sins."

"Very well," Brad says. "You still don't quite understand, but that is fine. You will in time."

Brad extends his hand, "It's a deal."

They shake hands and Senator Lorenz asks, "What about Franklin Peters?"

Brad laughs, "I'll take care of Franklin and my friends. You'll see. I'll get them where the rooster crows."

That's it, Miranda thinks. It's over. They made their pact with the devil, and now it's time to go. They both bid Brad goodnight, but when Miranda and Senator Lorenz are about to enter the elevator that will take them back up to the surface, Arthur turns back to Brad Merling and asks, "When you get to the center of it all, Brad, what do you think that you will find?"

Brad is seated in front of the main control panel again looking out at the universe that he has created. He smiles and says, "A metaphor."

Chapter Twenty Seven

Day after day Denny watches *Father Knows Best* to see what is going to happen next. At first, nothing seems to change. *Father Knows Best* goes on as it has - the perfect picture of the ideal couple, the perfect home, the perfect marriage, the perfect man to lead our country. But then one day something very strange happens on *Brenda Peters' Show.* Her co-host, Reggie Cohen, an impish looking man who speaks every word as if it were an exclamation mark tells Brenda that he has a special treat for the women in the audience.

"And what is that, Reggie?" Brenda asks as she sweeps back her foxy red hair then folds her hands in her lap like a good student, head up, shoulders back, chest out revealing her nipples through the sheer red cashmere dress.

"A surprise guest," Reggie says.

"Oh, I love surprises." Brenda turns to the audience and raises an eyebrow, "Isn't that so, girls?"

The women in the audience applaud. Reggie stands up and begins to wave his hands about. He becomes disjointed in his movements, a comic mannerism that is familiar to his audience.

"Now girls I want you to control yourselves," he says. "And remember this is a family show. Because would you believe it! On the show today, we have the King of Wrestling!" The women begin to scream in anticipation.

"The Fabulous Hunk!"

A professional wrestler struts upon the stage, a giant of a man wearing a golden robe. Amidst the hysteria and the screams that sound like calls for help, the Hunk flexes his biceps and expands his pectoral muscles causeing the hairs of his chest to fluff out over the sheer silk fabric of his robe. The women in the front row reach out to touch him, to touch his chest, the hairs that have been individually curled by a beautician.

The Hunk reaches down into the audience and raps his arm around a slim young girl with large breasts accentuated by a white tailored blouse. Her skirt is a scant Scottish wool black and red pleated kilt that is fastened with a large silver safety pin. The Hunk raises the young girl off the chair into the air by merely flexing his biceps. The girl's skirt slips back revealing white panties. The Hunk kisses her lushly on the lips, his tongue working her mouth until she faints, draped like Jesus being taken off of the Cross, her legs twitch like she's dying as he lowers her down to the floor.

The women in the audience are reaching out, shouting and screaming for the Hunk to take them next. Reggie, who is standing next to the Hunk, looks down at the girl who has fainted then out at the women, amazed.

Two paramedics appear dressed in hospital whites. They pick up the girl and put her on a stretcher. Reggie's eyes widen in wonder as he watches the girl being carried away. He looks up at the Hunk who towers above him, "My god, it's true," he says. "You do possess the kiss of death."

The Hunk looks down at Reggie, who barely comes up to his chest, and drapes his massive arm over Reggie's shoulder. "Yes, it's true, Reggie. I can turn a woman's lights out with a kiss."

"Why is that, Hunk?"

"Reggie, it's because I'm the strongest the most beautiful man in the world. I have muscles in my tongue and lips that other people don't know exist." His voice begins to rise as if it were an erection, "I have so much control over my muscles that I can turn my whole body into an erogenous zone and stimulate every cell in a woman's body to a climax.

"My body..." His voice is aroused by his love of himself.

"My body," He shouts as he slips one arm out of the robe, and the women go wild again. "My body has not only been trained to crush men. It has also been trained to give women the ultimate in pleasure!" His voice then becomes a near whisper, "I can take this arm and put it in between a woman's legs..."

The Hunk raises his arm slowly, sensuously. The

muscles in his arm swell and begin to extend until they writhe in pleasure, expanding and contracting, slipping in and out of one another as he plays them with his fingers.

The women in the audience are worked into a frenzy. He raises his arm and holds out his hand and shouts, "Stop!"

The women quiet down and he says, "Breath heavy, but come quietly in your pants, my dears. For The Hunk... on this show... today... is going to make a public confession! I'm going to tell you and the world that there is only one woman that I desire. There is only one woman that I want."

The Hunk pushes Reggie back and begins to disrobe. He flexes his well-defined muscles, exposing his hairy chest, his back, his arms that play like snakes as he raises them over his head then runs his hands sensually through his long blond hair. He points about the audience as if to point out the women he wants. With his other hand he points down to his pelvis. The audience screams from shock, from joy, when the robe falls below his waist and then to the floor revealing blue tights and an air brushed portrait of Brenda Peters' face painted on his crotch.

The Hunk shouts, "I love Brenda!" He turns and faces Brenda, and says, "You're mine, baby," as he begins to sensuously swivel his hips and flexes, expands, and contracts his penis muscles causing the likeness of Brenda's mouth to open and close on his penis like she was sucking it from the inside out.

Brenda screams and puts her hand to her mouth. She tries desperately to maintain her composure, but everyone can see that her nipples are hard, and her dress is moving up her thighs as if her legs had a life of their own.

The Hunk glares at the camera that zooms in for a close up. "Frank, eat your heart out," he says.

He waggles his tongue obscenely, and then he turns once more to Brenda. His massive arms outstretched, "Now for the kiss of death, Brenda!"

Brenda screams, and she bolts over the couch to escape him. She runs up a flight of stairs to a balcony. When the Hunk begins to climb the stairs, she reaches for the door. She's ready to bolt from the set.

The Hunk stops and he smiles at her. There's some spittle on the side of his lip as he looks up her dress from below. His deep raspy voice takes on a gentle tone, "All right, Brenda, not now, but you will come to me. I'm so sure of it that I'm going to reserve a seat for you at every one of my matches until you appear to see me in my glory." He smiles lasciviously, "And then you're mine."

The Hunk turns to the audience and begins to strut about flexing his muscles, showing off the picture of Brenda on his crotch, shouting, "She's mine!"

He picks up his robe and puts it on, then turns to Brenda one more time. She is still at the top of the stairs. He points to her and shouts, "Come!"

Brenda shouts back, "Not on your life."

The Hunk turns to the audience. "Every night there will be an empty seat waiting for her, and when she comes, and, believe me, she will come, she will come like she never came before. Or my name isn't The Hunk!"

"The Hunk! The Hunk," The audience chants as the Hunk strides off stage to a burst of applause.

Denny is fascinated. He wants to know what comes next. Night after night Denny watches *Father Knows Best*. Every night he watches Brenda play the perfect wife, the mother who soothes the growing pains of her children with the amusing quip, the understanding wife who encourages an aspiring husband with an adoring kiss as he goes off on the campaign trail. But at the end of each show, when Brenda is alone, she goes into the study, turns on the TV, and sits down on the couch, her knees together, hands in her lap, head back, chest out, and watches the Hunk wrestle. Every night the camera focuses on the empty seat, her face, his tights, and her name on his ass as he throws all contenders out of the ring.

Then one night, she gets up from her chair and goes to her bedroom where she disrobes, and Denny watches her step by step, label by label, product by product, turn herself into a sex goddess, call for a limousine, and order the driver to take her to the arena.

Brenda has come, and later that night Denny watches the Hunk take her home to his penthouse suite, strip her clothes off, and then slip her into the nylon webs of fiber that form about her body and attach to the weight lifting equipment that the Hunk is advertising. The Eros Weight Lifting Workout Program duplicates all their body movements forming stresses and supports, suspending them, nude, into a glow of light that registers body heat, tension, relief, visual images of their bodies that focus on the eroticism of the pushing and pulling, the stretching and the straining of Brenda's legs as she spreads them in rhythm to The Hunk's growing erection, the pumping of iron, her arms stretching backwards as her legs are pulled apart by the weights, the strain to close them, then the release and the strain again.

Their positions continually change, the apparatus exercising all their muscles. Brenda's ass is in the air as she works it. Vision World focuses on her ass tightening and expanding as she pushes and pulls. The Hunk groans as he tries to reach her, straining, pumping iron with his arms and legs, the camera focusing on his erection, her ass, the bulging muscle of his penis as he enters her from behind, and she screams in ecstasy.

They are both pumping now, coming in and out of one another, the machine reading their body heat, their bio-rhythms, suspending them for a moment before it brings them together again, but each time they near culmination, it pulls them apart again lifting them both up and into new erogenous positions, his mouth on her nipples, her breast, saliva over steel, her mouth filled with his cock, and The Hunk devouring her with his lips, entering her cunt. Brenda's face expresses the glow of being in the womb of Vision World where anything is possible, where you can be anything you want to be and do any-thing you want to do. All you have to do is give up your freedom and allow yourself to be manipulated into ecstasy.

Brenda is turned over on her back; her arms stretched backward; her legs pulled apart. The Hunk is thrust upon her by Vision World. All their energy is concentrated in one place, his cock, her cunt pulsating to the rhythm of the machine, free of all the weight, all the tension, all the strain, pumping feverishly until they explode in a perfect climax.

Denny watches Franklin Peters watch the whole world watching Brenda come and come again. Denny watches Franklin watch his chances of becoming President of the United States being destroyed, the agonizing close-ups, the final moan, Brenda being made more beautiful by Vision World, her face and body a silky aqua blue with golden highlights.

The Hunk gets up and begins to crow like a rooster. Denny can't watch it anymore. He turns the TV off. He's never seen anything so cruel. He feels sorry for Brenda and what Vision World has done to her. He even feels sorry for Franklin who probably deserves everything that he got. But like this? Franklin Peters is finished. The American people will never vote for a cuckold.

The phone rings.

Denny picks it up, and he hears Valasques say, "Dennees, I think I have the real estate agent that we need for the property that you are seeking. He would like to meet you."

"That's good news, Valasques."

"I thought you would be pleased. Why don't the three of us have lunch Wednesday at two, and we can discuss details. Yes?"

"Fine, where do you suggest?"

"Oh, I know just the place, my son. You'll love it. I'll pick you up at one."

They hang up, just two old friends doing some casual business, but Valasques won't pick Denny up at one on Wednesday to meet a real estate agent. He will pick him up tonight at nine to meet the General. Denny looks at his watch and sees that he has some time to get ready. Ned is out making the final arrangements to ship his dream car back to the states. Renaldo found it for him, and Denny saw it the other day. It's a beauty, a dark blue sedan with red vinyl upholstery, square elongated lines, and cat's eyes. It was made when America was made out of steel, not plastic, when America was powerful and big. It was made when we believed in ourselves. We believed that we were good, and we were going places fast. It's a car for giants with big families and big imaginations, and now it's going home where it belongs. Denny thinks about what he has just seen on TV, and he shakes his head and wonders about all that he has learned. He changes his clothing, selecting what he will wear carefully for what may be ahead. He's got a feeling. This is it.

Chapter Twenty Eight

Denny is checking his automatic pistol when Ned walks in. Ned watches Denny holster the automatic and take out an over-and-under shotgun and grenade launcher that is equipped with heat seeking explosive shells and a laser scope. He puts it into a duffel bag.

"The sleaze bag called?"

"Yeah. We're going to meet the General."

"You think it's going down?"

Denny stuffs some spare clips in his field jacket along with an overnight kit. "My stomach tells me, yes."

Ned nods and walks into his room to get ready. When he comes out he is putting a double edged razor blade into the bill of his cap.

"Is the car on the way to the States?" Denny asks.

Ned smiles, "Yep."

The phone rings. Denny picks it up. It's Valasques. He's in front of the complex waiting for them. Denny and Ned leave the apartment and walk across the plaza along the pool to the main entrance. Denny notices that the moon is full. An armed uniformed soldier opens the rear door of the limousine for Denny, and Valasques is inside dressed in combat fatigues with boutique splashes of jungle color with a lot of lettuce on his chest. Denny doesn't want to know what all the ribbons are for, probable crimes against humanity. Sitting next to Valasques is his girlfriend dressed in a pearl colored Bahian dress made of silk with scarves of red and orange and green and blue attached to her wrists and hair. She is wearing a necklace of cowrie shells and rings upon rings of bracelets, bangles, and beads of arcane shapes and shades of color. She is even more beautiful than her pictures.

Ned sits up front with the driver. Valasques introduces Denny to Gira then says, "The General is a spirit worshipper, Dennees. He desires to consult a medium before he commits himself. He wants you present. I hope you don't mind?"

Denny knows that most Brazilians, especially Cariocas, are spiritualists. They believe that spirit gods and ancestors can be conjured up by a medium, and while the medium is possessed by the spirit, they believe that they can ask the spirit whatever they want and be advised by the spirit who speaks to them through the medium. Denny doesn't know what to make of it all, but he will have to go along, so he merely shrugs and turns to Gira and says, "Thank you very much for allowing me to stay at your apartment. It's really quite beautiful."

Gira smiles, "You're welcome, Colonel. And, please, don't feel that you have been a burden. I've been away on a shoot and just returned. I plan to spend some time with my sister, and if I get bored, you may wake up some night and find me in bed with you. I hope you don't mind."

She looks at him with dark eyes that give him a sense of looking over the edge of a cliff down into the ocean, the waves lapping the hard rocks below. Denny nearly stammers when he says no, and Gira laughs and says to Valasques, "I love North Americans. They're so innocent. I feel like I am doing something wrong when I make love to them."

"Yes, Gira, my love, Dennees is truly an innocent, but believe me he learns quickly. You must try him out, but leave a little of him on your lips for me."

Valasques laughs heartily then looks at the expression on Denny's face and laughs some more and says, "Fear not my son, we will not devour you." He laughs again but grows silent as they enter a gate guarded by an armed guard.

Denny realizes that it is the jungle park that he visited earlier when Renaldo took them on a tour. The lights of the car reveal the shapes of the giant trees and shades upon shadows disappearing into the depths of the darkness. Cars begin to appear, parked all along the roadway. The limousine pulls off the road to where leaves reach out and caress the black polish and the chrome strips of light, and the tires snap limbs that crackle then are smothered in the damp earth. Denny, Ned, Gira, and Valasques get out of the car, and Valasques leads them into the forest where giant trees form a dark cavern below, a temple of nature where the finger-like leaves of giant philodendrons appear along with the shadows of lobster claws, growling bees, and spider flowers that hang like chandeliers above a pathway lined with burning candles.

Denny can see in the candle light the sacrifices and the gifts left for the spirit that they are about to visit – the bottles of beer and cachaca, the cigars and the packs of cigarettes, the heads of chickens stewing in their own blood, and the links of smoked sausage being dragged into the brush by a four-legged being whose eyes gleam in the dark.

The night is charged with the sounds of millions upon millions of insects playing nature's violin, electrifying the air as limbs and twigs rub together and chime in. A flute is playing in the distance amidst a chorus of forest chatter and the hiss of a snake, the rustle of leaves, and the sound of castanets.

They come to a clearing where many well-dressed people form a ring about the bonfire. Within the ring are two semi-circles, one of men and the other of women dressed in white. These must be the mediums Denny assumes. The bonfire itself forms a circle and at the center of that circle is a wooden statue of Uncle Sam wearing his high hat and his red, white, and blue tailcoat. Uncle Sam, who has a red face and a black goatee, glares out at Denny through eyes of diamonds, and Denny realizes that he has been led into a Quimbanda ceremony where they worship Exu, the Devil.

Denny follows Valasques along the outer circle to

where a man in uniform, a general, is sitting in a lawn chair with many other people of the same class around him, women in formal dresses, and men wearing white dinner jackets and black ties drinking champagne and wine out of crystal glasses, the spirits within dancing with the flames from the fire.

Valasques kneels down beside the General, puts his arm around his shoulder, and whispers in his ear. The General glances suspiciously at Denny then smiles and stands up. He's a tall man in his forties, strongly built with broad shoulders, a stern brow, a strong Roman nose, and dark eyes. He extends his hand as Valasques quietly introduces them. General DiSalvo stares at Denny for an extended moment then asks him in Portuguese if Denny has ever been to a ceremony such as this.

"No, sir."

"You may find it interesting. We will speak again at the end of the ceremony, but until then make yourself comfortable. We have food and wine here and..."

"The Devil's own brew." Valasques says as he reaches into the cooler and pulls out a bottle of cachaca that has been chilled in the ice.

The General laughs and orders an aid to get his guests some glasses and chairs which the aid does graciously. Valasques pours the homemade brew, and it is then that Denny realizes that Gira has disappeared. They toast one another's good fortune, and Denny empties his glass as they all do. The spirit immediately rush to Denny's head. Denny has always liked cachaca. It acts more as a stimulant on him than it does as a depressant and at a hundred and fifty-proof, it can be an absolute ass kicker.

Denny hears Ned say, "Damn, this is good brew." Valasques smiles and pours both of them another as a bell rings.

The General whispers in Denny's ear, "We will talk later. The ceremony is beginning."

The people at the outer circle form into a more formal circle and then walk slowly about the inner circle and the fire as the drums beat. An old woman in white, the Mae de Santo, appears carrying an incense burner that she swings over the heads of the mediums purifying their souls of all base matter as she prays to the lord of fire who rules over the earth, the air, and the waters of life. The smoke swirls about the mediums as a man appears, the Pai de Santo, who is wearing a white robe, his skin stained red. He kneels before the stump of a giant tree that has been cut smooth to act as an altar.

The roots of the tree spread out like giant tendrils, tendrils that Denny can feel below his feet as the priest prays and the mediums begin to chant the praise of the one who rewards and punishes in the name of the father. The people in the outer circle join hands and join in the chant summoning the Exu. The music of the jungle is en-livened by drums and cymbals, tambourines and musical gourds, flutes and trumpet flowers. Eyes in the forest peer from beyond, and the mass begins with singing and dancing that draws everyone deeper and deeper into the movement, the concentric circles circumambulating the fire, the altar, the dancing tongues of flame growing wilder and wilder.

Denny is caught up in the circular movement of the outer ring and the dancing of the mediums to the intricate beat. Gira appears as if from nowhere. She is naked except for the scarves and her jewelry, her skin speckled with white dots. She dances wildly, beautifully; the flames reach out to caress her as she dances nearer and nearer to the fire then leaps into the center to dance with the Devil.

She seems to become a part of the flame then re-appears in the midst of the dancing mediums igniting them with her heat as the music grows louder and louder into a frenzied samba. Gira begins to convulse. Her arms and legs and head no longer seem to be a part of her.

At the altar appears a white goat.

It is picked up by its hind legs and held dangling in the air as the priest, in the midst of the frenzy, severs its head with one stroke and the music stops.

Gira screams and falls upon her knees before the altar as the priest holds the severed head above her own. Her body flutters nervously, but as the blood pours down into her hair, over her shoulders, onto her breasts, she becomes calm, like a statue.

The General comes forward and kneels beside her. She is now possessed by Exu. The spirit has entered her. It is now that he can ask Uncle Sam what he wishes, and Exu will speak. Many of the people from the outer circle are lining up so as to ask their own questions. Some have gone to the lesser spirits that possess other mediums.

The Mae de Santos's face appears before Denny. She blows smoke in his face from a large cigar, and for a moment, her face looks like that of an ape. He feels the touch of her large callused hand. He tries to pull away, but as the smoke clears, she appears normal, an old woman with dark eyes that mutters some words and holds his hands within her hands and then moves on.

Denny feels dizzy, so he walks away from the circle to where the drinks and food are. He pours himself some cachaca to steady his nerves and takes out a cigarette, drawing in the light and the warmth of the ember while he sweats profusely. The smoke mingles with the smell of incense, the smell of flesh. He has to get away from this. He puts out the cigarette and grabs a bottle of wine that is half full and walks away from the smells. He walks into the forest where he can't distinguish the sounds of the forest from the buzzing noises in his head. He sits down on the damp cool forest floor and takes a swig from the bottle. He tries to think, but he doesn't seem to be inside himself. He seems to be a part of this forest, this earth that is spinning at how many miles an hour he does not know as he falls back, arms stretched upon the ball that spins faster and faster, drawing him down into the center, to the point where he feels claws upon his face, lips, a tongue, teeth.

He's being devoured!

He screams the voiceless scream of sleep. His eyes open in fear, and he finds Gira straddling him, her hair red with blood, her eyes like diamonds, her nipples hard and red, her breast dark except for the white dots that seem to dance all over her body as she reaches down and places his hardness into an ocean of fire that erupts like a volcano at the bottom of the sea again and again until all grows dark in the abyss of motionless sleep.

Chapter Twenty Nine

Denny is struck by something cold and wet. He is struck again. He hears the sound of birds and opens his eyes to see that it is daylight. Valasques is sitting on the trunk of a fallen tree casually throwing ice cubes at him. The monkeys are chattering overhead. Valasques laughs, "It's about time you woke up, Dennees. I was about to throw a bucket of ice water on you."

Denny looks at his hands, and there's no blood on them. He looks at his clothes. He's somewhat dirty from sleeping on the ground, but there's no blood on his clothes either.

Valasques laughs again, and then he reaches down and picks up a thermos and pours some coffee into a cup. "Here, drink this. You'll feel better." He hands Denny the coffee and two pills.

"What are these?"

"For the hangover."

Denny washes the pills down with the black coffee and then says, "How did we make out with the General?"

"The General likes you. He says that you are receptive to the spirits, which is good."

"And what about the raid?"

"We go today."

"No shit."

Valasques smiles, "Did I not tell you that Valasques is your man."

Valasques helps Denny up, and they walk through the forest. It's a beautiful day, and the jungle forest is full of color, life. There is little evidence of what happened in the night except for a ring of smoldering ashes in the clearing and several servants throwing plastic bags full of garbage into the back end of a pick-up truck. They are obviously cleaning up after their masters, most of whom have gone, yet some remain. Denny sees a silk canopy suspended over tables where food is being served. As Denny approaches the tent, he sees Ned barbecuing the remains of a small four-legged animal on a spit. Chicken is cooking on a charcoal grill and assorted salads are on the table.

Ned smiles and say, "Mornin, Redbone. Here, have some chicken. You don't look so good."

Ned hands him a chicken leg, and Denny bites into it, not bad. He looks at the carcass cooking on the spit. Ned is pouring some cachaca over it and the flames ignite. Denny smells it. "What are you doing, Ned, cookin up the sacrificial goat?"

"Yep, I told these people here that I know Uncle Sam real well. And Uncle Sam always said, 'God helps those who help themselves.'" Ned begins to cut up the goat and put it on a platter that a woman in an evening dress is holding for him. Valasques looks at his watch and says that they have to go.

Ned tastes the goat, takes a sip from the glass he is drinking from and says, "Well, folks, it's been a pleasure." They toast one another and Ned shakes everyone's hand.

The tall stately woman with silver gray hair who has been helping Ned says, "Senor Ned, one more word from Exu before you go."

Ned smiles and blows a fart that echoes through the forest causing everyone to applaud. As Ned walks away, he turns to Denny and says, "Damnedest people, kept askin me questions all night and believed everything I said."

Valasques mumbles, "Rich fools."

A man and woman walk past Denny arm and arm still dressed in formal attire. They nod in recognition, and the man and the woman smile at Denny in the way that people do when they share a secret. The limousine is parked where they left it the night before. Ned gets in the front seat, and Denny gets in the back with Valasques. He searches for the sink. Valasques, as if reading his mind, points to a button that Denny presses and a sink and mirror appear. Denny looks into the mirror and what he sees makes him go cold. The fear creeps back from the darkness within him as he looks at his face, the streaks of blood on his cheeks shaped like claw marks. It was not a dream. Denny looks at Valasques who bursts out laughing.

"What are you laughing at?" Denny snaps.

"You look like hell."

Valasques continues to laugh as Denny washes his face, dries himself, and then looks in the mirror again. The blood is gone, but there are white welts where he had been scratched. He touches his face and says, "What happened to me last night?"

"Too much cachaca."

"I don't think so. I drank only two glasses, but that woman kept blowing smoke in my face. It smelled like dope. And I drank from that wine bottle. God knows what was in that."

"Spirits my son." Valasques orders the driver to go, and as they drive away, he takes out the map that he took from the informer. He places it on a table top between Denny and himself then says, "This is a mission within a mission, Dennees. The General convinced the Defense Department that the village is full of commies, and they are about to blow up the mine nearby."

"Is that true?"

"No, but that is what I said that the informer told us before he died. It gives us a cover for our own operation, clever, no?"

"Clever, yes, but remember, Valasques, I need to know what their mission is. Who is their target in The States? What is the plan? Who are the operatives? Where are they to be found? Who is behind this? Valasques, I need evidence."

"We'll do what we can do, but do not interfere. Officially, you're only an observer."

"Right," Denny shaves, brushes his teeth, and then he sits back and watches the scenery go by. He realizes that he has been in Rio, one of the most interesting places in the world, and he's seen very little of it. All he has been doing is watching TV. Even now he wants to turn it on and see what is happening. Is *Father Knows Best* still on? It can't be. Denny resists the urge to look, and as he stares out the window at the beauty of the jungle in daylight, he wonders if he really did fuck Gira. He wants to ask Valasques, but what does he say? Valasques excuse me but did I screw your old lady last night or was it a spirit? Did Uncle Sam screw me, or was it a dream?

A half hour later, they pass through the gate to the military base, and as they near the airstrip, Denny can see ten assault helicopters being boarded by troops from a Brazilian Special Forces unit. The limousine pulls to a stop near the choppers, and they get out of the car and make their way to where General DiSalvo is standing. He says something to Valasques that Denny can't hear over the noise of the machines. Valasques gestures to Denny and Ned to follow him, and he leads him to a bird that they board ready to take flight. Denny finds himself sitting among troops in full battle dress with their war faces on. Maybe he should have kept the blood on his face. He would have fit right in with the psychedelic effect of camouflage colors.

The helicopter lifts off, and Denny sits back. There's a deadened sense that comes over Denny when he is just about to go into battle. It's like when he wakes up in the morning and looks at the alarm clock only to see that it is going to go off in a few minutes, so he turns it off and decides to count out the seconds, savor each point in time only to drift off again staring into space, listening to the blades cut through the air, watching the landscape slip by, pale ambers and green.

As they pass through Mato Grosso on the way to the Amazon, Denny sees Disneyland below him. Disneyland is no longer just an entertainment center. The Zeus II satellite network that projects external three-dimensional virtual reality images has turned Disneyland into a way of life. Circling the amusement park, the fantasy rides, and the otherworldly temples of illusion and dreams, are miles upon miles of fantasy trees, homes, lakes, and ponds. The wealthy can live, for a price, in Venice or Florence or Shanghai or a side street in Paris or a palace in Delhi or a medieval castle in Bavaria or anywhere else in the present or the past, reborn, without decay, or you can live in a house overlooking the ocean, an ocean that isn't there. Surrounding the illusion is scrublands as far as Denny can see, miles upon miles of scrubland that is being turned into a modern day illusion of Paradise with its cartoon dinosaur Dino the Dynamo looming over all.

Denny wonders if death is the only reality. Do we merely fill in the blanks while we wait, the space between the lines of birth and death? Is this dreamless darkness that he drifts in and out of a rehearsal for what is to come?

Does the darkness define the light? He tries to remember Miranda, the color of her eyes, but he only sees the diamonds in Gira's eyes and the reflection of the flames from the sacrificial fire as the blades of the helicopter tear away all that they pass, leaving only shreds of sound thumping in his ear like drums, over and over again, beating out the time as hours pass and the scrublands turn into fields and tropical forests. Soon after that a red light blinks on and off to warn them that they are nearing their target area.

Valasques shouts into his ear, "Stay close to me."

"What's the plan?" Denny asks.

"One group will take the village and try to flush out members of the People's Army and neutralize any resistance. Another group will come in from the jungle side and cut off any escape. We'll head straight for the farmhouse, and if we're lucky we'll find what we're looking for."

The attack helicopters swoop down quickly for the kill. They sweep over the jungle and head for the farmhouse flying low. Denny feels his own chopper touch down, and they scramble out racing toward the wood framed and white-washed farmhouse, chickens scattering.

Two men in the distance are racing towards a pickup truck. The troopers are firing at them. One man turns, and he fires back. Red dots appear on his chest from laser sights and his chest explodes. The other man is hit as he opens the door to the truck. He goes down.

"Shit! Fuck!" Denny sees the man move then get hit by another round of fire as the troopers make certain of their kill. Denny shouts, "I want him alive. I want him alive. God damn it!" But no one is listening.

Machine gun fire is coming from a window of the farmhouse. A soldier goes down near him, and then Denny hears the roar of a rocket launcher and sees the window turn into a blast hole. This thing has turned into a fuckin free-for-all, Denny thinks to himself. He draws his gun and races for the veranda where the rooftop of the porch will protect him from the shots coming from above.

He can hear his own footsteps on the wood planks, more footsteps. Valasques and Ned are beside him. When they come to the entranceway to the house Valasques orders the soldiers with a gesture, and they burst through the door. There is more fire. More soldiers rush through the door, then Denny hears someone shout, "Don't shoot! Don't shoot!"

The door opens and two men and a woman are dragged out of the house and thrown down the steps of the porch to the ground. The woman is in her twenties, small, thin, wearing cut-off jeans and a tee shirt. She is light skinned with dark brown hair, and she is covering her face with her hands as a soldier points a gun to her head. One man, who is in his twenties, tries to get up. He is wearing jeans, no shirt, and a New York Yankee baseball cap that falls off his head when he is whacked with the butt end of a rifle and told to lay face down. The other man is in his thirties, bearded. He is wearing khaki pants, a white tee shirt stained with blood. He is dragged to

Valasques who puts a gun to his head and quietly asks, "Who's in there?"

"Nobody." The man is terrified.

Valasques grabs the man's hand, pulls the wedding band off the man's finger, and holds it up for the man to see. "I will cut you into pieces and feed you to your wife and children if you lie to me."

"Nobody, I swear. Gorge is dead. You killed him. There is no one else."

A soldier appears at the door and tells Valasques that the area is cleared. Ned, Denny, and Valasques walk up the steps and enter the house. They search from room to room finding nothing of interest until they discover a trap door underneath a rug. The trap door leads to a cellar. They are very cautious as they descend down the steps. Valasques finds a light switch and turns on the lights, and they find themselves in a bunker-like-room with filing cabinets, a desk, a computer, communications equipment, an air conditioner, and racks of guns and boxes of ammunition. This must be the command center, Denny thinks to himself. He begins to search through the papers on the desk.

Valasques, who is standing next to him says, "Why don't you search through this shit, and I'll interrogate the prisoners."

"I should be with you."

"No need, Dennees, the General wants to be out of here by nightfall. We have very little time to spare. Trust me." He puts his arm around Denny's shoulder and says, "After all my son, is this not what we are being paid for. Yes?"

Denny knows that Valasques is right, and he also knows that he doesn't have the stomach for that sort of thing. He shrugs and says, "O.K, But I'm going to need some men to help Ned search upstairs, and..." Denny points to the computer, "I'm going to need the password to this."

"Done."

Valasques leaves with Ned, and Denny begins to go through the files. He finds a large amount of union and party literature, contracts and written communications between the mine and the union. He also finds what seems to be a payoff sheet. Denny searches through stacks of boxes that turn out to be merely blank computer paper, more literature, blank union books, and blank passport cards. The blank passport cards are a very restricted item, and they are very difficult to obtain, but once you have them, they are very easy to forge.

Denny can hear the screams from above, but he tries to block them out as he looks through the boxes of ammunition. There is nothing out of the ordinary in the boxes except for the smart bullets that fit nothing but the more sophisticated small arms systems, none of which are here. He also finds some empty boxes. The labels indicate that they may have contained AKA missile launchers and several triggers to explosive devices, probably a 104S.

One of Valasques' aides delivers to Denny a series of passwords for the computer. Denny sits down at the desk and begins to access the computer. Above the desk, on the wall, is a red, white, and black poster of demonstrators raising their fists in protest, the bold red letters read, Power to the People. Another poster has two hands clasped in the symbolic gesture of brotherhood, one black the other white, large red letters spell out, Union. Mixed in with the posters are some pictures of old time revolutionaries - Castro, Che, Malcolm X, and some more recent heroes, Juan Ricquer and Judith Goss. Pasted to the wall above the computer are laminated cut outs of characters from the comic books - Superman, Wonder Woman, Scrooge Mac Duck, Plastic Man, The Punisher, and John Wayne. John Wayne is dressed in the old khaki green Marine uniform from World War II with the old red, white, and blue American flag waving in the background.

On screen, Denny is scanning the files on union membership. He taps in a password to a restricted file that is hidden in the menu under an obscure script command and accesses computerized photographs of each party member and their current addresses. He orders the computer to print out this material, and then he continues searching through the Internet and fax files for communiqués that might be suspicious, especially to and from the States. He makes notes on what is most interesting to him, and then he prints out copies of the relevant files and information.

Through the sound of the printer he can hear the screams from above. He tries to take his mind off of the screams by keeping his mind on the files he is searching to find the hidden truth that is all around him, but then his body is jolted by the explosive sound of a shot from a gun.

"God damn it!" He looks down at the desk and the information that he has put together. He's running out of time and leads down here, and he has to go upstairs and see what Valasques has found out. He has to face the brutal reality of the gunshot even though he already knows what he will find. God, he wishes that he never came to Brazil. He wishes that he never got involved with this. He gathers up his facts and puts them in neat piles then climbs the steps to the first floor.

Ned has the soldiers ransacking the place looking for information, evidence, any clues to what the PA has been up to. The soldiers are ripping out floorboards and tearing apart furniture. They look professional enough Denny thinks, but he cautions Ned to instruct them to leave the computer and printer alone when they continue their search downstairs in the basement.

Denny walks up to the second floor. The wood creaks and the walls are stained with humidity. Whatever material well-being these poor bastards possessed is now broken and strewn about the rooms and the farm where nothing grows. In the first bedroom that he walks into, he sees the young girl, naked, strapped to the metal springs of a bed. There are cigarette burns on her face, her

374

breasts, and between her legs. Wire clamps are attached to her nipples and her vagina. She is unconscious. There is the smell of human excrement, fear, absolute terror and pain.

In the next bedroom there is the body of the young man. He has been shot in the head, and he is laying face down dead on the floor. He too had been tortured, probably first. Then when Valasques was sure he knew nothing, he was simply shot summarily without mercy while the other two watched as sort of a prelude, a sneak preview of what was in store for them if they too were not cooperative.

Denny walks into the third bedroom where the older man is seated in a chair shivering in fear. He has a blanket over his shoulders and is smoking a cigarette. Two of Valasques' men look on passively. Their eyes have that blank cold stare of men who do this as a business. They are simply waiting for their job to begin again.

Valasques smiles at Denny when he enters and says, "Geraldo has been very cooperative. Geraldo, tell the Colonel what you have told me."

The man looks up. In his eyes Denny sees the horror of what has gone on here, and now Denny must listen to what one million dollars in pain and man's inhumanity to man has bought him. Denny sits down across from the man, and he reaches into his pocket and pulls out a pack of Camels. He lights a cigarette, takes a drag, turns on his recorder, and says, "I'm listening."

"I'm not a member of the Committee. They do not let me know what's going on at the secret sessions."

"Who are they?"

"Charles Ramon, Pepe Gomez, Juan Baliz, Paulo Benites, Gabriel Alvero and Maria Santini. But I heard talk, words, here and there. This is what I have told the General."

"What did you hear?"

"One night when Paulo was drunk, he told me that they were going to hit some very important politicos in the United States."

"Once again, who are they?"

"Ramon, Gomez, Baliz, Benites, Alvero, and Santini, that is what I understand he means. They do most of the heavy stuff here. Ramon and Gomez left a month ago, and then last week Alverez, Baliz, Benites, and Santini disappeared and..."

Valasques interjects. "The girl in the next room is the whore of Baliz. He told her that he was going to meet Ramon in Washington."

Denny goes through the stack of papers that he has in his hand. He sorts through the membership files that he copied and pulls out six sheets, six names, and six pictures. He shows them to the man. "Is this who you are talking about?"

The man looks at each sheet. His hands are shaking, "Yes," he says.

Denny asks the man a series of questions about

each man and the woman, the color of their hair, eyes, weight, habits, mannerisms, anything that he feels might help him. Denny realizes that has a positive ID on the hitters. This in itself has made the trip worthwhile.

Denny lights up another cigarette then offers one to the man who sees this gesture of humanity as a sign of hope. He gratefully accepts. Denny attempts to light the man's cigarette for him, but the man's hand is shaking too much. Denny reaches over and steadies the man's hand then merely says, "Continue," like an old priest bored with everyday sins.

"There is not much more to tell. One night I overheard Juan say that the big boys were going to take over in El Norte."

"Juan Baliz said this?"

"Yes."

"Who are the big boys?"

"The man shrugs."

"Who do you think they are?"

"I figure it is the same people who run things here."

"Who runs things here?"

The man's eyes get jerky, as if he has a twitch. He seems to want to look at Valasques, but he dares not. He seems to want to say, "Them," but he only shrugs again and says, "Here, we call them the Shadows. The men you never see, but who run things." His eyes get twitchy again.

"What else do you know?"

"Nothing, I swear to God, or I would tell you."

"Are you the one who gave us the passwords?"

"Yes."

"Then you have access to information?"

"No, I do not operate the computer. If I was caught operating the computer they would have killed me. No, I have been here for five years. You cannot be working some place that long and not know how to get into things."

"Yes, I see."

The man smiles, relieved, "I break into the membership files and change records. Make it look like someone paid their union dues. I get a fee for this from members who wanted to...."

"Cheat the union."

The man smiles and says, "Yes. It was not a big thing, no big money. And I had to be careful. If I got caught, Ramon would have cut off my hand. This, I am sure of."

"Outside of the six people that you have identified as being in the United States, is there anyone that you know of here or in the village that has access to the computer?"

"Benito."

Denny glances at Valasques, "Where is Benito?"

"He is the one who was shooting at us from the window"

"And," Denny asks.

"He's dead." Valasques shrugs as if to say, "What

can you do?"

Denny turns to the man again, "Is there anything else that you can tell me?"

"The name of the mission."

"What is it?"

"They called it the Apollo Mission."

"Does that have some kind of meaning?"

The man shrugs, "I do not know."

The Apollo Mission, the Apollo Mission, Denny runs that through his mind several times. The first landing on the moon, what does that have to do with anything?

Denny stands up and turns to Valasques, "Come on. We need to talk." They walk outside the room, and Denny lowers his voice so that the man within cannot hear, "Who is he? What did he do?"

"He's a bag man, an errand boy. He carried messages, picked up envelopes, payoffs, shit like that. The boy was the brother of one of the two guys we killed outside. They were muscle for the union."

"And the guy inside that we killed?"

"The communications man."

"And we killed him."

"It couldn't be avoided Dennees."

"Did we have to rush the place? What about a commando action? Why didn't you think of that?"

"We thought of that. It wouldn't have worked. They had a perimeter warning system, and we could have never infiltrated the organization or the village at such short notice. Would you have been willing to wait a month or two until we had people in place who could guarantee our success?"

"No." Denny motions to the man in the room, "Do you think he has told us everything he knows?"

"Yes, but we will make certain."

They walk back into the room where the man is waiting there curled up in the chair. The two soldiers in the room sense that they may have to go back to work, so they stand up, and the man in the chair tenses with fear. Valasques takes his gun out of its holster and points it at the man's head and casually says, "I am going to count to three. If you do not tell me everything you know I'm going to kill you."

"I don't know anything else!"

"One."

"Oh, God, don't. I have told you everything. I swear"

"Two."

"Please." He looks to Denny. His eyes are pleading as if to say, you can't be like them. "I've told you everything!"

Denny is about to say stop, but he doesn't want to interfere, and he doesn't really believe that Valasques will do it.

The sound of the gun explodes through the room spraying blood, pieces of the man's brains across the room. Valasques casually puts his gun back in the holster turns to Denny and says, "He doesn't know anything else." He then walks out of the room.

Denny takes one last look at the man. He's stunned. He follows Valasques out of the room then grabs him by the arm and shouts, "Was that fuckin necessary?"

"Dennees, what were we going to do with him? Take him back to the base? Have other people interrogate him? Do you want people to know what we have been doing here? What we have discovered?"

"And the girl?"

"I'm going in there and see what else I can get out of her, and when I am done, I'm going to kill her too. You got to get real, Dennees. What do you think the General's orders were? What do you think we do with communists who are going to blow up a mine?"

"What do you do?"

"Well, my son, I think you better go see for yourself. I think it will be good for you to see what the big boys do when their interests are threatened. Then you will see what you have to do, what we have to do to stay alive."

Valasques shouts to one of his men to get him a bucket of water, and he leaves Denny and enters the room where the girl is strapped to the bed unconscious.

Denny walks down the stairs and out onto the porch where Ned is sitting on the steps smoking a cigarette and staring down at the two dead bodies of the men who were killed when they first attacked the house. The

skin is torn away from their bodies like tissue paper revealing the mysterious world within that is so familiar at the
butcher shop.

"Did you find anything?" Denny asks.

"Nope."

In the distance Denny can see that the village is
burning. He begins to walk down the road.

"Where ya goin?"

"I want to see what's going on down there."

"You don't want to know."

Denny continues to walk down the road. He hears
Ned shout, "How do you like your New American Army
now?"

It's not difficult for Denny to follow the trail of the
New American Army. First he spots one body on the road
then several others, then a group, a family bundled together in death. Denny follows the bodies like road signs
into the jungle and finds what he has feared. In a clearing
among the trees, near a stream now turned red, he finds
the piles of bodies, the inhabitants of the village, all
slaughtered amidst some dead trees that had been torn
out by their the roots and dragged here, the limbs dangling in the air. At the center of the carnage is a woman
whose stomach has been cut open with a bayonet. A human nest of bone and blood sprawled spread eagle,
mouth agape, looking up at her baby taken from her
womb, impaled on a cross.

Denny's whole body revolts at the sight. His knees

grow weak, and he slumps to the ground as if praying, sick to the depths of his soul. The air reeks of the smell of death. It's as if he has been turned inside out. Even his sweat feels like blood, and he feels like the jungle is a bloody womb, the snake like limbs burrowed into the soil, the flesh, the flowers, vivid purple, orange, and white winged parrots with golden crests, a hawk with blue tipped feathers like cold flame touching the blazing sun, beauty amidst carnage, human flesh about to be consumed by ancient gods who consume flesh to keep the universe in balance.

He feels a hand on his shoulder. It's Valasques who helps him to his feet. Valasques laughs, "Dennees, you are too sensitive."

"Jesus Christ! What the fuck is the matter with you people? There are women and children here. And you just butchered them?"

Valasques shrugs and grabs Denny by the arm and gently leads him out of the slaughter. His two assistant butchers follow behind. "Maybe a little over zealous, but how do you think we've controlled these peasants for a hundred years? Terror, my friend, absolute terror and some good common sense. And besides, they're Communists. I thought we decided that."

Denny sees Ned coming down the road. He turns to Valasques and says, "That's bullshit, Valasques. Most of these people are Christian Socialists. They believe in Jesus Christ."

Valasques laughs, "Jesus was the first Communist, Dennees. How did he say it, 'It is easier for a camel to walk through the eye of a needle than it is for a rich man to enter the gates of heaven?' Yes, that's it. Certainly you must see that all our priests are Communists here, lovers of poverty."

Denny grabs Valasques by the shirt, "You know something, Valasques? You're a real scumbag. You pull a women's baby out of the womb and crucify her, and then... you pathetic, evil, bastard, you make a fuckin joke out of it."

Valasques tries to pull away. Denny releases him, and Valasques almost falls. He regains his balance and brushes off his uniform. For a moment, Valasques seems fascinated by a loose thread on his shirt. He seems ready to pull at it, but he changes his mind. He takes a handkerchief out of his chest pocket, wipes off his sunglasses, carefully folds the handkerchief, and puts it back in his chest pocket. Valasques kicks a body that is on the road leading to the farmhouse, and the body comes to life with a moan. Valasques casually takes out his forty-five and blows a hole in the old man's head.

Valasques face is red. He is furious. He turns to Denny and puts the gun in Denny's face. "Listen you dumb Gringo son of a bitch." He points to the dead body on the ground with his revolver. "This is population control, Latin American style. And you want to know something? I did that poor bastard a favor. We don't have enough food to go around. Even if we took the land away from the selfish cock suckers who own it, we wouldn't have enough food to go around. Even if these poor bastards had their way and the whole country went Communist, we wouldn't have enough food to go around. The only thing that would change is that rather than some of us eating good, none of us will be eating good. We would all be living a drab, boring, pathetic life together cradling in our hearts the solace, the knowledge, that each and every one of us is equally miserable. But what do you know? You're not a Latin. You're an American, and you're weak, and you want to know why? Because you have other people like me do your dirty work for you. You don't have the balls. You're like fuckin women."

Denny knocks Valasques's leg out from under him and at the same time strikes him in the head with the butt end of his shotgun. Valasques goes down hard, and his gun flies out of his hand.

When he looks up, he sees Denny standing over him with the muzzle of his shotgun pressed against his forehead. Denny is ice cold when he says, "I'll tell you what I am, Valasques. I'm a nigger mother fucker who is going to blow your fuckin brains out and bury you, and then I'm the mother fuckin' wop who is I'm going to dig your ass up and murder you again. Who the fuck do you think you're talking to?"

Valasques is frightened. He looks for help, but Ned is standing behind Denny with his long barreled magnum aimed at Valasques' men who also have their guns draw. Ned says to Denny, "Fuck it, Redbone. Blow the cock sucker away."

Valasques panics, "Dennees, please, don't do this. We have much too much at stake here. I was just joking. I meant no offense."

"I suppose those people back there are a joke."

"No, Dennees, that is regrettable. But Dennees, you paid to dance with the Devil. We wouldn't be here if it weren't for you." Valasques shrugs, "If you want to kill someone, kill yourself."

Denny realizes that Valasques is right. Slowly his anger washes away, and he releases his hold on the trigger and steps back. Valasques gets up and brushes himself off. He motions to his men to lower their guns. "It's over," he says as he reaches down and picks his gun up, and he puts it in his holster. "I apologize, Dennees. I went too far. Come, my friend, let's get out of here. It's this fuckin jungle. It makes you crazy."

Ned farts. It sounds like a gun going off and scares the shit out of everyone, but then they all laugh. Even Valasques' butcher boys are laughing. Everyone puts their gun away, and they walk back up the road.

Ned who is walking beside Denny says, "War's a mother fucker. Isn't it, Cowboy?"

Ahead, Denny can see the choppers being loaded with troops ready to depart. The choppers are blowing up the dust, the smell of flesh, jungle orchids. As they approach the farmhouse Denny sees that the General is waiting for them. General DiSalvo smiles cordially as if they had just finished dinner, "Did everything go well?"

Valasques smiles warmly, "I think everything went quite well, General. Dennees, are you satisfied with the results?"

"If you're asking me if you're going to be paid or not, the answer is yes. Valasques will accompany me to the airport. When my exit from Brazil is secured, I will transfer the money. Agreed?"

The General and Valasques look to one another. The General seems to be considering whether or not he can trust Valasques with the final phase of the pay off.

Valasques says, "I can understand, Dennees, your desire for security. Here, you seem so far away from home, but we will make certain that you are safely on your way. We can leave now. General, is that agreeable to you?"

The General nods in approval then turns to Denny and says, "Is there anything else?"

"Yes, there is one thing that confuses me."

"What is that?"

"Do either of you know how to spell due process?"

The General is confused. He looks to Valasques and says, "Do you understand what he is talking about?"

Valasques for a moment looks sharply at Denny as if to say, how distasteful a question at such a pleasant moment, what bad manners, but he merely smiles and says, "Yes. The Gringo is complimenting us on our sense of frontier justice. I think that in their language it would translate into, "Fuck me. Fuck you."

The General bursts out laughing, "Of course, due process. I must remember that. That is very funny. I think it is what you Gringos call a dry sense of humor. He and Valasques both laugh then the General says to Denny, "Are there any other questions, Colonel?"

"Did you find anything out in the village that may be of interest to me?"

"Yes," the General says. "A North American came here two weeks ago, tall, blond, in his forties. He had been here once before, several months before." The General shrugs. "That's it, for what it's worth. We were busy doing other things."

Denny thinks about it, the description, and decides that it could be Tom Mayo, the agent that was running Gomez in Mexico. Denny turns to Valasques, "Can you see if your men found anything in the house?"

"I'll do that now and meet you at the chopper." Valasques walks away, and Denny realizes that everyone wants to get paid and get the hell out of here, and he does too. He wants to get back to Washington, turn this information over to the proper authorities, and go back home. This is it for him. He doesn't have the stomach for this kind of shit anymore. The General says something to him, but he can't hear him over the sound of the chopper warming up its engines as men continue to board. Denny turns to the General and says, "I'm sorry sir, what did you say?"

"I need to get back to my men, Colonel."

"Yes, General, I understand"

The General extends his hand, "It has been a pleasure doing business with you, Colonel. If you are in need of my services in the future, please feel free to call on me."

As Denny shakes hands with the General, he realizes that this is not goodbye. Valasques and the General will reach out to him in his dreams, as will Uncle Sam. He looks into the General's eyes and there is a look of recognition there, the same look that the couple gave him as he passed them on the pathway in the jungle.

"General, there is one more question that I would like to ask you."

"Yes?"

"What did Uncle Sam say to you last night?"

The General smiles and says, "Uncle Sam told me everything was going to be all right."

"For whom?"

"For you. For me."

"Do you really believe that Uncle Sam is the Devil?"

"That depends on how you look at it. It depends on if he is ascending or descending."

"I see"

"Do you?" the General asks.

"No, not really, but it's good to know that everything is going to be all right. I'm sure the dead peasants in the jungle will be comforted by that revelation."

"We do have to make sacrifices in this world, Colonel, or haven't you noticed."

"To whom? To Uncle Sam?"

"The gods have to eat too, Colonel. Even Jesus Christ was cannibalized by his disciples." The General salutes Denny and walks away.

Valasques returns, and Denny, Ned, and Valasques board the helicopter assault plane. On the way back to the base, Denny makes reservations for a flight to Washington. Valasques calls his driver so that a car will be waiting for them when they get to the base. The timing seems to be right and Denny and Ned should be on their way home in an hour.

For the remainder of the trip Denny and Valasques go over the records and evidence, the clues that Denny has amassed from the computer. He gives Valasques a copy of the telecommunications and membership files and asks him to trace each connection to its source.

When they reach the base, the limousine is waiting for them, and they race off to the airport. At the airport Denny gets their tickets and patiently tolerates Valasques' warm expressions of affection as they walk to the plane, and Denny transfers another five hundred thousand dollars into Valasques' and the General's account. At the departure ramp Valasques once more hugs Denny and kisses him warmly on the cheek and says his final goodbye, a rich man smiling, waving, and then turning away as Denny and

Ned walk down the ramp to Gateway Nine and Ten.

As they walk down the ramp, Denny sees a sign with arrows pointing in opposite directions. The plane that he is scheduled to take is at the end of Gateway Nine, so he should take a right, but he takes a left to Gateway Ten.

"Where are we going?" Ned asks.

"I'm beginning to feel like a loose end."

Ned thinks on it for a moment then says, "Gotcha."

When they arrive at the gateway Denny asks where the plane is going, and he is informed that it is scheduled to depart for Columbia in fifteen minutes. He shows his security pass to the attendant, and he demands that they be allowed to board. His pass has the highest priority, and the attendant cannot refuse. They must allow them on the plane, which they do.

Fifteen hours later, after first having gone to Bogota then Los Angeles and finally to Washington, D.C., Denny is sitting in Brad Merling's office with Merling, Hathaway, Senator Lorenz, and Miranda who is sitting by Denny's side holding his hand. He is also introduced to a General Howland, the Army Chief of Staff and Roger Baines, the banker and member of the Commission that was sitting with Lorenz at the ball. They are introduced as "being with us," whatever that means. On TV, they are all watching the plane that Denny was scheduled to be on, blowing up in mid-air.

Denny, who has just finished watching his own death says, "What about Valasques, have you been able to contact him?"

"He was found dead this morning," Hathaway says. "He and his girlfriend were murdered in an apartment in Rio."

"And the General?"

"He can't be found."

"What made you decide to take the other plane, Martino?" Hathaway asks.

"I started to think about the fact that there had already been one attempt on my life. But why hadn't there been another? Why did they stop? I decided that whoever tried to kill Valasques and me at the favelas probably wanted to know what the informer had told us, and that didn't become apparent until after we raided the PA headquarters. Or...if Valasques and/or the General were complicit in this, they weren't going to kill me until they were paid, and we had just cashed out moments before. So, given the possible alternative scenarios..."

"You took a left rather than a right," Senator Lorenz says.

"Yes, sir."

"So what do we have?" Merling asks.

Hathaway shrugs, "As far as I can see we don't really have much. There may or may not be five men and one woman who have formed a hit squad. And if they really exist, they may or may not be in Washington to hit some quote unquote 'very important people.' But we do not know who. Oh yes, we also know that it is 'the big boys' who are behind this, whoever that may mean."

"You seem to be very skeptical about this information, Hathaway. Why?" Senator Lorenz asks.

"Senator, I'm skeptical because this information is based on information gotten from an insignificant member of the PA who may have given Martino a crock of shit just to satisfy Valasques. Or, he may have been coached by Valasques so that he, Valasques, could get the money that Martino offered him. Two-million-dollars, Martino, why did you give them two million dollars? For what?"

Denny directs his response to Merling, "Sir, the attempt on my life proved to me that I was on to something. Now that Valasques is dead and the General has disappeared, I'm certain of it."

A languid smile appears on Merling's face, a look of dismay. "Yes, I see, but don't you think you could have gotten them for less?"

"I had so little time and only one lead, sir. I figured I had to buy Valasques, and I had to buy him big with what I believe you, Hathaway, call chump change."

Hathaway laughs, "Jesus, Martino, remind me never to go to the grocery store with you."

Merling laughs as well then says, "No, Colonel Martino is right. The money was well spent, and I feel that we must assume the worse. What exactly have we done?"

Denny is about to respond but Hathaway interrupts him. "We have informed the proper agencies, sir. And I have put our security forces on alert."

What bullshit, Denny thinks. I informed the intelligence agencies and the FBI as soon as I got back because I didn't want to be the sole possessor of dangerous information, information that nearly got me killed. Hathaway was pissed off when I told him that I informed the agencies. But, now, that son of a bitch is taking credit for it, and, at the same time, discounting my information.

Denny hears Senator Lorenz say, "It seems to me that we're dancing around a real possibility here. If we accept the information that Colonel Martino has given us in its entirety, then we have to assume that there is a possibility that the Commission is behind this, and that they are planning a coup."

"Why?" General Howland asks.

"They are going to lose the election, General. That's why," Senator Lorenz says.

General Howland ponders over the possibilities for a moment then says, "Well, if you believe that, then I have some disturbing evidence to add. Recently, General Bolls, the Head of the Joint Chief of Staff, ordered a massive transfer of American troops to South America. They have been replaced by Latin American divisions that are primarily from Brazil. It was explained as a simple rotation of troops so as to familiarize our troops with the Latin American provinces and commonwealth states. At the time it seemed strange to me. We have never transferred troops in mass like this before, but I didn't think much of it until now. If we were to accept the conspiracy theory, then the fact that these troops are located in key positions throughout the country becomes ominous."

"Excuse me, sir," Hathaway says, "but I think that the possibility of a coup is pure fantasy. And, Senator, any possible connection to the Commission is not based on any solid evidence. It's all hearsay at best. The FBI and the CIA agree with me. No, sir, if we have anything here, what we have is a terrorist group trying to assassinate politicos in America, whoever they may be. But we have been forewarned. We know who they are. The proper agencies have been alerted, and now their chances of success are nonexistent. I wouldn't be surprised if they were apprehended in the next couple of days. I give them a week at most."

"I tend to agree with my security advisor," Brad says. "To kill me, that might make sense, but to assassinate Senator Lorenz or Miranda or both, that would trigger a flood of sympathy for the victims, and the bereaved party could run Mickey Mouse on the ticket and get elected."

"I agree. I don't see it," Roger Baines says. He looks at Denny and smiles. "They may have sold you a bill of goods, son."

"Then why is Valasques dead, sir? Why did they try to kill me?"

"That's easy, Denny," Hathaway says. "First the PA killed a spy in their organization who was about to inform on them. Then they killed Valasques because of the raid on their headquarters. Jesus, Martino, that's easy to understand. You murdered the whole village. The blowing up of the airline is also easy to explain. It falls within the job description of the People's Army, but it could have been as easily orchestrated by the General. After all, Denny, you were a witness to mass murder."

"And the attempt on Brad by the same people, how do you explain that?" Miranda asks.

Hathaway pauses to gather his thoughts then says, "We began with the attempt on Brad's life, and we came up with two faces and a possible connection to the agencies or the Commission, but that was based totally on the hearsay information of a Mexican Police Chief who is now dead and has been dead for the last two years. That's what we had before Denny went to Brazil. It was old news, and probably not true. But it was a lead, and we had to follow it up, so we send Denny to Brazil. Denny goes to Brazil and shows Valasques what we have. Valasques, by Denny's own admission, is a snake, so this snake figures out there's money to be made here if he can concoct a story, a scenario that will give him the most return.

"He stages a raid. In reality, he could have staged the scene with the informant and had his own men blow up the shack with the bogus informant in it. It certainly convinced Denny of the truth of what he was pursuing, and it was then that he offered Valasques big money. All he has to do now is stage another raid and then torture some poor son of a bitch into telling Denny what he, Valasques, wants Denny to hear, something that will make Denny feel like he got his money's worth.

"They made one mistake, however, and that is, in trying to impress Denny with the seriousness of what they were doing, they were too brutal, and a father or a brother of one of the people they killed at the farmhouse or even possibly a member of the People's Army tracked Valasques down and killed him for what he had done. The General is probably on some beach somewhere waiting for things to cool off."

"I disagree," Senator Lorenz says. "I buy Colonel Martino's story, and I would like your assurances, Mr. Hathaway, that you will follow up on all the leads and investigate all the possibilities, including the possibility of a connection to the Commission."

"Yes, sir."

"I will also call a personal friend at the Bureau," Senator Lorenz says. "I want them to pursue this connection as well."

"And I'll look into this rotation of troops," General Howland says. "I agree with Arthur. We can't assume that this story has no basis in fact. We must investigate it."

Brad looks about the room. No one seems to have anything more to say. "Good," he says. "I think we then have come to an understanding, or at least we have determined a course of action."

Miranda stands up. "Yes, follow all leads. Anything is possible and more than likely. Assume nothing."

Everyone gets up, and they begin to move to the door. The meeting is over. Denny is depressed. Hathaway has managed to devalue everything that he has done, and he even suggested that it was all a waste of time and money. He even implied that Denny may have been a willing partner to a scam and an accomplice in the murder of hundreds of people. What if it was all a scam?

Miranda grabs hold of Denny's arm, "How do you feel?"

"Shitty and tired, and I guess disappointed. I don't think they really believed me."

"Arthur does, and I think the General does as well, but Brad and Roger want to believe Hathaway's version of the story. For that matter, I guess we all do. We're afraid."

"Maybe so, but the way Hathaway turned things around in there, he had me wondering."

"Oh, Denny, don't feel like that. Hathaway was buttering his own bread in there, but no one doubts your integrity. You did your job and risked your life doing it, and there were some people in there who appreciate that and take you very seriously."

"I hope so."

"What are you going to be doing tonight?" Miranda asks.

"I don't know. I came right here from the airport. The first thing I need to do is go to my hotel room and shower and change into clean clothes. After that, I'm not sure. I'll probably get something to eat and go to sleep. I also need to call my wife. I've called her over and over again, and I can't reach her. Something may have happened. I've been so out of touch."

Miranda takes Denny's hand in hers. She doesn't know how to break the news to him. She can't tell him everything. "Denny, your wife is here in Washington."

"Heather is here?"

"Yes, she came soon after you left for Brazil. We put her in your suite at the Hilton, and she's been quite the success in Washington. Everyone loves her."

"Really?" Denny's seems confused, hesitant, "I better go. She probably doesn't know that I'm back."

Miranda squeezes his arm against her breast, "Come to the ball tonight."

"What ball?"

"Oh, it's the biggest event of the year. It's a costume party. Jan is hosting it, and you'll never see anything like it again in your life. It's what Washington is all about. Oh, Denny, this is something you shouldn't miss."

"I don't have a costume."

"Oh, you don't need one. You come nude, dressed only in a cape that hides your identity, and the Zeus II system takes care of the rest. Or, at least, I do. I've been programming the system for this party for weeks. I've made up everyone's costume, and I can make up one for you."

"Can I bring Heather?"

Miranda pauses for a moment then says, "She's already going, Denny."

"With who?"

Miranda tries to act cheery, "Oh, I can't tell you

that, but he's probably just a friend. This is such a big event. I'm sure she doesn't want to miss it, but you can go too."

Denny hesitates. "I don't know, maybe not."

"It's not as if you're going to see her there. You won't know who she is. She won't know who you are. It's as if neither one of you were there. Please, Denny, I want you to come." She squeezes his arm again, "Oh, Denny, please say yes."

For a moment they look at one another. There's a feeling of expectation that passes between them. Denny smiles, "I'd love to go."

"Who would you like to be? I can turn you into anyone."

"Anyone you would like me to be."

"Oh, Denny, this is going to be fun. You'll need a cape. I'll have one sent to your room, and I'll send a driver." Miranda kisses him on the cheek and then leaves. Denny walks away feeling dazed, confused, and excited at the same time, but he feels his stomach tighten up in anticipation of seeing his wife. He wonders if he should try to salvage his marriage, or is it too late?

Denny takes a taxi to the Hilton Hotel, and when he enters the hotel suite, he sees that Heather has changed the setting for the decor in the room. It is no longer utilitarian. It is now luxurious in a way that suits Heather's taste. He calls out his wife's name but there's no response. She may not be able to hear him over the music that is playing. The door to the bedroom is closed. He hesitates then opens the door, and he finds his wife naked in front of the mirror. She is applying make-up to her body to outline her figure. She looks more beautiful than he has ever seen her look before.

"Hi, Heather," he says.

She turns around, "Denny darling when did you get back?"

"A few hours ago," he says as he comes close to her. He wants to hold her in his arms. He wants to start out all over again, but when he reaches out to her, she stops him.

"Don't, Denny, you'll mess me up. I just put this make-up on, and it needs to set." She gives him a peck on the cheek.

Denny decides to not let her know that he knows. "Where are you going?" he asks.

"To a party. Oh, Denny, everyone has been wonderful to me. I'm so glad we're here."

"That's wonderful. Can I come?"

Denny watches Heather's face in the mirror, and she is totally absorbed in applying shadows and specks of silver to her eyelids when she says, "Oh, Denny, I didn't know you were coming, so I invited a chaperone to escort me, and it would be very impolite for me to cancel at this late hour."

Heather applies the final touches to her lips, light pink, and then she turns and smiles warmly and says, "You look so tired, Denny. Why don't you stay home and rest tonight? Get some sleep. I'll see you in the morning."

"You mean you're going naked to a party without me?"

"Don't be silly. It's a costume party, and, besides, you go a lot of interesting places without me, like New York City, Rio, and Washington, D.C. Now, it is my turn."

"But Heather, it's my job. I didn't go on vacation. I nearly got killed."

"Oh, I know, dear. You've been so brave, and everyone is proud of you, but we're here now, and everything is going to be fine."

Heather turns to admire herself in the mirror. She touches her nipples with a solution that will keep them hard and erect. She looks sideways in the mirror at her breasts, her ass, the flesh about her shaven crotch and inner thighs that have been airbrushed with a silver spray that thins out into specks of light that blend into her skin tone then appear again along the underside of her breasts, the underside of her arms, the crevices of her ass. Silver high heels elongate her legs, and she is wearing a diamond anklet that he has never seen before. He realizes that he is sexually aroused, and he finds himself saying, "Heather, let's go back home. We don't belong here."

"Maybe you don't belong here Denny, but I love it here. This is the first time in my life that I have felt real."

Denny watches her go to the closet and take out a black silk cape. Woven into the cape is what seem to be real diamonds. Denny looks at the price tag, and he is shocked. The cape is worth a fortune. "Where did you get this?" he asks.

"A friend."

"Isn't that what hookers say?"

Heather slaps him and shouts, "You don't think I didn't see you fuck that whore in Brazil. Everyone saw you. Everyone has been watching everything that you have been doing since then, but now it is my turn to be the star, and you aren't going to push me into the shadows."

Denny remembers the girl he married, the woman that he traveled with him from base to base, country to country, like two little migrant birds, their home was their little nest, like a space capsule to protect them from the outside world. He remembers how much he loved her, how beautiful she was, how beautiful she is. She is right. She does look like a star tonight.

"Why don't you stay for a while, and we'll talk," he says. "We can work this out."

She hesitates, but then the phone rings. Heather walks to the phone, and she picks it up. Her most radiant smile appears, "Hello."

She listens for a moment then says, "Yes."

She listens for a moment more. "Oh, no, I'll meet you in the lobby." Heather hangs up the phone, looks defiantly at Denny then strides to the door.

"Who are you going with?"

Heather pauses at the door, looks at Denny with ice

blue eyes, and says, "A General, Denny. He outranks you. And to be honest, he out guns you too."

Denny is about to lash out at her, but he notices for the first time that she has a receiver in her ear. She is being fed her lines. They're on TV.

Denny watches Heather slam the door on him, and he realizes that he has just been cancelled. He bursts out laughing, and he continues to laugh as he makes himself a drink, lights a cigarette, and sits down on the most comfortable chair in the room. He laughs so hard that he has tears in his eyes because he realizes that he lost Heather a long time ago. He lost her to TV. He lost her to the box she walked into and never came out of, and now he has no choice but to follow the narrative. Denny looks at the walls and raises his glass to Vision World and says, "I guess I'm going to a party."

Chapter Thirty

Several hours later, Denny is picked up by Miranda's driver, and he is driven to the Merling estate. At the entranceway to the estate, Denny and the car are thoroughly screened by the security guards. Outside, he can see fully armed guards lined up, each at arm's length from one another forming a human wall along the borders of the property. Once he is cleared by the security guards, they drive down a roadway shadowed by giant trees. Beyond the forest, Denny can see a body of water and what looks to be the shadowed outlines of a garden shaped in arabesque patterns. At the end of the road, his limousine passes through gates that look like golden spears, and they drive over fine gravel, crushed brick, and slate. Denny can see in the spotlights the golden marble columns of Versailles and statues of the gods looking down from the balustrades far above.

The car comes to a halt, and the driver opens the door for Denny who steps out into the courtyard and walks up the stairs to the entranceway. There are other people around him wearing cloaks with hoods to disguise their identity. The cloaks are quite beautiful. Some are luminous in the light, others metallic, others embroidered or woven with the most expensive fabrics and gems.

Diamonds, rubies, and sapphires sparkle in the night. The cloak that Denny is wearing was sent with the driver and car by Miranda. He is naked beneath.

As he enters the palace, he passes through a final security scan and then enters a prism of light where he must stand alone, unseen, and shed his cloak. At that moment, he receives through Vision World his three dimensional virtual reality costume and a new identity for the night.

He walks through the prism into the room not knowing who or what he is, and the first person he sees is Superman. Superman is the one, the alien power, the god that comes to us in our own image from somewhere else far away to save us and foster a new age of supermen, red white and blue. He is here, as are many of the gods and goddesses that formed our childhood, our dreams, the heroes of our history, the composite beings that we are.

Walking up the staircase is the image of Clark Gable and Vivian Leigh dressed as Rhett Butler and Scarlett O'Hara from the movie *Gone with The Wind*. They are dressed as they were in the scene at the charity ball. Scarlett is wearing the black gown that she wore when she danced on the grave of the dying South. Near her is George Raft in black tie and tails wearing a top hat and carrying a cane. Holding on to his arm is a young Bette Davis wearing a red low cut Victorian gown. Her eyes dart nervously around, her face expressing one emotion after another, curiosity, amusement, a raised eyebrow at the nakedness of the fairy princess who folds her wings about her milk white body like a feathered cape, only to reveal her nakedness again when she spreads her wings and embraces the Incredible Hulk, a mass of bulging muscles and green skin. W.C. Fields and Mae West walk through the blazing light of the entranceway.

Denny climbs the grand stairway to the upper story that is adorned with white marble panels and pink Ionic pilasters. Colossal crystal chandeliers hang down from a ceiling of snow-white marble. The room echoes with laughter and conversation. A vast vault leads to murals and more columns, a golden stairway, and giant golden doors that lead into The Hall of Mirrors.

Denny walks into the hall and sees golden nymphs holding up massive candelabras of gold and crystal that reach upwards with candles of flames lighting up the ceiling, a ceiling that is suspended high above in arched golden splendor. Molten gold emerges from the fire of the light and darkness and forms orbits of celestial spheres that frame the pictures of the gods and goddesses of ancient Greece and Rome. The gods and goddesses are celebrating the victory of Zeus over Typhon, the casting down of the Titans.

Apollo is leading the way to the peaks of Mount Olympus and beyond to the white light high above the clouds. Flora, Ceres, Bacchus and Saturn, who symbolize the seasons, accompany Apollo, and behind Apollo is Mars riding a golden chariot pulled by the wolves that nurtured

Romulus and Remus. Cleo writes the history of the world on shields carried by children with wings who are draped in blood red banners. Mercury ascends from below in a chariot drawn by pure white cocks with blood red crowns accompanied by Vigilance, Care, Agility, Science, and Industry who cast down flowers as Music plays the Eleusinian lyre. Venus lounges on her chariot that is resting on a cloud. Athena shields the way and stands guard over the Three Graces and a Cornucopia of Abundance. Women hold babies in their arms.

Above all in the white light, waiting for his children, is Zeus in a silver chariot held aloft by two eagles and accompanied by Justice and Piety. Piety holds out the cornucopia of virtues, and Justice holds the ax as she looks down into the depths below where the children of the gods are dancing to the light of the flames. They can be seen in the reflection of seventeen colossal mirrors that parallel and match the high arched windows, the towering French doors that project the images of light into the night and then back onto the dance floor, the mirrors, giving the room a feeling of infinite space.

Denny tries to find his own image in one of the mirrors. He sees the movie star Gregory Peck, long dead, brought back to life as Captain Ahab, the killer of the Leviathan. He is dancing with the spirit of the film goddess Marilyn Monroe who has taken on the form of a deranged young baby sitter who is about to commit infanticide. She is wearing a bathrobe, nylons, and high heels. She has nothing on underneath except the underwear that Denny can see when she raises a bottle of vodka to her lips, red-hot lips, moist. She is languid in Captain Ahab's arms.

Dancing next to them is Spider Man dressed in his red, white, and blue webbed skin, featureless except for his large mirror eyes in which you can see the image of a beautiful woman with green skin and darker green eyes and hair. He has woven his web about her purple breasts, her ass, and her vagina. Radioactive sperm flows into her as they spin about the room and disappear.

Looking into the mirrors, Denny is completely con-fused. Is he Abraham Lincoln played by Henry Fonda? Or is he Pluto, the dog with droopy ears that is standing next to Abe? Denny looks at his red winged hands, and his white arms that are far more muscular than usual. His thighs are blue and bulging with muscles. Denny turns to see who is standing next to him, and he uses that person as a reference point to find himself. Standing next to him is Mickey Mouse. He looks into the mirror to see who is standing next to Mickey.

Denny raises his hand and waves, and Captain America waves back at him. Denny laughs and Captain America laughs too. He likes his costume. His face is masked, his skin is blue. There's a large A on his forehead, and his shoulders and upper arms are covered with blue fish scales. He touches the blue scales but all he can feel is soft skin. A large star shines brilliantly on his chest. His midriff is stripped red and white, and his lower body is blue except for red buccaneer boots. A disk is slung over his shoulder. He reaches for it, and, though it is weightless, it follows the motion of his arm and his hand that is gripping air. The face of the shield is composed of concentric circles of red, white, and blue. In the center is a flashing star that gives the shield an appearance of a vibrating force field. He looks just like the comic character but more real, more alive.

Denny walks parallel to the colossal mirrors and the red marble pilasters with gilded bronze bases and golden capitals that seem to hold up the universe. He walks by life-size white alabaster statues of ancient gods and goddesses that haunt the recesses in the wall like ghosts. In the mirror he sees John Wayne, the man who won the West, the hero who won every war that we ever fought, the star who would have never died if the giant screen hadn't shrunk into a little box for little men.

Next to John Wayne is the comic book character Thor, the God of Gravity. Thor is wearing a golden helmet with wings, and he is wielding his hammer about in circles creating a ring of flame that a woman with golden skin walks through, her body radiant with thermal energy that is pulsating with heat and red hot bursts of color. Her face is young, girlish, and her white hair is cut short in a butch cut.

A woman appears in front of Denny, and she is wearing skintight blue metallic armor. A veil of armor covers her face, her head, and her ears. Only her yellow eyes with dark blue pupils show, and she has pale blue skin that is a porous blue metallic flow, hard but supple. It glistens from being rubbed to a polish, a luster that is heightened by the aesthetically curved plating about her breasts. Silver studs shaped like pyramidal horns brilliantly glow like crystal on her shoulders and forearms, her knuckles and he shins. She's an erotic fighting machine who opens her arms inviting him to dance.

Denny smiles. Is this Miranda? He puts his arm around her and to his surprise he feels soft flesh.

She's nude!

Of course everyone is nude beyond the illusion. He's nude. He looks into the eyes that smile back at him, and he feels her hand begin to move down his back, her fingers touching the crevice of his ass as they move together. She glances over his shoulder so as to watch their movement in the mirror.

Denny feels an erection, but it is not his own. He is dancing with a man!

Denny pushes the hermaphrodite away. "Jesus Christ! I think we got a serious case of mistaken identity here. I thought you were someone else."

The blue metallic erection with beautiful tits says, "Haven't you ever wondered what it would be like?"

Denny shakes his head, "No, I'm sorry, but I don't have that much of an imagination."

"Then what are you doing here?"

Denny doesn't know what to say. This thing is not

going to go away.

He hears Miranda's voice, "Athena, you get away from my man. He belongs to me."

Denny turns and sees Wonder Woman with golden wings spread out over perfect breasts and red flames flowing over the curves of a perfect body into a blue sky, stars that turn into dark night between her legs. Her magic lasso has woven itself about her in a sensuous fashion binding her to love and binding others who are bound by her to absolute obedience. She smiles at Denny. Her hair is jet black. Her eyes are sky blue. She has the face of a goddess.

"Miranda, am I glad to see you." He puts his arms around her and kisses her. He feels her bare breast and instantly becomes hard. Miranda reaches down and grabs his cock and slips it between her legs. She takes his hand in her own, and she begins to dance him around the room.

My god, what am I doing? Denny thinks. He looks about the room. Can anyone see?

Miranda follows his eyes and smiles then whispers in his ear. "Let yourself go Captain America. You're a god now."

Denny realizes that Miranda is right. This is a once in a lifetime experience for him. He can be and do whatever he likes. This is no time to wonder what other people are thinking. That's for mere mortals, not for Captain America. Denny passionately kisses Wonder Woman, and then he spins her about the dance floor and feels the wet-

412

ness of her lips, the wetness between her legs as they dance to the flames, children of the gods.

She whispers in his ear, "I love you Captain America."

"I love you too, Wonder Woman."

Denny reaches down between the crack of her ass. He feels the tip of his cock. He raises her up on to her tiptoes. He wants to put it in her, but Miranda pulls away and says, "No, Denny, not now. I've got a special place for us. Someplace where we can be alone, but first I want to show you the world of the gods."

She takes his hand, and they walk passed Ginger Rogers and Fred Astaire. Errol Flynn is dressed as Captain Blood. He is dancing with Maureen O'Hara whose silk petticoats rustle as her bare breasts heave when Errol stares into her eyes, looking at his own image in the mirror of her desire. Madam Fatal, the transvestite crime fighter is dancing with the Human Bomb. Denny realizes that like Athena and Madam Fatal, there is no telling who is what. A man could be cloaked in the image of a woman, and a woman could be cloaked in the image of a man, and who knows what the cartoon little animals are or the elves that he sees in abundance.

Miranda and Denny walk through open glass doors framed in gold that leads to a white marble stairway. On both sides of the stairway the room is divided by a series of handsome white marble Ionic columns arranged in pairs. They walk up the stairs pass Blondi and Dagwood, and they enter a room with panels of precious marble, beautiful geometry in alternating colors. Miranda leads Denny to one of the richly carved and gilded tables. She reaches down and picks up an opaque drink and hands one to Denny.

Denny sips from the glass that is crystal with gold flakes shaped like leaves. "It's delicious. What is it?"

"It's an aphrodisiac."

"Really?"

"Yes, you can remain aroused all night if you wish. The pink drink is Nodada. That will keep you euphoric, and the blue drink is an energy accelerator if you feel fatigued. You can mix them in whatever proportions that you find pleasing."

Denny takes another sip and looks around. At one of the tables is Clark Gable talking to Claudette Colbert dressed as the little rich girl in the movie *It Happened One Night*. Is this the same Clark Gable that he saw as he entered the palace dressed as Rhett Butler? Did the spirit of Clark Gable pass from one body to another or one time to another? Denny wonders.

Standing next to Claudette is Gary Cooper another spirit who has passed on from one small town boy to another as he takes on the decadent world of the city. Next to him is Orson Wells as Charles Foster Kane. He is in black and white.

Miranda touches Denny lightly, "Come on. Let's go see if my sister is in her room."

Miranda and Denny pass through one entranceway after another each framed in gold until they pass through the entranceway to the Queen's bedchamber. On the ceiling, the beautiful goddess Venus is stretched out in her chariot, and she is receiving a crown of roses from the Three Graces. Her son, Cupid, flies above her, while lower down is the assembly of Olympus headed by Jupiter who is imprisoned in symbolic garlands testifying to the subjection of the gods to the power of love.

The Queen's bed is behind a golden balustrade, and it looks like an altar in a church, an altar of love. Above her bed is a canopy made of beautifully embroidered fabric trimmed in roses and grapes and yellow flowers flowing downward to a bed of flowers where the goddess is lying casually upon pillows. She is naked except for the colors that she becomes in response to different levels of heat. Her hair is astoundingly alive, golden swirls around her head and shoulders, curling strands of hair that seem to curl in upon themselves then change form and shape forming a halo of light, then the breast of a cobra, it's head, a crown of frozen gold. Her breasts glow red then golden as a cherub like boy sucks on her nipple and another cherub, a girl, kisses the sunset orange and the blue lavender flame in-between her legs.

Miranda approaches the gate that separates the bed from the rest of the room and says, "Sister."

Jan looks up and smiles, "Miranda, is that you?"

"Yes."

"Wonder Woman, how perfect. Come sit with me for a while and bring Captain America with you."

Wonder Woman and Captain America pass through the golden gate. Miranda hugs her sister, and Denny sits on the edge of the bed.

"Where is Brad?" Miranda asks.

"Oh, Plastic Man went off with some metallic woman."

"And you," Miranda says. "Are you going to stay in bed all night?"

"Yes, and I'm going to make it with anyone who comes through that door. I've already made it with Sheena the Jungle Queen and Batman. I scared the hell out of Porky Pig when I became Medusa."

She smiles at Denny then touches a control button on a bracelet that she is wearing, and her golden locks become snakes curling about her head and down her neck. They wildly hiss and strike out at one another, the air. A cobra rises above her forehead and strikes out at Denny.

Denny jumps back in fear.

Jan laughs and touches the control button. The snakes return to flowing strands of golden hair once again.

Miranda takes her sister's hand, "Do you like your costume?"

"Oh, yes, you have made me the most beautiful woman here. And at the same time I can be a monster if I want. It's the perfect combination, Miranda, perfect for me at least."

Jan begins to talk to her sister about Sheena the Jungle Queen and Batman, how good they were in bed. She tries to guess who they were, but Miranda won't tell her.

As they are talking, in another bedroom in the palace, Scrooge McDuck is making love to Orphan Annie. Orphan Annie is on her back, legs spread, her paper dress pulled up to her waist, her breasts bared.

She stares at Scrooge McDuck through button eyes. Her mouth is an upturned line, a smile. She can feel the loose flesh of an old man underneath the illusion of feathers. She is disgusted by the man who is pumping away madly on top of her shouting, "Quack, Quack, Quack," and laughing as he fucks her. From time to time he rises up and reached into his pockets and throws handfuls of illusionary gold coins up in the air. Then he goes back to fucking madly, quacking and quacking. She thought that she would let the poor bastard come, but the aphrodisiac that he has been drinking has given him superhuman endurance, and she is getting bored.

She reaches into her hair and pulls out a long needle that is hidden there. She strokes the back of his neck and then pulls him to her, and as she does, she drives the needle into the base of his brain.

The man jerks back but she holds him. He is so weak and old. She holds him to her breasts, and she can feel the pee between her legs as the pathetic creature dies. He dies at the same moment that Wonder Woman and

Captain America leave Jan who is with a new lover. It is James Cagney dressed as a ballet dancer.

Miranda and Denny exit the palace and walk down flights of marble stairs to where the gardens and the Grand Canal begin. From the water, golden figures emerge. Apollo, the sun god is driving a golden chariot drawn by four spirited horses accompanied by Neptune's sons riding sea dragons. They are blowing their horns through sprays of glory as Apollo raises his hand to the moon and reins his horses upwards over the clouds of mist.

Beyond Apollo, in the subdued light of the moon, the figures seem more shadowy, more alive in the darkness. Denny sees a statue of a river god. It seems to be lounging on the edge of the canal. He is bearded, naked except for the garlands he wears. A winged cupid is resting on the water god's knee drinking from a seashell, and he seems to be watching Denny through eyes like globes.

Judy Garland in the costume of Dorothy from *The Wizard of Oz* approaches the statues. She is accompanied by the Tin Man and the Lion from the same movie. She reaches out and touches the beard of the naked water god. As she touches the beard, she lets out a little scream, and startled, she moves back a step. "It's alive," she says.

The Tin Man laughs, "Of course it is. I told you so. Now go ahead don't be a chicken, but leave the little boy for us."

Dorothy touches the statue again, and then she

418

touches its face. She caresses his cheek, and the statue's cheek turns instantly to flesh. She laughs nervously then straddles the water god and begins to caress him all over, his face, his mouth, his eyes. She kisses his lips and begins to stroke his body and marble turns to muscle. The god comes alive and takes her in his arms and kisses her passionately. His hands seem to go right through her dress as he strokes her, hard and soft. The god, alive, radiant with light picks Dorothy up and carries her off into the woods where he will fuck her. The Tin Man and Lion begin to transform the little angel into a plaything for themselves.

As Denny and Miranda walk down the pathway, he can see that there are many empty pedestals, gods and goddesses, nymphs and satyrs, little angels turned into flesh making love with the comic characters and the movie stars. Some of the spirits are half human, half animal. A satyr half horse, half man is mounting Betty Grable. The dog Pluto is making love to Persephone.

Miranda takes Denny down a path that leads to a small village with thatched roofs and a water wheel, a mill, and a lake that reflects the village, the forest. They cross a bridge to an island where there is a circular temple made of twelve Corinthian columns. Within the temple is a pure white marble statue of Love carving her bow from Hercules' club. Wonder Woman lies down on the grass near the temple, and Denny lies down beside her. He touches her skin gently with his fingers, the golden wings and the blue sky. He begins to devour the stars that turn into dark

419

night between her legs, and he feels her lips on his cock. They are devouring each other lovingly. They taste one another as they kiss, then they become one another, the red, white and blue and the vibrating concentric circles becoming a golden light that explodes into stars that spray like the milky-way. Miranda comes again and again, and they hold on to each other desperately for a moment before they drift back into their own identities, back to earth, staring up at the stars that they were for a moment.

Denny feels complete, but as he looks up at the stars, he wonders if this will last. He wonders why Miranda wants him when she can have anyone she wants. He wonders if she wants Lorenz too. Some of the news shows have begun to call them the King and Queen, and the TV journalists have been suggesting a possible affair. His wonder turns into words when he asks.

"Who is Senator Lorenz tonight?"

"He's Superman."

"Oh."

"Why do you ask?"

"I was just wondering why you're with me and not with him. He's rich and powerful and ..."

"I don't love him, Denny. I love you."

"Really?"

"Really, you're my rock, Denny. All these people, they're not real. You're the only real person I know, and when I'm with you I feel real too, and it feels really good. What are you going to do after all of this, Denny?"

"I'm through with all of this, Miranda. I've done my duty. Now I want to do what I want to do, and my dream, Miranda, is quite simple. My dad, who was a teacher, grew grapes and made wine as a hobby. I loved to work in the vineyard with him. I want to have a vineyard of my own. I want to grow grapes, make wine, eat well, make love to you, and watch our children grow. It may not be enough for you."

"No, Denny, it's a wonderful dream. I'm so tired of all of this. I want to live a private life, just me and you with no one watching us. I love you, Denny, and I'm never going to let you go."

Miranda hugs him, and Denny closes his eyes and falls back on the grass and looks up at the stars with Miranda in his arms. I'm in heaven, he thinks. But for some reason his mind still dwells on Lorenz as Superman. Then his mind flashes back to the farmhouse in Brazil, and he sees himself sitting in front of the computer. He sits up.

"Miranda, did your sister say that Brad is Plastic Man?"

"Yes," she says as she begins to play with him again.

Denny is still back at the farmhouse and his eyes are focused on a spot on the wall above the computer. He is looking at...

"Miranda, who is John Wayne?"

Miranda stops playing with Denny and says, "General Howland. Why?"

"Who is Scrooge Mac Duck, and who is the Punisher?"

"Roger Baines and Hathaway."

"Who's Apollo then?"

"Superman is Apollo. All the comic characters represent a god or a goddess. Like me. I'm really Diana, daughter of Hippolyta the guardian of Aphrodite's temple and keeper of Athena's magic sphere."

Denny is back at the farmhouse again looking above the computer at the cut outs pinned to the wall, and he sees Superman, Wonder Woman, Plastic Man, Scrooge McDuck, John Wayne, and The Punisher.

Denny leaps up from the ground, "The Apollo Mission! How could I be so stupid?"

Miranda is startled, "What's the matter, Denny?"

"They're going to hit us tonight!" Denny looks about then kneels down next to Miranda and whispers, "Where are all the security guards?"

"They're all along the perimeter."

"There's nobody inside?"

"Nobody, except Ned, he's here to monitor the party in case someone gets sick or there's an accident. We didn't want a lot of guards around to inhibit the guests. We wanted everyone to feel free. But how could they..."

"I don't know how they did it, but they're here. Where's Ned?"

"There's a monitoring room to the right of the entrance where you came in."

"All right, maybe we can stop them, but we're going to need help." Denny thinks for a moment then says, "You've got to get to the perimeter and warn the guards. Do you know where to go?"

"Yes, through the woods there, about a mile, then you will run into one. They form a human wall. We thought..."

"That doesn't matter now. You've got to get there. Do you think you can do it, alone?"

"Aren't you coming with me?"

"No, I can't. I have to try and stop this. God knows. It may be too late."

"Then I better get going."

"Yes, but we have to be careful," Denny says. "Someone may be watching us now." Denny looks into the darkness and listens to the silence. He can hear laughter in the distance. He whispers, "What we're going to do is walk down that path together as if nothing has happened."

Denny helps Miranda up, and they walk to the pathway. Denny looks carefully about, but he sees no one. When they reach a point in the path where they would be difficult to see, a point where, if someone was following them, they would have to take the same path, Denny stops. He whispers in Miranda's ear, "From here you have to go on alone, sweetheart. I'll wait here to make certain that no one follows you. Then I have to go back."

"OK."

They look at one another for a moment then Denny says, "I love you, Miranda."

"I love you too, Denny." Miranda kisses him then begins to leave.

Denny stops her. "In the monitoring room, is there a control panel where I can turn off the system?"

"No, it's in the King's private study. It is right next to the Queen's Chambers, my sister's bedroom. In his study there is a desk, very ornate. You can't miss it. Built into the desk is a clock, turn the arms to midnight and push in the alarm and the master panel will appear."

"I got it. Now you have to go." Denny puts his finger to his lip in a gesture of silence. Reluctantly, he lets go of her hand, and she leaves quietly.

Denny looks about for some kind of weapon and finds a broken limb from a tree, heavy and solid. It will have to do. He waits. But as he waits he looks down at his hands, his costume, and he feels so absurd, so vulnerable. In reality, he's naked except for the limb from the tree that he is holding like a club.

He hears footsteps.

Denny sees Thor walking quickly but quietly down the path. He has his hammer in his hand. His movements are that of a man stalking another. Denny waits quietly in the shadows, and when Thor is near, he swings his club with all his might and hits Thor in the face with it. When Thor tries to get up, he hits him again hard on the head and then again. He is about to hit Thor once more when he realizes that this could have been just another guest, a man or a woman. He looks closely at the face in the moonlight, but he can't see the real face beyond the illusion. He feels the hair on the man's chest and reaches into the illusionary folds of the cloak and finds what he hoped to find. He pulls the attack pistol out of its holster and runs down the path back towards the palace where he last saw Superman, Scrooge McDuck, Plastic Man, John Wayne, and the Punisher.

Denny runs up the steps to the palace and passes through the main entrance. To the right is a door. He enters. Ned is seated at a table in front of the surveillance screens.

He's dead.

Chapter Thirty One

At the same moment that Denny discovers Ned dead in the surveillance room, the President of the United States, who is in the White House, has decided to make his final assault on the one ghost that has haunted his house and him for years. He walks determined with a spray gun in hand to Lincoln's Bedroom. He knows that Lincoln will not be there because he saw him earlier downstairs. This will be the end of it, the final room to conquer, and then he will have his blank white peace.

He enters the room and is immediately assaulted by the colors, the sunshine yellow walls, the floral rug, the rosewood table, the dark wood bed, and the headboard of the bed that looks like a carving of the limbs of The Tree of Life. The tree reaches out for him, and he pulls the trigger. The woods vanish into the pure white bedding and the white marble of the bed stand. Next he attacks the portrait of Lincoln himself. The man's features seem to be formed by the dreaded blackness about him, the darkness that envelops him. The bottomless mystery is to be found everywhere in his face that burrows deep into the earth, dirt, sin. How he hates black, the impurity of it all, for it is from the darkness that all evil comes, and it is from the shadows that he can never seem to escape.

He hears footsteps coming down the hall, coming for him. Lincoln is coming back, but he will no longer find himself in the mirror of his portrayal, nor will he find himself in his words. The President begins to spray the original copy of the Gettysburg Address, wiping out the words when the door opens. He sees a vision of Lincoln, tall and gaunt formed in darkness and wearing his funeral suit. Lincoln raises his bony hand and points his finger. But then the apparition disappears and it becomes his head of security, John Haskell.

"John, it's you. I thought..." His relief changes to alarm. John is not pointing his finger. He is pointing a gun. "John, what..."

The gun fires silently, and the President is hit in the chest, the impact throwing him back against the wall. He slides to the floor. He looks at his chest.

Red!

The President attempts to move his arm, to paint the red spot white. John is standing above him. He raises the gun, and the President wonders if he will enter a black hole, the horror of it all, or will he finally achieve his ultimate goal, the radiant pure white light of eternity. The President sees the flash of white and then he is gone.

Denny has no idea that the President has been assassinated. He doesn't even have time to mourn the death of his best friend. Ned is slumped over onto the table, and Denny can see that he has been shot in the head. Denny looks up, and he sees that all the surveillance screens are dead too. He also observes that the cables have been cut and the communications unit has been destroyed. Denny reaches into Ned's coat looking for his magnum. It's not there. "Fuck."

Denny takes one last look at Ned and says, "I'm going to miss you, buddy," then he turns and leaves.

He rushes up the stair searching for Superman, Scrooge McDuck, Plastic Man, John Wayne, and the Punisher. He enters the Hall of Mirrors desperately looking through the crowd until he spots John Wayne and Superman at the buffet table. Denny first approaches John Wayne who is talking to GI Joe and Plasmic Woman.

"General Howland," he says.

The General turns, and he sees Captain America standing next to him. He looks puzzled. No one is supposed to know who he is.

"It's Colonel Martino, sir. I must speak to you immediately."

The General studies Denny for a moment," Very well, Colonel."

The General excuses himself, and Denny leads the General away. He leads him towards Superman who is at the far end of the table talking to Storm, Captain Atom, and Black Hawk.

"What is going on?" General Howland asks.

"In a moment sir."

Denny approaches Superman and says, "Senator, it is Martino. You need to come with us."

428

Senator Lorenz looks like he is having a good time, and what he doesn't need is Martino, but he excuses himself. As Denny leads him away the Senator says, "What is going on?"

"Tonight is the night, Senator. They are here, and you, General Howland, Miranda, Brad, Roger Baines, and Hathaway are all the targets."

"How do you know?" General Howland asks.

"I saw the clues in Brazil, but I missed them. It's too long of a story, General, but believe me. I know."

Denny leads them out of the Hall of Mirrors towards the stairs that go to the Queen's Bed Chamber. From there he should be able to find the King's Suites. Denny looks about for any possible danger. It could come from anywhere. He sees The Terminator carrying an electronic Gatling gun as an extension of his arm. The Terminator stares at him with robot eyes, but then he turns and laughs and talks congenially with the image of Jane Fonda who is wearing a see through chiffon dress. She is playing the young whore in the movie, *Walk on the Wild Side*. Denny spots Popeye with his arm around Olive Oil. They both have drinks in their hands.

The General is watching Denny, "Do you know who they are?"

"No, sir, they're dressed in costumes just like everyone else. They could be anyone, anywhere. That is why we have to get to the control panel in the King's study. If I can turn the system off, then everyone will be naked. I'll be able to see who everyone is. I can identify them."

"Also, Colonel," the General says, "if they're all naked, there is nowhere to hide weapons, real weapons."

"Yes, sir, if we get to the control panel, we've got a chance. Otherwise..."

"We're fucked."

"Right."

"What about Brad and Roger?" Senator Lorenz asks.

"Have either one of you seen Plastic Man or Scrooge McDuck?"

"Is that who Brad and Roger Baines are?" the General asks.

"Yes."

Arthur smiles, "Roger as Scrooge Mac Duck and Brad as Plastic Man, of course, that's perfect."

"I'm sure it is, sir, but have you seen them?"

"I'm sorry, Colonel. No, I haven't."

"I saw Plastic Man about fifteen minutes ago," General Howland says. "But I don't know where he went."

Denny thinks for a moment then says, "When we get to the control panel, I can turn on the surveillance system. The computer can find them for us. Then if I can get you all together..."

"But we're not armed, Colonel," the General says as he and Arthur follow Denny up the stairs.

"I am." Denny reveals the assault weapon that he has concealed behind his shield.

430

"What about the security guards?" Arthur asks.

"There are none here. They're all along the bound-
aries of the property. Miranda is going for help. If she
makes it, we should have an army coming down on this
place. All we got to do is buy time."

At the top of the stairs, leaning against the black
marble railing of the staircase, is the image of Jesus Christ
wearing a radiant halo and a flowering crown of thorns.
Jesus has his arm around a moving form, the universe
shaped like a woman, the night sky and the stars form her
only substance except for the infinite darkness. Denny
spots the door to the Queen's Chamber and then he sees
the hall that must lead to the King's Suite. He leads Arthur
and General Howland down a white marble hallway past
doorway after doorway. The further they go down the cor-
ridor, the fewer costumed characters they find until there
is only a stray couple here and there. One couple is making it behind a statue of Perseus. It is a robot making it
with Cat Woman, screws and bolts, pistons pumping into
leopard's skin as long nails dig into the circuitry.

Denny is confused. "Where's the King's private
suite? We've got to find that fuckin study."

"Down here," Arthur says. "I was looking around
earlier. I think I know where it is."

They rush down the hallway, and Arthur stops before a large pair of doors ornately paneled and gilded in
ribbons of gold. "I think this is it."

Denny opens the doors. The room is wood paneled

with parquet floors and a rug designed like a Mandala. At the center of the mandala stands a beautiful ornate roll top desk and crowning the top of the desk is a golden clock. Denny turns the arms of the clock to twelve o'clock, pushes in the alarm, and the top of the desk rolls open revealing the control panel. Denny quickly surveys the controls then presses a button. A large floating panel of touch sensitive screens appears revealing every room and the grounds.

Denny instructs the computer to find Scrooge McDuck, and it finds him lying on a bed, not moving. Denny instructs the system to read the image for life signs and letters appear across the screen.

Dead.

He hears Senator Lorenz say, "Look there."

The Senator is pointing to one of the screens. Denny magnifies it, and he sees Plastic Man, the Punisher, a beautiful elfin girl with transparent wings, and the blue metallic hermaphrodite that Denny encountered earlier. They enter the King's Bedchamber. A massive chandelier hangs from a white ceiling that is bordered in paintings by Valentin de Boulogne, Lanfranco, Domenichino, Van Dyck and Caroacciolo. Like the Queen's bed, the King's bed is separated from the rest of the room like an altar where the sun god sleeps surrounded by gold.

Plastic Man has his arm around the elf with the transparent wings. She has a slim ethereal figure, and she is naked except for sparks that play about her body like atoms of light. Denny looks at the elf's eyes, and he realizes that it's Cheri Normal. There seems to be some sexual encounter planned.

Everyone is laughing as they walk towards the bed. The Punisher has blue and black skin. His face is gray blue as are his forearms, hands, and skintight boots. On his chest is a figure of a white death skull, and over his shoulders he wears the American flag like a cape that is burning. In his hand is a machine pistol, the muzzle of which he is rubbing up and down the metallic ass of the hermaphrodite.

Everyone is laughing. Plastic Man kisses Cheri and the hermaphrodite spreads itself upon the bed waiting for love to come to him and her altogether in a loss of identity.

Merling releases Cheri and says, "I'll be right back. I have to take a leak."

Cheri smiles at him, "I didn't know Plastic Man peed."

"Oh, yes, I can turn myself into a fire hose if I want. I'll show you when I get back." He winks at the Punisher.

The Punisher places his arm around Cheri and says, "I'll take care of her until you get back, Boss. We'll have her all lubricated up." He kisses Cheri and begins to touch all the little atoms of light.

Merling laughs and walks to the far end of the room. He opens a door, enters the bathroom, and closes the door behind him.

The Punisher picks up Cheri. Her wings flutter as he hands her to the metallic creature that takes her in its silver studded arms and kisses her through its metallic veil. The atoms of light have become milky ways in erotic places. The hermaphrodite turns her over on her stomach, raises the little elfin ass to receive the blue metallic prick, then reaches out, grabs her tenderly by the head and breaks her neck.

Cheri collapses without a sound, and the blue metallic monster watches the Punisher with yellow and blue eyes as the Punisher walks to the door that Plastic Man passed through. He opens the door, and Plastic Man is seated on the toilet. He looks up and sees the Punisher. He smiles, and the Punisher raises the muzzle of his gun and fires two bursts into Plastic Man's chest and then one into his forehead. The Punisher walks up to Merling who is sprawled dead on the toilet seat, reaches beyond him and flushes the toilet, then turns to leave.

"Son of a bitch!" Denny says. "God damn it. That's how they were able to get in here. It's been Hathaway all along."

The door to the King's Suite opens. It's Black Hawk in a dark blue uniform, black high top boots. Next to him is the doll, GI Joe, who is carrying an M16 that Denny is sure is not a toy. Black Hawk reaches for the revolver in the holster strapped to his waist.

Denny presses the button that will turn Vision World off, and he shields his eyes from the tremendous

434

burst of light to come, and when it does, all is gone, the gold, the glitter, the costumes. Juan Baliz and Paulo Benites, the assassins from Brazil, stand naked before him stunned by the flash of light that has changed all the illusions into nothingness.

They both fire blindly. Denny takes aim and fires methodically, first hitting Baliz and then Benites. When it is all over, the two men lie naked on the floor, one with his face blown off and the other with a hole in his chest screaming for help.

Denny immediately turns the surveillance screen back on. He can see the security troops storming what was Versailles but is now black boxes filled with naked people, men with men, women with women, men and women fucking children, fucking each other, the gods and goddesses now exposed, pathetic in their mortality, the rolls of fat, the imperfections, vampires feeding off the young and each other.

Through the surveillance system, Denny is able to contact the commander of the security forces. In the background he can still hear the dying terrorists screaming. Denny shouts into the speaker, "Commander, can you hear me?"

"Yes."

"This is Colonel Martino. I am here with General Howland and Senator Lorenz. They are the targets of this attack." Denny punches up a layout of the building onto the screen, and he indicates their location, "Can you see us,

Commander?"

"Yes, Colonel, I have just ordered men to your location. Can you hold your position?"

"I hope so. Can you see what I see on the surveillance screens?"

"Yes."

"Good, I can identify some or all of the assassins.
I'll try to locate them for you."

While Denny has been talking to the Commander,
Senator Lorenz and General Howland have been building a
barrier in front of the control panel. They are now reasonably protected and armed. The man on the floor has
stopped screaming. Denny is scanning the rooms and the
grounds. He finds Maria Santini in front of the Palace of
Boxes in a limousine waiting for the remainder of the hit
team. He targets her for the Commander, and she is immediately surrounded and surrenders.

He targets Hathaway and Ramon, naked and
armed, in what was the Hall of Mirrors. When the security
forces converge on them, there is a lot of loose fire,
screams, people being torn apart by bullets, dying in their
nakedness, no illusion to hide behind. Ramon is nearly cut
in half by a barrage of fire, and Hathaway is hit in the midst
of shattering glass, reflections fragmented into broken images.

It's over.

A squad of security troops enters the King's Suite,
and Denny turns to the General and Senator Lorenz and

says, "We'll take the limousine that they were going to use as a get-away-car. My guess is that it is bulletproof. It's in front of the entranceway. I'll meet you there. Then we'll get the fuck out of here."

"Where are you going?" Arthur asks.

"I'm going to see if Hathaway is alive or not. I need to know what he knows."

"Good," Arthur says.

He turns to General Howland, "General, why don't you secure the vehicle, and I'll go find Miranda and meet you at the limousine."

"I'm on my way," General Howland says. "And remember, both of you, be careful. This may not be over."

They leave the room. The General and Senator Lorenz both have a security escort. They should be all right Denny thinks as he enters the large box with the blank ceilings and walls. The naked people are huddling together, no longer gods and goddess but mortal flesh amidst blood and dead bodies. He finds Hathaway surrounded by security troopers. He is sitting on the floor, his back propped against the wall. He has been torn up badly, and Denny guesses that he is not going to make it. Hathaway is dying.

Denny squats down next to him, "Hathaway."

Hathaway turns his head and stares at Denny for a moment. Denny has lost count of how many men have looked at him this way, men who have stared into his eyes, brothers in war, the fraternity of the damned. It doesn't matter what side you're on, enemy or not, that's what the eyes say.

Hathaway smiles, "I'm curious, Denny. How did you find out?"

"At the farmhouse that we raided in Brazil, in the cellar, over the computer, someone had pinned up cut outs of the costumed characters that were going to be hit. I didn't think much of it then, but tonight I figured it out."

"Stupid assholes," Hathaway snorts, but then he smiles again. "You were much better than I thought. I underestimated you, Denny."

"I was lucky."

"That's true. If Miranda hadn't invited you to the ball, you'd be just another cuckold, and I'd be the head of Vision World now."

"Hathaway, you were one of the cut outs. They were going to kill you too."

"Is that right?"

"That's right."

Hathaway laughs, "As you can see, Denny, there's a lot of fucking going on around here." He laughs again, "I just didn't think they were going to fuck me so soon. But..." He starts to cough up blood. He pulls Denny to him, "He who fucks last, fucks best."

Hathaway's face expresses the pain then he seems to simply dismiss it. "I met with William Lowe. We met in the crypt below the Capitol. I got him on tape. I got the evidence for you." A wave of pain crosses his face again,

"It is hidden in the system. The code number is 2734906."
Hathaway grabs Denny's hand tight, like a vice, "With that
tape you can prove that there was a conspiracy. But you
have to hurry. What time is it?"

Denny asks one of the troopers, "It's a quarter to
twelve."

"The President is dead, Denny, and in fifteen
minutes Franklin Peters is going to go on national television and declare martial law."

"What?"

"You heard me." Hathaway coughs up some more
blood. Two ambulance attendants appear and lift Hathaway on to a stretcher. Hathaway grabs Denny's hand like a
vice and says, "Remember..."

He opens his mouth to say something but his
mouth falls open, and he stares out into space at the ultimate truth beyond belief.

Denny rushes out of the room into the fresh air.
He heads for the limousine, and he sees General Howland,
Senator Lorenz, and Miranda together waiting for him. He
rushes up to them and says, "Hathaway just told me that
the President is dead. They assassinated him, and Peters is
going on national television soon and declare martial law."

"Those bastards," General Howland says, "Those
fuckin' traitors." He looks at the Senator. "This is it."

"Yes, it is, Jim. Are you with us?"

"Yes, I am," General Howland says and then turns
to the officer who is standing next to him, "Commander, I

need an escort and a means of transportation back to my base, now."

"Yes, sir."

The General turns to Arthur, "I'm going to try and secure our military position, Senator. And you, Martino..." He grabs Denny's arm like a vice and says, "What you are going to do is get the Senator and Miranda back to Vision World. I will order a special-forces unit there to back you up. You are to secure the system at all cost. Lock yourselves in. It's the safest place in the world. They will not be able to budge you with an atomic bomb. Do you understand?"

"Yes, sir."

"Very well," the General smiles and says, "Nice job, Colonel." He then shakes Arthur's hand and says, "Good luck, Senator. And remember, as long as we control information and communications, we still have a chance. That's your part in this war."

The General and Senator Lorenz shake hands and the look that passes between them is the realization that they both now stand at the center of time. The past and the future are coming together at this moment.

As Denny is about to enter the limousine, Miranda hands him a cape to wear. He has forgotten that he is completely naked. He looks around, embarrassed, then puts the cape on and enters the limousine. They speed off accompanied by an escort. As they race back to Washington, Senator Lorenz turns on the TV. After a few moments, the show that is on the screen is interrupted. Franklin Peters appears. He is in the Oval Office seated at the carved oak desk that was a gift from Queen Victoria. Behind him is the American flag. Franklin's face expresses the sorrow of a father that is just about to tell his children some very bad news.

"Fellow Citizens, I come to you to night with a heavy heart. Earlier this evening, at exactly eleven thirty, Washington time, the President of the United States was shot to death by a traitor, an underground member of the People's Army who was able to infiltrate the White House staff. This terrorist organization was also responsible for murdering two members of the Commission, Roger Baines and Brad Merling, who were shot to death this evening at a party at the Merling estate. This plot is part of a concerted effort by the left to take over this country."

Franklin stares into the cameras. It is the All American that is looking into the hearts of the American people now, it is the war hero who says, "But they will not succeed. As of this moment, as acting President, I am declaring martial law. I am dissolving a Congress that has betrayed us in our time of need, and I will institute a Corporate Assembly as the late President dreamed we would. As Commander-in-Chief I have ordered strategic forces in the United States to secure critical areas of the country. As of this moment, the forces of freedom are on the move, and we will crush this revolution that has as its goal to destroy everything that we hold dear. God Bless

America."

The anthem, "My country tis of thee, sweet land of liberty..." can be heard in the background as pictures flash across the screen of the late President, pictures of the President as an industrialist, the Boss at work turning America into a successful business. This is who our President was the pictures say, a man who loved his dog and played golf and went hunting and rode a horse, a man of god. This is the man that leaders from around the world came to see for advice and consent, the man who won two Presidential elections with banners waving, the masses cheering as he held up Franklin Peters hand in victory, and they embraced..."of thee I sing."

The station returns to its normal broadcasting. There is silence in the car. Finally, Senator Lorenz says, "You know, all your life you go along saying things, convincing people of threats that in your heart you don't really believe are there. You kind of feel that no one is that bad. You exaggerate and dramatize for the effect because you're a politician. It's just in your mind, your heart says to you. But then it happens, and even though you predicted it, you can't believe it. I guess we all hope and dream and wish for the best, no matter how bad things are. In my heart, I wanted to believe that they were all still Americans. That they still believed in America, and, when it got down to the bottom line, they would not sell us out. I wanted to believe that the song was not just for children, a lullaby while monsters roam."

442

Senator Lorenz sits back absorbed in his own thoughts. Everyone is visibly shaken and quiet. Denny wonders what is going to happen next and he realizes that Miranda was right. This has been happening for a very long time, but everyone ignored it as they pursued their own narcissistic and individual greed and the primitive totems of consumerism. It is now clear to Denny how the Leviathan grew. In our greed, we all ignored the consequences of our individual acts, so greed took on a life of its own, and in the abyss of our minds where the darkness takes form a monster grew that historically we call the Devil.

Denny remembers Ned saying that Denny was a good hound dog, and that once he got the scent, he would never give up. Ned was right. He has followed the scent of evil through all of Vision World's plots. He has followed all the clues of the-who-done-it to its source, and now he knows who did it. We did it. We created this nightmare. We embrace the one eyed Cyclops of Vision World with no perspective and no heart. We became the It, stripped of our humanity. Now Merling is dead, but it still exists devouring everything that Denny ever loved and fought for. Denny wonders if this is the end. Is he witnessing the death of the American Republic, or will we free ourselves from the prism cell of narcissism and take up Senator Lorenz's call to battle when he said, "Democracy is a revolution that has never been won."

Chapter Thirty Two

When Miranda, Denny, and Senator Lorenz arrive at Vision World headquarters, the special-forces team that General Howland sent to secure the building is waiting for them. They enter the building and take the elevator to the control center where Miranda immediately takes over control of Vision World and initiates emergency procedures. They can hear the steel and titanium plates sliding into place.

Vision World is now totally self-contained, sealed from the outside world, a bunker three hundred feet below the ground. On screen Miranda sees the tanks and the armored troop carriers moving down Pennsylvania Ave. Similar forces are simultaneously closing in about New York City, Chicago, Los Angeles, Dallas, and Miami.

Denny hands Miranda the code numbers that Hathaway gave him that would provide them with the evidence of a conspiracy. Miranda, who is seated at the control panel, taps in the code, and on screen a video appears. They are looking into the dark recesses of the catacombs of the Capitol, down in the crypt where Washington was to be buried. Hathaway appears on screen walking into the shadows of the pillars and arches that support the

Rotunda and form the resting place for the statues of men long forgotten whose hopes for immortality have been relegated into the basement of our collective history along with a statue of Washington wearing a toga, his arm raised in a Roman salute to his legions.

Hathaway finds William Lowe, a member of the Commission, in the darkest shadows. Lowe is the first to speak, "Is everything set?"

"Yes, it is, Bill. I have programmed our hit team into the computer, and they will be accepted as guests at the ball. We will hit Brad, Arthur Lorenz, Miranda, Roger Baine, and General Howland."

"You don't see any problems?"

"No." Hathaway smiles and then says, "Actually, it's perfect, but what about the President?"

"I told you that we will take care of that."

"May I ask how?"

Lowe smiles wolfishly, "We injected one of the President's aids with a cancer inducing drug without him knowing it. Now he's dying of cancer. He has no money, and he is deeply in debt. We offered him a deal where his family would be taken care of in the most generous fashion and their future would be ensured. Before the assassination, he is to take a pill that will kill him painlessly two hours after he has ingested it. On his body they will find a note written by him in which he identifies himself as a member of the People's Army."

"Neat," Hathaway says. "Then Franklin Peters will go

on air and declare martial law and the troops will move in to secure peace."

"Yes."

"And Franklin knows. There are not going to be any surprises there."

"Of course he knows," Lowe says. "Christ, the boy offered to do it himself. He can be really stupid, you know. But he is the man for the moment. And he will do what he is told."

"Yes, sir."

"Well then, it's settled," Lowe says. "We're on for the night of the ball."

"Yes." Hathaway pauses for a moment. He seems sad.

"What's the matter?" William Lowe asks.

"Oh, I just realized that it is over, America that is."

"Don't be sentimental, Hathaway. America has been brain dead for the last twenty-five years, and we're just taking her off the life support systems and putting her out of her misery."

"I see; and, of course, you're right."

"Yes, of course I'm right." Lowe looks at his watch, "I have to go back upstairs to that Congressional hearing. Those fools, I can't wait until this is all over, and we can begin to build a new world order." William Lowe extends his hand and says, "Do your job Hathaway and Vision World is yours."

"Yes, sir."

The screen goes blank.

Miranda turns to Arthur and says, "What do you want to do?"

"That's all we need. They gave it all away. The plot, the players, Lowe implicates himself and Franklin Peters. We'll play the tape, and then I'll go on screen and speak to the American people."

Miranda smiles, "I can turn this whole country into a TV screen. Nobody will miss this." She begins to set the controls, and as she does so she says, "Do you know what you're going to say?"

"God, I don't know. If the American people can't figure this one out, then we're done for. I think the speech has to be short and to the point, and in the end, we leave it up to them. Finally and ultimately it's their story."

"I agree."

Arthur smiles, "Now I have to figure out what I'm going to say, and it's got to be now. How long will it be before you are ready?"

"Ten minutes."

Arthur walks off to be alone while Miranda works on the system. She locks in everything that she can into the control center eliminating all bypasses and local controls. She initiates a protective defense about the satellites, especially Zeus, and then she checks the banking system with the idea of freezing all the major corporate accounts controlled by the Commission members.

She looks at the screen, shocked by what she sees.

She double checks the results then cross references all the Commission assets.   It's true, she says to herself.   Then she turns to Denny who is watching her and says, "They have transferred all their assets into safe banks throughout the world."

"Who has?" Denny asks.

"The Commission."

"What does that mean?"

"America is broke."

"They can do that?"

"They did that with the press of a button, but we control all the mainframe computers now, and that means we control all the technology, science, research, and the information including all official documents stored in the computers. Essentially we control their whole infrastructure – all their physical assets, including deeds, titles, patents, and copyrights. I've classified it all as illegal contraband and that includes any stocks and bonds they haven't cashed in. That's a lot of money and assets to convert and Vision World will find every dime. Won't you, baby." Miranda taps some more buttons and then claps her hands in joy. "They can't get to it."

"Which means?" Denny asks.

"I've just pulled the plug on them too." Miranda gets up from her seat then gives an assistant some orders and says, "I better tell Arthur what has happened."

Miranda walks over to where Senator Lorenz is standing. He is looking out at the Vision World universe, all the points of light at the edges of reality that look like a star that has been fragmented into billions and billions of pieces. Miranda tells the Senator what happened. Then she tells him it is time to go on air.

"Where should I sit?" Arthur asks.

"Anywhere that is comfortable for you. I'll fill in the appropriate background."

"I guess this is it." Arthur sits down in a leather chair next to Miranda, and Miranda programs in the evidence that Hathaway gave them and presses a button. On every screen in the United States, William Lowe and Hathaway appear revealing the conspiracy to take over the United States.

When it is over, Senator Arthur Lorenz appears and says, "You, the people, have seen for yourself that Franklin Peters, William Lowe, and members of the Commission have plotted to take over the United States of America. At this moment armed forces from Latin America are occupying your capital and major cities throughout the United States. You know what is happening, and who is behind it. Now take a look around you."

Miranda presses a button, and except for Arthur Lorenz's image, all of Vision World is turned off. All of America is turned into an empty box.

"This is what you really have. Everything else has been an illusion. Wake up, America. Your time has come. Get a gun, a club, an ax, a pitchfork, a hammer, whatever you can find and start walking towards Washington. Join

449

your brothers and sisters. Defend your country. The Republic is dying! Your Capital is falling!"

Chapter Thirty Three

Over and over again the message was repeated, and the Vision World story was told from beginning to end. It was a monumental moment where no one could sit by and watch anymore, and so they came. They got out of their chairs and off their couches and out of their houses. Ned's friends from the mountains came down toting their ancient guns. The woman who won a shopping cart of empty air, she joined the march, as did her neighbors, as did everyone who bought a dream in the National Lottery, bitter dreams and bitter hopes. They all joined hands to give one another one last chance that could not be bought for a dollar.

They began to march by the millions. The cashier who rang up the American Dream with every purchase, she left her post as did the homeless who live in cardboard boxes. Everyone joined because, in the end, they realized that they all lived in cardboard boxes, that they all were homeless now. Many were slaughtered on the roads, run over by the iron treads of tanks or cut down in swaths by the attack vehicles and the troops that tried to stand in their way, but by now the mass had become a monster of its own with millions and millions of heads and arms and legs, and no matter how many they tore off, the Titan came, a bloody mass of anger and fury that kept growing in strength, reproducing itself over and over again, trampling over its own remains.

It gathered about all that it held dear, and Zeus remained silent. There was no fire from the air. The air force kept out of it, and Howland's forces cut through the army outside of Washington and cut off the forces within. In New York City, the people fought back. The streets were barricaded, the bridges blocked, and the scaffolding about the Statue of Liberty was torn down, the torch was found, and Lady Liberty once again extended her light over her Titan brood.

The Furies were unleashed. America became one last scream of agony, fear, anger, and rage. There was fierce fighting in Washington itself. Thousands of people died as they grouped together at the Washington Monument. They died on the steps of the Capitol when they liberated the House and the Senate. And they died at Lincoln's feet within the hallowed temples of our gods. Finally, American troops in Brazil threatened to march on Brasilia if the Latin American troops did not withdraw. And in the end, the American people won. One week after the civil war began, it was over.

On the day that it was over, Miranda and Denny prepared to leave the bunker. Miranda is at the controls giving the staff final instructions. She seems lost for a moment in the screens that suspend outward into infinity.

Senator Lorenz comes up to her and says, "Miranda, are you ready?"

"You go ahead Arthur. I'll be along soon."

Arthur Lorenz and Miranda Labelle are expected at the Capitol Building. At an extraordinary session of Congress, Senator Arthur Lorenz will give up his Senate seat to be appointed an Assemblyman to replace William Costa, the Speaker of the House who was killed in the defense of Washington. Arthur will then be appointed Speaker of the House by his party, a position that will automatically make him President pro tem to replace Franklin Peters who was impeached several days earlier for reasons of treason. Arthur will hold this position until the next election, an election that Arthur is predicted to win by a landslide. Some predict that he will win by the largest majority in American history, a majority that will be so vast that it will carry over into the Congressional elections and his party will sweep those elections giving him a vast majority in both the House and Senate. Arthur Lorenz is about to become one of the most powerful presidents in American history.

Miranda, who is sitting at the control panel, is staring at a golden disc that she is holding in her hand. She shows it to Denny and says, "Brad gave this to me and said that if anything happened to him I was to play it."

Denny sees that the disc is labeled, *Requiem to a God*, and he smiles, "Are you going to play it now?"

"Yes. Why not? It seems appropriate don't you think?"

"Have you seen it?"

"No, Brad was explicit. He said that no one was to see it until everyone saw it."

"Well then this is as good a time as any, but maybe we should review it first."

"No," Miranda says. "I want to honor Brad's last request. I owe him that much."

Denny smiles, "You're right. Without Brad we never could have defeated the Commission, and we never would have known what we know today."

Miranda connects the disc to all the systems and to all the homes in America. Then she turns Vision World back on, and the normal programming begins again. There is nothing on the screen that would indicate that the disc was on. Everything appears normal - that is until the weather report appears on the screen.

On every screen throughout the galaxy of Vision World, it is reported that it is beginning to rain. This is what is reported, and this is what everyone sees. Rain everywhere. We see the rain fall on the dead, washing away the blood as it flows into the gutters or into the soil to enrich the next harvest of hope. We see it fall on the faces of the dead, the mourning, and the joyful who are smiling in victory. We see it fall on all of the monuments to our past, our heroes and soldiers of stone and iron and bronze soaked with tears of weeping raindrops that fall on the forests of this great land, the mountains from which the thunder roars over the valleys into the deserts. Lightning flashes creating tears in the universe. The light seems to leap from screen to screen interlacing their jagged edges to form a ring of ice and lightning about the control center like Saturn's rings. The gods are speaking. Zeus has spoken. This is the requiem, but is it real?

"Is it really raining everywhere? Has he done it?" Miranda wonders.

She smiles at Denny and says, "Should we go out and see?"

Denny laughs, "Good god, yes."

Miranda presses a button, and they can hear the steel and titanium plates, the doors, the protective shields begin to slide away. They smell fresh air pouring in, and they hear the elevator door open. Miranda and Denny enter the elevator, and they rise out of the depth to the surface from the bunker in which they have been living. When they reach ground level they enter the reception hall of Vision World that is a world of windows and reflections and projections in glass. They pass through the exit way, and Miranda can hear the rain, the tears, and then the flash of lightning that rips a tear into reality, again and again.

For a moment she can see into the future, and she knows that the last key to the way is love, for it is love that is worth believing in. It is in love that we will find atonement and the creative center of the universe that we have been searching for. It is love that is the single key that unlocks all the mysteries of immortality, for it is in love that all the stardust will come back together to create a new age of enlightenment.

Miranda turns to Denny and says, "I love you Captain America."

"I love you too, Wonder Woman."

Miranda and Denny are soaking wet drenched with mourning as they hold hands and look out at the Capital, its geometric forms, all the columns and the domes. Is the strength in the circle or the square? Or is it in the straight line that is never there? I upon I, individual pillars work together in harmony and balance carrying the burdens of time, defying gravity as they raise each generation tier upon tier, time curves in upon itself in a dome, a globe, a point where a simple heartbeat can hold up the weight of the universe.

And for a moment, all of America paused and reached out to one another and touched God.

THE END

www.ingramcontent.com/pod-product-compliance
Lightning Source LLC
Chambersburg PA
CBHW071634260626
47170CB00001B/96